PRAISE FOR *Dumping Billy*

"A funny romantic novel."

—*Star*

"Sunblock? Lawn chair? Relax and read!"

—*St. Paul Pioneer Press*

"Hilarious and a real treasure . . . Lots of surprises and twists at the end . . . You won't be able to put this book down once you start, so read it when you have plenty of time on your hands!"

—Pelepubs Book Review

"Peppered with humor, wit, and sassy attitude that are sure to bring a smile to the reader's face." —Bookloons.com

"Full of quirky characters, hilarious situations, good and bad relationships, and sexy scenes. Olivia Goldsmith fans will cherish and enjoy this book and the unforgettable characters that she has created." —FictionAddiction.net

"As usual, the author writes with wit, humor, and a sharp eye."
—Romance Reader's Connection

"Goldsmith is in top form with this up-to-date story about the life and times of the thirtysomething set in New York City . . . Her often biting wit, cleverness, and bawdy language, as well as her ability to give readers satisfying characters with stories sure to intrigue, have kept this author at the top of bestseller lists for years. Goldsmith, one more time, leaves you turning page after page until, suddenly, you've read the whole thing."
—BusinessKnowHow.com

Also by Olivia Goldsmith

Dumping Billy

OLIVIA GOLDSMITH

WARNER BOOKS

New York   Boston

Grateful acknowledgment is made for permission to quote from "The Hokey Pokey" copyright © 1950 Sony/ATV Songs LLC. Used by permission. All rights administered by Sony/ATV Music Publishing.

Warner Books

Time Warner Book Group
1271 Avenue of the Americas, New York, NY 10020
Visit our Web site at www.twbookmark.com

Printed in the United States of America

Originally published in hardcover by Warner Books
First Trade Edition:
November 2005
10 9 8 7 6 5 4 3 2

The Library of Congress has cataloged the hardcover edition as follows:
Goldsmith, Olivia.
Dumping Billy / Olivia Goldsmith
p. cm.
ISBN 0-446-53110-3
1. Brooklyn (New York, N.Y.)—Fiction.   2. Bars (Drinking establishments)—Fiction.   3. Dating (Social customs)—Fiction.   4. Rejection (Psychology)—Fiction.   5. Female friendship—Fiction.   I. Title.

PS3557.O3857D86   2004
813'.54—dc22   2003059585

Cover design by Brigid Pearson
Cover photos by Microzoa/Getty Images (skyscrapers);
Mike Powell/Getty Images (woman)

ISBN 0-446-69505-X (pbk.)

To Nina

AND TO

Ethel Esther Brandsfronbrener Schutz
A lover of books, mangoes, oranges, and me

Acknowledgments

As this is my tenth novel, I'm a little late in acknowledging the gratitude I have for my readers. Writers have a lonely job, and the kind notes, the warm reception at bookstores, and the fact that you continue to buy enough books to keep me employed is a wonderful thing. There are not many writers privileged to not have a day job and I am grateful to everyone who has picked up and read one of my novels. I hope they have given you much enjoyment and diversion.

Special thanks to Jamie Raab for her belief in me and wonderful nurturing; thanks to Larry Kirshbaum for laughing at my jokes and feeding me lunch; thanks to Nick Ellison just for being Nick; thanks to Onieal's Restaurant, my unofficial office, and the wonderful staff, including: Chris Onieal, Nicole Blackham, Kristen Collen, Kristin Prinzo, Jaqueline Hegarty, Anna Schmidt, Stuart Bruce, Lauren Reid, and Jodie McMurty.

Special thanks to John Claflin of Colours who has not only built (and painted!) my home but has gotten me out of hot water time and time again. Thanks also to Jed Schutz for all his help; Roy Greenberg for his good humor and legal expertise; PG Kain for his creativity and input; and as always, Nan Robinson for her enormous contribution. For anybody else I left out, you know who you are. Thank you.

Dumping Billy

Chapter One

Katherine Sean Jameson sat behind her desk and looked at her client. Being a therapist was never easy, but with a client who needed this much help and had this much resistance, it was really tough. And heartbreaking. To the casual observer, Kate was just a mildly pretty twenty-four-year-old (though she was actually thirty-one) with long curls of wild red hair.

Now, as she looked at Brian Conroy, she unconsciously twisted those curls into an impromptu bun at the nape of her neck with a practiced motion and pushed a pencil through it to hold it in place.

"So what do you think?" Kate said, and almost bit her tongue. Despite what laypeople believed, a good therapist didn't sit around all day saying, "What do you think?" She'd have to try a different approach. She was wasting her own time as well as Brian's. Why was it the clients she loved most were so often the ones she could help the least?

It was warm. Kate's office was not air-conditioned, and the breeze from the open window felt good on the back of her neck. Brian, looking at her intently, was sweating, but it could just as easily have been from nerves as from the early spring heat.

Kate sat silently. Silence was an important part of her work, though not something that came naturally. But she had learned that at times stillness and space were all that were needed.

Not today, apparently. Brian pulled his eyes guiltily away from her own and looked around the office. The walls were filled with pictures done by children—some of them very disturbing. Kate watched to see if Brian's attention focused on one.

Kate stifled a sigh. She was trying to wait Brian out but was conscious of their time ticking away, and for his sake she needed immediate results. Brian was obviously in crisis. She looked with compassion at her eight-year-old "client." His teacher said he was constantly disrupting class and showing signs of obsessive-compulsive or maybe even schizophrenic behavior.

And disruption simply wasn't allowed at Andrew Country Day School. A private school in the best neighborhood in Manhattan, it accepted only the best and the brightest—of students and staff. Every amenity was provided, from an indoor swimming pool to a state-of-the-art computer center to language lessons that included Japanese and French for six-year-olds. That's why there was a school psychologist. Kate had gotten the plum job only recently, and Brian, like other kids who showed the slightest "difficult" behavior, had been immediately remanded to her office. Nothing was to disrupt the smooth daily ingestion of information by the children of the elite.

"Do you know why you've come here, Brian?" she asked, her voice gentle. Brian shook his head. Kate rose from her desk, moved around it, and sat on one of the small chairs beside the boy. "Can you guess?" He shook his head. "Well, do you think it's for eating gummy elephants in school?"

He looked at her for a moment, then shook his head again. "There's no such thing as gummy elephants."

"Gummy rhinos?" Kate asked. Brian shook his head again. "Eating peanut-butter-and-raccoon sandwiches at your desk?"

"It wasn't for *eating* anything," he said. Then he lowered his voice to a whisper. "It was for talking. Talking in class."

As Kate nodded, the pencil fell out of her bun, and her hair cascaded over her shoulders while the pencil clattered to the floor. Brian smiled and actually let a giggle escape before he covered his mouth. Good, Kate thought. She leaned closer to her little patient. "You're not here just for talking in class, Brian. If you were just talking in class, then you'd be sent to the principal's office, right?"

Brian's adorable face gazed up at Kate with terrified eyes. "Are you *worse* than the principal?" he asked.

Kate felt such empathy for the boy at that moment that she was tempted to take his hand in hers, but he was so anxious that she feared he might shy away. This kind of work was so delicate—like dealing with Venetian spun glass, where the slightest jar could shatter it—and she often felt so clumsy.

"Nobody is worse than the principal," Kate said. Then she smiled and winked at Brian. None of the kids at Andrew Country Day liked Dr. McKay, and—as so often was the case—their instincts were good. "Do I look as bad as Dr. McKay?" Kate asked, feigning shock.

Brian shook his head vigorously.

"Well. Thank goodness. Anyway, I do something different. You aren't here to be punished. You didn't do anything wrong. But everybody hears you talking—even though you're not talking to anybody." She watched as Brian's eyes filled with tears.

"I'll be quieter," he promised. Kate wanted to scoop him up onto her lap and let him cry as long as he needed to. After all, his mother had just died of cancer, and he was still so very young. Kate's own mother had passed away when she was eleven, and that had been almost unbearable.

She dared to take one of the boy's hands in hers. "I don't want you to be quiet, Brian," she said. "You do what you need to. But I'd like to know what you're saying."

Brian shook his head again. His eyes changed from tearful to frightened. "I can't tell," he whispered. Then he turned his face away from her. He mumbled something else, and Kate managed to hear only one word, but it was enough.

Go slow, she told herself. Go very, very slowly and casually. "You're doing magic?" she asked. Brian, face still averted, nodded but didn't speak. Kate was already afraid she had gone too far. She held her breath. Then, after a long moment, she lowered her own voice to a whisper and asked, "Why can't you tell?"

"Because . . . ," Brian started, then it burst out of him. "Because it's magic and you can't tell magic or your wish won't come true. Like birthday candles. Everybody knows that!" He got up and walked to the corner of the room.

Kate actually felt relieved. The boy wasn't schizophrenic. He was caught in a typical childhood trap: total powerlessness combined with hopeless longing and guilt. A toxic cocktail. Kate gave him a moment. She didn't want him to feel trapped. Yet he shouldn't be alone with this pain. She approached him slowly, the way you might move toward a strange puppy. She put her hand on the little boy's shoulder. "Your wish is about your mother, isn't it," she said, her voice as neutral as she could manage to keep it. Brian didn't need any of her emotions—he needed space for his own. "Isn't that right?"

Brian looked up at her and nodded. His face registered a cautious relief. The dreadful burdens of childhood secrets always touched Kate. Though she was a long-lapsed Catholic, she still remembered the power and release of the confessional. She had to serve this child well. "What are you wishing for?" she asked, her voice as gentle as she could make it.

Brian began to cry. His face, usually so pale, flushed deep rose. Speaking through his tears, he said, "I thought if I just said 'Mommy, come back' a million times that she would be back." He sobbed and put his face against Kate's skirt. "But it isn't working. I think I've said it two million times."

Kate's eyes filled with tears. She took a deep breath. She could feel the heat of Brian's face through the thin fabric of her skirt. The hell with professional detachment. She scooped Brian into her arms and carried him over to one of the chairs. The boy nestled against her. After a time he stopped crying, but his silent neediness was even sadder. They sat for a few moments, but Kate knew their session was nearly completed, and she had to speak. "Oh, Brian, I am so sorry," she told him. "But magic doesn't work. I wish it did. The doctors did everything they could to help your mommy. They couldn't fix her, and magic can't fix that. It's not your fault that the doctors couldn't save her." She paused. "And it's not your fault your mommy can't come back." Kate sighed. Breaking children's hearts, even to help them, had not been part of her job description. "But she can't, and your magic can't work."

Brian suddenly pushed against her, wriggling his way out of her embrace. He stood up and looked at her angrily. "Why not?" he demanded. "Why can't my magic work?" He glared at Kate for another moment, then pushed her hard and barreled out of the room, nearly knocking over the dollhouse. The office door crashed and rebounded open. From down the hall, she heard a voice—Elliot Winston's—try to stop Brian. "Shut up, you stinky dick!" Brian shouted. Kate winced and listened to the little boy's footsteps recede.

A moment later, Elliot stuck his head around Kate's door. "Another satisfied customer?" he asked, his eyebrows raised nearly to his receding hairline. "Perhaps you should have stuck with French."

Kate had majored in French as an undergrad. For a while, she had even considered continuing her language studies in graduate school. She had never regretted not doing so, because her work with the children was so satisfying, but occasionally, particularly at moments like this, Elliot—one of the math teachers and her best friend—teased her about her choice.

"As I recall, the German for 'stinky dick' would be *riechende Steine*. What would you say in French?"

"I would say you are very annoying," Kate told him. "That's good enough. And I would also say that Brian and I are making some progress. He expressed some of his true feelings today."

"Well, he managed to express his feelings about me and my genital odor. Congratulations on your progress." Elliot stepped into the room and sat beside the dollhouse in an overstuffed chair—the only piece of adult-size furniture in Kate's office aside from her own desk and chair. Elliot was dark-haired,

average in height, slightly overaverage in weight, and possessed of a much higher than average IQ. As usual, he was
wearing wrinkled chinos, a baggy T-shirt, and a clashing open-
necked shirt on top. Putting his feet up on the toy box, he
opened his lunch sack.

Kate sighed. She and Elliot usually had lunch together. But
today Elliot had had the dreaded cafeteria duty and was just
now, at nearly two-thirty, getting a chance to eat. She delighted
in his company, but she was melancholy from her session with
Brian. Elliot, fresh from the horror of the lunchroom, was
blithely unaware of her mood as he pulled out several items
and tore into a sandwich that smelled suspiciously like corned
beef.

"Brian's in Sharon's class, isn't he?" Elliot asked too casually.

Kate nodded. "Poor kid. His mother dies, and his teacher is
the Wicked Witch of the Upper West Side." She had to smile.
Neither she nor Elliot had much use for Sharon Kaplan, a truly
lazy teacher and a deeply annoying woman.

"So aside from a recently deceased mom, what's bugging
Brian?" Elliot asked.

Kate felt too fragile for their usual badinage. "You have mustard on your chin," she told him, but as Elliot reached up to
wipe it away, the glob fell onto his shirt.

"Oops," he said, and dabbed ineffectually at his shirtfront
with one of the hard paper towels from the school's bathrooms.
The yellow splotch looked particularly hideous against the
green of his shirt. Watching him eat, Kate often thought, was a
spectator sport.

"He believes that magic can bring his mother back," she said,
sighing wistfully.

"See? See what I mean? They're all obsessed with witches and
wizards. Damn that Harry Potter!" Elliot said, and took another
huge bite of the sandwich. "So what's your prescription?" he
asked, forcing the words out while chewing his food.

"I want him to give up the magic and get in touch with his
anger and pain," Kate answered.

"Oy vey!" Elliot said with the best Yiddish accent a gay man from Indiana could manage. "When will you give up on this quest to get every little boy at Andrew Country Day in touch with his true feelings? And why discourage magic in his case? What else does the kid have?"

"Oh, come on, Elliot! Because magic won't work, and he mustn't think it's his fault when it fails." She shook her head. "You of all people. A trained statistician. A man who could trade this job in, triple your salary, and become chief actuarial at any pension fund. *You're* telling me to encourage magic?"

Elliot shrugged. "Haven't you ever had magical things happen?"

Kate refused the bait. Elliot, raised in the Midwest and stoic to the bone, had once told her, "The unexamined life is the only one worth living." He often challenged her about the efficacy of psychology. Now, just to annoy her, he was going to take a perverse stand on magic. "If you think you're going to start an argument today," she warned him, "you're out of your mind." Then, to annoy him—as well as for his own good—she added, "I didn't think corned beef was good for your cholesterol."

"Oh, what's a few hundred points one way or the other?" he asked cheerfully, swallowing another mouthful.

"You've got a death wish," Kate said.

"Ooooh. Harsh words from a shrink." He winced mockingly as he opened a Snapple.

"Look, I'm leaving," she told him, gathering some notes from her desk and putting them into her file cabinet. If she left now, she'd be able to do a bit of shopping before meeting her friend Bina. She took a lipstick and mirror out of her purse, dabbed the color over her mouth, and smiled widely to make sure she didn't have lipstick on her teeth. "I'll see you for dinner."

"Where are you going?"

"None of your beeswax."

"A secret? Come on. Tell! What if I threw a tantrum like Brian?" Elliot reached into the toy box at his feet. Then he hurled a stuffed bear in Kate's direction. "Would you tell me then?" The plush missile hit her squarely in the face. Elliot curled up in the chair, held his hands in front of his face, and started to beg rapidly. "It was an accident. I'm sorry, I'm sorry, I'm sorry."

"I'll show you sorry," Kate warned. She threw the bear back at Elliot, but it missed him.

"You throw like a girl," Elliot taunted. Then he picked up another animal and threw it at Kate. "Duck!" he called as he reached for yet another toy to throw. It was indeed a duck, yellow and fluffy.

"Duck this, you math nerd," Kate almost shouted as she grabbed a fuzzy rabbit and pummeled Elliot's head. It felt good to blow off some steam.

"Abuse! Abuse!" Elliot screamed in delight as he rolled off the chair to protect himself. "Teacher abuse! Teacher abuse!" he continued to yell.

"Shut up, you idiot!" Kate told him, and rushed to close the office door. She turned from it just in time to get a stuffed elephant right in the face. It stunned her for a moment, then she grabbed the pachyderm and lunged at Elliot. "I'll show you abuse, you sniveling cholesterol warehouse," she threatened as she fell on top of Elliot and beat him repeatedly with the toy.

Elliot fought back with both an inflatable flamingo *and* a stuffed dog. He might be gay, but he was no wussy. When both he and Kate were exhausted, they sat panting and laughing together in the big chair, Kate on top. The door opened.

"Excuse me," said Dr. McKay. Despite his words, he wasn't the type to excuse anything. "I thought I heard a ruckus in here."

George McKay, the principal of Andrew Country Day School, was a hypocrite, a social climber, a control freak, and a very bad dresser. He also had a knack of using words no one else had used for several decades.

"A ruckus?" Elliot asked.

"We were just testing out a new therapy," Kate said quickly. "I hope we didn't disturb you."

"Well, it was certainly loud," Dr. McKay complained.

"From the little I know of it, AAT—airborne animal therapy— can frequently be noisy," Elliot said, poker-faced, "although it's having significant measurable success in schools for the gifted, where it's being pioneered. Of course," he added, "it might not be right for this setting." He nodded at Kate. "I'm not the expert," he said as if he were deferring to Kate's professional judgment. She smothered a laugh with a cough.

"We'll put this off until after three o'clock, Dr. McKay," she promised.

"All right, then," he said primly. He left as suddenly as he had arrived, shutting the door with a firm but controlled click. Kate and Elliot looked at each other, waited for a count of ten, then burst into giggles that they had to stifle.

"AAT?" Kate gurgled.

"Hey, straight men love acronyms. Think of the army. He'll be on the Internet in less than ten minutes, searching for 'airborne animal therapy,'" Elliot predicted. He stood up and began collecting the stuffed animals. Kate got up to help him. The irony of the situation was that Elliot had helped Kate get hired, and since then George McKay had told several teachers that he suspected them of having an affair. Ridiculous as that idea was, the sight of the two of them in the chair was not one to instill confidence in Dr. McKay, who had frequently announced at teachers' meetings that he "discouraged fraternizing among professional educational co-workers."

When Kate and her "professional educational co-worker" finished laughing, she stood up, smoothed her skirt, and put her hair back up, this time with a barrette she found in her drawer. Elliot was standing still, looking down at the chair. He heaved a dramatic sigh.

"Oh, shit!" he told her. "You crushed my banana." He held up the mangled fruit from his lunch bag, which had slipped under them during the battle.

Kate turned, struck the pose of a femme fatale, and rasped, "How times have changed. You used to like it when I did that."

Elliot laughed. "I'll leave all banana handling to you and Michael."

Kate and her new boyfriend, Dr. Michael Atwood, were going to dinner with Elliot and his partner, Brice. It was Elliot's introduction to Michael, and Kate felt a little flurry in her stomach at the thought. She hoped they liked each other. "If I don't leave now, I'll be late tonight," she told him.

"Okay, okay."

She grabbed her sweater from the back of her chair and moved toward the door.

"So you like your work so far," Elliot said, watching her. As she passed by, Kate nodded. But she kept moving: She knew what was coming. "And even though I helped you get the job, you're still not going to let me know where you're going?"

Kate didn't bother to answer as she sailed out of the room, Elliot scrambling to hurry after her. Elliot was what people in Brooklyn called "a nudge."

Chapter Two

In all the years Kate had known Elliot—over ten now—he'd always managed to cheer her up when she was sad and support her in her successes. Now, as they walked down the corridor to his classroom, she glanced at him affectionately. The stretched-out orange T-shirt, the ugly green overshirt decorated with mustard, the slight love handles, and the wrinkled chinos didn't make him look like much, but he had a keen mind and was a loving and generous friend. She felt a swell of gratitude toward him. As always, he had cheered her up and helped her make the break from school.

Kate was proud of the work she did with these kids. She had learned a lot from them, too. For one thing, the school catered to the children of the rich and successful, but Kate saw that money, privilege, and education brought on as much misery as had her own deprived childhood. She had lost her resentment of those with money, and she was grateful for that. She had not picked her calling for the money it earned; in fact, she regarded her work as a kind of vocation. It was one thing she never made light of, and she often found it hard to leave her work behind at the end of the day. But tonight she had to, to help Bina prepare for her big night and then, later, to introduce Michael to Elliot and Brice at dinner.

She waited just inside Elliot's classroom as he chucked the offending lunch sack in a bin and started messing about in his untidy desk.

"You know, it's very hard not to keep thinking about Brian. He's so adorable, and has had a really difficult time. And I think the disappointment when his magic doesn't work, which of course it won't, could cause real problems later." Kate sighed. "Boys are just so much more fragile than girls."

"Tell me about it." Elliot sighed deeply, too. "I'm still getting over the time Phyllis Bellusico told me I smelled."

"Did you?" Kate asked, ready to be either his straight man or his audience. She was used to Elliot's shticks. Since college they had been amusing each other with dark humor from their childhoods.

"Well, yes," Elliot admitted reluctantly, "but I smelled *good*. I should have. I'd dumped an entire bottle of my mother's White Shoulders into my underpants."

"Pee-yuw," Kate said, imitating any one of her school "clients." "Maybe Brian has a point. I'd have to agree with Phyllis. And this happened . . . ?"

"In third grade, but with a little more therapy and Brice's love and support, I expect to get over it in the next decade."

Kate loved it when Elliot got going. She had to laugh. "Boys. They always break the thing they love."

"Not if they can kill it," Elliot replied bitterly. He had been tormented by kids in school. After a moment he said, "I have to go to Dean and DeLuca to get rice for our dinner tonight. Brice is making his world-famous risotto. You can tell Michael it's your recipe. The way to a man's heart . . ."

Kate looked up with a suspicious glance. "Yeah, and please be on your best behavior. Elliot," she began, "can't you just—"

"No," Elliot retorted, "I can't just anything." He walked over to her and gave her a quick hug. "I don't want to discourage or criticize you. I just want to make sure you know what you're doing."

"Oh, God! Who knows what they're doing when they try to find a soul mate?"

"Well, you have a point there. But I don't want you to be hurt again, Kate." He paused.

Kate knew where he was going, and she didn't want him to. Her last entanglement had ended so badly that she didn't know how she would have gotten through it without Elliot. She had invested a lot of time and emotion in Steven Kaplan, all of it worse than wasted. It had left her more suspicious and distrusting of men than she liked to admit. One of the good things about Michael was that she could trust him completely. He might not have Steven's banter and easy charm, but he had substance and achievement and sincerity. At least she thought so.

"That's why you're meeting Michael."

"Ever since Steven, I get to meet your *new* boyfriends. I'd like you to just find the right one and make him an *old* boyfriend."

"He's thirty-four. Old enough?"

Elliot rolled his eyes. "I worry about you."

Kate looked directly at Elliot. "This one is different. He's got his doctorate in anthropology, and he's very promising."

"Promising what? You always think they're different, and you always think they're promising, until they bore you, and then—"

"Oh, stop," Kate interrupted. "I know: I won't pick losers on account of my father, and I won't pick winners on account of my father. Yadda, yadda, yadda."

"Don't leave out your fear of commitment, yadda."

"I'll have you committed if you bring that up one more time. How come for thirty-one years you're allowed to be a gay bachelor—in both respects of the phrase—and then one day you hook up with Brice. Bingo! But since then I'm neurotic for not doing the same."

"Hey, I don't want you to hook up with Brice," Elliot cried in mock protest. "We're both strictly monogamous."

"I can't tell you how relieved I am to hear that," Kate retorted. "But don't project your fears onto me. It isn't easy to find a kindhearted, dependable, intelligent, sensual single man in Manhattan."

"Tell me about it!" Elliot exclaimed. "I had to try almost every guy on the island before I met Brice."

"Try not to be bitter, Elliot. I try so hard not to be." She reached up and wiped off a remaining bit of banana from his mouth with her thumb, then gave him a little peck on the lips. "Do you really have to be gay?" Then she smiled. Elliot was everything to her except her lover. And sometimes she thought that's what made her love him the most. Elliot was safe. Unlike the other men in her life, Elliot would always be there.

"What makes you think I'm gay?" Elliot asked with wide-eyed innocence. "Is that your professional opinion, doctor, or just a guess? Is it my spectator pumps?"

In fact, Elliot was not a flamboyant homosexual. He didn't look or act like what Kate's old Brooklyn crowd might have called "a fag," and like most of the young gay men in New York, he didn't go in for the high-maintenance *GQ*. Elliot looked and acted like a grade school math teacher—no, what he looked like, she thought affectionately, was a classic nerd: The only thing missing was the broken glasses held together with tape.

"How did a little queer kid from Indiana get to be so well-adjusted?" Kate asked him, also not for the first time.

Elliot reached over, took one of Kate's hands, and held it in both of his. "Listen closely," he told her, "because I am going to tell you something from Indiana about getting in touch with your true feelings." He looked at her intently and asked, "Are you listening? Because I am *not* going to repeat this." Kate nodded, and Elliot continued. "I got in touch with my true feelings by learning how to mask them very early in life. When you realize that your true feelings are most likely going to get the shit kicked out of you, you learn how to hide them and nurse them inside of you for as long as you have to until you find a safe place to express them." He smiled and gave Kate's hand a gentle squeeze. "You and Brice are where I can express them. And I don't recommend kids try to find a best friend and lover when they're in Andrew Country Day."

"I hear you," Kate agreed, and thought of poor Brian again.

"So, what *are* you doing now before dinner? Feel like making the trip to Dean and DeLuca with me?"

Kate noticed the time—she'd have to hurry now—and gathered up her backpack and cotton sweater. "No can do. I must run. I have a date."

"You're meeting this early with Michael?" Elliot asked, surprised. "You have a date with him *before* he's coming to dinner with us?"

"It's not with Michael."

"You have another date with someone else before Michael? And I don't know about it?" Elliot's voice rose with shock and offense. "How could that happen? On average we speak six point four times a day in person and two point nine times by phone. A date I don't know everything about is a statistical improbability."

Kate rolled her eyes and decided to put him out of his misery. "It's just a date with Bina. Barbie's told her Jack is finally popping the question tonight—they're going to Nobu because Jack wants to make it really special—and to help prepare her, I'm taking her out for a manicure." She wiggled her fingers in the air. "They should look good for the ring," she said in an accent similar to Bina's Brooklynese.

"You're kidding! And you didn't tell me?" Elliot asked.

She shrugged, slipped on her jacket, shouldered her bag, and started toward the door. "I guess not."

Elliot followed her to the school door. "The fabled Bina and the much-sought-after Jack. Together at last."

"Yep, wedding bells have broken up that old gang of mine," Kate said. "Bye-bye, Bitches of Bushwick. It's only Bunny and me left unmarried." She looked down at her Swatch, refusing to acknowledge the depression this thought gave her. "Gotta go."

"Where are you and Bina getting together?" Elliot demanded.

"In SoHo," Kate answered as she pushed against the bar of the school safety door.

"Oh, good. I'm going that way. Just let me pick up my stuff."

"Forget it," Kate told him sternly.

"No. No. Wait for me!" he begged. "We can take the subway together, and I can finally meet Bina." Kate tried to keep her face still. Elliot had waged a year-long campaign to meet her old Brooklyn gang. But Kate didn't need it. In fact, as she'd made it clear more times than she could count, she loathed the idea. She'd tried in the dozen years since she'd left home to erase most of the dark memories of her troubled background, and though she was still close friends with Bina Horowitz and occasionally saw her other old pals, she didn't need Elliot's jaundiced eye appraising them.

Kate gave him a look. She disappeared out the door, then called back, "You need to meet Bina like I need another unemployed boyfriend."

She thought she was safely away and down the steps of the school when she heard Elliot behind her. He had on a madras hat and was clutching his backpack with one hand while he ran in a crouched posture that was a cross between Groucho's walk and a begging position. "Oh, come on," he pleaded. "It's not fair."

"Tragic. Absolutely tragic. Just like so many things in life," Kate told him, and kept on walking while he flapped at his other backpack strap.

"How come I never get to meet any of your Brooklyn friends?" he demanded. "They sound so fascinating."

Kate stopped in the schoolyard and turned back to Elliot. "Bina may be a lot of things, but fascinating is not one of them." Bina Horowitz had been her best friend since third grade and was still, in some ways, the most dependable. Kate had spent every holiday and most summer vacations at Bina's, partly because the Horowitz house was so clean and orderly and Bina's mom was so kind, but mostly because it allowed Kate to avoid the empty apartment that was her home or, worse, her father, who was too often drunk.

If Kate had perhaps outgrown Bina, who'd dropped out of Brooklyn College and worked at her father's chiropractic office, it didn't stop her from loving her. It was just that they had different interests, and none of Bina's would appeal to Elliot or any of her other Manhattan friends.

"Elliot," Kate said sternly as they made their way down the street. "You know your interest in Bina is only idle curiosity."

"Come on," Elliot coaxed. "Let me come. Anyway, it's a free country. The Constitution says so."

Kate snorted. "Unlike the U.S. Constitution, I believe in the separation of church and state."

"No," retorted Elliot, "you believe in the separation of gay and straight."

"That's not fair. You had dinner with Rita and me a week ago." She wasn't going to let him manipulate her with his politically correct blackmail. "You're not meeting Bina because even though she's my oldest friend, you have nothing, absolutely nothing, in common with her."

"I like people I have nothing in common with," Elliot argued. "That's why I like you and live with Brice."

"Don't be greedy, you're getting to meet Michael tonight," said Kate. "Isn't that enough for two yentas like you and Brice?"

"Yeah," Elliot conceded, giving in. "It will have to do."

Kate laughed and said, "Come on, I'm going to be late for my girlie date. Let me give you the same advice I gave Jennifer Whalen, my student, a few hours ago. 'Try to make your own friends, dear.'"

They were at the IRT subway entrance. She gave Elliot a big smile and then hugged him good-bye. He shrugged, admitting his defeat. As she descended into the shadow of the subway, Elliot shouted after her, "Don't forget; dinner's at eight!"

"See ya there!" she yelled back, and ran to get the train.

Chapter Three

Kate and Bina walked down Lafayette Street, gazing in the windows of the fashion boutiques and art galleries that lined the SoHo strip. Kate looked and felt at home in SoHo. She would have liked to live in the neighborhood, but it was far too pricey for a school psychologist's salary. Her apartment was in Chelsea, but Kate could pass as a downtown hipster. Bina Horowitz, on the other hand, was still all Brooklyn: her dark hair too done, her clothes all "matchy-matchy," as Barbie used to say back in high school. Short, a little dumpy, and wearing too much gold, Bina stuck out like a sore thumb among the modelesque shoppers converging in one of the coolest sections of downtown Manhattan. That didn't stop Kate from loving her friend dearly, but she was grateful for all she herself had learned about style from Brice, college, Manhattan boutiques, and her current New York friends. She'd left her Brooklyn look far behind, thank goodness.

"My God, Katie, I don't know how you live here," Bina said. "These people in Manhattan are the reason girls all over the country go anorexic." Kate just laughed, though Bina wasn't far from wrong. Bina continued to crane her neck at every opportunity, slowing them down to look at a pedestrian painting of a nude, or a dress shop window where the clothes were torn into strips, and to marvel at the boutique called Center for the Dull. Kate had to explain it was just a clothing store like Yellow Rat Bastard—a store Kate didn't shop in, although she had one of their shopping bags.

"Why all the confusing names?" Bina asked. "And isn't it hot?" she added, fanning herself frantically with a flyer for a failing Off-Off Broadway show that some guy had just shoved into her hand as they walked by. He hadn't tried to palm one off on Kate, but then she didn't look like the kind of person who accepted garbage.

"Just calm down," Kate said. She tried to quicken their pace—the salon was notorious for demanding promptness—but Bina was Bina, and she simply couldn't be rushed or silenced. The Horowitz family had taken Kate in when she was eleven, and Kate knew practically everything about Bina. Kate had once done the math and realized that Mrs. Horowitz had fed her more than five hundred meals (most of them made with chicken fat). Dr. Horowitz had taught her to ride a two-wheeler bike when Kate's own father was too drunk or too lazy (or both) to bother to do it. Bina's brother, Dave, had taught the two of them to swim in the municipal pool, and Kate still swam laps whenever she could.

Back in Brooklyn, when Kate had had no other outlet and longed for more sophisticated friends—like Elliot and Brice and Rita—with whom she could banter or talk about books, Bina had sometimes annoyed her. But now that she had a circle of intellectual, cosmopolitan pals, she could give up the frustration over Bina's provincial interests and conversation and simply love her good heart.

"It's really hot," Bina repeated—a habit she had when Bina was paying no attention to Kate's response.

"Is it hotter in Manhattan than it is in Brooklyn?" Kate asked her, teasing.

"It's *always* hotter in Manhattan than it is in Brooklyn," Bina confirmed, completely missing Kate's irony. Bina definitely had an irony deficiency. "It's all these damned sidewalks and all this traffic." She looked up and down Lafayette Street and shook her head in disgust. "I couldn't live here," she muttered, as if the choice were hers and million-dollar lofts were an option she and Jack could consider. "I just couldn't do it."

"And you don't," Kate reminded her, "so what's the problem?"

Bina stopped fanning herself abruptly, looked at Kate with a wide-eyed appeal, and meekly asked the question that she always asked midway through one of her anti-Manhattan tirades. "Am I being horrible?"

Kate felt a rush of affection overcome her annoyance and, as always, remembered why she loved Bina. Then she gave her the answer that she always did: "Same old Bina."

"Same old Katie," Bina responded in the litany they'd used to make peace and settle differences for two decades.

Kate grinned, and the two of them were right back on track. Kate could neither imagine introducing Bina to her Manhattan friends nor envision life without Bina—although she sometimes tried. Bina absolutely refused to grow, and that was both irritating and comforting to Kate—and sometimes downright embarrassing.

Just as they crossed Spring Street, Bina, as if reading Kate's thoughts, virtually shouted, "God, look at him!"

Kate turned her head, expecting at the least to see a mugging in progress. Instead, across the street she saw a pierced and tattooed guy going about his business, not the slightest bit fazed by the local wildlife. Kate didn't even comment; she merely looked down at her watch. "We can't be late," she warned Bina. "I have something special reserved." And to change the subject, "So have you picked out a manicure color?"

Bina dragged her eyes away from the local sideshow with obvious difficulty and focused instead on Kate. "I was thinking of a French manicure," she admitted.

Kate felt distinctly unenthusiastic, and it must have shown. Bina had been having the tips of her nails painted white with the rest a natural pink since high school.

"What's wrong with a French manicure?" Bina asked defensively.

"Nothing, if you're French," Kate retorted, having conveniently forgotten her teenage days when she, too, thought a

French manicure the height of sophistication. Bina looked puzzled by Kate's remark. Kate had forgotten Bina's irony deficiency. "Hey, why not just try for something a little more up-to-date?"

Bina held out her hands and studied them. Kate noticed she was still wearing the Claddagh friendship ring Kate had given her for her sweet sixteen. "Go for something . . . daring," Kate suggested.

"Like what?" Bina asked, again defensively. "A tattoo on my fingernail?"

"Oooh, sarcasm. The devil's weapon," Kate said.

"Jack likes French manicures," Bina whined, still looking at her left hand. "Don't push me around like you always try to." Then she dropped her hands to her sides. They were both silent for a moment. "I'm sorry," Bina said. "I'm just a little nervous. You know, I've been waiting for Jack to propose for over—"

"Six years?" Kate asked, forgiving her friend. She had to start remembering to stop giving unwanted advice, which was difficult for a woman with her temperament in her profession. She smiled at Bina as they continued to walk down the street. "I think that on your first date with Jack, you started designing the monograms for your towels."

Jack and Bina had been going out for so many years. He had been her first and only real love. He'd made her wait while he finished college, got his degree, and became a CPA. Bina giggled. "Well, I knew right away he was the one. Such a hottie."

Kate reflected on the wide variation of people's tastes. To her, Jack was so far from a hottie that he left her ice cold. Of course, she'd never, ever, in all the six years of their courtship revealed that to Bina. And Bina had thought Steven was sour and gaunt, while to Kate he'd been—

"I just can't believe that he's leaving for Hong Kong for five months tomorrow, and tonight's the night," Bina chattered on, interrupting Kate's thoughts. Kate smiled at her.

There were few secrets among Kate's old Brooklyn posse, so when Jack had consulted with Barbie's jeweler father to get "a good deal" on an engagement ring, the news had traveled faster than e-mail among them. The day Bina had waited for for so long had finally arrived, but when Kate glanced at her friend, she noticed something odd: Bina seemed anything but happy. Surely she couldn't be having second thoughts. But Kate knew Bina well enough to see that something wasn't right.

Oh, my God, thought Kate. Bina has changed her mind, and she's afraid to tell anyone. Her parents—especially her mother!—will be beside themselves if . . . "Bina, are you starting to have doubts?" she asked as gently as she could, stopping to look at her friend. "You know, you don't *have* to marry Jack."

"Are you crazy? Of course I do! I want to. I'm just nervous that . . . well, I'm just nervous. Normal, right? Hey, where is this place, anyway?"

"Just to the left on Broome," Kate said. And if Bina didn't want to talk about her nerves, it was fine, she told herself. Give the girl a little space. "This is the Police Building," she said as a diversion while they passed the domed monument that Teddy Roosevelt had built when he was chief of police. "It's condos now," she went on, "and they found a secret tunnel from here to the speakeasy across the street, so—"

"So the Irish cops wouldn't be caught getting drunk," Bina said, then stopped in embarrassment. Kate just smiled. Her father, a retired Irish cop, had died three years ago from cirrhosis of the liver, and Kate couldn't help but consider it a release for both of them. It was the Horowitzes who couldn't get over it.

"No harm, no foul," Kate told her. "We're almost there and we're only four minutes late. You're going to like this place. They have great nail colors, but just in case, I brought a few alternatives for you." She scrambled around in her Prada bag—the only purse she owned, and she carried it everywhere. It had cost her an entire paycheck, but every time she opened it, it gave her pleasure. Now she pulled out a little bag. It contained three nail polishes, each one a wildly different seductive shade.

Bina took the bag and peeked into it. "Ooooh! They look like the magic beans from 'Jack and the Beanstalk,'" she said. Then she started to giggle. "Get it? Jack and his beanstalk?" she asked, raising her eyebrows suggestively.

Kate gave Bina her "I'm not in the mood" look. Clearly her moment of nervousness had passed. "Hey, spare me the details of Jack's beanstalk or any other part of his anatomy," she begged. "Consider that your bridesmaid's gift to me." She took Bina's arm to get her around the guy selling used magazines on the sidewalk and across to their destination.

Just then, as they crossed the street, Bina stopped—as if the Manhattan traffic would wait for her—and pointed to the corner. "Omigod! That's Bunny's ex."

Kate looked in the right direction as she simultaneously pulled Bina's arm down. She was about to tell her not to point when she caught sight of one of the best-looking men she had ever seen. He was tall and slim, and his jeans and jacket had the perfect casual slouch. As a cloud moved, light from the west fell on that corner and reflected off his hair as if he had a halo around his head. He had stopped for the light, and before he began to cross the street, he fished in his inside pocket. Kate couldn't help following his hand, and as he crossed the street she turned her head to get a look at his buns. She always had a weakness in that area, and this guy was . . . well, his buns must have come from the very best bakery.

"He went out with Bunny?" Kate asked. Of her posse, Bunny was probably the most garish and certainly the dimmest bulb.

Bina nodded. Kate could only see that in her peripheral vision, because she couldn't tear her eyes off the man just twenty feet away.

"Are you sure that's him?"

To Kate's good luck, the guy stopped at the corner across from them and turned downtown in their direction. Kate stood rooted to the spot, although it was a few steps off the curb. She thought that he looked at her. Just then a taxi honked, the driver deciding he would warn them before he ran them over. At a shriek from Bina, Kate pulled her eyes away, and the two of them scampered across the street. By the time they had walked single file between parked cars and gotten to the sidewalk, the Adonis had put on sunglasses and was striding away.

"What color do you think I should do for bridesmaids?" Bina asked.

Kate suppressed a groan. Bev had had them all in silver, and Barbie had picked a pistachio green that not even a blonde could wear without looking sallow. "How about basic black?" Kate asked, but she knew there wasn't a hope in hell. She sighed. She and Bunny would be the last of their high school crowd not to be married—at least there was still Bunny. Kate would try not to mind, but everyone else would. No one at Bina's wedding would leave the naked state of her left finger unnoted. "Please, Bina! Don't make me walk down that aisle again. Why not just make me wear a sign that says 'Unmarriageable'?"

"Kate, you have to be my maid of honor. Barbie was always closer to Bunny, and Bev . . . well, Bev never really liked me."

"Bev has never liked anyone," Kate informed Bina, not for the first time, and took her arm. "Hey, I'm really touched." The pair came up to the door of the salon. Kate held the door open for Bina, who nervously stepped inside.

Chapter Four

Kate knew the spa was unlike any place Bina had ever seen in her life—a sort of postindustrial French boudoir with Moorish touches. That was exactly why she had chosen it. Not to show off, but to make it very special for her friend. "This is," she informed Bina in a dramatic stage whisper, "the most expensive spa in the city of New York." She studied Bina's face to make sure what she was telling her was sinking in. "And I mean the *entire* city," she continued.

"Wow," was all Bina could manage, looking around at the sheer curtains, the concrete floor, and the Louis XVI bergere armchair.

Kate smiled and walked up to the counter. A chic young Asian woman smiled back and, without speaking, raised her perfectly shaped eyebrows. They did a good brow wax here. "Kate Jameson," Kate announced. "There are the two of us here," she added, because Bina had disappeared shyly behind Kate. "For manicures, pedicures, and toe waxing."

From behind, Bina whispered, "Toe waxing?" but Kate ignored her. "We have a reservation. I have the confirmation number."

"It will be just a moment," said the beautiful receptionist. "Please, have a seat."

Of course, that was difficult with just the one antique armchair, but Kate motioned for Bina to sit and she did, albeit gingerly.

Then she looked up at Kate and grabbed her hands. "Oh, Kate. I'm nervous. What happens if I go through all this and it jinxes me? What if Jack doesn't—"

"Bina, don't be silly. You can't 'jinx' things." Kate sighed. "I just spent an hour trying to convince an eight-year-old that magic won't work. Don't make me repeat myself."

"Look, I know all about you. Little Miss Logic. But I'm superstitious, okay? No black cats, no hats on the bed, no shoes to friends."

"Shoes to friends?"

"Yeah. You give shoes to a friend and she walks away from you," Bina said. "Don't you know that?"

"Bina, you are truly crazy," Kate said. "Anyway, this is your big day, and I want to be a part of it. So relax and enjoy. Everything will be fine, and tonight with Jack will be wonderful."

Bina still looked doubtful. She craned her neck and looked around again. "It just must be so expensive," she said. "You know, I can have all of the same things done in Brooklyn at Kim's Korean place for about one-quarter the price. And I bet it's every bit as good, too."

Kate smiled. "Maybe—maybe not. But here you have ambience."

"Well, my mother would say, 'Ambience, schmambience, paint my nails.'"

"You know I love your mother, but sometimes she's not exactly au courant." Bina looked perplexed. "And by the way, how do you spell schmambience?" Kate asked with a smile.

"You don't," Bina told her. "It's Yiddish. It's a spoken language."

Kate laughed. This was typical of the verbal exchanges she and Bina had been having since Kate first entered the Horowitzes' household and Mrs. Horowitz pronounced that Kate's father knew *"bupkis"* about raising a *"sheyna maidela."*

At the time, Kate didn't know that *bupkis* meant "virtually nothing" or that *sheyna maidela* meant "pretty little girl," but she figured it out from the context. She learned what *putz* and *shnorrer* and *gonif* meant, all of them words that sounded better and more accurate than their English equivalents.

Kate had celebrated every holiday at Bina's house—even if they weren't Kate's holidays—and learned to love sweet noodle kugel. When the time came for Kate's first Holy Communion, Mrs. Horowitz sewed up Kate's white dress and bought a headpiece. (When Bina wanted a white dress and headpiece, too, she got one, though Dr. and Mrs. Horowitz drew the line at allowing Bina to get on line with the little Catholic girls for the ceremony.)

Kate, told by a priest in her catechism class that trick-or-treating on Halloween was a mortal sin, felt tremendous disappointment. When she shared this with Bina's mother, the reassurance Kate got was, "Sin, schmin! Do your best with that *meshugene* in a dress and go out to get your candy. Don't worry about it."

"But I don't want to go to hell after I die," Kate told her tearfully.

"Hell, schmell," Mrs. Horowitz responded. "Trust me, there's no such place except here on earth." She drew Kate onto her lap and held her close. "There's only heaven, honey," she whispered. "And that's where your mama is."

Somehow, Mrs. Horowitz's complete conviction sank in. A few months later, after catechism, when Vicky Brown told Kate and Bina that Bina's Jewish mother was going to hell after she died, Kate turned to Vicky and declared, "Hell, schmell! What do you know?" After that, Kate and Bina made a pact to stick up for each other.

Maybe it was from that day they became known as the "Witches of Bushwick." As teenagers, their posse grew, with Bev and Barbie and, later on, Bunny, but they stayed the same, though in the neighborhood their nickname changed to "Bitches." Then Kate drifted from the group.

Bina was still holding on to Kate's hand. "Oh, Kate," she said, and squeezed hard. "I'm so excited! Tonight's the night I get proposed to by the man I love."

"Don't forget to act surprised," Kate warned her. "You don't want Jack to know you already knew."

"I wish Barbie hadn't told me that he bought the ring." Bina sighed. "I'm so nervous. Why couldn't she just have let it be a surprise for me?"

"Oh, honey." Kate laughed. "You don't want surprises. You want to look your best."

Just then another Asian woman even more beautiful than the receptionist walked into the waiting area. "Kate Jameson?" she asked. Kate nodded. "We have your room all ready. Follow me, please."

Kate and Bina followed her into a small room, and Kate sat in one of two facing chairs. Each was thronelike, with a built-in foot Jacuzzi already filled with delightful-smelling bubbling water. The softly lit room, all in soothing sea blue, also had two glass tables on wheels prepared for hand pampering. Two young Asian women knelt on blue silk pillows on the floor beside the foot baths. They helped their clients out of their shoes and indicated that they should plunge their feet into the fragrant Jacuzzis in preparation for the pedicure. Bina looked across at Kate in amazement. Kate merely smiled at her. The air smelled of freesia, and Kate took a deep, appreciative breath. If she had to pay half her salary check for the "ambience, schmambience," it was *so* worth it. The second beautiful Asian woman came back into their blue heaven and asked the pair, "Would you like bottled water, coffee, tea, juice, or champagne?"

"You're kidding!" Bina almost squealed.

"Champagne, I think," Kate replied as if Bina hadn't reacted. Bina didn't usually drink, but, "This is a big celebration," Kate told her.

In the moment of silence that followed, Kate closed her eyes, and the image that came to her, unbidden, was the long, lean jeans-clad guy whom Bina had pointed out. She must have been wrong. Bunny could never have dated someone like that. She mused about it for a moment or two and, guiltily, compared what she had seen to Michael. Michael was just a little too broad in the beam, and there was something about his walk. . . . Kate shook the thoughts from her head as unworthy. "What's his name?" she asked Bina.

"Whose name? Jack? His name is Jack." Bina gave her a look, then laughed. "You're so funny." Kate blushed and decided to forget about the guy on the corner.

"Kate, this is so nice of you," Bina began as one of the two pedicurists began to massage her feet. She giggled, pulled them away, and giggled again.

"Oh, just relax, Bina," Kate told her. "Breathe." For a moment the two were silent. Kate closed her eyes and let herself feel the strong hands work her heels and instep.

Bina leaned forward to whisper across the small room, "Is this really where Sandra Bullock, Giselle, and Gwen Stefani get their manicures?"

"Yup," Kate said. "And it's where Kate Jameson and Bina Horowitz have their manicures, too."

"Soon to be Bina Horowitz Weintraub," Bina reminded her. "Oh, Kate, I love Jack so much. I'm just so . . . so happy today, and so glad I'm sharing part of it with you. I just want you to find your Jack and be as happy as I am."

Kate laughed. "As your mother would say, 'From your lips to God's ears.'" Before Bina could speak, the door opened and the woman entered with a tray holding two flutes of champagne. She offered one to Kate and one to Bina.

"Enjoy!" she said as she glided from the room.

Kate felt a slight change in her emotional landscape. There was a time when she thought she might be drinking champagne to celebrate something with Steven, but she had been very wrong. She wondered if the time would come when she and Michael . . . She pulled her thoughts away and focused on the moment.

Bina looked at her glass. "I don't think I should start drinking this early in the afternoon."

Kate rolled her eyes. Bina never wanted to drink. "Oh, come

on, Bina. Live a little," she said, lifting her own flute. "To your wedding!"

"Oh, Kate!" Bina was clearly touched. Both girls took a sip of their champagne. Then Kate started looking through the polishes. "Boy, I bet Bunny wishes she were in my chair," Bina said, leaning back.

"How *is* Bunny?" Kate asked. Bunny was a dental hygienist whose record with men was admittedly poor. Again Kate thought of the delicious-looking man they had seen outside. Bunny's ex? It was hard to believe.

"You don't want to know," replied Bina.

Bina was right. Kate *didn't* want to know. Bunny was really more Bina's friend. She'd entered Kate's life in junior high, taking the Bitches to five and changing her name—Patricia—to begin with B so she'd fit in with the gang. Kate had drifted from the group by then. She spent more time studying and reading. While the others were worrying almost exclusively about hair, makeup, and boys, Kate was focused on SAT scores and college scholarships. And when graduation day came, the other Bitches set their sights on nondemanding jobs, good marriages, and babies, while Kate declared that she was not just going to "sleep-away" college, but also intended to become a doctor of psychology.

As Bev put it, "She thinks she's who the fuck she is." If it hadn't been for Bina, that would've been the end of Kate's association with the Bitches and everyone else in Brooklyn. But Bina made friends for life. At first Kate had resented what she had considered Bina's "clinging." Then she realized that there was no one who knew her the way Bina did. And while she'd prefer to forget much of her other "backlash" from Brooklyn, for Bina's friendship she was grateful.

She finished her glass of champagne and was immediately brought another. Bina was still talking about Bunny.

". . . so the guy drops her like a rock. You saw him. I mean, Bunny should have known he wasn't for her, but she took it hard. And now she's on the rebound. She's already going out with another guy—Arnie or Barney or something—and she's telling Barbie they're getting serious."

Big news flash. Bunny picked one inappropriate man after another, always insisting they were "serious" and always being disappointed. Classic repetition compulsion, Kate thought, but what she said was, "Denial ain't just a river in Egypt."

"What?" Bina paused for a moment. "Oh! I get it!" She paused again, then made her voice falsely casual. "How are things going with this Michael?"

"All right," Kate said noncommittally, and shrugged. She liked to keep a low profile on her dating life with Bina and the others, or else the Horowitz family would be sending out engraved announcements. "He's very smart and seems promising. We're going over to Elliot and Brice's tonight for dinner."

"Who's Brice?" Bina asked.

Kate sighed. When it came to Brooklyn, Bina remembered what day of the month each of her friends had their periods, but outside Brooklyn . . .

"Elliot's partner."

"Elliot who?"

"You remember, Elliot Winston. My friend from Brown. The guy I teach with."

"Oh, yeah. So if he's a teacher, how does he have a partner?"

"His *life* partner, Bina," Kate said, exasperated.

Bina paused, then dropped her voice. "Are those guys gay?"

Yeah, and so is your unmarried uncle Kenny, Kate thought, but all she did was smile tolerantly. So what if Bina's gender politics were way behind the times. She decided to change the subject. "So what color are you going to go with? Remember, every shade goes with a diamond!"

"I don't know. What have *you* picked?"

Of course the question was completely irrelevant, but Bina was like that. Before she selected anything from a menu, she had to know what you were having.

"Same old Bina," Kate said, smiling at her irrepressible friend.

"Same old Katie," Bina said, slurring her words a bit. The champagne was clearly starting to get to her, and looking at her friend, ready to take such a big yet inevitable step, Kate shivered. Jack had never been her cup of tea—and he certainly was no glass of champagne—but he seemed loving to Bina, her family liked him, and . . . well, looking across at Bina, Kate had to admit that Jack was probably a good match. She was torn between bursting into tears and laughing out loud. Bina smiled at her, slightly cross-eyed. "I love you, Katie," she said.

"I love you, too, Bina," Kate assured her, and it was true. "But no more drinks for you. You've got a big night ahead of you."

Bina took a last sip of champagne. Then she leaned over, close to her friend. "Kate," she whispered. "There's something I'm dying to ask you."

Kate steeled herself. "Yes?"

"What's a toe waxing?" Bina inquired.

Bina's tone made it sound obscene. Kate laughed. "You know how sometimes there is a little bit of hair on the knuckle of your big toe?" she asked.

Bina pulled her foot out of the Jacuzzi and studied it. "Wow," she said. "Look at it. Eeuuyew." One of the Asian women turned to look at the other, and both started to giggle. Bina's face turned a bright pink. "It's kind of icky," she admitted. "Like Bigfoot. God, Katie, you're making me feel like a freak. But I never noticed it before."

"Well," Kate continued, "after it's waxed off, Jack won't, either. You can let him kiss all your little piggies with pride. So, what color have you picked?"

Bina turned her attention to the gift bottles from Kate and the others arranged beautifully along the wall shelf at her elbow. "They don't have most of these colors in Brooklyn," she admitted.

"Just one more reason why I live in Manhattan," Kate declared. "Step up to the plate. What's it going to be?"

Bina looked down at the Asian girl already working on her left hand. "Do you do French manicures?" she asked.

Chapter Five

Kate's Manhattan apartment was undeniably small. Still, she had been lucky to find it. It was in a brownstone on West 19th Street, on a tree-lined block close to the seminary, a very desirable location. The apartment was on the first floor, above street level, and consisted of a large room that had once been a parlor, a small bathroom and smaller kitchen behind it, and then a cozy bedroom.

The main room faced the back garden, which unfortunately belonged to the apartment below. But at least she had quiet, a green view in summer, and a chance to watch the snow in winter. She hadn't had much money to spend on furniture, but Elliot, always alert for bargains, had helped her find and carry home the sofa—a small one with blue-and-white awning stripe. She had found an old wicker rocker in a thrift store, and after it was sprayed blue, it made a comfortable, if slightly rickety, seat.

Max, who lived upstairs, had recently helped her put up bookshelves that now filled in the recesses on either side of the fireplace. Max was a friend of Bina's brother and he worked on Wall Street with Jack, his cousin. He'd introduced Bina to Jack, so when Kate had heard that he was searching for an apartment, she'd let him know about the one about to become available in her building. Max, who would be forever grateful, had also been interested in her, but Kate couldn't get up any enthusiasm. He was nice and good-looking, but they had nothing to talk about, although Max didn't seem to mind that. And though her father had given her precious little advice about life, he had expressed his philosophy to "never crap where you eat." She had managed to handle Max diplomatically, though, and they were friends as well as good neighbors. Though Max would never need to stop by to borrow a cup of sugar, he might well ask for a cup of coffee, a shot of vodka, or, less frequently, a fix-up with some girl Kate knew.

Kate opened the curtains. It looked like rain. She threw her purse on the sofa and hurried across to her bedroom. The beauty treatment with Bina had taken more time than she'd expected, and she had only a half hour before Michael came over. Although she had been cavalier about it with Elliot earlier in the day, Kate was actually a little nervous about bringing Michael over. Introducing a boyfriend to Elliot was like taking him home to meet her family, and she wanted everything to go smoothly.

Kate's bedroom was really just a part of the larger room that had been partitioned off. Its biggest disadvantage was the smallness of its closet.

But she lived with it, as most New Yorkers did. Kate decided she didn't have the time to shower, so she selected the Madonna blue sleeveless dress she'd just bought and ran into the bathroom. She had enough time to wash her face, take her hair down, brush the cascades of wavy red that fell below her shoulders, and pull out her makeup bag for a quick fix.

She never wore much makeup. Her skin was pale, and she'd finally outgrown the tiny freckles, no bigger than pinpoints, that used to dance across her cheeks and the bridge of her nose—a sort of Irish trail. Now her face was simply creamy, and most of the time she only bothered with lipstick so that her hair didn't overpower the rest of her face.

She had only ten minutes before Michael was supposed to arrive, though he was often a little late. That, she'd come to understand, wasn't because he was disrespectful—Kate hated lateness as a pattern and thought it a narcissistic trait—but because he was often so wrapped up in his work and thoughts of his research that he occasionally forgot to get off the subway or he overshot the bus stop.

She smiled at the thought of him. He had a good mind, good hands, and a strong jaw. She liked his silver-rimmed glasses, his earnest eyes peering through them, and his dedication to his work.   .

She had only recently begun sleeping with him: She wasn't usually so prim, but her affair with Steven had left her more cautious than she had been before. They had met at her friend Tina's; Tina and Michael worked at the same university. Tina hadn't "fixed them up" because she hadn't thought that Michael was Kate's type, but since Steven, Kate wasn't sure what her "type" ought to be. Michael's courtship had been slow but steady. When they had finally taken the plunge, Kate had been delighted to find he was caring and generous in bed. And it seemed as if he were just as taken with her. But this was the point of the relationship where things could go on for a long time without actually moving forward. Kate had spent nearly two years with Steven, a writer, and had been hurt when she realized that he would never want to marry her or possibly anyone else. She didn't want to spend another year only to have that happen again.

She sat on her bed and looked down at her painted toes. For a moment she could even imagine being envious of Bina, who had her life settled. But she reminded herself that Bina had put in her six years with Jack. She knew she wanted children but wouldn't marry just for that. The work she did with Brian and the others at Andrew Country Day would hold her until she was ready to have a normal family of her own.

And Michael seemed like a possibility. They had not yet discussed exclusivity, but, as he called her almost every night and since they saw each other regularly, Kate thought the talk would be only a formality. She wasn't in a rush and wouldn't make ultimatums. Still, deep down, she wanted to know her goals were shared.

Kate slipped into the silk dress and scrambled under the bed for her high-heeled sandals. Black and strappy, they would show off her newly painted toenails. They were killers to walk in, but she didn't have to walk far to Elliot's.

When there was a knock at the door a few moments later, Kate was ready. She clicked across the floor and opened the door. But it wasn't Michael. Max was there, holding a bouquet of snapdragons and statice. "Hey," he said. "You look great."

"Thanks." Kate smiled briefly, trying to show she didn't have the time to chat. Max held the flowers without moving. He had an adorable smile; one of his incisors showed because it had moved up onto the tooth next to it, and Kate found that appealing. But Max was a bit like his incisor: He often tried to push in where he didn't belong. There was no harm in him, though, and no denying he was a likable guy.

"Are those for me?" she asked.

"You betcha," Max said. "The green market was open when I walked by. The snapdragons reminded me of your hair. You can't say no."

Kate didn't. But as she took the bouquet, she worried that Max might still have a crush on her. She didn't want to encourage him, nor did she want to be rude. She tapped across the living room floor to the tiny excuse for a kitchen and fumbled for a vase. Max followed her and stood in the doorway. Kate filled the vase and couldn't help but smile when she saw the red snaps with the orange centers. "I wish I could wear two of these as earrings," she joked.

"You don't need any earrings," Max said. "You look perfect. And as cool as a cucumber."

Kate took the flowers and set them on her small dining table. They did make a pretty spot of color. "Thanks, Max," she said, and kissed him on the cheek, leaving a small imprint of lip gloss.

"Where you off to?" he asked.

"Oh, just dinner at Elliot's." Max, an accountant and actuarial, occasionally enjoyed talking higher math with Elliot. She hadn't yet told Max about Michael.

"Well, that dress is wasted on him," Max said, and to Kate's dismay, he sat down. It wasn't that she had any reason to feel guilty, but she didn't want Michael to arrive and find another man in her apartment or to have to introduce them to each other. Michael didn't seem overly possessive. On the contrary, he seemed a little nervous. But Kate wanted him to feel secure, so she also wanted Max to get up and go, although she didn't want to have to ask him.

Max shifted position on the striped sofa and pulled some envelopes and a rolled-up magazine from his back pocket.

"Oh, here. I picked up your mail."

Kate smiled and tried to hide a sigh. There were no separate mailboxes for the four tenants of their brownstone, and mail was left on a radiator in the vestibule. "Are you being so nice to me because you wanted to borrow a bottle of Absolut?"

"No, I try not to rustle booze until it's Absolut necessary."

Kate gave him another obligatory smile. He was a nice guy, but a little tiresome. "Well, hey, I've got to go."

Max got up and ambled over to the door. "Whatever." At last she saw his back and closed the door. She took the mail he had brought and walked over to the wastepaper basket beside her desk. She tried to smooth out *The New Yorker;* picked up a catalog from Saks, tore it in half, and threw it into the basket before it could tempt her; filed a bill from Con Ed next to her checkbook; and threw away all the junk mail. Then, at the bottom of the small pile, she found an almost square envelope addressed to her in gold calligraphy. Oh, my God, she thought, has Bina jumped the gun and sent out wedding invitations before the proposal?

She turned over the ominous communiqué and saw Mr. and Mrs. Tromboli's address written across the back. Kate's hands began to tremble. She slit open the envelope and accidentally tore off the corner of the enclosed pasteboard. She pulled out the inevitable: an invitation to the wedding of Patricia (Bunny) Marie Tromboli to Arnold S. Beckmen. For a moment, Kate felt dizzy. How could this have happened? What had Bina been saying earlier about that Brooklyn guy who had broken Bunny's heart? Now Kate felt her own heart quiver. With Bina engaged and Bunny about to get married, she would be the last of her old friends to be single. When they started having children, she would really be alone. And Bev was already heavily pregnant; inevitably, young mothers got involved with playgrounds, preschools, play dates, and pregnancies—the four Ps. Four peas in a pod, the Bs would be busy reproducing, and Kate would be closed out of the circle completely.

She put down the invitation, feeling a little dizzy. Then the buzzer rang. She and Michael had no time for a drink now, and she had no desire for one, either. She hit the intercom as hard as the wedding invitation had hit her, and when he said hello, instead of inviting him upstairs she told him she'd be down in a minute. Stuffing the stiff card into her purse, she told herself she wouldn't think about the Bunny situation; but on her way down the stairs, careful not to trip in the sandals, the idea of Bunny reproducing like a rabbit came to her. As much as she loved the children at school, and as dedicated as she was to them, Kate felt mournful. She knew she would always make do if she didn't have a child of her own to raise and love.

Michael was standing in the vestibule. He was wearing pressed chinos, a white Oxford shirt, and a tweed sports coat. It was a little heavy for the season, but Kate had noticed that he was always careful to dress conservatively and just a little "scholarly." He was both a good-looking and a nice-looking man, just slightly taller than Kate was in her heels, and she liked his abundant curly brown hair. "Hi," she greeted him, trying to put away her concerns the way she had stuffed Bunny's wedding invitation into her bag. They kissed, just a peck on the lips. "You've had a haircut," she said.

"Nope, just had my ears lowered," he replied.

Kate wished he hadn't cut his hair, especially just before meeting Elliot and Brice. It made him the tiniest bit geeky looking, but she put that thought out of her mind as well. Michael looked fine, and he was a decent human being. He had put himself through undergrad and graduate school on scholarships and various jobs. He'd already published papers in important journals and was poised for a brilliant career in academia. He was well-read, well-informed, and well-intentioned, as far as she could tell. The fact that he'd been married—but for only one year, when he was too young to know any better—made him look even better in her eyes. He knew how to commit, even if it had been to the wrong woman.

Now he looked at Kate, and his deep brown eyes sparkled behind his glasses. "You are breathtaking," he said, and Kate smiled. The cost of the dress was well worth it.

"We'd better go," she said. "Brice hates late guests when he's cooking." Despite her words, Michael pushed her gently against the doorway and kissed her. He was a good kisser, and Kate let her tongue and mind wander. Then Max, clothed for the gym, came bounding down the stairs. They pulled apart, but Max, of course, had seen them. He raised his eyebrows as he walked past them, Kate's lip gloss still on his cheek.

"Dinner at Elliot's?" he asked as he walked by and down the stoop. Kate felt a twinge of guilt. Of course, she *was* going to dinner at Elliot's, but by withholding the information that she was going with an escort, she now looked like a liar. Michael, unaware, took her hand and they walked outside and down the steps.

Kate couldn't help but think of her two years in Catholic school. Sins of omission and sins of commission: She thought she remembered they were equal. She promised herself she would find some way to apologize to Max later.

Now she took Michael's arm as they walked down the shady street. Chelsea was very pretty west of Eighth Avenue. "Let's walk through the seminary garden," Michael suggested. Kate smiled her agreement. At this time of day, the block-size park enclosed by the church and seminary buildings was at its most lovely. They walked arm in arm.

"Kate, stop for a minute," Michael said. "I have something for you."

He fumbled around with his briefcase straps for a moment. He had given Kate a gift before—an out-of-print English psychology book by D. W. Winnicott. It had been very thoughtful, and just now she expected another book. But instead he took out a small, oblong box wrapped in silver paper. Unmistakably a jewelry box. "Do you know today is our three-month anniversary?" he asked. Kate actually hadn't, and she was really moved that he had. "I saw this and thought of you," he said. He handed her the box, which she unwrapped. Once she opened it, a thin silver bracelet with a tiny K hanging from it was revealed. She looked from it to the expectant expression on Michael's face. It wasn't anything she would have chosen for herself, but it was very sweet nonetheless.

"Oh, Michael. Thank you." They kissed again, and this time there was no interruption.

"Do you like it?" he asked.

For a moment, Kate thought of sins of omission again, but even Sister Vincent couldn't believe they would extend to this. "Yes. It's lovely. Would you fasten it for me?"

Michael leaned forward and fiddled with the tiny clasp. It took a moment, but at last he had it around her wrist. She stretched out her arm. "It looks very nice," she said.

"It looks great!" Michael said, and tucked her arm in his.

Kate felt better than she had all day.

Chapter Six

Brice and Elliot met three years ago but had moved in together only in September. Brice's stylish retro furniture in orange and lime green had taken precedence over Elliot's collection of thrift shop purchases and off-the-street finds. Their two-bedroom apartment in a Chelsea brownstone near Kate's had large windows in the living room overlooking a tiny backyard. An old refectory table was set before the windows, and despite their protests, Michael and Kate were given the chairs that faced the garden view.

"The tulips are just over and the roses haven't started, so it's not at its best," Brice said apologetically as he seated them; then he excused himself to bring dinner in from the kitchen. Kate noticed they were using Brice's good glassware and Havilland china, and she was touched. Elliot brought in a wine cooler and set it on the oak credenza.

"A coaster! A coaster!" Brice exclaimed, and slipped one under the crystal cooler. Kate suppressed a smile.

In a few moments, dishes were being passed around. Elliot, standing, began to pour wine into the waiting goblets. Michael picked up his glass and almost ostentatiously set it upside down. "None for me, thanks," he said.

Kate winced. She should have seen this one coming. Michael didn't drink at all, just said he didn't like it. Given her father's bad habits, it seemed a good trait to Kate, but she knew it wouldn't go down well with Elliot. He prided himself on his wine cellar—even though it was actually in the linen closet—and he must have taken pains selecting this Pinot Grigio.

"Don't you drink?" Brice asked, his brows slightly raised. Kate could imagine the talk afterward: "Is he an alcoholic, is he in AA. No? Then he's a control freak or a born-again Christian." Oh, it would be endless.

"I prefer to keep a clear head," Michael answered.

"Yeah. You never know when someone might need to see through it," Elliot muttered beside Kate's ear as he reached for her glass.

Once all their plates were filled and the drinking crisis was past, they began on Brice's famous appetizer: a beautiful, multi-colored vegetable terrine. There was some cursory conversation, but the tension seemed thick in the air, especially between Elliot and Michael. Of course, Elliot was always very protective of Kate. And he had already registered his dislike of this accomplished and nice-looking new boyfriend. The fact that Michael was a bit priggish and overly fastidious wasn't lost on Kate, but he did have other, compensatory traits.

"There's a good chance I'm going to get that Sagerman grant," Michael said to Kate as they finished the first course. "I saw Professor Hopkins, and he told me that the committee discussions seemed to be very . . . well, promising." Kate saw Elliot and Brice exchange a look. It was rude of Michael to ignore them, even briefly, but he was a single-minded academic.

Kate held back a sigh. Even when she and Michael were alone, it was sometimes difficult to remember all the cards in his academic deck. Now, to make the conversation general it would be necessary to explain to the others about the Sagerman Foundation, Michael's interest in a postdoctorate appointment, and his complicated relationship with his mentor, Charles Hopkins. It was the kind of thing that made a difference to a couple but didn't make for good dinner talk.

"Great," Kate said.

No one else spoke. Elliot refilled their glasses, and Brice

passed around the second course. Kate looked at it and knew that her friends had spared no expense to impress Michael. This was Brice's risotto with truffles, and she knew what truffles cost. They all took a bite of the steaming rice. As the awkward silence stretched out, Kate turned to Brice in an attempt at light conversation. "Brice, this risotto is really delicious."

"Very good," Michael agreed.

Brice beamed at the compliments. He was proud of his cooking, his design sense, and his extensive collection of pristine Beanie Babies arranged meticulously on a series of long floating shelves over the credenza. Kate had watched Michael notice them and avert his eyes. He was not, she had to admit, very playful in his attitude to decor or dining chitchat.

"So, what happened at the salon this afternoon?" Elliot inquired of Kate.

She smiled. She knew him so well: He was taking pity on her and trying to make the dinner less painful. And he also figured she'd spill her guts more readily just to keep the conversation going. Nice try, she thought, but it wouldn't work.

"Oh, I just had my nails painted," she said. She showed ten gleaming fingertips and still managed to hold the fork. "Do you think Dr. McKay will feel they're subversive?" The previous semester, the principal had declared toe rings subversive, and all the kids had to remove their socks and shoes to have contraband foot jewelry confiscated.

"That and cock rings," Elliot said.

"Elliot, please!" Brice reprimanded. "Not in front of the Havilland." He flashed a smile at Kate and Michael.

Their conversation continued in fits and starts, but Kate knew Michael was not a hit. Of course, Elliot had really liked Steven and that hadn't worked out, so . . . perhaps Elliot's first impression was not as important as she had thought it was.

"Salad or cheese and fruit before dessert?" Brice asked. "I have lovely Bosc pears."

"No thanks, Brice," said Kate.

"None for me," Michael agreed. Across the table, Elliot stood up and began to clear away the dishes. "It was very good," Michael added.

Even to Kate it seemed a bland thank-you. "Wasn't the terrine terrific?" she prompted. She looked at Michael, who in turn looked at the empty serving plates with an expression of confusion.

"Which was the terrine?" he asked.

Kate's face flushed pink. She knew how much effort Brice had put into the dish. "The vegetable pâté," she explained to Michael.

Elliot, still picking up plates, circled around behind Michael. "With your head so clear you probably just call that 'thick dip,' huh," he said.

Kate winced. From behind Michael's back, Elliot held his nose and gave Kate a thumbs-down sign, almost dumping the plates he had gathered.

"Watch out for the Havilland!" Brice warned again.

"Elliot, you don't have to do that," Kate said, referring both to his comments and the clearing.

"Oh, but I do, I do," Elliot replied, grinning.

She gave him a look. Clearly they needed some private time in the kitchen. "I'll help you clear," she offered, noticing Michael didn't even attempt to help.

Brice began to protest and rise as well, but Elliot shook his head and looked pointedly at Michael. Brice gave him a pleading look, but Elliot leaned close and whispered, "Somebody has to talk to him."

Brice gave Michael a weak smile. "So, what's new in anthropology?" he asked Michael in a bright voice. "Is the Sugerman grant a sure thing?"

"Sagerman," Michael corrected. "From the Sagerman Foundation for the Studies of Primitive Peoples."

Kate sighed, picked up some glasses, and followed Elliot into the kitchen. It was small but efficient, with black-and-white floor tiles, red walls and cabinets, and the latest stainless-steel appliances. Kate tried to prepare herself. Elliot was silent as he put the dishes in the sink. Then, as she knew he would, he turned to face Kate, his hands on his hips like an accusatory nun. "Where did you dig him up?" he demanded. "This guy's the worst of the lot."

"Oh, Elliot! He is not," Kate protested. "And keep your voice down."

"Come on, Kate. Wake up and smell the primitive peoples. He's dull, he lacks humor, and aside from his haircut, I don't see anything superior about him," Elliot said.

You *would* like that haircut, Kate thought. "*You* come on, Elliot," she whispered. "You never like any of my boyfriends."

"Neither do you," Elliot retorted. "Not since Steven. And this one is not only boring, he's also self-involved, pompous, *and* a homophobe."

"He is not!" Kate exclaimed. "You blame everything on that."

"Kate, the guy didn't address a single word to either of us through the whole meal."

"That doesn't make him a homophobe. Maybe he's just shy. Or doesn't like you personally," she added. "It could happen." She put the wine goblets—one of them clean—on the counter.

"Doubtful. And he's probably an alcoholic. That's why he doesn't drink. Anyway, coming here to dinner is like meeting your family," Elliot explained as he rinsed a plate. "He should at least pretend to like us, since we're in loco parentis."

"Well, loco, anyway," Kate agreed. Elliot made a face. She opened the dishwasher and started to put in the china.

"Oh, no." Elliot sighed. "Not the Havilland. It's a hand-wash job. Brice wants gold leaf, Brice washes it." He rinsed his hands. "We better get back in there. At least the coffee ought to help get things moving. Would you fill the creamer?"

Kate nodded and opened the refrigerator. "Hey, Elliot, I've told you before. It isn't easy to find a good, interesting, educated stable man who doesn't want to date a supermodel."

"You may be right," Elliot agreed. "I certainly don't think you'll find him in the Sub-Zero. But you could take out the profiteroles."

"Very funny." Kate pulled out a quart of milk and a pint of half-and-half and placed them on the counter. "I admit you didn't see him at his best. Trust me. Michael is much better one-on-one."

"I bet." Elliot smirked.

Kate ignored his innuendo. "No. Honestly. Evidence. He can be funny. And he's really smart. He got his doctorate at twenty-one, was teaching at Barnard when he was twenty-four, and is considering his postdoc. I think he's going to get tenure at Columbia."

"I didn't ask for his curriculum vitae," Elliot snapped as he popped the chocolate sauce for the profiteroles into the microwave to heat. "He's just dull. Your father was an alcoholic and you never knew what to expect when he came home. Your mother died before you hit puberty. I know you want a responsible male, someone you can depend on. But this guy isn't just stable, he's inert. Where's the magic between you? And he's not nearly good enough for you. Don't let your snobbishness over academic achievement blind you."

"I won't," she assured him, but a nagging voice at the back of her mind wondered about that. Despite all her professional training and the analysis she herself had been required to undergo, she still sometimes felt that much of what she did was a reaction to the desperate childhood she'd had.

Elliot shrugged, turned around quickly in order to pick up the tray of coffee cups, and knocked over Kate's purse, which had been sitting on the counter.

"There goes my cell phone," Kate said.

"Is it the Havilland?" Brice called from the living room.

"No. It's the Melmac," Elliot yelled. "He's obsessed with the damn stuff," he told her.

Then he knelt to pick up Kate's handbag and all the objects that had scattered over the floor. "I'm so sorry. I think I broke your makeup mirror."

"Uh-oh. It was a magnifying one. So do I have fourteen years of bad luck, or just seven years of more intense bad luck?"

"Stop it, Kate. I'm a statistician, a mathematician, not a superstitious bumpkin."

"But you talk about magic . . ."

"Not Harry Potter magic. Not superstitious nonsense. I'm talking about magic between two people."

"Need any help?" Brice called. "We're waiting out here."

"No, dear," Elliot responded. He handed Kate her purse. Kate, kneeling beside him, picked up the rest of her items and threw them in. "Hey, what's this?" Elliot asked. Kate looked up. He was waving an envelope in the air.

"It's an invite to Bunny's wedding." Kate sighed.

"Bunny of the Bitches of Bushwick is getting married?" Elliot asked. "When did this happen? You never tell me anything."

"Hey, I got it today. And you're on a need-to-know basis." Kate stood up. "Can you believe it? She was just dumped by a guy a month ago. I don't know where this came from."

"Brooklyn. And on the rebound," Elliot said. "Can I go? Please, can I go?"

"No," Kate replied. "See, this is another valid reason why I shouldn't break up with Michael. With Bina getting engaged and now this, I have to go with someone viable."

"But Michael is so—"

Elliot didn't get a chance to finish his critique. Suddenly there was a loud and frantic pounding at the front door of the apartment. "What in the world . . . ?"

The two of them hurried into the living room just as Brice was striding to the door. He turned back to look at Elliot, who shrugged. Brice opened the door. A woman, her hair wild, her face covered by her hands, threw herself into the room, sobbing uncontrollably. Everyone stood in silent amazement, and Brice actually took two steps back. It was only after a moment or two that Kate saw the woman's fingernails and realized, with a horrible shudder, that she had a French manicure.

"Bina!" she gasped. "Oh, Bina! What's happened to you?"

Chapter Seven

Bina looked around her wildly. "Katie! Omigod. Oh, Katie!" Then she threw herself onto the sofa and heaved with sobs. Kate stepped forward and put her hand gently on Bina's shoulder. Could she have been raped? Had someone mugged her? Her clothes were such a mess and her hair was so disheveled that for a moment, Kate thought only of physical calamities.

Elliot stood looking down at the weeping woman on his couch. "It's Bina?" he whispered. "This is the famous Bina?"

Kate ignored him. "Bina? Bina dear, what's happened?"

Bina shook her head violently. Kate sat and put her arms around her sobbing friend. "Shhh," she crooned, stroking Bina's hair. All the times Kate had witnessed Bina's hysterical outbursts over the years, at sleepovers and parties, flashed through her mind. It was a familiar sensation, kneeling with her arms around Bina. Then she looked up and remembered that they had an audience—and that this drama was playing out in Manhattan on a borrowed sofa. She hoped the whole thing wasn't as bad as it seemed. Then a new thought occurred to her. "Bina, how did you find me here?"

"Max," Bina said, struggling with her tears. "He heard me crying in the hall and told me where you were." She took a gulping breath and burst into tears again. Elliot and Brice drew closer to the couch, like rubberneckers, while Michael had withdrawn to a spot behind the dining table. Kate couldn't help but think that she was watching them all react in predictably typical fashion for men: Michael, the straight male, retreated in the face of emotional turmoil, while Elliot and Brice jumped right in.

She looked back at her friend. "Bina, what's happened?" she asked again.

"Choked," Bina wailed as fresh tears streamed from her eyes.

"Are you choking?" Kate asked, confused.

"I can do the Heimlich. Does she need the Heimlich?" Brice asked a bit too hopefully.

Bina, still sobbing, violently shook her head no.

Kate took Bina's hands in her own and spoke to her firmly but gently. "Who choked? Who's choking, Bina?" She turned to Elliot. "Would you please get her a glass of water?"

Elliot, turning to Brice, repeated the request. "Brice, get her a glass of water. This is better than *One Life to Live*."

Brice didn't budge. "*One Life to Live?* This is better than *The Young and the Restless*." He turned to Michael, still in the corner behind the table. "Put down the linen," Brice told him. "You get the water."

Michael seemed all too happy to leave the scene, and he disappeared into the kitchen. Bina gave another wail.

"Bina, you have to calm down," Kate said. "And you have to tell us what's wrong." Bina took some trembling breaths and got the sobbing under control. It occurred to Kate that she might have had an accident; maybe she was ill. "Does something hurt?" she asked.

Bina nodded.

"Do you need a doctor?" Kate continued.

Bina nodded more vigorously. "Yes. Jewish and unmarried. The kind who likes my type and who's looking for a serious commitment." She broke out into sobs again.

Elliot and Brice moved even closer to the circle. "Uh-oh," Elliot said. "Kate, check out her hand." He and Brice exchanged meaningful looks.

Kate, not quite understanding, thought of their manicure that afternoon. "Bina, have you hurt your hands?" She looked down at Bina's hands but didn't see anything more alarming than the French manicure.

"Not her right hand, Kate," said Brice. "Her *left* hand. Second finger from the pinkie."

Kate finally understood. She wrapped her arms around Bina and said, "Oh, my God. Jack . . ."

"Jack choked," Bina told her. "He had the ring in his breast pocket. I could see the bulge the box made." She began to cry again. "Oh, Katie! Instead of asking me to marry him, he asked if we could spend this time apart . . . exploring our singleness."

"That son of a bitch!" Kate, who thought that she understood enough about people and their motivations to be surprised at nothing, was shocked. While Jack had finished school and moved into corporate life, Bina had waited, worked, and collected every issue of *Bride*. She'd watched as all her other friends became engaged, she'd relentlessly thrown shower after bridal shower, a virtual preconnubial fountain. And now, when it was her turn at last, Jack had choked? "That goddamn son of a bitch!" Kate was ready to spit.

She looked up to see that Michael had returned from the kitchen just in time to hear her undeleted expletives and recoil at the outburst. Lucky she hadn't called Jack a motherfucker, she thought as she watched him approach the sofa and gingerly offer Bina the glass of water. Bina ignored the offer.

"I can't believe it!" Bina said, wiping ineffectually at her face and only making the raccoon eyes worse. "He got the ring from Barbie's father. Mr. Leventhal gave him a break. It was princess cut, Barbie said—just under a carat and a half." She paused for breath while Michael gaped and Elliot and Brice shook their heads in sympathy—and almost in unison.

"Everyone will know," Bina said, and began sobbing again. "I can't believe he'd do this to me. Just drop me. And shame me in front of everyone."

Kate took a napkin from the table, dipped it into the water, and held up her friend's face to mop up. "Bina, honey," she said with all the assurance she could muster, "you've been going out with Jack for six years. You grew up together! He loves you." She wiped mascara from under Bina's eyes. "Blow your nose," she said, and Bina did. "Look, this is just a temporary thing. Sometimes it happens. Picking a life mate is a serious decision. It isn't that Jack doesn't want to marry you. It's a lot more probable that he just got frightened. I'm sure he'll call you tomorrow."

"Tomorrow he'll be in Hong Kong. With my ring! I'll be dumped in Bensonhurst and he'll be the Christopher Columbus of singleness," cried Bina, who had a penchant for wildly inappropriate metaphor when under pressure.

"Maybe you should drink the water," Michael said awkwardly, and pressed the glass into her hand.

Bina looked down at the glass. "Is there strychnine in it?" she asked without lifting her eyes.

"Uh . . . no," Michael replied.

In a single smooth motion Bina dumped the water out over her shoulder and down the back of the sofa. "Then what good is it to me?" she said to no one in particular. She fell back onto the sofa and burst into a fresh batch of tears.

"That was a gesture," Elliot said, grabbing a napkin.

"On Fortuny fabric," Brice added. "This is *so* Brooklyn."

"I knew I'd love Brooklyn," Elliot said.

Kate looked up over Bina's head and gave the two of them a warning squint, her blue eyes narrowed to lizard slits. She wondered if she could get her friend home to her own apartment, but either getting a cab or walking back with Michael seemed impossible. Better to deal with it here and then go home. But first she needed to free the frightened Michael and stare off the spectating twosome—though, to be fair, it was their own home. "I'm sorry, guys," Kate said, looking up at the three men. "It looks like we might have to put off dessert."

"Don't be ridiculous," Brice said. "In times of pain, nothing works better than drowning your problems in profiteroles."

Elliot nodded, but Michael began backing toward the door. "I think you're right, Kate," he agreed, relief shining from every pore. "I'll just see myself out." He picked up his briefcase and headed out the door into the foyer. "Have a nice evening," he said, and closed the door behind him.

Kate jumped up. "Just a minute, Bina," she said, giving another narrow-eyed glance at the guys as a deterrent, and ran to the hallway. She was just in time to see Michael step into the elevator. "Hold it!" she called, got to the button, and pressed it. Michael stood in the fake mahogany cab like an insect suspended in amber. "You're leaving like that?" she demanded.

"Like what?" he asked, looking down at himself as if she were commenting on an unzipped fly.

"My friend just had her life shattered and you go out the door saying, 'Have a nice evening'?" Kate had learned not to expect too much of a date in the early stages of their mating dance, but Michael was *way* out of tempo. "Have a nice evening?" she repeated, mirroring him.

"Kate," Michael began, "Bina is your friend, not mine. I don't really think it's my place—"

"To be what? Nice, kind, caring? Can't you just pretend to be sensitive?"

Kate realized she was holding him hostage and took her finger off the button. The door closed slowly across his miserable face. She turned away, hoping he would press the open button and return, at least to give her a kiss and a moment of sympathy, but the elevator door remained as smoothly closed as Michael's emotions. She shook her head to clear it. She had to return to Bina.

She entered the apartment and found, to her surprise, that Bina had stopped crying. She was sitting up on the sofa beside Elliot, who was holding her hand and sharing his own heartbreaks. ". . . and then he said, 'I'm going back to my place to get my things and move in.' I was thrilled, just thrilled, so I said, 'Can I come and help?' And he kissed me and said, 'No, sweetie. It won't take but a few hours.' And I never saw or heard from him again."

Bina shook her head in mute sympathy.

"Just as well," Brice said. "Street trash. It's all worked out for the best." He kissed the top of Elliot's head. Kate saw Bina blink.

"Well, let me bring out the profiteroles," Brice said, and headed for the kitchen.

"Meanwhile I'll get a blanket," Elliot offered, and disappeared into the bedroom. Bina nodded gratefully to Kate.

Kate, with nothing else left to do, sat beside her. "I'm sorry," she said, comforting her friend now that they were alone. "You must be devastated."

"Oh, Katie, how could he do this? Who does he think he is? The Magellan of certified public accountants?" Bina asked. "How could he?"

Kate looked into her imploring eyes, but she had no easy answers. "Even if he leaves for Hong Kong, he'll have that long flight alone, he'll miss you, he'll remember the good times and how much he loves you. . . ." She paused, hoping that all she conjectured was true. She wanted to comfort Bina, but not lie to her. If an eight-year-old like Brian had to face the death of his mother, Kate believed it would be best for Bina to face the death of her relationship with Jack, if that's what it was. But it couldn't have suffered a mortal wound. Bina was lovable, and Jack, slow moving as he was, had always seemed to adore her. "I'm sure he'll call. Even if he leaves for Hong Kong, I bet he sends you a ticket to join him and proposes there," Kate ventured hopefully.

"Men are just funny. . . ."

"Not homosexual ones," Elliot said as he walked back into the room carrying a knitted afghan throw. "We're fucking hysterical." He knelt beside Bina and wrapped her up in it. Brice came out of the kitchen carrying a full tray, which he put down gracefully on the coffee table. Arrayed before them were four dessert plates, the plate of profiteroles, a silver server of piping hot dark chocolate sauce, lace-trimmed napkins, a crystal shot glass, and a frosted bottle of Finlandia. "All for you," Brice said.

Bina looked at the tray. "I'd love some dessert, but I don't drink," she told him.

"You do tonight, honey," Brice said, and poured her a shot. "Chocolate and alcohol together beat the shit out of Prozac."

Bina looked at him, at the brimming shot glass, and to Kate's utter surprise she took it from him and knocked it back.

"Good girl!" Elliot said. "And here's your chaser," Brice added, and handed Bina the pastries. "You know what they say: Just a spoonful of sugar . . ."

Bina picked up the plate to dig in.

"Wait just a minute," Brice said. "The doctor is in." He took hold of the silver pitcher, raised it theatrically, and poured the bitter chocolate over the ice-cream pastry.

Kate looked at the three of them, entranced, not sure if she was experiencing pleasure or discomfort. Her two worlds had merged here on the Fortuny upholstered sofa, and all one could have said was that it seemed quiet on the western front. Then Brice filled the shot glass again and handed it to Bina, who, docile as a kosher lamb, drank it down. That broke Kate's trance. "Guys, this is more serious than something a drink and an overdose of carbohydrates will cure," she told them.

"Honey, there's nothing that will cure this. But alcohol and sugar will temporarily dull the pain," Brice replied. "Trust me. I know."

Bina, fully involved with her dessert, looked up from it with a dazed expression on her face. Elliot wiped the chocolate from around her mouth with the lace napkin.

"Who are these guys, Katie?" Bina asked, looking at Elliot and Brice with some confusion. "Are they therapists, too? They're very good."

"No, dear. This is my friend Elliot, who works with me at school, and his partner, Brice," Kate told her. Bina smiled, but it was obvious that Kate's words were merely washing over her. She realized just how drunk Bina was.

"Why am I here?" Bina asked. "And why are they roomoots?"

She slurred her words, and only God knew how slurred her mind was. Again Kate wished that she hadn't mixed Brooklyn with Manhattan. They were parallel universes and, like parallel lines, should never touch.

Despite her concern, however, Kate was slightly amused watching Bina's expression—surprise mixed with curiosity and a soupçon of horror—as she looked from Elliot to Brice and back. At Bina's next words, however, her amusement dissolved, and she cringed in anticipation.

"Oh, so *you're* the—"

"Mathematical one," Elliot finished for her.

"And I'm the emotional one," Brice said with an exaggerated sigh. "Somebody's got to do it."

Kate had to get Bina home and onto her own couch before it became necessary to carry her. She knew once Bina was forced to stay here, Brice and Elliot would dig themselves in deeper. They were kind, but they couldn't help Bina now, and Kate knew she had a big job to do.

"You're coming to my apartment," she said. "It isn't far, and you could use the fresh air."

"She's welcome to stay here," Elliot offered, and Kate knew his kindness was mixed with equal parts of curiosity.

"Show's over," she said. "Say good night, Gracie." She pulled the dazed Bina up from the couch and began to walk her to the door.

"Good night, Gracie," Elliot and Brice chorused.

Chapter Eight

Later, Kate could not remember much about the nightmare of getting Bina back to her apartment that night. It was called "selective memory" in her textbooks—some things were just too gruesome to keep in your consciousness. In the four long blocks from Elliot's apartment to Kate's, Bina alternately wept, sang, tripped, wailed, and sat down at one point on the sidewalk, refusing to move. Kate didn't think Bina had tried to throw herself in front of a bus or wet herself, but she couldn't be absolutely sure of either. It was lucky that Max had been home and heard her trying to get Bina up the stairs. Asking no questions, he took over. Kate didn't remember if he carried Bina up the stairs in his arms or over his shoulder. She did remember holding Bina's head as she vomited violently and washing her up. Max left her to that thankless task. Kate made an executive decision not to put Bina in her bedroom but instead to tuck her up on the sofa. Made in haste, it was a decision that Kate would not regret.

The next morning Kate was up early, brewing coffee, laying out the Tylenol, and waiting to call in sick to work. One look at the bedraggled, unconscious Bina gave Kate a pretty good idea of how she was going to spend her next twenty-four hours. She took down her favorite coffee mug. It was the only gift she could remember her father giving her. A ceramic one, the handle shaped like Cinderella. When she was little Kate used to imagine that Cinderella was bending over the top of the mug and looking into whatever liquid would be put there, as if it were a wishing well. She thought of calling Mrs. Horowitz or even trying Jack before he left, then thought better of it. Kate didn't mind being involved, but she didn't want to become the puppeteer pulling strings. Bina—despite many childlike qualities—would have to decide on her own what actions to take, and Kate would support her as best she could.

When the phone rang, Kate glanced at the caller ID, picked up the receiver, and without preamble said, "Yes, she's still sleeping. No, I'm not going into school today, and no, you can't come over."

"Good morning to you, too," Elliot's voice said briskly. "Can I at least drop off a couple of bagels on my way up to Andrew?"

"Forget it. I don't think Bina is going to want to eat anything, and if she does, I have plenty of saltines." Kate poured the hot coffee into her Cinderella mug. She was careful, as always, to avoid the little blond head peeking over the rim.

"God, Brice and I feel so bad for her."

"At least you're not feeling as bad as her . . . I mean, she is. Bina doesn't have the genetics to handle a hangover," Kate told him. "You shouldn't have let Brice pour that booze down her throat."

"Well, he's not apologizing for getting her drunk, and I think it was the best thing for her," Elliot began.

"Well, it wasn't the best thing for me," Kate retorted, peeking at Bina. It wasn't a pretty picture. "I've had quite a mess—literally and figuratively—to clean up."

"Oh, the poor girl," Elliot said, his sympathy real. "How can I help?"

"Short of teaching Michael to deal with human feelings and finding Jack and slapping some sense into him, I don't think there's much you can do," Kate told him.

"Yeah, I told you Michael was a dud. What went on between you two in the hall? I'll bet he got a pounding."

Kate thought of Michael's face before the elevator door closed and chose to change the subject. She spilled some coffee as she moved her mug to the counter beside the refrigerator. "I don't think there's much anyone can do, but I'm taking a sick day."

"Maybe you should call it a mental health day," Elliot said. "Except for once this one isn't about you. Do you want me to take the day off, too? The kids have standardized testing most of the day. I can keep you company and help with Bina."

"Forget it. I know you're just afraid you're going to get my cafeteria duty," she joked. "Anyway, you had your first and last dose of the Bitches of Bushwick. It ought to be enough Brooklyn to last a lifetime." Before he could protest, she added, "I have to go. She's waking up."

"I'll call you later," she heard him say as she put the phone down.

She quickly poured a glass of club soda—her favorite remedy for the dehydration of a hangover—and walked from her kitchenette into the living room with her mug in one hand and the drinking glass in the other. Bina groaned, put a hand to her forehead, and then opened her eyes, which she closed again quickly. "Oh, my God," she said, and Kate wasn't sure if it was a reaction to the light or a remembrance of things past. She groaned again.

"It's okay, Bina, drink this." Kate held the glass in front of her friend, and Bina squinted at it.

"What is it?" she croaked.

"Well, it's not vodka," Kate told her. "Come on, sit up and take your medicine."

Bina did as she was told, took the glass, drank three or four big gulps, and then began to choke. She put the glass on Kate's coffee table, and Kate moved it onto a coaster before she went to Bina's side. "Omigod," Bina repeated. And Kate knew that this time she had remembered Jack and the night before. Bina looked up at her. "Oh, Kate. What am I going to do?"

Kate sat in the wicker chair and reached for her friend's hand. "Bina," she said, "what happened last night?"

"You were right about the French manicure," Bina said. She shook her head, and Kate could see the physical pain register on her face. She went back to the kitchen and brought her three Tylenols and a couple of vitamin Cs.

"Here," she said, thrusting them into Bina's hand. "Take these. You'll feel better." She left Bina again and went back into the kitchen, where she took out her emergency stash of saltines. Bina had just downed the last pill when Kate returned. She didn't want them all to lie there on an empty stomach, so she handed Bina a saltine. "Eat it," she said.

"Oh, please," Bina responded in a world-weary voice.

"Eat it," Kate commanded, "and now tell me what happened last night." She watched as Bina made an entire meal of the saltine, taking many tiny bites and washing them down with the club soda. The moment she was finished, Kate handed her another saltine and refilled her glass. "Good girl," she said. "So what happened?"

Bina lay back among the cushions and put a hand across her forehead. This time the tears were silent. Kate rose, went to her bedroom, and came back with a box of tissues. Wordlessly, she handed one to Bina, who mopped at her eyes and began to talk in an unsteady voice. "You know that I was meeting him at Nobu, and I was excited because it's one of the kinds of places you go to."

Kate almost smiled. Nobu was one of the most expensive, stylish Asian restaurants in the city, and she couldn't afford to eat there even on her birthday.

"Anyway, the place was beautiful, and when I walked past the bar I could see that all the women looked better than I did. I don't know why, because their clothes weren't as good as mine—at least they didn't look as good, but somehow they looked better, if you know what I mean." Kate just nodded. "Anyway, when I got to the dining room, the hostess wasn't there. I looked around, kind of self-conscious, then I thought I saw her. She had her back to me and was talking to some guy at a table and she was holding his hand up and laughing. When he laughed back, I realized it was Jack. I nearly plotzed."

Kate had a vision of Bina going into hysterics and throwing a scene in the middle of the Zen of Nobu. God, she thought, that would end a romantic evening quickly. Bina did tend to overreact. "So did you . . . ?"

"For a minute I didn't do anything," Bina said. "I couldn't believe it. Then I walked over to the table and—"

The phone rang, and Kate looked at the caller ID. "It's your mom," she said.

"Don't pick up!" Bina nearly screeched.

Kate let the phone ring until the answering machine kicked in. Mrs. Horowitz's concerned voice came on, and Kate turned the volume down. "You will have to tell her what happened. After you tell me, of course," Kate said. "And she must be concerned. Where does she think you are? Did she know about your plans last night?"

Bina covered her eyes again. "I can't talk to her now," she said. "And I didn't tell her anything because she would have nudged me to death. But I'm sure she knew about the ring, and I'm sure she knows Jack is leaving." She stopped for a moment and began to wail. It was a high-pitched keen of misery. "He's leaving tonight. Omigod, he's leaving tonight."

Kate crouched at the edge of the sofa and took Bina in her arms. She felt her friend tremble against her, shaking with every sobbing breath. "Bina, you have to calm down and tell me what happened. We can probably fix this."

Bina shook her head silently but lowered the volume of her crying. Just then the phone rang again. Reluctantly, Kate left Bina and went over to it. It was Michael. Kate looked over at Bina, who had turned on her side and was sobbing quietly into a bunch of tissues. She picked up the receiver.

"Kate, you're home?" Michael asked.

"Yes." She didn't need to tell him anything more. He knew that she was usually in her office by this time, and as a postdoc he might have had the brains to figure out that based on what he had reluctantly witnessed the night before, she might not show up at school.

"Hey, Kate, I . . . I just wanted to apologize."

Kate softened. She sighed but covered the mouthpiece to be

sure that Michael didn't hear it. She had learned that there were two kinds of men: those who apologized and continued their behavior and those who apologized and stopped it. She hadn't known Michael long enough to know which type he was. The way she looked at things at this point in her life, most relationships were compromises, and all men had to be looked at as fixer-uppers. "Okay," she said to Michael with a voice as neutral as she could manage.

"I'm sure I looked like an unfeeling jerk last night. You know, it's just that . . . well, your friend was *very* dramatic."

That pissed Kate off. "I suppose a little drama is warranted when your entire life is ruined." She purposely kept her voice low and looked over at Bina to make sure she went unheard. What good was an apology, she thought, if it was followed by a further injury?

"I've done it again, haven't I?" Michael asked. He might not be empathetic, but he wasn't stupid, Kate reflected. "Look, let me take you out to dinner one night this week," he said. "Let's talk about it. I know I can do better."

Fair enough, Kate thought. But it couldn't be in a restaurant. There should be a lot of talking, a lot of negotiating, and maybe some conciliatory sex. "Why don't you come over for dinner," she proposed. "But not tonight." She looked over at the sofa again. Bina was just raising her head. "Gotta go," she said. "Let's talk later."

"I'll call you this evening," Michael promised, and Kate hung up. She returned to Bina's side. Bina, her eyes red, but not as red as her nose, looked up at her.

"How can we fix it?" she asked.

Kate sat down and the wicker creaked. "Well, to know that, first I have to know exactly what happened."

"Well, I went over to the table, and Jack was laughing, and the Chinese woman—who was smaller than a size two and taller than I am—looks at me like I'm the busboy. But Jack, he jumps and pulls his hand away. 'Hey, Sy Lin was just teaching me how to say hello in Mandarin. Nee-how-ma!' So I look at him and say, 'Me-how-ma, right back atcha.' Then I turn to Sy Lin and said, 'How do you say good-bye?' So she just gives me this smile, does one of those look-overs—you know, the way Barbie does when someone is dressed really badly—and then looks at Jack and says, 'Enjoy your dinner.' Oh, and just to make it a really bad omen, she was wearing the color nail polish you picked out. I should always listen to you."

"Bina, don't be silly. This isn't about manicures. So what happened next? Did you pitch a fit?"

Bina began to cry again. "That's the worst part," she said, gulping back her tears. "I didn't do anything. It was Jack, Jack who—"

The phone rang again. Kate stepped over and looked at the handset and saw that it was Elliot's cell. "Wait a minute," she told Bina, who ignored her anyway. Kate picked up the phone.

"Okay. Don't worry about a thing," came Elliot's voice. "We've got the situation under control. Brice and I are on our way with bagels, cream cheese, and lox. We also have two pints of hand-packed Häagen-Dazs," he added. "Rocky Road and Concession Obsession. And that's not all. I have a couple of ten-milligram Valium that Brice 'borrowed' from his mother's medicine cabinet. We're the rescue squad. Don't try to get in our way. Besides, we're practically at your door."

"Elliot, this is serious," Kate admonished.

"That's why Brice and I took half a day off from work. Well, that and intense curiosity."

"The two of you are gossipmongers," Kate said.

"You betcha. Don't let Bina say another word until we get there, because even though I'm a social idiot, Brice knows how to fix up anything that's interpersonal. I hang the shelves."

Kate found herself holding a dead phone and looking at her almost dead friend. Maybe some food, ice cream, muscle relaxants, and diversions were just what she needed. But first she had to get the rest of the story.

"Was that Jack?" Bina asked.

"No," Kate admitted. She sat down again. "Tell me what happened next." And then the doorbell rang.

Chapter Nine

It's Jack!" Bina shouted, and virtually levitated off the sofa. "Oh, my God! It's Jack and look what I look like!"

"It isn't Jack," Kate told her, and watched Bina struggle with both relief and disappointment simultaneously. "It's Elliot. He's the only one who can get into the building without my having to buzz. He has a key to the downstairs door."

Kate went to the tiny foyer and looked through the safety peephole. There was Elliot, smiling and gesturing to Brice, who was beside him and holding up the promised goodie bag. Reluctantly, Kate turned the knob and opened the door. If she didn't do it, the guys would come in anyway—Elliot had a spare set of keys for emergency purposes (like the time Kate locked her purse in the office and got halfway home before she noticed), and he wouldn't hesitate to use it.

Kate opened the door, and Elliot and Brice almost tumbled in. "Is she okay?" Elliot whispered.

"No," Kate told him.

"Well, is she better?" Brice asked.

"No," Kate repeated.

"Then it's a good thing we came," Elliot said.

"I told you," Brice responded, and then the three of them stepped into the living room, like all those clowns emerging from a tiny car at the circus. At least it felt like a circus to Kate.

"Oh, Bina! You poor girl," Elliot said, and flew across the living room to sit beside her in Kate's one good chair.

"Don't worry about a thing," Brice said, and began unpacking the shopping bag onto Kate's coffee table. "What's the last thing you ate? And when was it?"

Bina, a bit dazed, tried to answer him. "Well, I thought I was going to eat last night with Jack, but then I never finished the meal. I was too upset. Then I couldn't find Kate. I remember having some vodka. . . ."

"Well, you need one of these," Elliot said, and took out a waxed-paper parcel and handed it to her.

She opened it up. Kate winced at the poppy seeds that went rolling off the bagel, and onto the sofa, the floor, the rug, and places that wouldn't be found for months to come. "Oh, I can't eat," Bina said.

"You have to keep up your strength," Elliot told her.

Kate nodded. "It would be good for you to have some breakfast," she coaxed. "Just take a bite."

Brice nodded, moved to the foot of the sofa, sat down, and rearranged Bina's feet so they were on his lap and covered with the quilt. "Now, just tell Uncle Brice all about it," he said, his voice a combination of mockery and sincerity.

"I can't believe yesterday was supposed to be your big night and nothing happened," Elliot said. "You must be so distraught." At that point Kate realized she was fairly distraught herself; she took a throw pillow from the sofa and sank to the floor on it beside the coffee table.

"Tell me about it! I thought Jack was nervous. Like he was making sure the ring was still safe. Jack Weintraub was finally going to propose to me, and he was nervous. You know, he's such a perfectionist—Barbie said he insisted on a perfect stone: flawless D color."

"Flawless D!" Brice said approvingly.

"Right. See? I love him for a reason. He knows things. He wants things right. And I thought he wanted me to be happy. So I was happy, and I decided to forget about Tokyo Rose."

"Oh, forget the hostess," Kate pressed. "Unless he asked *her* to marry him. You didn't fight over her, did you?"

"We didn't fight at all," Bina protested. "I was a little upset about the dragon lady—it just isn't like Jack to flirt with strange women—but I couldn't have loved him more. Anyway, he raised his glass of champagne, and I think he was about to make a toast when he realized I didn't have a glass. So he tried to get a waiter or a waitress, and they were nowhere to be seen. So Jack says he has to go to the men's room and on the way he'll order me a drink. But I think he might have been looking for the hostess. . . ."

"Her and many like her, the man-whore," said a heated Brice. "I just hate it when a man—"

"Hey. Don't make this personal," Elliot said, cutting him off with a meaningful look.

"Focus, darling," Kate said, touching Bina's face. Kate was quickly losing hope that a simple phone call before Jack got on the plane might put things right.

"Okay. So he excused himself and headed for the men's room. I watched him walk away from the table. I couldn't help thinking he was so handsome."

"I know. Men are so cute from behind," said Brice.

Bina nodded solemnly. "I mean, people are like 'Jack is just ordinary,' but that's what I like about him," she continued, either ignoring or oblivious to the sexual connotation of Brice's comment. It seemed to Kate as though Bina were bonding with Brice the way she did with her girlfriends. "Jack reminds me of the Goldilocks story," Bina went on. "He's not too tall or too short, he isn't too skinny or too fat, he isn't too handsome or too ugly. He's just right," she said. "At least just right for me." Then she realized anew where she was and what had happened. "He *was* just right, but I wasn't just right for him. Maybe it's me that's ordinary."

"Oh, Bina," Kate said, and put her arm around her friend, squeezing tightly. "You're not ordinary." That might not have been totally true, but that she was at the very least Jack's equal was a sure thing. Kate had never met anyone more ordinary than Jack. "What happened then?"

"Jack was gone for a little while. So finally that stupid hostess came back and asked me if I wanted a drink. I told her that my boyfriend was getting me something, and she said, 'Your boyfriend? He said this was a business meeting. Otherwise I would have given him a more private table.'"

"The bitch!" Elliot and Brice said simultaneously.

"Yeah. The beautiful, thin, exotic bitch," Bina agreed bitterly.

"This is not productive," Kate said. No matter what the story was, she was going to be sure they didn't criticize Jack too much, because when he and Bina patched things up—and they would—Bina would forever remember any criticism. Kate had learned that lesson the hard way with Bev, before she married Johnny. "Bina, you are so beautiful. Any guy in the world would be lucky to share the same air as you," she told her friend, and meant it. Every bit of Bina's soul was generous and giving. Her heart was loyal and loving. And she had an adorable, round little face and a curvy figure. Kate stroked Bina's dark, shiny hair. What the hell was wrong with Jack? It must have been a panic attack. Commitment was a very frightening prospect. "Didn't you tell me just last week that Jack said he found you beautiful in so many ways?"

"Honey," Brice said with a tilt of his head, "greeting cards can tell you that."

"No, he said I was too beautiful and too good for him," Bina corrected.

"Uh-oh," Brice and Elliot said again in unison, and exchanged a look.

Kate gestured to them behind Bina's head. "Well, anyway, Bina, you *are* beautiful, and I am sure Jack still feels the same way."

"Yeah? You haven't heard the end of the story," Bina said.

"We're trying to," Kate told her, attempting not to snap.

"Go on. Get it all out," Elliot advised.

"Well, of course I was hating this . . . woman." Bina paused, and Kate was pleased that she didn't stoop to any slur. "So I told her to go away. Jack finally came back with my drink and said—and you won't believe this." Bina mimicked Jack's deep Brooklyn baritone voice: "'I looked at you from across the room. You looked good from over there.' Was that a compliment or a diss?"

Kate pursed her lips but refrained from speaking. It seemed clear that her theory was right—Jack needed distance in both senses to see Bina. But up close and intimate, his anxiety paralyzed him. If only he could have stayed at the bar and proposed by cell phone, Kate thought ruefully.

"I just gave him a look," Bina continued.

"And what did he do?"

"Well, I think he saw my reaction. He asked if something was wrong. He sounded so sincere, so concerned, that I felt bad, and I figured I had to let up on the poor guy. I thought he was a nervous wreck about proposing. Also, to tell the truth, Jack has never been . . . well, let's just say he's careful with his money."

"Oh, hell," Brice said. "Let's say he's cheap." Bina opened her eyes wide, and for a moment Kate thought her friend was going to giggle.

"Go on," Kate said.

"Well, I just shook my head and suggested that we make a toast. And all he said was, 'To us.' I waited for more, you know, like 'And to our future as Mr. and Mrs. Jack Weintraub, the perfect married couple,' but there was nothing more." A tear slid down her cheek, and Brice took her hand.

"So?" Kate prompted. She wondered what time Jack's plane was actually taking off, whether he planned to be on it, whether he had called the Horowitz household, whether he had called his cousin Max across the hall.

"Then he said he really wished he didn't have to take this trip, but said some of that stuff about markets misbehaving. So I suggested that in the future maybe we'd make the trips together."

"What did he say to that?" Kate asked.

"Well, of course then the waitress shows up before he can

answer. Just my luck. And you know it takes Jack a long time to order. And then he has to make sure none of the things on his plate are going to touch any of the others."

Kate had forgotten about that phobia. She nodded to Bina.

"So we had our drink, and it seemed that the dinner was going fine until I told him how much I was going to miss him. I mean, that's okay to say, right? The guy is going away for months and it's halfway around the world. Jack and I haven't been separated by more than ten miles since we first started dating."

"Really?" Brice asked. "That's so romantic!"

"It's true, right, Kate? She was there the night Max—you know, Kate's neighbor who now lives across the hall—had the party where I met Jack."

Kate rolled her eyes. Bina had a habit of playing what her friends called "Jewish geography." Kate had gotten her apartment because Bina's brother knew Jason, the building owner's son, from summer camp and he had told Bina, who had told Kate about it. Kate got the place. Later she and Bina had been invited to a Manhattan party by Bina's brother, which had been thrown by Max at his old apartment. And Bina—on one of her infrequent trips across the East River—met Jack, Max's cousin, there. . . . Well, it could go on endlessly, between Hebrew schools, summer camps, bar mitzvahs, weddings, cousins, and on and on and on.

"The weird thing is we had grown up together in Brooklyn just six blocks from each other, but we were introduced for the first time that night, and we haven't been apart since. I mean, he took me out for a drink after the party and asked me out for the next night. And that weekend he came over for dinner with my parents and brother and . . . well, there we were, saying good-bye to each other for a very long time. So I thought it was appropriate to say I would miss him. And I thought it would be good to kind of, you know, get him started. I mean, we were finished with our appetizers and entrées. Did I have to wait until he popped the question?"

"Men spook easily," Brice offered. "I remember the time when Ethan Housholder told me—"

"Not now, Brice," Kate interjected.

"Right, sorry. Continue, honey."

Kate had to admit that Bina couldn't have two more sympathetic listeners than Brice and Elliot. And sometimes simply talking was the best therapy. But then, just when she thought they had gotten safely out of the water, Bina began to cry again. Elliot's soft pats and Brice's coos of sympathy only made it worse.

"Well, it was like all the color drained out of his face. And then he said, 'Bina, you know I have to be in Hong Kong for almost five months, and that's not going to be easy.' He kept touching his breast pocket, and the tension was almost overwhelming. I couldn't help but think, Here it comes. Then he just sat there. I wanted to scream, *Why don't you just take the damn thing out of there and ask me to marry you?* But, nothing. The man just sat there and then looked down and finished eating his fucking chicken Rangoon."

Chapter Ten

What did you do?" Elliot asked.

Kate was afraid that she would hear that Bina had become hysterical, attacked Jack physically, made a huge scene, or something even more dramatic. But Bina surprised her.

"I went to the ladies' room, of course."

"Of course," Brice agreed. "I can't tell you how many times I wished I could go there myself."

"So, anyway . . . ," Bina continued. She opened her eyes wide and they glazed over, as if she could see the scene replaying itself.

Kate, Elliot, and Brice all held their breath. Then the phone rang. "Shit!" Kate said, and grabbed for the receiver, peering at the number. "It's your mother again," she said. "I think you'd better talk to her."

"Kill me first!" Bina pleaded. Kate froze for a moment. She couldn't bear to explain the situation to Myra Horowitz, and she didn't have the heart to give the phone to Bina. But she couldn't refuse the call again. . . .

"I'll take it," Elliot said.

"Don't be ridiculous," Kate told him, realizing he was getting deeper and deeper into her Brooklyn life. She pressed the answer button.

"Katie! Thank God! Listen, do you know where Bina is?"

"She's fine. She's right here with me," Kate told Mrs. Horowitz, telling only one lie, not two.

"Well, put her on."

Bina was shaking her head wildly, putting her hands in front of her face as if to ward off a blow.

Kate was grateful for every moment she had spent at the Horowitz house, because even with her training it took more than therapeutic skills to talk Mrs. Horowitz down. Kate said soothing words, then distracted her with questions, then reassured her, then sent her love to Dr. Horowitz. All the while Elliot circled his hand, telling her to move it along, while Brice pulled his index finger across his throat, giving her the sign to cut it short. As if she wanted to be the middleman! Finally she hung up.

"At last," said Brice.

"So you were in the ladies' room," Elliot prompted.

"Yeah. You know, I just wanted to be by myself for a minute, just long enough to get it all together again," Bina said. "So I fixed my makeup—and I still had to give the woman there a dollar, even though I hadn't used the toilet—but I just looked at myself in the mirror and said, 'Bina Horowitz, this is the night that's going to change your life. Be nice and be happy.'"

"Good for you," Kate said.

"So I get back to the table and Jack stands up. He always does it when we're in a fancy restaurant. So he leans over to help me into my chair, and . . ." She gulped. "The ring box slipped out of his pocket. It was like a car accident in one of those movies. I saw it all happening in slow motion. The ring box fell over and over and over. The moment the box hits the floor, Jack lets go of my chair. The ring flies out of the box and he scrambles to retrieve it. I'm as frozen as a Swanson TV dinner, and I see the ring skid across the floor, and that stupid bitch hostess bends *all* the way over and picks it up."

"Wow," was all Kate could say.

"Wow indeed," Brice added.

"What did you do?" asked Elliot.

"I just sat there, like the turkey dinner that I am, and I realize that Jack, on the floor, can see up the woman's skirt—well, it was *so* short, and she bent right over. And not from the knees like you're supposed to, but from the waist. And she isn't wearing any underwear."

"What?" all three said in collective amazement.

"None. And Jack is on the floor, looking straight up her—well, up her—"

"We get the visual," Kate said.

"So did Jack. Everyone was looking. I think that was when he lost his mind. It must have been then. So Jack manages to get off the floor and tear his eyes off that woman's naked crotch, and she turns around and hands him the ring. He stands up and puts it in his right pocket. Then he scoops up the box and puts it in his left pocket." Bina stopped for a moment and shook her head. "He walked back to the table." She turned to Kate. "I couldn't stay happy anymore, Katie. I told Jack that if he was trying to make it a memorable evening, he was succeeding. I mean, I could have smacked him, I was so mad. And you know what the asshole said?"

"What now?" Kate asked.

Bina, using her Jack voice again, said, "'This isn't how I want to remember you, Bina.'"

"Uh-oh. Here it comes," Brice said.

"Wait for it," Elliot warned him.

"Please, you two—it's like Tweedledee and Tweedle Very Dumb," Kate admonished. "Let the woman finish her story, which, I pray, is almost over."

"Almost," Bina said. "So, I was wondering which pocket my ring was in now. It made me think of that game, Katie, that my father would play with us when we were little girls. You know, when he would have surprises for us and we would have to guess which pocket they were in."

Kate nodded, almost smiling in remembrance. Dr. Horowitz had been so kind to her. He used to give his daughter her allowance every Sunday morning, and since her father was usually sleeping one off on Sunday and rarely gave her money, Dr. Horowitz always gave Kate the same allowance as well: A big Sunday event was going to the candy store and agonizing over Junior Mints or Bit-O-Honey. Not to mention the Betty and Veronica comics. Bina and her family were good people, and she hated hearing how she'd been subjected to this hurtful slapstick. But maybe the situation could be salvaged. After all, Bina and Jack had years of history and were made for each other. "So then what?" she asked.

"Well," Bina continued, "Jack then looked me in the eyes and said, 'Bina, I have something I want to say to you.' And I'm thinking at least someday we'll tell our grandchildren about all this and laugh! But then Jack says, 'I have to be honest; Hong Kong is far away from here. Very far away.' Like I didn't take geography, right? So I think maybe he's going to want to elope. It would break my mother's heart, and I want the dress and all, but I was like dying by now. I kept waiting for Jack to reach for the ring, but his hands are staying folded together on top of the table. He takes a deep breath, looks up to the ceiling, and says, 'I think it would be unfair of me to leave and ask you to just wait for me.' I told him I agreed, and I looked down at my hand to get my finger ready. But then he said, 'I think this time apart might be a good chance for us to . . . well, for us to . . . I think this might be a good chance for us to explore our singleness.'"

"I could kill him, Bina," Kate said.

"Oh, me first," Brice added.

There was silence in the room. Kate, Elliot, and Brice sat there with their mouths opened wide, until Bina started sobbing again. All three snapped back into action. Kate moved closer on the sofa and held Bina. "Oh, honey," she said. Brice got up, took a cushion, and put it under her feet as if she had internal bleeding. Elliot got up, went into the bathroom, and returned with a wet towel, a glass of water, and a blue pill. Ever neat—except in his clothes—he looked for a coaster. Before Kate could hand him one, he found a piece of cardboard.

"Take this and drink all the water," he told her. Bina did as she was told without question.

"What was that?" Kate asked.

"Oh, I just felt she needed a visit from cousin Valerie," Elliot told her. It was his code word for Valium, and Kate knew a blue one was ten milligrams.

"She'll sleep for a week," Kate said.

"What a good time for that," Elliot told her.

"Okay, Bina. Tell us what happened next."

"I just ran out," she said. "Well, ran as best I could in my heels. I went straight to your apartment, Katie, and when I couldn't find you, Max helped me. You can't believe how hysterical I was." Kate silently disagreed with her on that. Bina blew her nose and continued. "Max was home. And he told me he thought you were out to dinner and where Elliot lived, and I went straight there in the pouring rain, and . . . Omigod!"

"What! What is it, Bina?" Kate cried.

Bina reached over to the coffee table and picked up the coaster for the water. It was Bunny's wedding invitation. "Bunny? Bunny is getting married?" she asked.

"Is that a bad thing?" Elliot wanted to know.

Bina ignored him. "Why didn't you tell me, Katie?"

"I just found out. I got the invitation yesterday."

"Oh, this is it! I'm glad I didn't see my mail. But this proves I'm a loser," Bina wailed. "Bunny! She just broke up with a guy. That one I showed you on the way to getting a pedicure."

"The guy was getting a pedicure?" Elliot asked. Kate gave him a look.

"Bunny is going to be a bride, and Jack is off to become the Marco Polo of singleness. Why don't I just open my veins?"

"Well, it's very messy, for one thing," Brice told her. "And it's almost impossible to get blood out of clothes. Very cold water and hydrogen peroxide—"

Bina put the pillow over her face and wailed into it. It wasn't that she was competitive with Bunny, Kate knew. It was just that Bunny had been the last to join their group, hadn't had a date to the prom, had never been pinned. Bunny didn't do well with men, picking a string of bad boys and scoundrels. One she had lived with had stolen everything—even her sofa and kitchen table—when she went away for the weekend. "How can Bunny be getting married? She just got dumped by that guy we saw in SoHo. She's only just met Barney or whatever." Bina squinted at the card. "And how did they get invitations so quickly? They must be Xerox copies."

How had Bunny met someone? Kate wondered why it was so much more complicated for her than for Barbie and Bev and Bunny. When Kate found a warm man, he was often devoted to her, but just a little . . . dull. Or second-rate. And when she found a man with a first-rate mind and an engrossing career, a man like Michael, he lacked emotional heat. Of course, she reflected, Bina's father, a successful chiropractor, had doted on her. So in spite of her current troubles, it seemed only natural that she would eventually find a successful accountant who doted on her. Kate sighed. It didn't bode well for her. "Bina, everything is going to be okay," Kate promised.

"Fine for you to say. You've got that doctor Michael to go with. What am I going to do? Go with my brother?"

"Oh, I don't think Katie will want to bring Michael all the way across the Brooklyn Bridge," Elliot began. He turned to Kate and gave her a little smirk. "Unless you want to prep him for his journey to Austin, you know, a little bit at a time."

Kate grimaced at him. Elliot turned back to Bina.

"Anyway, if my calculations are correct—and they always are—we have here two women who need dates," he announced, "and two men with an insatiable curiosity for the customs and rituals of deepest, darkest Brooklyn."

"Really?" asked Bina.

"Not only that, but I have fabulous formal wear. I'll definitely be better dressed than the bride," Brice said.

"In a dress?" Bina asked, her voice about to rise into hysteria again.

"No. A great tux. Armani. And I'll do your makeup. You'll look absofuckinglutely great, and all your friends will want to know who the great-looking guy you're with is. You can tell them whatever you like. I once passed as the prince of

Norway." Brice turned to Elliot, gave him a loving but exasperated look, and then stared at Kate. "I know what he looks like in a rented tux," Brice told her. "You're on your own."

"Thanks," Elliot said. "No offense meant, I'm sure, and none taken. So it's set. Brice and I will take you two girls, and we will all have a wonderful time."

"Maybe that's a good idea," Bina said. "But right now I think I have to take a little nap."

Kate watched as Bina's eyes fluttered shut. "You guys must be joking," she said. "No way."

Chapter Eleven

Kate and Bina, both carrying presents, were waiting for Elliot and Brice three blocks south of St. Veronica's Roman Catholic Church, the place where Kate had made her First Communion in the dress Mrs. Horowitz had sewed for her. Kate, all grown up now, was unaware that in the simple calf-length navy blue dress that set off her fiery hair, she looked stunning. She didn't think of her Communion dress; she was just grateful that she didn't have to wear one of the loopy bridesmaids' gowns she was usually stuck in.

Bina, at Kate's side, looked totally Brooklyn and smelled like fear. She wore a pink dress that poofed at the skirt. Her dark brown hair was done up in lacquered swirls of French twist curls as if she were going to their senior prom. Sal, the hairdresser who had "done" both of them for the prom, had probably done Bina this time, too.

"Is it going to be a high mass?" Kate asked, remembering her boredom at the standing, the kneeling, and the standing again in the interminable services of her youth.

"Mass, shmass," Bina said dismissively. She craned her neck, looking for the guys. "I'm safe during the ceremony. It's afterward that I'm dead meat."

"Bina, this isn't a firing squad. These women are your friends," Kate tried to assure her. "You've known them forever. They're not going to judge you."

Bina turned back to stare at Kate. "Are you kidding?" she

asked in amazement. "That's exactly what they're going to do. That's what friends are for."

"Hey, look: We got a great strategy," Kate reminded her. "Everyone may assume that Elliot is Michael; it will take a while to straighten that out, which will distract them. If Bev opens her big mouth and calls him Michael, I can do half an hour of material to make it look like I'm embarrassed. And everyone knows Jack left. So showing up with Brice will just daze and confuse them, or maybe even blow them away. I mean, he *is* gorgeous."

"Yeah," Bina agreed dispiritedly, "but he's no Jack." Jack had gone to Hong Kong without calling, and Bina had heard nothing from him since. Now, she looked up and down the street again. "Where are they?" she whined.

"They'll be here," Kate reassured her, looking down the all too familiar Woodbine Avenue. She felt slightly dizzy, and she wasn't sure if it was the heat or the location. Returning to Brooklyn and the old neighborhood gave her a kind of vertigo.

"But what if they don't show up? I'll have to go in alone. I can hide in the back during the ceremony, but if at the reception I have to go Jackless and ringless, they'll all want to know the reason he broke up with me, and—"

"Bina, calm down," Kate said with more than a bit of concern in her voice. For the past two weeks, Bina had been spending every day and almost every night alternating between Max's and Kate's. After a few days, Kate had remonstrated, but Bina refused to cross the bridge. "I can't go home. Everything reminds me of him," was Bina's first excuse. Kate had been happy, at first, to provide Bina with a safe haven, but after four days she'd insisted that Bina call her father and mother herself and break the news. Dr. Horowitz had threatened to fly to Hong Kong right then and there to "knock that *pisher's* block off," but Bina had implored her father to stay in Brooklyn and had thereby kept Jack's block safe. Mrs. Horowitz, in the face of all the evidence to the contrary, remained convinced that her daughter was engaged.

"I can't take this," Bina said. "I'm melting from nervous perspiration. I'll never wear this dress again." Kate thought that was probably a good thing. Just then, a black Lincoln Town Car pulled up and Elliot and Brice emerged.

"You're late," she said in place of a greeting, but she was happy to see the two of them.

"Well, hello to you, too." Elliot smiled, his usual cheerfulness intact. "Who's late?" He looked at his watch. "You said the ceremony was three o'clock. It's two fifty-seven."

Kate sighed. "Being on time is late in a situation like this."

"Haven't they heard of fashionably late?" Brice asked.

"This is Brooklyn," Kate reminded him. But as she looked both men over, she couldn't be angry.

"Wow," Bina said. "I love your outfits."

Kate smiled. "You two do clean up well."

"Of course," Brice said. "We're gay." With that he grabbed Bina's arm. "But not for this afternoon." He lowered his voice to a baritone. "This afternoon I'm devoted to you. Can't keep my hands off you." Bina actually smiled.

"Shall we, honey?" Brice asked. Bina nodded. "Hmm. Who did your hair?" Kate heard him ask Bina, that "anything she can do I can do better" tone in his voice.

"Sal Anthony. He has a little shop at the corner of Court and—"

"Burn it down," Brice ordered. "And we'll see if we can't soften it up a bit."

"He's so bossy," Kate said softly to Elliot.

"Yeah. Isn't it great?" Elliot asked.

They got to St. Veronica's and walked up the formidable stairs to the entrance of the church. Once inside, Kate indicated the way to the ladies' room downstairs.

"Follow me, princess," Brice told Bina, and led her off to the basement.

Coming in at the very last minute wasn't a bad strategy, Kate thought. There was no time to meet and greet—and to be interrogated. Kate and Elliot left the foyer and took a place in the next-to-last pew. Soon Brice and Bina joined them. They tried to be unobtrusive, but by now everyone was waiting for the ceremony to begin, and with their entrance, heads turned. Then, to Kate's relief, in only a moment the organ began to play the "Wedding March."

Bunny, a meringue of tulle and taffeta, began to make her way down the aisle on her father's arm. There was the usual "oooh" from the guests. Oddly, Kate felt tears well up in her eyes. She'd never been very close to Bunny—she couldn't honestly say she even liked her. But the tears were there nevertheless. She wondered if she was simply being empathetic for Bina, who must be finding this almost unbearable, but it felt far deeper than that.

Kate blinked away the moistness, then took a chance and looked around at the other guests. She wondered if they had as many doubts and fears as she did about picking a mate for life. Certainly Bina and her other friends had talked of little else for many of the years they were in school together. Boys, and then young men, who was going steady, who was breaking up, marriages, and honeymoons were the fodder of many—maybe most—conversations. Yet despite all the talking and all the romantic notions, hopes, and dreams, Kate didn't see intelligent or realistic choices being made, and she also didn't see any marriages or relationships she envied.

She wondered sometimes if her view was darkened by her early home life or her professional training. But the truth was that she remembered very little of her parents' marriage and didn't believe that it was bad or violent. Her father's serious drinking had started after her mother's death. So why was she so frightened? Was everyone frightened and they just hid it better?

So what was Bunny doing now? She'd just met this guy. Was she simply on the rebound from whoever had dumped her? Or was she smitten, deep in that sex haze of infatuation that never seemed to last longer than several months? How could she be taking these steps so quickly down the aisle beside her father?

Though a lapsed Catholic, Kate was still idealistic enough to believe marriage should be forever.

Here, standing in St. Veronica's watching Bunny meet the groom at the altar, she felt an uncomfortable combination of jealousy and fear: jealousy because she doubted she could give herself to Michael or any man without hesitation; fear because she wanted to and might lose her opportunity to do it. Though she had made up with Michael, his lack of compassion for Bina had made her look at him in a new way. Would he always dwell on his own issues and concerns and be insensitive to others? He had seemed sincere in his apology, but Kate felt it was important to watch him. Above all, she needed a partner with empathy for others.

She sighed. Beside her, Elliot gave her a smile, then returned his gaze to Bunny. Maybe it was Manhattan. Here in Brooklyn, love seemed so much easier, Kate reflected. Young women met young men. They dated for a while and either broke up or made a commitment to make a commitment. Women pressed for marriage, and the men, albeit sometimes reluctantly, seemed eventually to fall into line. It was expected. And families, ever present in the background, pushed for it.

Of course, there were the exceptions like Jack, but despite this glitch, Kate felt almost certain that he could get over the hump, have some fun in Hong Kong, and return to Bina, the woman he loved. But for how long, if they married, would they love each other? Looking at the older couples in the pews beside and ahead of her, Kate saw bored, middle-aged men and stoic or overly sentimental women. Many held handkerchiefs or tissues to their eyes. When Kate saw an older woman cry at a wedding—and she'd been to lots of weddings—she often thought they cried because unconsciously they remembered their own hopes and the subsequent disappointment that marriage had brought them.

Kate stood there, between her two best friends and between two worlds, and realized that she was not only envious, but also very, very sad. Even if Michael wound up being the right man for her, she simply couldn't imagine wearing the gown, she certainly wouldn't be in a church, her father couldn't walk her down any aisle, and it seemed impossible she'd feel the joy that she'd glimpsed on Bunny's veiled face. Worst of all, she'd probably want Elliot as her matron of honor, which would cause all kinds of difficulties and hurt feelings among her old crowd.

Kate had to smile at the thought. Of course, Elliot would love it. She looked over in his direction and saw that behind Bina, Elliot and Brice were discreetly holding hands. It was so sweet that Kate, without a tissue, again felt tears fill her eyes. She was so happy for Elliot, who had searched and searched for a wonderful partner. But it sometimes made her feel more lonely than she had felt in years.

"Having fun?" Elliot asked in a whisper as he nudged her out of her reverie.

"Just thinking," Kate murmured.

"Bad idea at any time," Elliot advised. "*Particularly* bad during rituals." He flashed Kate another quick smile. "And did I tell you, you look extremely fetching in that dress?"

Kate smiled but put a finger over her curved lips. Religion was serious in Brooklyn. The ceremony was beginning. And so was the trouble.

Even though she was not Catholic, and was standing yards and yards from the altar, the moment the priest began to speak, Bina began to sob. At first they were silent, shoulder-shaking sobs. For a few moments Kate didn't notice them. But by the time Bunny and her groom had knelt and stood up and knelt again, Bina was audible halfway up the nave. Kate and Elliot eyed each other, then leaned forward and gave Brice a look. He already had one arm around Bina's shoulder and shrugged in the traditional "what else can I do?" gesture.

Kate looked toward the altar, desperate to think of options. A little crying at a wedding was acceptable, even mandatory, but this was getting out of hand. For no reason, her eyes focused on the incense-filled censer hanging from the hands of an altar boy. Really handy looking. For a moment she wished she could get hold of it and give a swing at Bina's head. Not to crack it hard, of course, merely to knock some sense into it. It was going to be difficult enough to get through the reception without Bina blowing her cover now by making a spectacle of herself.

Already a few heads had turned toward them. Kate smiled and nodded, wiping at her own eye as if acknowledging everyone's tears of joy. "So beautiful," she mouthed to someone's mother. Brice, in a moment of brilliance, turned Bina to him and planted a kiss on her lips. For a few moments, Bina's total surprise silenced her. Elliot, putting his arm around her neck from the other side, discreetly covered her mouth with his hand. Bina took the warning and they all watched as the couple stood up, knelt yet again, then stood up and faced each other.

"Is this a wedding or an aerobics class?" Elliot asked. Kate almost laughed out loud, but just then the couple got to "love, honor, and cherish," and Bina cut loose, crying louder than the baby somewhere up front.

Before everything got completely out of control, Brice reached over, turned back Elliot's cuff, and removed a straight pin. Then, without a moment of hesitation, he stuck it into Bina's upper arm.

Kate, shocked, was not as shocked as Bina, who yipped, shut up, and looked from Elliot on one side to Brice on the other. Brice just leaned forward, whispered in her ear, and, magically, the crying stopped.

At last the service was over, the bride and groom kissed, and Brice and Elliot had to let go of each other's entwined hands to hold Bina's down so she didn't cover her face and begin to sob again. "Hey, look," Kate said, taking Bina by the shoulders. "Pull yourself together. This isn't the worst part. The worst part is about to begin."

"Oh, boy!" Elliot said. "Will there be a family feud?"

"With guns?" Brice added hopefully.

Kate ignored their remarks. "We have to get Bina out of here before the rest of the rabble," she told them.

"You aren't kidding. Just look at her." Elliot tilted his head toward Bina.

Kate had to agree. Bina's makeup was mostly smeared off her face, and mascara had run down her cheeks. Kate gestured, and Elliot tapped Brice on the leg.

"Time to go now," he told Brice.

"No fucking kidding," Brice responded. "The last thing Bina needs right now is to have rice land on her face. It would stick."

Elliot nodded, his face scrunched up at the thought. Then they all crept quietly out of the pew, out of the foyer, and out of the church.

They were lucky to snag a passing cab—not so easy in a borough dependent on car services. They piled out at Carl's of Carroll Gardens, where everyone in Brooklyn, it seemed, had their wedding reception.

"Well, here we go," Kate said as they stood before the entrance. She gave Elliot a nervous smile, and they linked their arms and went through the revolving doors together, followed by Brice and Bina. Fortunately the reception area was empty except for a few bustling waiters who had seen a lot worse than Bina's ruined face.

"Where's the bathroom?" Brice whispered in Kate's ear. "I'm going to take Little Miss Three Mile Island in for a makeup makeover. She's had a serious meltdown."

"It's down the hall to the left," said Kate. She had been to this banquet hall many times in the past. Maybe a dozen people she knew had gotten married here, but it would be a quiet day at Andrew Country Day School before *she* ever would. Assembly-line wedding, with the same music, the same guests, the same MC, the same cake. "Take her away," Kate said. "And Brice, darling, please be gentle."

"I'll do my best," he said, and started to push Bina from behind. "Come on, honey. Time for some surgery from Dr. Brice."

Kate heard Bina's nasal protesting voice trail off as she and Brice disappeared down the hall. "Well," she said, turning to Elliot. "Are you ready for your first Brooklyn reception?"

"Oh, Katie! This is going to be so much fun," Elliot said, grinning wickedly.

"Cut the 'Katie' before you get your tongue cut out," Kate warned him. "I've got a mission. Let's see where we are supposed to sit, change it if we can, and then avoid everyone until we've regrouped."

"Sure. I'm happy just to gape." Elliot craned his neck almost the way Linda Blair had in *The Exorcist*. "Where do they get these smoked mirrors? Are they left over from the sixties or can you still buy them?" he asked, his voice low. It was kind of like Halloween in Greenwich Village. Then he looked down at his watch. "Kate, I'm going to look around some, then maybe check on Brice and see what he's doing to Bina. I'll be back soon. You wait here for the resurrection." He sauntered down the hall.

Once alone, Kate walked over to the gift table and placed her box from Tiffany's right in the center. She knew it wouldn't be the only one there wrapped in distinctive robin's-egg blue, but she was fairly certain the beautiful cut-glass bowl would be the only gift that actually came from Tiffany's. Those blue boxes were often more highly prized than the contents they carried and were passed around over and over, filled with gifts from Bed Bath & Beyond or Pottery Barn.

The reception area was beginning to fill up. After about fifteen minutes, Kate began to wonder why Elliot hadn't come back with Brice and Bina. She could hear more cars pulling up outside. It wasn't only Bina who would be tortured at this event. Kate was definitely not in the mood to deal with all these people—well-meaning or not—asking her about her "love life" and whether "wedding bells" were in her future, too. People from the old neighborhood neither thought deeply personal questions were off-limits nor took notice of how she had managed to add a "Dr." before her name. All everyone here would talk about was when there would be a "Mrs." in front.

She put all this out of her mind because she had a goal to achieve. She had to get over to the table where the seating plans were and make sure her party of four was at the same table. Then she had to get into the closed banquet hall and move the place cards on that table so that Bina would be tightly cordoned off from attacking hyenas, the type that tried to take down a straggler or the weakest member in the herd.

She approached the assignment table with complete authority. If she didn't, she might get stopped by one of the staff. They were used to unmarried women putting themselves beside bachelors, bitter aunts removing themselves from tables with their relatives, even parents who moved their kids to other tables so they could eat dinner in peace. Kate quickly spotted her card: "Miss Katie Jameson and guest," table nine. She shook her head. Not only had the "Dr." been omitted, but she didn't even get her full name. And she hated being called Katie, but Bunny and her mother wouldn't care about such subtleties.

Two cards above her own was "Miss Bina Horowitz and Mr. Jack Weintraub." That was something Kate knew she couldn't afford to let Bina see. Bunny's mother obviously hadn't remembered about Jack's trip. Kate picked up the card, turned it over, and, using a black marker she had put in her purse for this very purpose, wrote, "Miss Bina Horowitz and guest" on the back of the card and replaced it. She hoped that Bina wouldn't turn the card over and that Brice would be smart enough to pocket it.

So far, so good, Kate thought. Next, and last, was getting to the actual table to manipulate the place cards. If Bina was seated next to Bev or Barbie, she wouldn't last five minutes. Of course, they might be seated in the traditional boy-girl-boy boring arrangement. Kate sighed, thinking of one more dinner beside Bobby, Barbie's excessively dull husband. She walked to the closed entrance of the banquet hall, and as luck would have it, a hassled-looking waiter came out. She grabbed at the door closing behind him as he departed with an armful of linens and stepped into the room.

A sign read "Tromboli-Beckmen Wedding Saturday." Under it was "Eisenberg Bar Mitzvah Sunday." Kate surveyed the room. The interior of the hall was Bunny Tromboli's dream come true, amazingly close to Kate's nightmare. The decorations, the centerpieces, the candles—everything was a middle-class version of photographs Bunny had been clipping and saving from society pages since she was ten. All of the Bitches except Kate had done the same. Kate sighed deeply. Whenever she had allowed herself to envision the elements of a dream wedding, the major emphasis had been on the groom, not the flatware.

Yet despite the inconceivably garish tablecloths and place settings—hot pink and orange, a combination Kate saw no use for in either clothes or furnishings, along with black dinnerware and centerpieces that looked like patent leather with flourishes of net—there was something lovely, calm . . . even magical about a vacant room prepared for but empty of revelers. She allowed herself to pause for a moment to take it all in. Then the colors and her mission moved her forward. She found table nine, looked it over, and moved the cards so that the lineup on their side of the table was Elliot, then Kate, then Bina, and then Brice. She had to juggle Bobby and Johnny, Barbie's and Bev's husbands, to get it to work out, but in a few moments it was done. She pulled out the four chairs for her party and leaned the backs against the table—a very déclassé way to show the seats were taken and to ensure that nobody reedited her editing.

The noise of new arrivals outside the banquet hall had gotten much louder, and then, without warning, the doors swung open. The guests began to pour in. Kate, not wanting to be found alone in the room, a target worse than a lonely duck before the hunter's blind, decided to make her way out to the terrace that ran along the east wall of the room. She would wait outside, get a breath of air and a bit of privacy before the onslaught. Once her crew came back, there would be enough people and enough noise to allow her to slip back inside, find the Trouble Trio, and begin the minimum required mingling. She'd mingled at dozens of weddings before, and she could do it again, she told herself.

Out on the terrace, Kate had a moment to reflect. She was overwhelmingly glad that she had not invited Michael to the affair. She would have been self-conscious and, although she shouldn't be, rather ashamed. The clothes, the accents, the loudness, the . . . well, the vulgarity of it all, made her wince. She was used to it, and loved many of these people, but she did not want to have to translate them for Michael or anyone else. At the same time, she wasn't enjoying how much Elliot and Brice were enjoying their Brooklyn visit. It was too much like a visit to Great Adventure Safari Park. They were observing the wildlife with the detachment of another species.

Kate peeked into the room. It wouldn't take long for it to fill. And then Elliot and Brice would get to talk to the creatures they had been observing at church. Somehow, while it was all right for Kate to think of these people as strange, she didn't like the idea of outsiders observing them in that way, not even Elliot and Brice. Yes, she reflected again, it was the right thing to do to leave Michael out, and how on earth would she have managed Bina without the help of the guys?

She continued to watch as people entered, rearranged their own place cards, hugged or kissed one another, and went for the drinks. Even through the windows, she could hear them speculating about the estimated per plate cost of the upcoming meal, where the bride had bought the dress, whether there was a bun in the oven . . . and then Kate saw Elliot, Brice, and Bina enter the room. She had to admit it: Bina did look a thousand times more sophisticated with the terrific makeup and more gentle upswept hairstyle Brice's lengthy ministrations had created. Kate reached for the handle of the French door to let herself in, only to find that it had locked itself behind her. She tried the second one, then the third. All locked.

Stranded. She knocked on the glass and tried desperately to get someone's attention, but the hall was abuzz with noise. She could make out older female guests loudly declaring the ceremony to be the most beautiful they'd ever seen, while the men called across the room to one another, inquiring about the outlook for the Mets.

In moments, the room had changed from tranquil to chaotic, from empty to full, and myriad poof skirts and dangerously high hairdos blocked her line of vision. She had lost sight of her friends. Kate thought she caught a glimpse of Brice and someone who might be Bina, now on the side of the room opposite their table, but she couldn't be sure. She ran back down to the remaining doors of the terrace to try to get in, but they were all locked. Well, she would just have to wait until someone—

Just then, a tall blond stepped out the door at the other end of the terrace. What a relief!

"Wait!" Kate yelled. "Wait! Hold the—"

But before she could finish her sentence or make a move, he had turned to the side and the door slammed behind him.

Chapter Twelve

Damn it," Kate muttered. She walked over to the slammed door and tried the handle, but it was locked. Meanwhile, the guy had moved to the ivy-covered wall and was looking around casually. He was, she couldn't help but notice, one of the best-looking men she'd ever seen. His blond hair must have had a dozen shades in it—the kind of hair women paid hundreds of dollars to salons for but never achieved. He was probably only a little over six feet tall, but his wide shoulders and the way his jacket tapered from them, along with legs that didn't quit, made him incredibly well proportioned. Kate wondered whether his upper arms were muscled and cut in the way she found so attractive. She could barely see his profile, but even from here she could tell that he didn't have the usual pale coloring of a blond. There was a golden tone to his skin that . . . well, he was altogether a golden guy, the type who is all looks and no substance.

Then he saw Kate and turned to face her. From a full frontal, he was—if it was possible—even more alluring. To her dismay, Kate felt a blush rise from her chest to her neck, but he didn't seem to notice. He just asked, "At the risk of sounding clichéd, what's a pretty girl like you doing in a place like this?" He took a few steps toward her. "And you look distressed. Um, in the damsel, not the furniture, sense." He smiled. The smile was the coup de grâce. It was marvelous the way his teeth lightened his face, how parenthetical dimples formed around it, and how his eyes, unlike most people's when they smiled, stayed wide open. He was what might be called *un canon,* a living embodiment of male beauty.

Kate took a step back. She was suspicious of men this good-looking and with charm as well, but she couldn't help staring. Something about him looked familiar, but she would never have forgotten him if they had met. Perhaps he was a newscaster or someone she had seen on television. She forced herself to take her eyes away from his.

"You could have helped by holding the door open," she said, trying to keep her embarrassment from showing. "Now we may have to wait until someone from the Eisenberg bar mitzvah lets us in tomorrow afternoon." The words had come out more sharply than she'd meant them to. He cocked his head and observed her. She felt self-conscious at the way he looked at her. Not because it was a once-over, merely because it was so intent—as if he were memorizing every detail of her, from her exposed collarbone to her Jimmy Choo shoes. She turned and looked in at the party through the long window.

"Would that be such a bad thing?" he asked.

Still peering through the window, Kate could see Bina at the far side of the room, flanked by Brice and Elliot, who was looking around, presumably for Kate. Oh no, she couldn't let Bina sit down among their old crowd without her protection! There would be a feeding frenzy. She rattled the door handle. No luck. *"Merde!"* she said.

"Ah. Parlez-vous français?" he asked, almost too quickly.

She turned away from the party to look at him. This guy wasn't just an average hunk. He had the smile of a man who knew he was more than handsome and irresistible to women. It was a well-practiced smile that bathed Kate in warmth. She felt as if she were the first woman in the entire world to ever see such an expression of welcome. The guy was absolutely gorgeous, what French slang would describe as *"un bloc."*

"Oui." Kate blushed and cursed the paleness of her skin. She

might as well have her feelings written in neon on her forehead. *"Je parle un petit peu, mais avec un accent très mauvais,"* she told him.

"Mais non. Pas mal. Vraiment."

Handsome as the guy was—and his accent was perfect—Kate was in no mood to test her skills in a foreign tongue right now, though the thought of his tongue provided a momentary distraction from her desperation. She turned and tried once again to open the doors, but they were clearly catch locks, openable only from the inside. "We're stuck out here," she said.

"What an unexpected bonus at an affair like this. Maybe it's an omen," Mr. Gorgeous continued. "Maybe we're not meant to participate in the Bunny Tromboli and Arnie Beckmen nuptials." He leaned back on the terrace railing, crossed one foot in front of the other, and gave Kate an appreciative once-over. "Personally, I would take that as a gift."

Kate was too uptight to flirt or respond to compliments, especially from a guy as practiced at them as he obviously was.

"You don't look like you're from around these parts," he said, doing a passable Gary Cooper accent. He even looked a little like Cooper, and he probably knew it.

Kate had always preferred slightly nerdy boyfriends, no matter what Elliot said. They were more real, more sincere. Ever since a really handsome Oxford exchange student had asked her on their first date, "How can I possibly keep from falling in love with you," and subsequently dated her roommate a week later, she'd been wary of charm. *"Et vous?"* she asked, just as a test.

"Oui, je suis un fils de Broooklyn," he answered with a mischievous smile.

"Your accent is perfect," Kate observed admiringly.

"My French accent or the Brooklyn one?" he asked, and smiled again. Looks like his should be against the law, she thought, and despite herself, she couldn't resist glancing at his hand, checking for a wedding band. There was none. Not that it mattered to her, she told herself. She didn't know what this guy was about—the answer was probably *rien*—and she didn't have the time to find out.

Turning, she peered through the glass. She could see that Elliot had found the table and their place cards. She couldn't see his face, but she could see Bev Clemenza and her husband, Johnny, headed directly toward him. Predictably, Barbie and Bobby Cohen were right behind them. "I have to get in there," Kate said in a panic. She grabbed the knob and shook the door frantically.

"Are you a friend of the groom or the bride?" he asked her.

She knocked again on the window. "Bride," she answered tersely, then realized how rude it sounded. "Bunny is one of my oldest friends," she added. Through glass she watched in a paralysis of horror as Elliot shook Bobby's hand and then Johnny's.

"A much older friend, right?" the charmer asked, and moved beside her.

Kate was not in the mood. "Bunny and I have been friends since grade school," she told him, waving wildly through the glass, hoping someone would notice the movement. "And yes, in fact, Bunny *is* older—by almost a month. But we didn't let that come between us."

"So what's the problem if you miss some of the earlier festivities?"

"I have to be there to support a friend from my posse."

"Your posse?" he asked, and smiled. "Anyone I know?"

"Bev Clemenza, Bina Horowitz, Barbie Cohen."

"You're kidding!" he began, and he stepped away to get a better look at Kate. She turned to him, just for a moment.

"C'est incroyable, mais vraiment." What was it, she wondered, with the friggin' French? She looked back in at the party. God, the DJ was starting to play! "You must be one of the infamous Bitches of Bushwick," he said. "I've heard about *you* girls."

"Excuse me?" Kate asked, turning to him in surprise.

"How come I've never met you?" he asked, oblivious to her hostility. Typical narcissist, Kate thought.

He looked over Kate's head into the room and pointed. "I already know Bev, Barbie, and, of course, Bunny. All the busy Bs. Who are you? Betty?"

"My name is Katherine Jameson," Kate told him.

"I'm Billy Nolan. Why haven't I met you before?"

"I left Brooklyn to go to college."

"I left Brooklyn to go to France. What did you do in college? And where have you gone since?"

"I got my doctorate. I live in Manhattan now." She paused. "Look, Billy, I have to get in there."

"I'm willing to cover my hand with my jacket and bust through the glass, but it . . ."

"It might be a bit much," Kate finished for him.

"They'll open the doors once it gets too hot in there," he said, sitting on the balustrade. "Have you noticed how no one from Brooklyn ever outgrows having their name end with an 'e' sound? Barbie. Bunny. Johnny. Eddie, Arnie." He chuckled. "Here in Brooklyn I'm never William or even Bill. I'm Billy."

He held out his hand, and Kate couldn't resist shaking it. She tried to appear casual, despite the thrill that ran up her back, causing hairs on her neck to rise. "Do you prefer Billy to Bill?" she asked.

"Hey. We're in Brooklyn," he answered. "Go with the flow. Here I'm Billy Nolan. And should I call you Dr. Katherine? Kate? Kathy or Katie?"

"Oh, please, Kate. Not Katie. I hate it," Kate confessed. "Oh, look, they must be playing their song."

To her complete surprise, Billy stood up, grabbed her hand, and started to dance. Before she could make a move, he stopped abruptly. "'Doo Wah Diddy' is their song?" He made a face, looking puzzled in a really exaggerated way, his head cocked to the side.

Kate laughed. "Well, maybe not."

"I hope not. If it is, I give the marriage three weeks. You have to at least *start* with some romance."

She bet he did—and that for him romance wore off fast. Kate looked him over. The sun glinted on his golden hair. He was one of those very few lucky Irish with the kind of skin that tanned and made their blue eyes bluer. "So you don't think you can keep romance going?" Kate asked him.

"If I thought that, I'd be married." Billy Nolan laughed, and from nowhere the phrase *coup de foudre,* a lightning bolt, entered Kate's mind. He was something—and he knew it, she reminded herself.

"Ah. The tyranny of commitment," Kate said, nodding.

Billy reacted with widened eyes. Then he clutched at his chest. "Now they're doing the hokey-pokey!" he said, as if that upset him.

"So unusual at a Brooklyn wedding," Kate agreed a bit sarcastically. They always played the hokey-pokey or the alley cat or both. She looked in the window, where dozens of old ladies were dancing, their backs to them. "We definitely won't be able to get their attention now."

"Uh-oh. I think I'm in trouble," Billy said, and began to shake. Kate wondered if he was still reacting to the word *commitment*. "Good thing you're a doctor," he said.

Kate looked at him suspiciously. "Why is that?"

"I may need treatment right now. I have a terrible phobia of the hokey-pokey."

"Really?" Kate said. She didn't need this kind of banter now, but as long as they were stuck outside . . . "As I say in my practice, 'Why do you feel that way?'"

"It seems obvious," Billy told her. "Did you ever think about it?"

"About what?"

"About the song? I mean, 'You put your left foot in, you take your left foot out.' Yadda, yadda. You do the hokey-pokey and you turn yourself around. And that's what it's all about." He did an exaggerated shiver.

"So?"

"Well, what if that *is* what it's all about? What if life is just putting one foot in front of the other and that's it? Doesn't the thought terrify you?"

Before Kate could decide how tongue in cheek he was being and come up with an answer, the doors at the other end of the terrace flew open and a big guy in a wrinkled blue suit stuck his head out. "Hey, Nolan!" he shouted. "Get your ass in here. Arnie wants to talk to you about the toast."

Before he vanished again, Billy shouted: "Larry! Hold that thought and that door!" He gracefully ran the length of the terrace, catching the handle just in time. Then he turned back to Kate, held the door ajar, and said, "After you, *chère mademoiselle.*"

Kate felt her cheeks color again but wasted no time stepping through the doors and into the crowded room. She was about to thank Billy when she heard Bev Clemenza's high-pitched voice screech, "Katie! Katie! Over here," and didn't dare look back.

Chapter Thirteen

As Kate crossed the room toward her posse, she almost felt a gravitational pull back toward Billy Nolan. She was deeply embarrassed by the strength of her attraction and decided to put it out of her mind. He was just a superficial Brooklyn flirt. And she had an important job to do now.

"Katie!" Bev called again. Kate didn't want to see how terrified Bina was going to be. Though it wasn't her choice, she bitterly regretted that she hadn't been beside Bina during the first few critical minutes. As she moved through the crowd—now twisting again as they did last summer, or at the last wedding—she silently cursed Billy Nolan and the time on the terrace, diverting as it had been.

At last she managed to get across the dance floor and could clearly see table nine. Luckily, Bina was still somewhere in the crowd and Elliot had apparently abandoned the table for greater intrigues. There was Bev, her frosted hair slicked back and her visibly pregnant belly stretching her unsuitable Lycra dress. Barbie, with her big hair hanging halfway down her back, was already seated, too. Barbie's dad, in the jewelry trade, had been more successful than the other friends' fathers had been. She'd always had more clothes, trips to Florida, weekends in the Poconos, and things that seemed enviable at the time. But now she was a Brooklyn wife, a buyer for a women's clothing store on Nostrand Avenue. Her husband, Bobby, was in insurance. Kate could look at her now and feel no envy at all.

Barbie sat beside Bobby, her plunging neckline revealing the half of her breasts not covered by her push-up bra. Kate averted her eyes, but the husbands were, in their own way, more difficult to look at. If each of them hadn't been wearing a bow tie and cummerbund that matched his wife's dress, Kate wouldn't have been able to tell Bev's and Barbie's husbands apart. They were nice-looking Brooklyn boys, but neither of them was the kind of handsome that Billy Nolan was. And behind their eyes was none of the genuine intellect that Michael possessed. The thought of Michael trying to communicate at table nine raised goose bumps on her arms. "Hey," Bev yelled. "Look who's here."

For a moment Kate thought she was being greeted, but Bev was staring past her. Kate turned to see Billy Nolan join the wedding party at the head table, talking to the groom. Bunny looked down from the dais and gave Kate a quick wave and a big, proud smile, while taking Arnie's arm. Kate waved back, but her eyes strayed to Billy, talking earnestly to the groom, then laughing with him. Well, there would be no laughs at table nine, Kate reminded herself. She forced herself to turn back to her own companions.

"Wow, Kate, you look great!" Bev said. "Of course, you're a Scorpio and your ruling planet has come out this month, so no wonder."

"Yeah, there's that. And the sale at agnes b.," Kate said with a smile. Kate's simple dress, sleeveless and high collared, with a placket that covered the buttons, was the antithesis of all the overdone outfits of her old friends. If she but knew it, she easily looked the most elegant woman in the room. It was always curious to Kate that while her Brooklyn crew never missed an issue of *Vogue, Allure,* or *Cosmo,* they never seemed to dress any differently from the way they always had. Or if there had been a change, it seemed merely to be that blouses had gotten tighter and patterns had gotten louder. Bev, despite her belly, was wearing a black-and-lemon tiger-striped Lycra thing. Barbie wore a tight, strapless dress in a Hawaiian floral print, all banana leaves and toucans wreathing (and writhing) around her torso. Kate could never quite decide if their taste was unbelievably bad or whether hers had been permanently repressed by the nuns at Catholic first school.

"You could use some accessorizing," Barbie opined by way of a hello. "A scarf, or maybe a pendant." Barbie herself was wearing an emerald—no doubt real—that was suspended just above her cleavage.

"I have to wait until I get the chest and the gem for it," Kate said smoothly.

"You are so cynical," Bev snorted. "Such a Scorpio." Since she had become pregnant, Bev, always a horoscope reader, had *really* gotten into astrology. Hormones or something, Kate thought. Or perhaps the feeling of being out of control and the comforting compensation of a system to predict the universe. Kate turned to face the wedding hall again, to try to spot Bina and the guys. She was getting nervous about them. At last she saw Elliot making his way across the room. He arrived carrying three drinks.

"For you, and you, and you," he said, and gave each of the women a cosmopolitan.

"Ooh. Thanks," Bev said, "but I can't."

"What a gentleman," Barbie said appreciatively, then dug Bobby in the ribs.

"This is my friend Elliot." Kate took Elliot's arm.

"We've already met," Elliot said. Kate raised her eyebrows. "Out in the reception area. Your friends are as unique as you are, Katie."

"Oh, we're very unique," Bev said.

"Where's Bina?" Kate asked Elliot out of the corner of her mouth. She scanned the room and saw Brice and Bina making their way toward the table.

Bev tugged on Kate's elbow. "Hey, that guy with Bina, is he her date or what?"

Barbie raised her highly waxed eyebrows. "I love the tuxedo," she cooed. "Armani."

Kate had to smile. If Judaism was a religion to Bina, fashion had always been Barbie's creed. And Kate remembered that Brice had predicted the impression he would make.

"But do you think Jack would approve?" Barbie asked. "I mean, he's gone only a couple of weeks and she's . . . Does he know?"

Kate shrugged. Let 'em guess. Keep 'em busy and distracted.

"His name is Brite or something," Bev said, rubbing her belly.

"Brice," Kate corrected.

"So, what's this guy Brice's sign, anyway?" Bev asked.

"I think he's a Taurus, you'll have to ask him," Elliot said, holding out a chair for Kate, who was grateful to sit down. It was going to be a bumpy ride.

"Oh, Katie, a Taurus! Not for Bina!" Bev complained. "Dangerous while her fiancé is gone."

"Oh, he's a dangerous man," Elliot agreed.

"Is he on the cusp?" Bev added, hopeful.

Kate didn't need or want to explain that Brice was way over the cusp as a mate for Bina. "I think they're just friends," she said.

"That's not what it looks like to me," Barbie said as she joined Kate on her other side. "And he's *gorgeous*. Like a *GQ* model. He'd be perfect for my cousin Judy. What does he do?"

"He's an attorney," Kate told Barbie.

"In a big firm or a solo practitioner?" Barbie asked.

"You'll have to ask him." Kate sighed. Same old Barbie. Putting everyone in boxes, fixing them up with one another. She turned to watch Brice and Bina, who were caught in the electric slide on the dance floor. She couldn't help but smile a little at Brice's artful moves as he sidestepped between the slides, dragging Bina behind.

"What happened to Michael?" Bev asked. "Is that all over?" Except Bev pronounced it "ohvah." They all dropped final r's and added inappropriate ones at the ends of words that didn't have them.

But Kate didn't have time to consider diction, because at that moment Bina and Brice arrived at the table. Bina said, "Hi there, everyone," and sat down immediately without making eye contact. In fact, the only contact she seemed interested in was grabbing what would have been Jack's waiting glass of wine with her right hand and pinning down Kate's hand with her left. To Kate's astonishment, she knocked back an entire glass.

"Hello," Barbie said, but not to Bina. She leaned over the table and extended her hand to Brice while exposing more breast than most foldouts did and a lot more than Brice needed or wanted to see. Well, maybe she was trying to scoop him for her cousin, Kate thought charitably.

Meanwhile, Bina picked up Kate's wineglass and drank off half of that. Before Kate could say something to slow her down, eagle-eyed Bev noticed. "Since when do you drink? Capricorns don't drink!" she cried.

"Plus ça change, plus c'est la même chose," Kate said, surprising herself. Obviously her encounter on the terrace had had an effect after all.

"What?" Barbie and Bev asked in unison. Kate just smiled and shrugged.

"Bobby, Johnny, this is my friend Elliot, and this is Bina's friend Brice," Kate said to the men, interrupting a deep conversation about the pros and cons of moving some football team to Dallas. "Elliot, Brice, meet Bobby and Johnny." The husbands nodded a greeting in unison.

"What do you boys think of them moving the Rangers to Dallas?" Bobby asked.

"I'm not really into spectator sports," Elliot said.

"Oh, I love football. Tight ends, wide receivers. *You* know," Brice said, smiling at them.

For a moment, the two husbands looked confused. "You a Jets or a Giants fan?" Johnny asked, a little suspicion in his voice.

"Definitely a Giant. Love a 'Giant'—"

"Brice!" Elliot said, trying to interrupt.

"—game," Brice finished, and Kate let her breath out.

Bev and Barbie, now also totally confused, stared across the table and looked the two men over more carefully. Kate knew they were setting them up as potential husbands for their two poor, unmarried friends. Ha! When should she thwart them by breaking the news that Elliot and Brice were already married—to each other. But, as Kate hoped, they were at least temporarily distracted by their looks. Well, the delusion would do for now.

"What's your sign?" Bev asked Brice.

"'Do Not Enter,'" Brice replied, raising his eyebrows and smiling innocently.

Elliot, always ready with a peacemaking lie, smiled at Bev. "Oh, he's a bull," he said, and gave Kate a nudge under the table, as if she wouldn't get the joke without it. On the other side, Bina was still clutching Kate's right hand with her own.

"Hmm. A Taurus," Bev murmured, reappraising him.

Meanwhile, Bina reached out and picked up the cosmopolitan Bev had refused. In another moment she'd gulped it down.

"Bina!" Barbie exclaimed. "What are you doing?"

"Yeah, you have to pace yourself," Bobby advised.

Brice nudged his chair closer to Bina and took away her empty glass. They had created a Bina sandwich, insulating her from her friends. Bina reached out for Brice's glass of wine. He paused for a moment, then shrugged and handed it to her. She downed it in a few breathless gulps. Bev and Barbie stared at Bina. Kate could see Barbie reevaluating Brice as a candidate for Judy.

There was a moment of complete silence. Then Barbie asked the dreaded question. "Bina, you have to tell us about Jack's proposal. Let's see the ring." Kate clenched Bina's hand and tried to change the subject.

"Look at the bracelet Michael gave me," she said hurriedly, holding up her wrist for them to see the sad little silver chain and the thin charm that hung from it.

They barely glanced at Kate's wrist. With her usual amount of discretion, Bev opened her mouth. "Yeah, what happened to

Michael the doctor?" she wanted to know. "Bina told me about him."

"Why isn't he here? Is he gone already?" Barbie asked.

Kate shook her head. "He's away at a conference. Elliot is a nice change." Elliot and Kate exchanged looks of love. Barbie raised her eyebrows.

"What is Michael's sign, anyway?" Bev asked.

"Well, I'm not sure, but I think it might be—"

"Wait a minute," Barbie interrupted. "What's going on here?" Kate watched suspicion bloom on her face. "Bina, the ring!" she exclaimed. Then suddenly, without a moment's notice, Barbie reached across the table and grabbed Bina's wrist, yanking her hand from Kate's grip. There was a moment of total silence at table nine. Bina's naked hand, still French manicured, lay like a dying whitefish on the hot pink tablecloth.

Chapter Fourteen

Where the hell is it?" Barbie demanded. "My father sold Jack a perfect stone." She looked down at the ringless finger and then back up at Bina, whose face was scrunched up as she tried to hold back tears. "Wait a minute!" Barbie said as the light began to dawn. To her credit, there was true concern in her high-pitched voice. "Bina, is everything okay with Jack?"

Two waiters arrived and began distributing plates of chicken and vegetables. Kate hoped it would give Bina a distraction, but she paid no attention to the bland food in front of her.

"Yes . . . in a way," Bina managed. Bev and Barbie exchanged looks, then frowned.

"Okay. How is it okay?" Barbie pressed.

"Well, after his trip we'll get . . . we'll probably get engaged then, after—"

"I knew it!" Bev exclaimed. "Mercury is in retrograde!"

"Very true," Brice said. "It's affected my whole law practice."

But the distraction didn't work. "You lost him, Bina!" Barbie said. "After six years on the hook, you still couldn't reel him in?"

"Barbie!" Kate remonstrated. Elliot put his arm protectively around Bina's little shoulder.

"Oh, God! Are you holding up okay?" Bev asked with genuine sympathy.

"Yes . . . and no," Bina said, and then began to cry outright.

"Well, is it yes or no?" Barbie asked.

"Looks like no to me," Johnny said, pushing away his plate and rising. He shot a look at Bobby, who nodded, wolfed down one last forkful of chicken, and pushed back his chair. "Uh, we'll get some drinks," he offered, and he and Bobby abandoned the table.

"Honey, is there anything we can do to help?" Barbie asked.

"Well, I've been staying with Kate, and Elliot, Max, and Brice have been a major support," Bina told her friends through her tears. "Look, I'm fine," she began. "I cried for a little while, but now I have found"—she looked fuzzily at Brice—"a new focus."

"Right!" Barbie chimed in. "Focus on the possibilities." She smiled at Brice. "You miss one bus, there's always another. A door closes and a window opens. You lose one house and you find one next door."

"Wrong street," Elliot muttered to Kate, who shushed him.

Kate couldn't let the charade go on. "Brice and Elliot are here together," she said.

"Well, we can see that," Bev said.

"No, I mean they're *really* together." Kate watched as the realization of what she said slowly dawned on all of the guests around the table. Despite *Queer Eye* and *Boy Meets Boy*—or maybe because of them—the old Brooklyn crowd felt that gay was a reality, but only on TV.

There was a pause. At last Bev spoke. "No wonder you guys are so well-dressed."

Barbie turned to Bina. "And just because you're desperate now, showing up with these guys doesn't mean there can't be a—" she cleared her throat—"a straight guy in your future. No offense meant."

"No offense taken," Elliot assured them.

"Yeah, look at Bunny," Bev said, waving her hand with its unbelievably long nails toward the bridal table. "Less than two months ago, she got dumped. Then she met her Arnie . . . and everything turned around."

"I don't want everything to turn around," Bina sniffed. Kate was actually grateful for the wine Bina had consumed, because without it there would be floods of tears. "I want Jack. . . ."

Eventually the waiters returned and removed the dishes, replacing them with a limp salad. A waltz began, and the seductive swell of Strauss drew their gazes toward the dance floor. At first, Kate was glad of any diversion, but then she realized the only two dancers were Billy and Bunny, whom he was twirling expertly around the floor. Kate, along with every other woman in the room, admired his moves, his mastery, and all the rest of him. His grace made Bunny look good. Spontaneous applause broke out, and then other couples started to join them on the dance floor. Kate was about to casually ask about him when Bobby and Johnny finally returned to the table, carrying a tray full of drinks. Kate was thankful for hers but had trouble swallowing at the sight of Bina guzzling down a Jack Daniel's with Coke.

"Oh, look at Bunny! Thank God she lost those last five pounds," Barbie said. "I told her not to buy a size six when you're an eight. It wasn't like she had eight months to lose the weight. She'd been on the Häagen-Dazs diet after she got dumped the last time. Then bim bam boom, and she's getting married."

"It was in the stars," Bev said dreamily.

Kate was distracted from the conversation as the waiter stepped in to pour coffee. "She bought the dress three weeks ago," Barbie told them. "And they only got this date at all because another couple eloped. It's too bad. If she had done some Pilates, she could have worn a bias cut. They're big now."

"Stop!" Kate interjected. "She looks beautiful because she's happy."

Brice looked out at the couples on the dance floor. "I'm not sure I like her dress, but I like her taste in grooms," he said, snapping a Polaroid of Bunny and Billy as they passed by. There was greater interest and enthusiasm in Brice's voice than Kate would've preferred, but it didn't seem as if anyone else noticed.

"Oh, that is *not* her husband!" Barbie sneered. "That's Billy." Apparently a raw spot had been touched. "He's the guy who dumped her, but he introduced her to Arnie."

Kate leaned back to see around the waiter who was carrying the tray of dessert. Then, as clear as a movie flashback, Kate remembered the glimpse she had gotten of the man in SoHo, the one Bina had pointed out. Of course. She *had* seen him before.

"See, Bina? It could happen to you," Bev said, her voice warm with encouragement. "I'll do your chart and see what's up. It could be a Taurus," she added archly to Brice.

"And what a lucky Taurus he would be," Brice said gallantly. He sat back in his chair and picked up the developed picture of Billy. "Ooh, pretty," he said to himself, and slipped the photo into his pocket.

"Sure," Bina slurred.

"One day dumped and the next engaged," Barbie told her.

"I have not been dumped!" Bina exclaimed.

"Can you believe Billy's actually the best man?" Barbie asked the table at large, apparently still stuck on the subject.

"Didn't you date him right before you met me?" Johnny asked his wife. Bev blushed as she nodded that she had indeed dated the man in question. "I went out with him for a few weeks, right before we met, but it didn't work out." She leaned over and kissed her husband. "Anyway, he's an Aries," she offered by way of explanation.

"He's an asshole," Barbie clarified. "He's the asshole who dumped Bunny."

For once Kate was forced to agree with Barbie. Her assessment of the guy had been right: too good-looking, too facile, too smooth.

"Good old Billy," Bina said, clearly close to drunk. "Let's drink to 'Dumping Billy.'"

"Dumping Billy?" Elliot asked with interest. "Why do you call him that?"

"Because he's turned dumping women into a major lifestyle," Barbie told him.

"He's not really a bad guy," Bev said. "It's hard for an Aries to commit."

Johnny snorted. "I can't believe you actually dated him."

"Well, I wasn't the only one," Bev replied, on the defensive, "was I, Barbie?"

"No," Barbie said bravely, "Billy was the last guy I dated before I got married to Bobby. But he didn't mean a thing to me. When I broke up with him—"

"Excuse me?" Bev asked. "Reality check. He broke up with you."

"Whatever. He's not really so terrible. He's fun, and he's got a great sense of style. It's just that the word *commitment* isn't in his vocabulary."

Brice leaned across the table to whisper to Kate, "Elliot was so right. This is so much better than *The Young and the Restless*. But a lot less realistic."

"That's because soap operas are art, and this is not real life," Kate told him. She didn't even want to imagine the feedback she'd get from these two after this nightmare was over.

She looked over at Elliot, who had taken out a pencil and paper. "Let me see if I have all the facts right," he said to himself. She wondered what in the world he could be up to. But before she got a chance to ask, Bina stood up unsteadily and decided that this was the moment to announce to the assembly just how unhappy she was.

"Ladies and gentlemen," she said, "you are looking at Bina Horowitz, loser and future spinsper."

"Spinster," Brice corrected.

"Whatever," Bina said, and tried to climb up on her chair. Elliot caught her before she fell, but he couldn't stop her from raising her voice. "Single women can have children, you know. Not just Rosie O'Donnell. Michael Jackson did it, and he wasn't even a woman. I'm a woman, goddammit!"

Despite the incredible din in the room, people were beginning to stare. Luckily, at that moment, the sound system crackled and Billy Nolan's voice covered Bina's.

"Excusez moi," Billy tried once, and then tapped the microphone and said more loudly, this time in English, "Excuse me.

Everyone?" The chattering continued until finally he tapped the microphone so firmly that the high-pitched squeal of feedback quieted the crowd. "Stop talking!" Billy nearly shouted at them all. It was a perfect opportunity to get Bina calmed down. Kate and Brice tried to take her by the hand as she resisted. Meanwhile, over the speakers Billy Nolan seemed to be having trouble of his own. "Jeez, I know it's imp-possible for B-Brooklyn women to b-be quiet, b-but if you could just g-give a guy a b-break here."

Kate cringed as he struggled to overcome his stammer. Kate looked down at the bracelet Michael had given her and sighed. Then she turned to see what Elliot thought of Billy, but he didn't seem to be paying attention. In fact, he looked as if he were trying to solve a math problem. As the best man started to lift his glass in a toast, Elliot was scribbling frantically on his napkin with a pen.

"I raise *my* glass to Arnie and Bunny," Billy began. *"À vous, mes amis. Toujours l'amour."*

"Oh, Jesus," Barbie spat, rolling her eyes, "he's pretending to be French again."

"Who in the hell does that guy think he is?" Bobby wanted to know. "Speak English!" he shouted from the table.

"Sorry"—Billy blushed—"English it is." He took a deep breath and continued. "I, uh—I introduced Arnie to B-Bunny," he said quickly. "I've known Arnie for years, and B-Bunny . . . well, I've known her, too!"

Kate frowned at the chorus of salacious hoots and catcalls that caused Bunny to blush and Arnie to hang his head. Kate wondered about Billy's stammer. If he was putting it on, he was an even bigger asshole than she suspected. Fortunately he made the rest of his toast French free and brief.

"Congratulations to Arnie and Bunny!" he said. "They're good p-p-people. And marriage is a beautiful thing . . . to witness from afar. To Arnie and Bunny." He lifted his glass to signal that he was finished.

The crowd cheered and clinked their glasses with their silver-ware, and Arnie and Bunny obligingly kissed. When the cheering and jeering stopped, Kate turned to the others at the table and asked, "Did you two really date him?" Bev and Barbie nodded ruefully and shrugged.

At that moment the band started playing again, and people drifted back onto the dance floor. This should have been all right, since it would make slipping out unnoticed easier. Except Elliot stood up and excused himself from the table. "Where do you think you're going?" Kate asked. "We ought to get Bina out of here."

"I'll be right back," he said, and hurried into the crowd.

Kate kept hold of Bina and watched as couples did the twist and slow-danced to "Every Breath You Take." Finally, Elliot returned. He had a self-congratulatory look on his face.

"Where have you been?" Kate demanded. "We must take Bina home. She's all ready to start doing the hora all by herself."

"I was just doing a little probability research," Elliot replied.

"Great!" Kate snapped. "Why? Going to set up a whole new group of word problems for third-grade math in a wedding hall? If X serves four cocktail wieners to three guests and Y serves two stuffed—"

"Look, statistics are involved," Elliot said, "but no word problems will be solved. Merely a romantic one. You'll see." He turned to Brice. "Get her left arm," he said, pointing at Bina. "And I'll get her right."

Without a word, the two men surrounded Bina and coolly and unobtrusively led her away from the table, across the room, and out the exit. Kate followed, forbidding herself to turn and take one last look at Billy Nolan.

Chapter Fifteen

Some days later, as Kate finished her notes and was ready to lock them in her file cabinet for the night, the phone rang. She hadn't seen Michael for over a week. He'd been off on a seminar, and she'd been held hostage by Bina since the wedding. Tonight he was coming to dinner, and she expected his call. She lifted the receiver.

"Kate?" It wasn't Michael's voice, nor was it a voice she recognized. Male, youngish sounding, but deep.

"Yes, this is Kate Jameson."

"Hi. This is B-B-Billy Nolan." The stammer gave him away, even if he hadn't identified himself by name. Kate felt the color rush to her face.

"How did you get my number?" she asked. "My number here at work." What nerve! As if it wouldn't have been inappropriate enough to have him call her at home. Kate always worried about protocol. After all, this was her first professional job. Now this . . . this . . . jerk had her work number. She'd kill whichever one of the Bitches had given it out.

"Look, I hope this isn't a b-bad time."

She'd had a rough afternoon. Stevie Grossman, a fifth grader, was showing disturbing signs of schizophrenia, very unusual in a child his age. Kate knew he needed to see a psychiatrist—she had a friend at the Ackerman Institute for the Family who might help—but both his parents and Dr. McKay were trying to minimize the boy's troubles in the face of her professional advice. And now this bozo—albeit gorgeous bozo—was calling her at work? "I'm afraid it is," Kate said coldly. How many women had he scored with? Did he expect to add her name to the list?

"Would there be a better time?" Billy asked.

"I'm afraid there wouldn't be," Kate said. She should have hung up the phone at that moment, but something, she wasn't sure what, tugged at her. It was hard for her to be really rude. "I'm sorry. I have to go." She placed the phone back in its cradle as a twinge of guilt doused the tiny glow of pleasure she felt from the call. She was seeing Michael in just a little while. Who did Billy Nolan think he was?

She put the thought from her mind, gathered her things, and locked her office. As she passed Elliot's third-grade classroom, she caught a glimpse of him teetering on a chair, sticking transparencies on the windows. "Math Is Fun!" they said. He was hanging them so they showed their faces to the outside world and read backward to the class.

"Well, that ought to convince them," she teased. She needed her dose of Elliot to cheer her up. "Good for the dyslexics, at least."

Elliot whirled, startled by her voice, and nearly fell off the chair. He grabbed at the window to steady himself, then looked down at her and smiled. "Nice to see you, too." He sighed. "Andrew Country Day. Home of learning for learning's sake."

Kate walked in and took a seat in Elliot's chair, putting her feet up on his desk. Maybe he could suggest something she could do to convince Stevie's parents to get him professional help. He could be pretty resourceful. But he beat her to the punch.

"How's Bina doing?" he asked, swiping at her feet to get them off the desk.

"As well as can be expected," Kate said, shrugging. After the wedding, Bina had agreed to go home to face the music and begin her "exploration of singleness." Somehow that had translated into coming over to Kate's constantly for sympathy and getting gossip about Jack from Max.

"Poor Bina," Elliot said. "I really like her."

"So do I," she agreed. "She's like a sister to me."

"I liked Bev and Barbie, too," Elliot said. "What a hoot."

"Well, I wasn't as close to them," she reminded Elliot. "But I'm glad you and Brice had fun."

"Fun? Brice hasn't talked about anything else since. He's dying for the next installment."

"There is no next installment. It's not a soap opera. It's life, sort of. Bina is back managing her father's office. Maybe she'll meet some guy who needs a spinal adjustment."

"I'd like to see Bina," Elliot said.

"Look, Brooklyn isn't a spectator sport." Kate stood up. She didn't want to hold her friends up to derision and criticism, even if she did so herself. "Bina is very low. She had a lot invested in Jack." She sighed. "I've gotta go. I have a date with Michael tonight."

"Sit down another minute," Elliot requested, for once without saying a word against Michael. Kate was surprised enough to do it, but only at the edge of the seat, ready for a quick exit if he got started. "Look," he said, "I think I have a way to help Bina."

"Oh, Elliot. Please," Kate began, rolling her eyes. "Unless you have a written proposal from Jack in your pocket, there's nothing you can—"

"Just listen," he told her. "This might be as good as a written proposal."

Kate looked at him skeptically, as if he were about to reveal the secrets of the mummy's tomb.

"Remember how at the wedding Barbie said she got dumped by that gorgeous guy?"

Kate couldn't believe it. Was she going to be hounded by mentions and visions of Billy Nolan? She would never tell Elliot about the call or he would become hysterical. "What gorgeous guy?" she asked.

"The best man. Billy," Elliot reminded her. "Remember? The one who looked like a much more handsome Matt Damon?"

"Oh, yeah. The toaster. What about him?" Kate said, trying to look bored.

"Well, Barbie dated him."

"Barbie dated everyone," Kate said. "She'd just about run out of Brooklyn guys and had to start on Staten Island."

"Try to hold your focus," Elliot said. "As you may or may not remember, Bunny also dated and got dumped by Billy. Right before she married Arnie."

"Bunny had really bad luck with men," Kate said. "So?"

"Well, she had good luck, as you call it, after Billy . . . if you consider Arnie good luck."

Kate shrugged and tried to remember if she had picked up her white blouse from the dry cleaners or not. She wanted to wear it tonight. "And your point would be?"

"Well, Bev had dated Billy, been dumped, then got married, too. When I noted this odd probability, my brilliant mathematical mind went into high gear and I started to do some digging."

"And?" said Kate.

"And so," Elliot continued, sounding a little annoyed, "I went on a little fact-finding mission and found out six women at the wedding dated Billy and got dumped by him."

"So he's a slut," Kate said. She thought of the way Billy had charmed her on the terrace, his phone call, his incredible good looks. She was surprised there weren't thirty women there he'd disappointed. "Wow, Elliot. You're a regular Sherlock Holmes."

"You're not getting the picture here. You remember how I had to help you with statistics?"

"How could I forget? You remind me at every possible opportunity."

"Well, I'm a genius," Elliot told her. "Geniuses are always disrespected." He spoke primly, holding his nose a little higher. "Stay with me here, Kate. You'll see. All six of these women, after getting dumped by Billy, *married* the very next man they dated."

Kate shrugged. "Anyone would look good after that guy. He's just a player." Even to her, her voice sounded too bitter. A little flirt and a phone call. What was Billy Nolan to her?

"Kate. Kate! Don't you get it!" Elliot almost shouted, clearly exasperated. "It's not about him. It's about what happens *after* him. Do you know the statistical likelihood of this phenomenon?"

"Obviously not," replied Kate, who was getting pretty irritated herself by now. She stood up. She wouldn't have time to stop at the cleaners, and if her white shirt wasn't at home, she'd wear the green silk one. She picked up her purse. "Gotta go."

"Kate, I've worked it out, and the probability ranges from one in six million and three hundred and forty-seven to one in eighty-two million six hundred and forty-three. And that's *with* standard deviation."

"Talk about deviation," Kate said, "when do you have time to shampoo your hair?" She got to the door. Then she stopped for a moment. "Anyway, how does that help Bina?"

"Don't you get it?" Elliot yelled. "We *use* it in Bina's favor."

She stopped. Then she turned around. "Use it?" she asked.

At that moment, Dr. McKay showed up in front of Kate like a migraine on a sunny day. "Is there an altercation going on in here?" he asked.

"Certainly not," Elliot assured him. "We were testing the acoustics of this room. For some reason, the students in that corner near the door don't hear all of the class discussion. Kate thought it might be the corkboards."

Kate nodded. "Proust and all," she said.

Dr. McKay blinked, and Kate almost laughed out loud. He was so easily impressed by literary allusion. "Oh, I see. Well, that will suffice for now," he said, and was gone as quickly as he had appeared.

"He thinks we're having a lover's quarrel," Elliot said.

"That, or he's going off to bake some madeleines." Dr. McKay brought his own baked goods to every cake sale. "So just tell me what the point of all that was before I run for the subway."

"The point," Elliot told her, "is that Bina is supposed to explore her singleness, right? So we get her to date Billy, get her dumped, get her to see Jack, and wham, bam, thank you, ma'am, he'll ask her to marry him."

Kate could hardly believe what she'd just heard. "And I thought Stevie Grossman needed therapy," she said. "Elliot, you're certifiable. Next you'll tell me to adopt Bev's black magic and that Bina needs to be a Pisces so she can swim to happiness."

"Kate," Elliot said, his voice deepening as he got more serious, "we're talking statistics and probability here, not astrology. I'm not Bev. I calculated it out, and it's as close to a sure thing as possible."

"Oh, come on, Elliot!" Kate exclaimed. "You've lost it. I don't even begin to have the time to tell you how flawed your plan is."

"Try," Elliot challenged her.

"Number one: Bina doesn't want to date anybody else. Number two: Billy is an asshole who has slept with every truly attractive girl in Brooklyn—and possibly lower Manhattan. Number three: Bina, as much as I love her, couldn't pick up a guy if he had a handle on him, much less get a date with Billy Nolan. Will that suffice for now?"

"Okay," Elliot conceded. "But give me one more good reason it won't work."

"You're insane." She began to walk down the hall.

"You won't be saying that when I am Bina's matron of honor," Elliot called after her.

Jesus, Kate thought, McKay would be on them in a private school minute. She turned around to face Elliot. "No, Elliot. Just no."

Elliot examined her face. "Who tutored you so you passed your GMATs?"

"You did." Kate sighed. She knew the litany.

"And who graduated top of his class from Columbia?" he asked her.

"You did, but—"

"And who was invited to accept an adjunct professorship and a grant at Princeton?"

"You, but that doesn't—"

"But that doesn't mean that you can still doubt my abilities?" He shook his head. "In the land of the blind . . . Kate, this is an absolutely fascinating finding, and a tremendous opportunity to exploit, and you are calling it hooey?"

"I don't think I ever actually used the word *hooey,*" she said, and lowered her voice. "That sounds more like something McKay might say."

"But you know I'm *never* wrong when it comes to numbers," Elliot told her, grinning.

Kate looked down at her watch and then again turned to leave. Let him screech down the hallway if he wanted to. "Elliot," she said as she began to walk, "I don't believe in magic, I don't believe in superstition, or horoscopes, or coincidences that predict the future. Now I've got to go. I've got a date with Michael, and I haven't shaved my legs in a week."

"Ah, yes, Michael," Elliot said, walking past the lockers. "I thought—"

"I would rather not go into your thoughts right now." She got to the entrance. "Bye, bye."

Elliot put his hand on her shoulder. "Look, Kate, this doesn't involve just you, it involves Bina and *her* future. At least let me present the facts to her. It ought to be her decision."

Kate looked back at her friend, shook her head, and shrugged. Then she hurried down the steps on the way to her date.

Chapter Sixteen

Kate strolled along Eighth Avenue with the pleasant anticipation of the weekend before her. She decided that after the Bina siege, Bunny's wedding, and Elliot's insane reaction, she wouldn't allow herself to think about any of it. She wouldn't even think about her little clients at school. She had done a bit of what she thought of as indulgent grocery shopping: stopping at some of the superb food specialty stores in her neighborhood and buying prepared curry chicken salad, a bunch of perfect red grapes, and poached sole with lemon-zest garnish.

Friday afternoon was a special pleasure to Kate. She had finally reached the point in her adulthood where she had hired a cleaning lady. Teresa came for only half a day each Friday, but the $50 was well worth it, because at the end of a hard week, Kate could look forward to walking into a vacuumed, dust-free living room and a bed freshly made up with clean sheets. When she remembered her teenage years, she thought of the reluctance she had felt in going home to the four dirty rooms that she shared with her father and the misery of shopping for the cheapest basics—sardines, canned soup, and cold cereal. She would open the door fearfully, never knowing what she would find inside. All this had given her an enormous appreciation now for the security of knowing what to expect when she opened her own door, as well as a pride in the order and cleanliness of her apartment.

She passed by a Korean market, and her eyes were drawn to roses of an unusual apricot color. It would be nice if Michael brought her flowers, but if he didn't, it would be lovely to have some of these roses in a bowl in the living room and a vase beside her bed. She stopped, and when the old merchant offered her "special discount two bunches for ten dollars only for pretty lady," she smiled at him, took out a $10 bill, and walked away with the paper-wrapped roses tucked under her arm.

Kate turned the corner to her block. Many of the windows were open, and as she walked by the brownstones, she could see people in basement kitchens preparing dinner, others in living rooms with books or a glass of wine, and even a few children playing on the stoops and tiny yards in front of the buildings. When she got to her stoop, she strode up the steps quickly, had her key ready, entered the vestibule, and managed to pick up her mail and get up the flight of stairs to her apartment without dropping the delicacies, her purse, the flowers, or the mail.

She entered her small but orderly space and sighed, kicking off her shoes and leaving them at the door. It was past five, and she needed enough time to put away the food, arrange the flowers, take a shower, and change her clothes. She would have to rush. She was just putting the last rose into the vase for her bedroom when the phone rang. She picked it up while she carried the flowers to her bedside table. She checked her caller ID. She simply didn't have time for another call from Bina. Cruel as it might be, they were starting to annoy her.

"Look, I don't want you to be angry," Elliot's voice said.

"I'm not angry, I'm just in a rush."

"Of course you're not angry yet," Elliot said. "I don't want you to be angry after I tell you what I'm going to tell you."

"Is it that I look fat in the skirt?" she asked. "It's too late for me to take it back now. You told me it looked good." She put the flowers down and stood back to get the full effect. The room looked charming.

"I know you're just joking, but I'm serious. Don't be mad. I'm inviting Bina to brunch on Sunday."

Kate, in the act of slipping out of the new skirt while she

cradled the receiver between her shoulder and her neck, nearly dropped the phone. "Why would you do that?" she asked. "Why in the world would you do that?"

"I knew you would be mad," Elliot said. "But I've done a little more sleuthing, and—"

"Who are you? Nancy fucking Drew?" Kate asked. "No one does sleuthing, no one drives a roadster, and no one is inviting my Brooklyn girlfriend to their Chelsea apartment for brunch except me—and I'm not even sure *I'll* do it." She hung up her skirt and was delighted to see that she *had* brought home her white sleeveless blouse from the cleaners. She would wear it with the top two buttons undone and the gray pants from Banana Republic. But first she'd get rid of Elliot and stop this stupid plan.

"Kate, it isn't just Barbie and Bunny. There are six women who have dated Billy, and right afterward—right after he dumped them—they got married to other men."

"Are you still on that?"

"The statistical probability is almost unheard of. You owe it to Bina to—"

"Elliot, I don't know why you've gotten this bee in your bonnet, but kill it right now." Kate, truly annoyed, put her clothes on the bed and held the phone so that she was speaking right into the mouthpiece. "You only want to have Bina over so that you and Brice can watch her up close and personal and then make fun of her later."

"That is so unfair! This is just a way to help Bina."

Kate looked at the alarm clock on her dresser. "Michael is coming over. I have to go. Bye." As she replaced the phone on the receiver, she could hear Elliot whining.

"But Kate—"

She rushed into the bathroom, showered but kept her hair dry, got dressed, and primped for a few minutes in front of the steamy bathroom mirror. Then she picked up her hairbrush, went into the kitchen, and began brushing out her hair while she poured herself some peach iced tea.

Since their reconciliation after the night of Jack's failed proposal, she and Michael had begun to slip into that comfortable stage where both of them assumed that they would spend most of the weekend together and called each other just about every day. Although it was a hot day, Kate kept the window open and she sat at it, sipping the tea and waiting for Michael's arrival. She had only to toss a few greens and take out the rest of the food and they would be ready for a pleasant dinner. She had a bottle of Frascati chilling in the refrigerator, and the table was set. Michael, as usual, was just a little bit late, but Kate didn't mind. It gave her more time to enjoy the peace of her apartment and the pleasant view of brownstones.

Last winter, after she had broken up with Steven, when the trees were bare, the view had seemed gray and empty, just like her life. Elliot had nursed her through, and time . . . well, time had passed and done what it does.

She smiled for a moment, grateful that she had put those days behind her. It was funny; someone should write a book about the new, twenty-first-century stages of commitment and separation in relationships. Perhaps she would suggest it to Michael. Each action represented either a step in growth or a diminishment in love and trust. First a couple only had each other's home numbers. Then they exchanged phone numbers at work. Then there was the important moment when you programmed both numbers into your home and cell phones, followed by the ceremonial leaving of the toothbrush, followed quickly by the leaving of personal hygiene products—deodorant, moisturizer, a razor. Then, most symbolically, came the critical exchange of keys. Eventually, of course, each of these actions was reversed. Kate didn't know when Steven had wiped her name from his cell phone, but she remembered clearly the day she had deleted his.

While she and Michael had not yet exchanged keys, Kate felt that they were moving nicely from the dating phase into what she would call "a relationship" if the word didn't make her wince. And that was a relief. When she was in her twenties, it had seemed that dates had either been more casual or guys had played games, and when they parted after a time together, Kate never knew if they would call her the next day or the next week or even ever. Maybe it was because she was in school and there was a big pool of people to date, so it was easy to meet someone to replace the someone of the previous month. Now, however, since Steven, she felt some kind of shift. Dates always seemed to be an assessment on her part of the chance for a long-term hookup, and if she didn't feel a strong level of interest from a man, she found herself losing interest in him.

As she looked down at the street, thinking of him, Michael appeared around the corner. From her vantage point, she could observe him and remain unobserved. There was something about his walk that, seen from above, looked a bit prissy, but Kate put the unworthy thought out of her mind.

"Yo, Michael!"

Down below, he stopped, looked up to the trees for a moment, and then caught her waving from the window. "Hey," he yelled up. "Sorry I'm late."

She hadn't meant to make him feel guilty. She just shrugged, smiled, and gestured for him to come up. She left the windowsill and buzzed to unlock the downstairs door, then opened the door to her apartment and waited for him.

She heard his steps on the stairs before she saw him, ignored his second apology, and kissed him instead. He held her for a moment, and it felt so good that she was disappointed when he let go. But dinner was pleasant, and Michael was appropriately grateful. She talked about the progress she was making with Brian Conroy, the motherless little boy, and about some trouble they were having with two brothers—twins—who kept trading places and confusing not only the staff, but their classmates. Michael told her about his week. All of his news lately had been about the mutual courtship between him and the Sagerman Foundation. He was still hoping for an offer to chair a department at the University of Texas. Kate wasn't sure whether or not she was included in his Austin plans. He didn't speak about it, and she didn't ask. Did he plan for her to go? Or would he bring it up at some point in time? Maybe he only wanted to be offered it and then wouldn't accept. Austin . . . Kate tried to put it out of her mind. Texas was not for her.

When dinner was over, Michael helped her clear the table and produced a white paper box containing a poppy seed pound cake for dessert. "I have some vanilla ice cream that might go well on top of that," she told him.

"I can think of something that might go well on top of something else before dessert," Michael said. He took her hand. "Did I tell you how pretty you look?"

She shook her head. "Are you telling me now?" she asked, hoping for more.

Instead he looked down at her. "You have a problem with the buttons on your blouse." From his height he could see her modest cleavage. She smiled up at him. "You've made a mistake." He put his hands on the next button. For a moment, she thought he was about to button her up, but then she realized what he was doing. "You silly girl. You've neglected to leave them all open," Michael said. And in a moment, he had undone them.

In a few moments more they were on her bed, and she was—in the Victorian sense—being completely undone. After Steven, with whom she'd shared such an intensely passionate relationship, Kate had been afraid that anyone she slept with would be a second best; but what Michael lacked in humor, he more than made up for in bed.

Kate was so engrossed in her own thoughts that when she felt his hands move deftly over her body, she had to rouse herself to put her arms around him and do more than simply lie back and enjoy it. Together they kissed, fondled, and held each other. When Michael pressed his hands against her shoulders and rolled onto her, she was more than ready.

Chapter Seventeen

When Kate awoke on Saturday morning, she was smiling. She stretched out, arching her back in the delicious relaxation of postsexual languor. Her smile widened as she thought of the weekend of leisure ahead of her. She wanted to snuggle up and whisper a thank-you to Michael, perhaps even entice him into an encore, but when she turned on her side, she realized he was gone. It took her a moment to remember that he always ran for an hour between six and seven. "No matter what," he'd told her when they'd first met, and she'd admired his self-discipline. Now she was just disappointed. He'd come back wide awake, he'd shower, and he'd want coffee, which she'd have to serve him.

Kate sighed, lifted herself up, saw that it was a quarter to seven, and lay down again. She considered her options: She could get up, shower, and begin to make breakfast, or she could go back to sleep and wait for his return. Despite wanting some snuggle time, she knew if she waited for Michael, he would go straight to the shower, thoughtfully leaving her alone to sleep. He'd probably read the *Times* quietly until she got out of bed. She decided to replay last night's sex in her mind and was just closing her eyes when the phone rang. No one would be calling her this early on a weekend morning except . . .

"Hello, Elliot," she said. "Do you know that it is ten minutes to seven on a Saturday morning?"

"Am I interrupting something?" Elliot asked coyly. "I can call right back. Or does he take longer than a few minutes?"

"Elliot! You are interrupting my sleep," Kate said. "What's the emergency?"

"Look, Kate, I don't want you to be mad."

"Mad? What have you done?"

"Look, I know how you are. And I didn't mean for it to be more than Bina, but she told Barbie, and you know how *she* is . . ."

Yes, Kate reflected, she did know how Barbie was, but she didn't need to hear about it, and certainly not from Elliot before seven A.M. on a weekend.

"I had to do it. The mathematics and the potential for happiness here were just too big to be ignored."

"Elliot, what are you going on about?"

"About the brunch. I had already told Bina about the findings, and she wanted to hear more, and Brice suggested a brunch, but then I was going to cancel after I spoke to you. Now, though, she's invited Bev and Barbie. And Bunny is back from her honeymoon, so Bev told her, and now—"

"Oh, God," Kate cried. "Don't tell me you bothered Bina with this geeky idea of yours. Stop it, Elliot! And what does it have to do with the others? Or a brunch?" She had hoped for a Bina-free weekend, a time to relax with Michael and refuel. She tried to focus on what Elliot was saying, but she wanted to be unfocused, soft and fuzzy and feminine and pampered. "Elliot, don't get Bina crazy with your nonsense."

"You don't understand the clarity and magnitude of the numbers, Kate," Elliot told her. "Since Bina talked to the girls, they found two other cases where a woman married *immediately* after Billy broke up with them."

"So what?" Kate heard the door to her apartment squeak open. Maybe, if she got up right now, she could negotiate a little more time in bed. She liked Michael sweaty, but he was too fastidious to comply with her wishes. Still, there was a chance. . . .

"I have to go," she told Elliot.

"I understand," Elliot said meaningfully. "Have fun. Just close your eyes and think of England. And be here tomorrow at eleven-thirty."

"I hate you," Kate said.

"But doesn't it feel good, in a strange and exciting way?" Elliot asked. "Eleven-thirty tomorrow. Be there or be . . . talked about."

On Sunday morning, Kate knocked on Elliot's door at a quarter to eleven. She wanted to arrive before the Bitches, lay some ground rules, vent a little anger, and limit the way Elliot and Brice would toy with them.

"Kate!" Brice shouted in false surprise when he opened the door. "You're early! Whatever could be the reason?"

"I thought perhaps I could help you get ready by putting some ground glass in the chicken salad," she said with an insincere smile.

"My, my. Little Miss Hospitality," Brice said.

She stepped past him and walked into the apartment. She had a bone—well, more like a whole skeleton—to pick with Elliot.

Her quarry was standing at the sofa, barely visible, behind an armload of charts and graphs. When he saw her he dropped everything onto the coffee table. Brice, never dumb, disappeared into the kitchen, from which delicious smells were emanating. "What's all this?" she asked Elliot, who had begun to sort out the charts, placing them on an easel.

"This is the evidence," Elliot replied. "I thought putting the facts right in front of Bina's eyes would convince her."

"Elliot, I absolutely forbid this. You are not allowed to interfere in people's lives in this way."

Elliot gave an exaggerated blink, lowered his chin, and looked over his glasses at her. "This from a woman who is attempting to reshape two dozen kids at Andrew Country Day."

Kate bristled. "My work is very different. I'm professionally trained to assess and assist children, some of them in crisis, while they are developing their personalities. I am trying to prevent future problems. You're dealing with adults, you have no training, and you're going to *create* future problems."

"I beg your pardon, Dr. Jameson," Elliot said, "but you forget that I am a professional in my field, and this data is astonishing." He touched the charts for emphasis. "And I'm dealing with adults who have free will. Bina doesn't have to listen to me. She is not a captive audience."

Kate did not like the implication; her kids were not captive, but maybe she was being a little unfair to Elliot. Maybe he was only trying to be helpful, even if it ended in heartbreak.

"Just take a look, Kate," Elliot coaxed.

Kate picked up the first chart. She had no idea if what she saw there was true or not, but if it was accurate, it was fascinating. She looked at the other carefully constructed models, then sighed. Elliot had put in a lot of work, and it was impressive, but she was not going to budge from her veto. Elliot was smart. He knew Bina and the others would be gaping and amazed by the brightly colored charts and graphs, just the way tourists in Times Square were stunned by the lights and ads. But tourists didn't change their lives based on a huge Pepsi ad.

"Kate, it really can't hurt. At the very least, it's a distraction for Bina, and that's what she needs right now. She can't keep herself in her father's office and wait for something to change."

Kate thought of the three or four long messages from Bina on her answering machine each night when she got home. "Okay," she said, "but I want you to play this down, not up. It may be Fun with Math for you, but it's Bina's life. Anyway, even if all of this crazy nonsense is true, a troublemaker like Billy Nolan would never be interested in dating someone as ordinary as Bina Horowitz. So don't get her hopes up."

Elliot nodded vehemently. "No hopes up," he said.

Brice came back out of the kitchen carrying two bottles of white wine. He put one down and popped the cork on the other. "Bottoms up," he said, pouring a glass and handing it to Kate. Just then the buzzer rang. "I'll get it," Brice sang as he strode over to the door and opened it. "Hello, ladies!" he greeted the group.

And there they were, in all their splendor, the Bitches of Bushwick. Barbie came first, wearing a bright pink halter top with a leather jacket over it. She was followed by a nervous but hopeful-looking Bina. Next came Bev and her belly, and then in walked Bunny, who had returned from her honeymoon and had the tan to prove it.

"Hi. You're Bunny the bride," Brice said. "I'm Brice, and that stud muffin over there is Elliot." The girls giggled, except for Bunny, who actually blushed. Without the "breaking in" that had happened at table nine, Kate could see that the adventure wasn't comfortable for her. She had grown up in a strict Italian Catholic home where, Kate was sure, homosexuality was synonymous with sin, perversion, and the molestation of little boys. Brice, sensing her hesitancy but never one for subtleties, threw his arm around Bunny's shoulders. "We didn't have a chance to talk at your wedding. But it was beautiful. Absolutely beautiful!"

He couldn't have said anything better. "Wait till you see the video!" Bunny exclaimed, suddenly ready to bond.

Kate winced. The ordeal of watching that video might be worse than going to the event itself, but Brice was all enthusiasm. "Oh, you *have* to show us. And what a dress!"

"Size six," Bunny said proudly. "Priscilla of Boston."

"I knew it!"

"She got lucky," Barbie told him. "It was a special order, but the bride was pregnant and didn't tell. By the time the dress arrived, well, you can imagine."

"I got it at cost," Bunny told Brice.

The attention seemed to relax her. Soon they were all standing around the buffet, filling their plates and—with the exception of Bev—drinking wine. Kate looked around at them covertly. Bev's belly looked as if it had doubled in size since the wedding. Kate tried to avoid staring at it in horror, although she couldn't escape a twinge of jealousy as she felt her own flat stomach.

Elliot, too, was caught by Bev's very apparent expansion. "Wow," he said to her. "Are you going to go into labor right here, or are you carrying twins?"

"I know, I'm huge and I've got months to go." Bev looked down at her belly and shrugged.

"Remember after graduation how you dieted all summer and were a size four by September?" Bunny asked. She was the group's weight historian and could tell any one of them what they had weighed at any event or moment since they'd met.

"I'm trying to cut back on eating so much," Bev explained to Elliot. "I think I've gained about forty pounds." Despite the confession, she piled her plate with Nova, cream cheese, a poppy *and* a sesame bagel, and, with a final guilty flourish, some herring in cream sauce. "Unless I give birth to a thirty-five-pound baby, I'm gonna be in big trouble," she said, and laughed.

"Do you want a girl or a boy?" Elliot asked her.

"Doesn't matter," Bev said, waddling to the sofa from the buffet, Bina and Bunny right behind her. "Johnny says he just wants it healthy."

"He'll get healthy when he sees your ass after the baby is born," Barbie said, snickering.

Kate never stopped being astonished by the way the women passed over cruel taunts without a ruffled hair. She watched as they sat down and checked out the apartment around them as if they'd just stepped into a den of unimaginable iniquity. It was a big adventure for four girls from Bushwick to finally see the inside of a homosexual couple's apartment—even Bina hadn't really had a chance to look around the last time she was there. Kate could only imagine what they thought they were going to find. And she wasn't going to point out that Bunny's uncle Tony and Barbie's youngest brother were most certainly gay but hadn't come out. Anyway, it must have been reassuring to see that there was nothing terrifying or exotic about Elliot's home—thanks to Brice, it was all done in stylish taste (though the Beanie Babies were a little camp). The situation made Kate smile. She knew how frightening good taste could be to someone from Bushwick.

They all sat on various perches like colorful birds with big mouths. Toucans, maybe, Kate thought. Despite their provincialism (and some morbid curiosity), it was really moving to see that all the girls had shown up for Bina. Kate loved them for that.

Barbie, of course, was the most brazen. She looked around as if she were assessing everything. "How much does a place like this cost in Manhattan?" she needed to know.

"It's a steal," Brice obliged willingly. "It's stabilized. We're still paying only eighteen a month."

"Eighteen dollars a month for rent?" Bina asked in utter amazement. "My grandmother's apartment on Ocean Parkway is rent-controlled, but she pays sixty-six bucks a month."

The better-informed Bunny was not as confused. "Jeez," she spat in disgust, "for eighteen hundred dollars a month, you'd get three bedrooms and a balcony in Brooklyn."

"Honey," Brice replied, "call me crazy, but I'd rather have a closet in Manhattan than a palazzo in Prospect Park."

"I thought you guys were all out of the closet," Barbie said, grinning and obviously pleased with herself.

"Sweetie, some of us were never in it," Brice said. There was silence for a moment.

Almost desperately, Kate spoke first. "Well, isn't this nice?" she chirped, turning to Elliot as if to say "I told you so." "Finally, all of my girlfriends together in one room."

Bina let out a rather nervous giggle in response, but Bev just agreed. "You have a lot of girlfriends, Kate. But then you're a Scorpio. Scorpio women always have lots of girlfriends."

"And lots of boyfriends," Elliot added sotto voce.

"So you have some plan to kill Jack the scumbag?" Barbie asked.

"Not exactly," Elliot told her. He put down his fork, stood up, and self-consciously stepped next to the easel. He looked first to Bina and then back to Kate. He placed one hand on the first chart, turned it over so they could all see it, and said, "As Bina knows, I made an incredible mathematical discovery while we were at Bunny's wedding."

"Like what?" asked Bev.

"Probability," Elliot said. "Some events can be predicted because of constancy and reliability of past data."

"Huh!" Bina said. Kate suppressed a giggle. Poor Elliot.

"This helps us take down Jack the scumbag?" Barbie asked.

"Hey, what good would that do anyone?" Elliot asked. "What if I told you that instead of revenge, I've found a surefire way to get Jack to propose to Bina?" he asked the room. "And marry her."

Bina dropped her coffee spoon, Bev choked on a mouthful of bagel, and Barbie and Bunny began to murmur together appreciatively. Only Kate let out a snort of derision. "Elliot!" she warned. Then she turned to Bina. "Remember, this is just a theory, a suggestion, Bina. It may not be correct. You don't have to pay any attention to it. Personally, I think it's a lot of hocus-pocus."

Elliot looked down at her from his full height. "Kate," he said, "I think we all know your views on magic. So it's a good thing this has nothing to do with it. This is mathematical theory put into practice."

"What's wrong with you, Katie?" Bev asked. "Such a spoilsport."

"What are you actually talking about?" Barbie asked.

Elliot nodded and pointed to the chart and said, "These statistics are . . . well, they are just incredible. But they are absolutely accurate. I've done a bit of research and worked out the probability, and you'll see that even with a differential for the—"

"Is he a college teacher or something?" Bina whispered to Kate.

Kate snorted. "He's an obsessive neurotic gone compulsive."

"I know. Isn't he wonderful?" said Brice, placing his hand over his heart.

Elliot was in his teaching mode and ignored them both. "Remember how Bev and Barbie both said that they had once dated that Billy guy who had just dumped Bunny?" He turned to her. "No offense."

"None taken," Bunny said. "When I dated him I was a size four—and weighed one hundred and sixteen pounds. My personal best."

"Well, we both got dumped by him, too," Bev added.

"Which was just fine with me," Barbie assured everyone. "The guy's a jerk."

"That's right," Elliot said, nodding to Barbie, "and right after that you met Bobby and got married."

"Well, it wasn't right after. It was at least three weeks." Barbie paused, then added, "And Bev got married to Johnny right after she got dumped."

"My Johnny and I had our moons in Venus. It was fated," Bev observed. No one paid any attention to her.

"So at the wedding, Elliot . . . well, began to snoop," Brice explained.

"I collected data," Elliot corrected Brice with dignity.

"Did I tell you about Gina Morelli and Nancy Limbacher, Elliot?" Bev asked, already eager to be part of the plan. "Billy dated and dumped them, too."

"I found that out on my own. Both of them married right after Billy Nolan. They were at Bunny's wedding."

"Sure. I worked with Gina, and Nancy is best friends with my cousin Marie," Bunny said.

"Marie Genetti?" Elliot asked. "Billy dated her, too."

"He dated Marie? You're kidding. She never told me!" Bunny exclaimed.

"So now we know that Billy Nolan has dated and dumped every woman from here to Albany. Who cares?" Kate spat out angrily. She thought of him charming her on the terrace. And to think that she'd been attracted to an idiot like him.

"Bina should, and as her friend, so should you," Elliot told her. "I did some digging, and I made some calls. Everyone this guy drops gets married."

"How did you find that out?" Barbie asked. Kate smiled. As the professional gossip of the group, she must be feeling a bit defensive.

"He pretended he was doing an article for *Jane* magazine," Brice told her proudly.

"You're a regular Columbo," Bev said admiringly.

Elliot laughed and acknowledged Bev's compliment with a slight bow. Then he turned back to his first chart. "Look at this," he said, pointing. "All five of these women dated William Nolan." On the chart were the names of each woman and the date, time, and place of their first encounter with Billy Nolan. "Now here," he said, flying to the next chart, "is a time line that follows the period of each relationship. Please note that where Billy drops out there is a segment of between three point two weeks and four point seven months before each woman marries." The room was silent. Even Kate was momentarily impressed.

"Was the bastard going out with Gina Morelli the same time he was dating me?" Bunny asked.

"From the data I've collected, he only goes out with one woman at a time. Anyway, that doesn't matter," Elliot said. "The point is"—he indicated the first chart—"soon after each woman got dumped by Mr. Nolan, each met or returned to another man—and sometimes, as in Bunny's case, she was introduced to that man by Billy himself. In all cases, that very next man was the one they married." He stopped and looked at Kate and the Bitches with a broad smile, as if his message were perfectly clear.

"Wow, congratulations, Elliot—it's quite an achievement," Bev said, more serious than was necessary.

"Right. Now you qualify as the biggest gossip in all five boroughs," Kate said coldly.

"Yeah. What's the big deal?" Bunny asked. "We all know that Billy Nolan is the biggest player that has ever lived."

"But you didn't know this," Elliot said, and flipped over a third chart. On it was a row of fourteen names with a column listing the time each had dated Billy and another column with wedding dates beside each name—except two. "It isn't *most* of the women Billy Nolan dates. It's *all* of the women Billy Nolan dates."

The women examined the list.

"Don't you get it?" Elliot asked. "Do you know the statistical likelihood of this phenomenon?" He flipped to his next chart. "I've worked it out with and without the standard deviation, the probability ranges from one in six million three hundred and forty-seven to one in eighty-two million six hundred and forty-three."

Kate wondered about the two out of the fourteen but figured she'd get her chance to debunk all this later.

"I don't get it," Bunny admitted. "I don't think even Billy Nolan could date and dump eighty-two million women. It's just not humanly possible. Are there even that many women in New York?"

"He doesn't have to date eighty-two million women," Barbie told Bunny dismissively, "he just has to date Bina. Right, Elliot?"

"Really? Really, Elliot?" Bina asked, her voice filled with more hope and animation than it had since the afternoon of the manicure.

"Oh, Jesus H. Christ," Kate said, no longer able to control her disgust. She stood up and started to pace around the room. "Elliot, you know I don't approve of this whole scheme. It's just ridiculous."

"Be quiet, Kate," Bev said, "I'm trying to understand this." She narrowed her eyes and looked at Elliot. "You're saying that anyone who dates Billy gets married right afterwards?" she asked.

"Everyone?" Bina asked.

Kate felt she couldn't let this go on. Instead of spending the morning in bed with Michael, then reading the *Times* together and having a nice meal before they parted, she was stuck with this bunch of maniacs and a berserk plan. She never thought any of them would buy it. "It's a bunch of superstitious crap," she told Bina and the rest of them.

"This isn't about superstition," Elliot insisted, sounding hurt. "These are the facts."

Bunny kept staring at the charts and now tried to sound smart. She used to do it in sixth grade to about the same effect. "Are you saying that the odds against Bina ever getting married are about eighty-two million to one unless she dates Billy Nolan?" she asked Elliot.

"Well," Elliot said, pretending to give the ridiculous question some thought, "that's not *exactly* what I'm saying. I can't compute the odds of Bina getting married. I don't have enough data. But the odds are eighty-two million to one in her *favor* if she does date Billy."

Kate saw Bina pale and felt her own face grow warm with anger and agitation. She was about to speak when Barbie stood up and brushed off her skirt.

"Then it's settled," Barbie said. "Bina has to go out with Dumping Billy. That's all there is to it. After all, what has she got to lose?"

Bina stood up, too, but she hesitated before she spoke. "Elliot, I appreciate all the time you must have put in this, but I'm not interested in dating anyone except Jack." Kate watched as tears filled her eyes. "I just want Jack back."

"This is a way to *get* Jack, Bina," Elliot said. "You date Billy, then get dumped, then see Jack and . . . voilà!"

Kate turned to Bina. "This is all ridiculous. I didn't know it was quite *this* insane, but I promised him I'd let him show you—"

"Why is it insane?" Bev asked.

"Well, it's a long shot that we could get Billy to go out with Bina in her current state," Barbie said, then narrowed her eyes speculatively. "But if we did some work on her . . ."

"Just look at the numbers, sweetheart. The numbers don't lie," Brice said to Bina. He took her hand in his, but he was watching Elliot with the look of a proud mother on his face.

Kate was sure that Bina, monogamous for so long, wouldn't consider this nonsense.

"They *all* got married?" Bina asked Elliot in disbelief.

"Yes. Well, to be totally accurate, one joined a convent, and one came out as a lesbian," Elliot confessed, "but both are hooked up, one to God and one to her girlfriend. So that makes fourteen for fourteen."

"Isn't he wonderful?" Brice asked no one in particular.

"He's absolutely nuts," Kate snapped. "Bina, don't even consider it."

"We'd have to time it so that Jack was back at the strategic moment—just after the breakup," Bev said.

"And to be safe, we have to make sure he drops her," Elliot cautioned. "I have no indication of what happens to his partner after she dumps him."

Bev and Barbie laughed. "No one dumps him," Barbie said.

"Of course, he's gorgeous," Bev said (it sounded like "Ov cous, he's gowjus"). "But that doesn't explain it. That only explains why he gets women."

"And probably why he dumps them," Elliot said.

"No," Bunny told him. "To be fair, he is always nice, and he seems . . . well, I don't know." She thought for a minute. "Like really disappointed when things don't work out."

Elliot took a deep breath. "I don't really care about his psychology," he told them. "The key question is why women marry right after he leaves them."

Kate wondered, too.

But Bina wasn't listening; she was staring at the charts before her. Kate knew how desperate she was. Elliot, seeing that he had Bina hooked, asked, "Do you want a detailed cross section?"

Kate could see Bina's love for Jack and the longing for him written all over her face. "I don't need one. I'll do it!" Bina exclaimed.

"Bina!" Kate cried, shocked.

"Then it's all settled," Bunny said, and stood up. "I gotta go back to Arnie."

"Well, we're not exactly finished," Barbie said in the tone that had driven fear into many preteen girls in their junior high days. "He doesn't go out with just anyone. He looks for a certain . . . style." She preened for a moment. "Do you think Billy would go out with *Bina?*"

"Barbie!" Kate turned from Bina to Barbie, shocked yet again. Despite the usual cruelty of the girls to one another, this went too far.

"The boy is certainly hot," Brice said to himself, pulling out the Polaroid from the wedding. He put it on the table.

"Very hot," Bev said, also looking at the photo while pretending to fan herself.

"Good point," Bunny agreed. "Maybe Bina would be out of her league."

Before Kate could jump to Bina's defense, her friend took control. "I'm still in the room!" Bina suddenly exploded. "Why are you talking about me like I'm not here?"

"We're sorry, Bina," Kate said, apologizing for the group. She could feel her friend's mortification at having been reduced to a statistic. And for what? All she really wanted was to be with Jack.

"We didn't mean to hurt your feelings, honey," Bev said, and put her arms around her friend as best she could manage.

"Look, no one said you couldn't become Billy's type," Barbie said by way of an apology.

"Right. We only wanted to help, not to hurt," Elliot added.

"And to make it up to you . . ." Brice began to mime a drumroll. "A makeover!"

Once the magic word had been spoken, Kate knew there was no going back.

Chapter Eighteen

Kate sat in her office and tried to put the problems of Bina, Jack, Billy, and what for a moment she was thinking of as "the rest of that nonsense" out of her mind. Bina's makeover and the idiocy of getting Billy to date her was not as important as the problem facing her at the moment. Jennifer Whalen, a pretty and neatly dressed nine-year-old, was sitting in front of her doing what she seemed to do best.

"So my father opens the door to the limousine and Britney Spears steps out. And she came into our building and right up to our apartment. She even had dinner with us. We had meat loaf. And if you don't believe me, she gave me this bracelet." Jennifer pulled the elastic of the bead bracelet she had around her wrist. "See? I have proof."

Kate withheld a sigh. She knew there was no point in discussing this particular lie or any of the other whoppers that Jennifer had told not only her classmates, but also her teachers. The question was why Jennifer needed to lie. Did she crave attention? She was a middle child, with an older sister at Andrew Country Day and a year-old brother at home. Had the baby usurped her position in the family constellation?

Or was it feelings of inferiority? Kate knew that both Jennifer and her sister were receiving financial aid because their family, though well-off by Kate's childhood standards, were only middle-class and could not afford full tuition for both girls. Maybe Jennifer felt inferior to her friends simply because their homes were bigger, their school vacations were often spent in Aspen, the Hamptons, or even Europe, and Jennifer couldn't compete.

The worst-case scenario, of course, was that Jennifer might be showing early signs of a delusional problem. However, as Kate looked at her, she felt that she was studying a healthy, outgoing little girl who doubtless knew the difference between fantasy and reality.

Kate didn't want Jennifer's lies to continue, but neither did she want to argue with her. She had listened quietly without showing much reaction. She could, of course, recommend a therapist for the child, but she and Jennifer had a good rapport. This business was always tricky, but Kate thought of a quote from A. S. Neil: "Sometimes you simply have to trust your instinct with children. Analysis with them is an art, not a science." She decided to take a chance.

"Want to know a secret?" she asked. Jennifer nodded. "I'm going to get married. And I'm going to have a really big wedding. It's going to be in a castle, and Justin Timberlake is coming." Jennifer's eyes opened wide. "He's going to bring *NSYNC, but my sister is really angry because *she* invited the Backstreet Boys, and you can just imagine what would happen if they came, too."

Jennifer's eyes were popping, and she nodded. "I bet they hate each other," she said.

"They do. And they all hate my husband-to-be. Do you know who I'm marrying?"

Jennifer shook her head back and forth, her mouth opened slightly.

"Dr. McKay," Kate said.

Jennifer's face froze. Then Kate watched as doubt, then disbelief, then relief, and even, perhaps, understanding bloomed on it like one of those flowers opening in time-lapse photography. "No way!" Jennifer said.

"Way," Kate insisted, and nodded. "Know what else? We're both going to ride white horses down the aisle of the church."

"No way!" Jennifer repeated more vehemently. Then she started to giggle. "Dr. McKay on a horse!"

Kate laughed, too. Then she paused. "I really like you, Jennifer. You know why?" Jennifer shook her head. "Because you are smart and cute and funny. And you have a great imagination. You have a gift for fiction."

Jennifer frowned. "What does that mean?"

"It means that I think you could write really good stories. Or maybe books. Or maybe movies."

"I could write down a movie?"

"Sure." Kate nodded. "Movies all start from someone writing down a story." She didn't want to start another round of lying. "Not every story is good enough to be a movie, but once you write one down you never know what could happen." She paused, letting the compliments and the idea sink in. "Of course, it isn't easy. Do you think you would like to have some special time with Mrs. Reese?" Joyce Reese was the creative writing teacher for the sixth grade and a friend of Kate's.

"I'm only in fourth," Jennifer said, but that, of course, added to her enthusiasm.

"That's true," Kate agreed, "but I would say that you could probably write sixth-grade stories. Maybe even eighth-grade stories. If one was in the school magazine, everyone would read it."

Jennifer stared at her. The two of them sat like that for a few moments in silence. Kate could see the child's mind working behind her gray eyes. "Britney Spears didn't come to my house," Jennifer said.

"But it was a good story," Kate told her, keeping her tone neutral. "If you tell it like a story or write it down like one, people would want to hear the next part. They'll think you're special because you can make up really good stories."

"But then they get mad," Jennifer said. "They get mad when it isn't true."

"Did you feel angry at me when I told you about my wedding?" Jennifer sat for a moment, looking down at her nails. "First I liked it. I thought it was a secret. But then when I knew you were . . . lying . . . I got a little mad," she admitted.

Kate nodded. "That happens when you fool people. They get mad."

Out in the hall, the bell rang. In a moment, they could hear the sound of doors being thrown open and the noise of classes getting out.

"Why don't you come in and visit with me next week? And in the meantime I'll talk to Mrs. Reese."

Jennifer nodded.

"But now, I'm sorry, but you'll have to go or you'll be late for the bus."

Reluctantly Jennifer stood up. "You told a lie," she said.

"Don't tell anyone," Kate whispered. "And especially don't tell Dr. McKay."

Jennifer laughed. "*Nobody* would want to marry him," she said, and marched out of Kate's office.

Kate had just gotten home, thrown her purse onto the sofa, and kicked off her shoes. She hadn't even had a chance to sit down before there was a knock at the door. God, she wasn't in the mood for a visitor! She turned around and opened it. Max stood there, still dressed in his suit and tie, clearly just back from work, though he was not usually home until after dark. He was leaning against her doorway, one arm raised, his head resting on his inner elbow. He must have been away during the last weekend because he had a bit of a tan. It made his blue eyes bluer. "Hi," she said.

"Hi," he returned. "Is Bina here?" he asked, his voice low.

Kate felt a stab of irritation. Since Jack had flown the coop, she'd felt like Bina Central. "No," she snapped. "You can call her at home."

"No, that's a good thing," Max told her in a normal tone. "See, I want to show you something, and . . . well, I don't know if she should see it or not." Kate rolled her eyes, but she let Max take her hand to lead her up the stairs.

His apartment door was open. Inside was the usual requisite bachelor setup: black leather couch, workout equipment, an expensive stereo, and the pile of newspapers that seemed a requirement for all male apartments. Max also, of course, had the latest titanium laptop, and it was that toward which he led her.

"I want you to look at this and tell me what to do," he said. He loosened his tie before he hit a few keys. For one crazy moment, Kate thought he might be asking her opinion about some stock meltdown, but she had never had a share of anything in her life except a dorm room. But instead of charts, graphs, or analysis, the screen filled with a photo. It was Jack, bare-chested, standing on a balcony with a view of a beautiful harbor behind him and an equally beautiful woman next to him.

"Oh, my God," Kate said. "Where did you get this?"

"He e-mailed it to me today," Max said. "Do you think I should show it to Bina?"

"Do you think I should set fire to your hair gel?" Kate asked. The thought of Bina seeing this grinning ass literally made her sick to her stomach. When she'd found out Steven had been cheating on her, she'd been so distraught that she couldn't get out of bed for three days. Bina would just collapse.

Unconsciously, Max smoothed down his wavy hair. "I didn't think so, either," he said. "But, you know, I feel responsible for this. I introduced them and all. . . ."

Kate felt her irritation melt away. She had always thought of him as a stereotype, a kind of Wall Street/jock/yuppie clone. When he'd had girlfriends for any length of time, he hadn't seemed particularly committed or passionate. Now, however, his concern seemed genuine and moving. She began to feel a new warmth toward him and a little guilt over how she may have misjudged him.

"I know Jack, and he is a one-woman guy." He shook his head. "I saw Bina. I know what this has done to her, and I told her that he was just talk. I mean, who would think Jack . . ."

Max stared at the picture displayed on the screen. Kate could feel him getting lost in it for a moment. "She is very pretty," he murmured.

"Well, I hope they're very happy together," Kate said tartly. "I'm sure they share common goals and interests."

"Hey, he isn't married!" Max protested. "Even Jack isn't that stupid."

"How do you know?" Kate asked.

"Read the e-mail," Max said, and displayed the message from Jack.

What a place! The views are incredible, electronics are cheap, and the women are incredible and cheap. You gotta come! Money is king here, and the dollar rules.

Kate didn't bother to read any more. "He is disgusting," she said. She turned away and started to walk out of the apartment.

"So you don't think I should show this to Bina? Right?"

"Right, Einstein," Kate said, and ran down the stairs to her own place. As she walked in her door, the phone began to ring. She grabbed it and saw Elliot's number on the caller ID. "Shoot me in the head," she said into the receiver.

"And a good evening to you, too," Elliot said. "I didn't catch you during dinner, I hope, but Brice and I are getting together with Bina on Saturday morning for the big renovation. Are you in?"

Kate hesitated for a moment, torn between the news from upstairs and her disapproval of the whole scheme. Wasn't a makeover a kind of lie not much different from little Jennifer's stories? It was a visual way of saying you were someone different. But Jack's e-mail had shocked her. "I'm in," she said.

It was only after she hung up that she realized her commitment would mean canceling Michael. They spent every Friday night together and each Saturday. After Steven's unreliability, Kate appreciated the fact that Michael saw her every Wednesday, Friday, and Saturday night. During the week, they usually went to a movie and stayed at her house afterward. They alternated places on the weekends.

Perhaps Michael was a little too routinized, because he always seemed upset when she had to change their schedule and apologetic when he—rare though it was—had to do the same. Well, Kate would regret the pleasant, leisurely Saturday they would lose, but perhaps she could persuade him to work while she was off with her friends instead of on his usual Sunday night. She picked up the phone again and, feeling uneasy, dialed Michael's number.

Chapter Nineteen

Two days later, the Bitches, accompanied by Brice and Elliot, were walking down Fifth Avenue. They had all insisted on being a part of Bina's makeover.

"All I can say is it's about time," Barbie said. "You're starting to look like an Orthodox Jew."

"It's the hair," Brice agreed. "It looks like a bad wig."

"Brice!" Elliot warned before Kate could.

"The truth hurts," Bev said, patting Bina's arm and then her own tummy.

"I think I need to, uh, go to the bathroom," Bina said. "I'm so nervous. Jack liked my hair."

"Not enough," Barbie said.

"Don't worry. They have a ladies' room at Louis," Brice told her, and took her into a marble lobby. Kate shook her head. The whole crew knew she disapproved, but they ignored her except Brice, who turned to her and said, "You know, while we're here Pierre can cut your hair, too."

"I don't think so," Kate snapped. She loved her hair long. So had Steven, and so did Michael. It was sexy and easy to put up if she had to. Now, completely offended, she joined the party as they got onto the elevator to go up to the fourteenth-floor salon overlooking St. Patrick's Cathedral.

"Wow!" Bina said as she stared out at the skyline. "It looks almost as good as Epcot." Kate rolled her eyes.

Brice didn't bother with the view. "Pierre, please," he told the woman at the desk. "Tell him it's Brice and we have a cut with him and a consultation with Louis." Bev, Barbie, and Bunny looked at one another, obviously impressed. All those years of reading *Allure* magazine had familiarized them with Louis Licari, the god of hair color. And Brice had just called him by his first name. "Now c'mon. I think we can do everything your head needs here," he instructed Bina as he clutched her hand and escorted her to the stylist's chair.

"Except get it examined," Kate muttered. She looked over to Elliot, but he just shrugged. Barbie, Bunny, and Bev were right behind them. Kate was delighted that Bina was getting so much help and attention. It was just what she needed at a time like this. But, oddly, she also felt a bit of envy. She had never asked for help when her crisis with Steven had taken place, not that the Bitches would have been much help.

Bina spent four hours at the salon. While they were there, Barbie got a good cut, Bev had a facial, and Bunny got a massage—as a belated wedding present from Brice and Elliot. Kate merely had a manicure and didn't even care for the color she'd selected. But it was Bina who was transformed. Her hair had been lightened a bit around her face, and then streaks of ash blond made the dark brown of her natural color glow. Kate was stunned by the subtle artistry of it. The style, a chin-length, undercut masterpiece, made it seem as if Bina had a head of moving light, a kind of nimbus of hair. Even Kate had to admit the transformation was remarkable.

"Holy haircut, Batman," was all Elliot said as he looked up from the papers he was marking. Bina giggled and shook her head from side to side. The nimbus moved like a saintly glow in a chapel. The receptionist and two cashiers oohed and aahed, as they were paid to do. Barbie, Bev, and Bunny kept cooing like demented pigeons. For an insane moment, Kate wondered if she should get her own head shorn. Maybe a haircut, a few highlights, and a makeup makeover would . . . She took a deep breath. Then she got a grip.

"Okay," Brice said. "We did the drapes. Now on to the uphol-stery." He looked at Bina's outfit, an old Gap blouse and a charity skirt. "First stop, Prada!" he called, and the entire group headed outside and into two taxis.

Before Bina even had a chance to take note of the ambience or the price tags, she was standing in front of a three-way mirror while a saleslady pinned up the hemline on a skirt that, in Kate's opinion, was already far too short and far too tight. It draped to one side, exposing a thigh. "Do you really think this is *me?*" Bina asked the admiring group.

Barbie backed away from Bina and gave her an approving once-over. Kate remembered squirming under those looks back in tenth grade. Barbie liked what she saw. "Isn't it nice to wear something red? It's the new beige, you know," she confided.

Kate didn't have a clue as to what that meant, but she thought that Bina looked ridiculous. But that didn't stop them from buying the skirt and moving on to Victoria's Secret. Brice picked up a Wonderbra and then handed it to Bina.

"Here you go, honey," he said. "Every girl needs a little support."

"Don't forget this." Bunny handed her a lacy black thong.

Bina looked down at the bra and dental floss in her hand. "I'm not wearing these." She lifted up the thong and held it two ways. "I . . . I don't even know how to wear this," she admitted. "Besides, I'm not sleeping with him. My underwear isn't relevant." She looked at Elliot. "The charts didn't say I had to have sex with him, did they? Because I'm not doing that."

"Honey, it's not about having sex, it's about feeling sexy," Brice said. "And if you feel sexy, you'll look sexy to others. Right, Elliot?"

"I plead the Fifth," Elliot responded.

"Bina, you're a Capricorn," said Bev, "and trust me, they need all the help they can get when it comes to attracting men. See what it does for you."

Bina disappeared into the dressing room and came out with her eyes and breasts bulging. She'd put her blouse on to step out of the dressing room, but she hadn't buttoned the top two buttons. Barbie leaned forward and unbuttoned the third. "Now, that's a nice rack," she said.

Bina stared at herself in the mirror. Then she turned to Kate. "I wish Jack could see me now," she said. Kate's breasts, unexposed, felt a stab of sympathy for her friend. Cheerful little Bina, a cupcake of a girl, now looked more like a Pop-Tarts pastry and still she thought only of Jack. She was doing all of this because of him, and Kate honestly couldn't decide if it was an act of self-mutilation or love. She doubted that any of this would make a man like Billy Nolan want Bina. After all, she was still "Bina, the good girl from Ocean Avenue." At least, she decided, it gave Bina something else to concentrate on, and who knew? Looking like a hot tamale, she might meet someone else. One thing Kate did know was that while she could go on without Michael and even without marriage to anyone, Bina always had only one goal: marriage and children, preferably to and by Jack.

"Hey. Turn around," Bev said. "Let's see if there's a panty line."

"How can there be?" Bina asked. "There's hardly any panty." She turned as directed. "This is so uncomfortable," she said.

"Beauty has to hurt," Bunny told her.

At Tootsie Plohound, Bina once again followed Barbie's directives and bought her first pair of serious "fuck me" sandals.

"You need a low-cut top," Bev said, taking inventory of their progress to date. "I mean, you've got 'em, and you've lifted 'em, might as well show 'em. And you've always had a small waist, so we should find something tight." She looked down at her own stomach. The Lycra she was wearing couldn't be any tighter without crushing the fetus, Kate thought.

"Yes, that would complete the outfit," Brice agreed.

As the seven of them walked down the busy West Broadway sidewalk, Kate had to marvel at how seamlessly Elliot and Brice seemed to join in with her Brooklyn friends. She'd avoided this for years and never introduced Bina and the others to Rita, her friend from graduate school, or Maggie, a choreographer she'd met in her exercise class. Somehow she hadn't thought a mix like that would work as smoothly, and she suspected it was because Brice and Elliot were observing all this as they participated.

But while everyone else seemed to be enjoying themselves, Kate was feeling distinctly uncomfortable. She had worked diligently for as long as she could remember to change her style, her look, her vocabulary . . . well, almost everything that she had believed didn't reflect who she was or wanted to be. She thought she had succeeded in creating a unique persona. Hers, she felt was valid. Now, watching Bina's instant transformation, she wondered if it wasn't valid as well, even if it had been overseen by others. After all, Kate had made all of the changes to herself based, in part, on what others—even if they were people in magazines or strangers she'd observed in Manhattan—had shown her.

As Elliot led the way to hail yet another pair of cabs, Brice took stock. "Give me half an hour in Make Up For Ever and I'll have you looking like a queen," he promised.

A look of horror came over Bina's face. "I'm not changing my makeup," she protested as the cab pulled out into the traffic.

"You have to *wear* makeup if you want to *change* makeup," Bunny said sharply. She reached into her purse and pulled out a lipstick tube. "Just try a little of this."

"Oh, leave her alone!" Kate begged. She wondered what all the criticism and change was doing to Bina's self-esteem. But Bina took the tube and applied it. It was awful—it made her look like Mrs. Horowitz at a funeral.

"I don't think red is her color," Kate objected, and then realized she had now added to the critique.

"I agree with you there," Brice said from the front seat beside the driver. He handed Bina a tissue. "I see you more in a sizzling salmon."

By the time they were ready to head home, Bina had charged

more on her credit cards in one day than she ordinarily spent in three months. Kate was exhausted but happy to see that Bina finally seemed to be enjoying herself, even if it was over silly things and a harebrained scheme. It was the first day she had paid more attention to herself than Jack since he'd left. Elliot helped Bev waddle up the steps of Kate's building.

"A fashion show!" Brice demanded once they were inside. Barbie, Bunny, and Bev added their chorus, and so did Kate, a little reluctantly. Having all of them in her living room felt not just crowded but claustrophobic. It was a clash of cultures and sexual orientation in the tiny space that was, in a way, sacred to her. But Kate was the only one who seemed disoriented. Bev had her feet up, her hands over her belly, Barbie sat primly in the rocker, Bunny stood in front of the fireplace, glancing every so often at her honeymoon tan in the mirror that hung over the mantel, and Brice was busy going through the bags, while Elliot just sat back on the sofa, smiling to himself.

Bina took the shopping bags into Kate's bedroom and, a few minutes later, returned completely transformed. There was a moment of silence. Kate was shocked. In a single day, Bina had changed literally from head to toe, and she could barely recognize the hot little number pirouetting in front of them. She thought of Billy Nolan and the look he had given her out on the terrace. Would a man who had approved of her style and looks want a woman arrayed the way Bina was?

"Wow! You look great!" Bev said, breaking the silence.

Then Elliot gave an excellent wolf whistle, and Barbie, Brice, and Bunny began to applaud. Kate joined in. "Okay, so now all we have to do is bring you over to Billy and serve you up on a platter," Elliot said.

"How?" Bina asked, as if playing the trussed fowl on a plate came naturally.

"We go to his place of business," Elliot said, "the Barber Bar in Williamsburg. Then we—"

"Is that where he works?" Kate interrupted. Elliot ignored her and laid out the time, the rendezvous spots, the assault on the watering hole, and all the rest as if he were the Iron Duke planning an invasion.

"Now, not that you can't do it, but let me come over and do a touch-up to your hair and makeup next weekend," Brice said. "And I'll have a surprise for you."

"I'll hafta be surprised later," Bev said. "I need to get home for my Johnny."

"Sure, Bev," Barbie said. "Bunny, are you in?"

"Sure," Bunny said.

Kate looked at her and wondered if Bunny had enjoyed her honeymoon, especially after . . . after Billy. Then she wondered if she'd like to go on a "honeymoon" with Michael. They had spent one weekend at the Jersey shore, which had been pleasant. Two weeks, though . . .

Kate brought her focus back to the party that was breaking up. "We'll see you all later," Barbie told them. "Oh, Bina, I'm so excited for you. Good clothes open all doors." Kate tried not to laugh. How had Barbie's mother known in advance how to name her so accurately?

There were many kisses and hugs, and then the three women disappeared out the front door.

Bina was left with Brice and Elliot, who were walking her to the subway. At last Kate was left alone. She wondered what Dr. and Mrs. Horowitz would say when Bina walked in the door. Mrs. Horowitz had a mild heart condition; maybe she should call ahead to prepare her.

It wasn't until Kate was in bed, just at the edge of sleep, that she wondered again what she would look like after a makeover. Then she closed her eyes and slept—poorly—for the rest of the night.

Chapter Twenty

Kate sat in her office across from two identical twin boys wearing identical green corduroys and white T-shirts, each with the same picture of a *Tyrannosaurus rex* clawing across his chest. Each had a name tag stuck to his shirt—one reading "James" and the other "Joseph." Kate was perched on the front of her desk purposely, to appear to tower over the two small third graders. The three of them had been talking for a while already, and Kate thought she'd cleared up the situation.

"Now, I am going to take you back to Mrs. Gupta's class, James," she said, pointing at one of the boys—the one who was wearing the "Joseph" name tag. "And you, Joseph, are to go back to Mrs. Johnson's," she said sternly to the other boy. "Where each of you belongs," she added.

The Reilly twins were good boys, well behaved and intelligent. But they had been assigned separate classes this year with the consent of their parents, and since the separation, they had developed a bad habit of fooling not only their classmates but their teachers and even Dr. McKay about their identities. They switched at will, but when Kate suggested to their parents that the third graders might be better off if they dressed individually instead of in matching clothing, they had insisted that it was up to the boys. And the boys still wanted to dress alike.

Lately, the mischief had escalated, but Kate felt her talk about trust and fooling people had penetrated into the strange and interesting world of twinship. "So we're agreed?" she asked.

Just then the phone rang. Kate turned her back to the twins and reached for the receiver. "Dr. Jameson," she answered.

"Dr. Jameson? This is Dr. Bina Horowitz. I'll be at your office ready for our conference tomorrow at six. I've been told we have to consult with Dr. Brice first," Bina said.

"No one is listening in, Bina," she told her friend. Years of eavesdropping by her mother on the extension had made Bina paranoid. "Come on over for Operation Ridiculous. I'll be there at five. Gotta go. I'm working."

Kate hung up and turned back to the twins. "I want the two of you to exchange your name tags now," she said. They nodded, peeled off the sticky-backed strips, and handed them to each other contritely. Her phone rang again. She sighed and turned her back on the twins, who quickly retraded name tags and seats.

"A Dr. Michael Atwood is here to see you," Louise, the secretary from the front office, informed Kate in her nasal voice.

"Thanks, I'll be right out," she said, and cradled the receiver. This was unexpected. Michael was nothing if not a creature of habit. Kate wondered what had prompted such a spontaneous visit.

Kate's mind was so preoccupied with these thoughts that she didn't notice the twins' subterfuge. "Remember," she said to them absently, "it isn't just a trick to switch places. It's unkind to fool people. And after you fool them, they won't trust you when you want them to. Understand?" Normally, she wouldn't have repeated herself, but she was a little thrown by this surprise and was anxious to hear what Michael had to say.

The twins nodded innocently. She hopped off her desk and took each boy by the hand. She led them out the door and down the hall. Michael was standing at the far end. He gave her a big, if somewhat sheepish, smile, which Kate did not acknowledge. Instead she stopped in front of a classroom door and nodded for "James" to go in. "Joseph" let go of her other hand, gave her a triumphant smile, and raced to another door on the opposite side of the hall.

Only then did Kate smile back and walk up to Michael. "Nice surprise," she said to reinforce his spontaneous behavior. "What are you doing here?"

"I thought I'd see you in action. Very stern." He smiled. "You're such a natural with kids."

"Thanks," Kate replied. She wondered—just for a moment—if he ever thought of her as the mother of his children, but then she stopped herself. It was too early for that.

"You almost ready to go?" he asked. "Do you mind that I dropped by?"

"Not at all," Kate said. "I like it." And she did.

"I have something else I wanted to show you before tonight," Michael said, reaching into his briefcase. He pulled out an academic journal with a bit of a flourish.

"Oh, Michael! Your article!" He had been working on this piece for months. He had even gone into the field for research. It meant a lot to him and to his career. Kate was delighted for him.

"Hot off the press from the University of Michigan's *Journal of Applied Sciences,*" he said proudly.

Kate gave him a big hug. "I'm so pleased for you," she said. "What a great surprise!" She took the journal and opened it to the article. He had already marked the page with a bright red sticker. She smiled at that. There were things about him that were . . . surprisingly childlike. It was endearing.

They walked back to her office. "That's the very first copy," he told her. "I thought as soon as you were done here we could go out for a drink and then maybe dinner." She smiled at him and nodded. "I'm looking forward to our weekend," he said, and he put his arm around her and nuzzled her neck. She felt his stubble tickle her and giggled, just as Dr. McKay appeared at the door.

"Excuse me," he said.

Michael pulled away, and Kate did her best not to look like a guilty schoolgirl. In fact, she found herself having to suppress a smile, since Dr. McKay's face clearly showed his confusion as well as his disapproval. She could imagine him trying to decide whether she was two-timing Elliot or had moved on, slutlike, to a new man. Since it wasn't his business, she smiled at him. "Yes, Dr. McKay?"

"There seems to be a problem with the Reilly twins," Dr. McKay told her. Kate could see him trying to keep his eyes off of Michael.

"I know," she told him. "I had them in my office and we had a talk about it. Dr. McKay, I would like to introduce Dr. Michael Atwood."

Dr. McKay nodded curtly in Michael's general direction, then turned back to Kate. "I know you saw them," he told her, "but apparently they pulled a switcheroo again."

"Oops," Kate said. "I guess I'll have to do some more in-depth work with them," she told him.

"I guess you will." Dr. McKay turned and disappeared.

Michael looked at Kate. "'Oops'?" he asked. "Is that a Freudian or a Jungian term?"

Kate had to laugh, though she felt some embarrassment and concern. Well, she would deal with it on Monday. Now she had to deal with her changed plans for the weekend.

As they walked out of the school and passed the playground, Kate took Michael's hand. "I'm so glad you came to the school," she said. "It gives us some extra time together." Michael nodded and smiled. So much for the setup, Kate thought. "The thing is, Michael, I have to go out tomorrow night."

"Tomorrow night? But it's Saturday."

"I know. But it's Bina . . ."

"Oh. Bina."

"It will just be for a few hours," Kate told him.

"A few hours on Saturday night," Michael said, and Kate could hear the reproach in his voice.

"I'm sorry," she said. "It's not going to be fun. I just have to." As she voiced the words, she felt annoyed with herself and him. She didn't have to apologize. Why did she feel so guilty? It was a small change, and it wouldn't hurt him to learn to be a little more flexible.

Michael nodded, then looked down at his shoes for a moment. Kate watched him adjust, and then he put his hand in his pocket, pulled it out, and opened his fist. There, nestled in the palm of his hand, were two shiny keys on a new key ring. "Well," he said, "I'm glad I got these for you. It'll make Saturday more convenient. You can let yourself in to my place."

Kate took the keys as if they were a piece of jewelry. Indeed, exchanging keys was the equivalent of what getting pinned had been decades ago. It was a sign of trust and commitment. "Oh, Michael," she said, taking the keys. She kissed him, then realized that she would now have to give her keys to him. She also realized that she didn't really like the idea.

The next evening, a guilty Kate and a new, hot, trendy Bina met Elliot and Brice at Kate's apartment to do a hair and makeup touchup and begin their trek into Brooklyn. Kate looked down at her own simple blue knit dress—short, but with a turtle-neck—and felt distinctly underdressed, though she knew it was flattering. Steven had liked it. Then she reminded herself that this was about Bina, not her. Billy meant nothing to her.

"This is even better than that trip to Nevis last fall," Brice said. "The cultures of indigenous people have always fascinated me."

Kate cleared her throat to catch Brice's attention and gave Bina a sideways glance. Bina, however, was too absorbed in trying to learn to walk in the "fuck me" sandals to notice Brice's comment. Brice, taking pity on Bina's poor soul, not to mention poor soles, cocked his head and said, "Think up, dear. Lift! Lift!"

Bina jerked her shoulders up higher, and in just a moment the look of total concentration on her face passed into a smile. She took a few tentative steps, then walked around Kate's small living room almost confidently. "Hey! Wow!" she exclaimed. "Thanks, Brice. That really works."

Kate couldn't resist. "Brice," she asked, "where did you learn about walking in stilettos?"

"Hey, is there a party going on?"

The voice, muffled by the door but clearly Max's, stopped the conversation. Elliot, closest to the entrance, reached out and turned the knob. Max, with his dry cleaning hooked over his shoulder and a bag of takeout in his other hand, was staring across Kate's living room at Bina. His eyes moved up and down, and Kate watched as both hands opened in surprise and the takeout and plastic-wrapped dry cleaning fell to the floor. For a moment, despite the spills, Max couldn't pull his eyes away. "Bina?" he asked. "Is that you?" Then, as if waking from a spell, he looked down, flushing with embarrassment. He crouched to pick up the hangers while Elliot went for the plastic containers of what looked like Chinese food. Fortunately, they hadn't spilled their contents.

"Hi, Max," Bina said. Kate had to turn away from the wreckage in the hallway because she could hardly believe it was Bina who had managed to pack so much flirtatiousness into the two syllables simply with her tone. In all the years she had known her, Kate had never heard a coy sentiment escape Bina's lips. But there was definitely something new, some come-hither timbre, packed into her words. Suddenly Kate felt that perhaps Bina could manage to nail a date with Billy Nolan.

"Here's your dinner," Elliot said cheerfully to Max, handing the bag back to him. "Gotta go."

Kate grabbed her purse and ushered Bina out the door behind Brice's broad back. Unfortunately, she had to stop to lock the door, and in the moment it took her to do so, Max, still immobilized, asked Bina, "What happened to you?"

Bina opened her mouth, but before she could put her sandaled foot in it, Brice intervened. "Only I and her hairdresser know for sure. Toodles." He took Bina's hand and led her to the stairs.

As Kate followed them, she turned and saw Max, still frozen, above her. "Don't worry. It wasn't Bina," she told him. "It's Bina's evil twin."

The taxi had sped across the bridge and now seemed lost in Brooklyn. "Do you know where this Barber Bar is?" Kate asked.

"Sure," Elliot said. "We'll stop right here. It's just a block or two, and we're meeting the others on the corner. I need some time to coach Bina." Turning to her, he said, "Now remember, if you want this to work, you have to remember LAID."

Kate sighed. "If that's a requirement, we may as well go home now. Bina already made it clear that she's not going to sleep with that man."

"I thought I didn't have to go to bed for this to work," Bina whined. "I love Jack and don't—"

"Oh, calm down, both of you," Elliot interrupted. "Not *laid*, LAID. L-A-I-D," he spelled. "God, I hate acronyms. They're so military and butch. Anyway, it stands for lick, arouse, ignore, and disturb."

"What am I supposed to lick, Elliot?" Bina asked him, her voice tentative.

"Your lips," Elliot answered.

"And that's all you lick, missy!" Kate added.

"And that will arouse him?" Bina frowned. "And what do I ignore?"

"Him!" Elliot answered, as if to say, "Uh, duh!"

"And why?" Kate demanded, not liking this acronym at all. She was only afraid that Billy would ignore Bina and the entire plan would fall apart.

"Because he obviously has intimacy issues," Elliot explained, turning to Kate with exasperation. "God! You're the shrink, not me."

"I don't get it," Bina admitted.

"If you ignore him, he won't be afraid of you," Elliot said. "And if he's not afraid, he'll ask you out again. We just have to get past the two-point-seven-month requirement."

"Fine," Bina said good-naturedly. "Then what?"

"Disturb," Elliot answered.

"That should be easy," Kate told them. "Just tell him why we're doing this. I think Billy Nolan would find this whole idea very disturbing."

Elliot ignored Kate. "Try to be just disturbing enough to be a challenge, but not challenging enough to be a turnoff. You get it?" he asked.

"I—I think so," Bina stammered.

"Well, come on, kids," Brice said as the cab pulled over to the curb. "The Bitches and Billy are waiting!" He looked at them and started to laugh. "This is a little like the Osbournes visiting Sesame Street."

The cab had pulled up to the subway stop at Bedford Street, where they had all agreed to meet. Bev and Barbie were already there. Bev was looking *very* pregnant, while Barbie appeared to have raided the closet of a fifteen-year-old girl.

"I haven't had a night out with the girls in I don't know how long!" Bev squealed.

"Me either. Biological girls, at least," Elliot said, looking lovingly at Brice, who had immediately gotten into a "deep" conversation with Barbie about hemlines.

"We're going to meet Bunny at the bar," Bev told them.

"Isn't she newly married?" Kate asked in disbelief. "They're barely back from their honeymoon. Doesn't she want to spend her weekend with Arnie?" Once the words were out of her mouth, she realized how her new culture was colliding with her old.

"Hey, she just got married to him and finished their honeymoon. How much do you expect?" Bev asked.

Kate had to smile. The gang had a very split but pragmatic view of marriage: that it was necessary to have but easy to ignore. The girls hung with the girls, and the guys hung with the guys.

Now, however, as she looked at her motley crew, she began once again to have serious doubts about the whole expedition. Quietly she pulled Bina away from the rest of the group. "You don't have to do this, you know," she said in a near whisper.

"Kate," Bina began, "after I've dedicated years of my life to him, he wants to explore his singleness. Who does he think he is? Ponce de León?" She looked over at Bev—more specifically,

Bev's swelling belly. "Neither of us has found the fountain of youth. Don't you worry about your biological clock?"

Elliot, having overheard the entire conversation, chose this moment to break in. "Like every modern girl," he said, putting his arm around Kate, "Kate has had her eggs frozen for future reference."

"You have?" Bina said in awe.

"Really?" Barbie joined in.

"Don't listen to him. He's crazy," Kate told them as if his nonsense didn't embarrass her, although a telltale blush was tingeing her cheeks. "Anyway, where the hell is this place?" she asked, refocusing attention on the task at hand.

"I think we turn down at the next corner." Bev indicated a side street. "Bunny gave me these directions. I know it's here somewhere." They turned the corner. "There should be a barber's pole—"

"There it is!" Brice pointed down the block to a barely visible red-, blue-, and white-striped pole, and they all walked toward it.

Chapter Twenty-one

Since I'm supposed to meet Billy here, I'm buying." Bina's voice cut through Kate's thoughts. "What's everybody drinking? Beers?"

"I'll help," Kate offered. "The rest of you see if you can find us a table. And if we're not back in ten minutes, send a search party."

Kate led Bina through the crowd to the bar. "Try to get Billy's attention," she said. She could see him down at the end of the bar. His white shirt emphasized both his wide shoulders and his tan. Kate wondered briefly if he was so vain that he went to a tanning parlor, but there wasn't time for much reflection. "Call him," she told Bina.

"Call him what?" Bina asked.

Unfortunately, at that moment a different bartender, older, balding, and with a beer belly, approached them from the other end of the bar. "What'll it be, ladies?"

"Omigod!" Bina whispered to Kate. "That's not him."

"Great pickup line," Kate told Bina. Turning to the bartender, she said, "Thanks anyway, we're just looking."

Kate did a quick scan of the crowd at the bar. It was clear that it was far busier at Billy's end and that a gaggle of girls had monopolized the stools. A younger man had crouched under the bar top and began taking drink orders. She grabbed Bina and pulled her through the crowd to the other end of the room, and then, mostly by pushing and a couple of shoulder moves, she got the two of them right up to the bar again, this time at the right place.

Waiting to be served, Kate sighed. She felt way too old for the bar scene. Did that mean she was getting old at thirty-one? At least this place was a little more imaginative than most, she had to admit, looking around. The old barber chairs, obviously restored, were still screwed into the black-and-white marble floor, and the bar, a dark mahogany, was backed by what must have been the original mirror and shelves of the barbershop. Among the vodkas and malt Scotches lined up, there were also antique shaving cups and old bottles of hair tonic, aftershave, and the like.

The place had obviously been expanded from the original barbershop. Aside from the bar and the row of chairs where people clustered, there were banquettes along the far wall and tables and booths in the back. The noise was deafening, like screams of laughter in a subway tunnel, and Kate thanked God that she had chosen not to bring Michael. The scene was so . . . outer boroughs.

Bina looked behind Kate. "Omigod! It's really him."

Kate kept her back to the bar, facing away from Billy and toward Bina. "Yep. Elvis has not left the building. Get on my left and get his attention," she commanded, hoping it would work.

"What comes first?" Bina asked desperately. "The lick or the annoy?"

"Just call his name and order our beer," Kate told her, turning toward the bar to help her. Billy, his teeth as white as his shirt, his hair more golden than Kate remembered, finished pouring a drink for another customer. She gave Bina an elbow poke. "Say something."

"Billy! Here," Bina gasped. Perhaps he heard the urgency in her voice, because he came right over.

"What'll it be, ladies?" he asked, flashing his perfect Crest commercial smile. Kate turned away, but it was too late. Billy looked straight into her face, and she didn't think it was her imagination that she saw his eyes widen in recognition. She elbowed Bina again.

"Two pitchers of Shirley Temples and a beer," Bina sputtered, and then flushed bright red.

"Better line, but not effective," Kate said softly to Bina, who had apparently frozen with an exaggerated smile, her eyes bulging.

Billy narrowed his eyes for a moment and searched Kate's face, but Kate was careful to keep hers perfectly blank. "Is this for a whole table of designated drivers and one drunk?" he asked, grinning. He ignored Bina's embarrassed giggle and looked directly at Kate.

"It's two pitchers of beer and one Shirley Temple," Kate replied, not as amused.

Billy wouldn't take his eyes off Kate. "At the risk of sounding like a cliché," he began, "haven't we met before?"

"I think you met my friend Bina. At Bunny and Arnie's wedding," Kate said. "Bina, this is Billy." She noticed how Billy did not even look in Bina's direction, but rather kept his gaze on her. Her face felt hot beneath his stare.

"Nice to meet you," Billy said to Bina without so much as a nod in her direction. "But you and I," he said, still looking intently at Kate, "we met—"

"Bina lives here in Brooklyn, too," Kate interrupted, pulling her eyes away from him and focusing on her friend.

"Oh, yeah? Nearby?" Billy asked, glancing over at Bina for the first time.

"Well, kind of. In Park Slope," Bina replied much too anxiously.

Billy began to pour the two pitchers of beer. "Hey, there's a big difference between Park Slope and Williamsburg, Reina."

"Bina, her name is Bina," Kate snapped.

Billy shrugged and handed over the tray with the drinks on it. Kate took the tray and hustled Bina to the table where the rest of the group was sitting.

"That was him!" Bina exclaimed.

"Who?" Elliot said slyly.

"*Him!*" Bina squealed.

"Mel Gibson?" Bev asked, playing along.

"Bill Clinton?" Barbie joined in.

"It was Billy," Kate said in an aside to Elliot, "but he didn't have the ightest-slay interest-ay." Elliot grimaced. It was becoming clear that Bina was going to need all the help she could get. "Well, here are your pitchers, ladies," Kate said, handing over the tray. "I'm going to run to the bathroom."

She made her way through the crowd to the tiny one-stall bathroom. It was surprisingly clean. She had just entered when she heard two voices just outside the door.

"Hey, did you see the way that redhead looked at me?" said the first. It was a thick voice, raspy and guttural: the older bartender, the one Kate heard customers call Pete. "Man, she's hot! Did you see the eyes on that girl? And she had two other beautiful things." He snickered suggestively.

"What redhead?" This voice Kate recognized immediately: Billy Nolan.

"The one who carried off those two pitchers of beer."

"She wasn't looking at you," Billy said with thinly veiled contempt.

"You know," Pete grunted. "You do all right for yourself, but sometimes you miss the subtleties. She wants me."

Kate heard Billy groan, and then the two were quiet for a moment. Billy's voice broke the silence. "Susie was in earlier."

"Shit!" cried Pete. "And I missed her. She was so fucking hot. Why'd you dump her?"

"I dunno," Billy answered. "Anyway, she comes in and tells me that—"

"Don't tell me," Pete interrupted, "she's engaged, right?"

"How did you know?" Billy asked.

"Billy—buddy, look. I don't know what it is that you do to these women, but once you date them they become like marriage roach motels. Other guys check in, but they don't check out."

Kate was finished, and she really didn't want to hear any more. But even as she flushed, washed her hands, and hit the dryer button, she could hear the men still talking.

"Usually it wouldn't bother me," Billy said, "but I was at Arnie's wedding a few weeks ago and I realized that I'm like the last single guy out of all my friends."

"You're a bartender," said Pete. "Bartenders are supposed to be single. You're not the marrying type. Besides, what's happening with Tina?"

Kate had heard enough. She opened the door quickly, hoping to get back to the table before Billy and his friend were finished with their break, but she was moving too late. Just as she stepped into the passage beyond the rest room door, she found herself face-to-face with Billy Nolan.

"Whoa! Slow down, Red," he said as Kate tried to continue on her way without speaking. She ignored him. The hallway was narrow, and a guy pushed past them and nudged her up against Billy. He steadied her with a hand on each shoulder and looked at the passing customer. "Hey, watch it!" he shouted. He looked again at Kate. *"Je pense . . . ,"* he stopped. *"Je n'oubliez pas,"* he said, slipping into French.

What was it with this guy and French? Kate wondered. "I haven't forgotten you, either," she admitted, but as a throwaway line.

"Right. We discussed existential issues. I always like to combine Sartre and weddings," he added, and Kate couldn't resist smiling, though she tried. This guy was impossibly self-assured. How could she entice him to date Bina? "So what are you doing on this side of the river?" Billy asked.

"Having a drink with my friends in that corner," Kate said, pointing to their table. Just then Pete tapped Billy on the shoulder from behind.

"Yo, Bill," he said. "Forget the conquest. There're customers waiting."

Kate blushed against her will, angry at the thought of being considered "a conquest." "See ya," she said, and forced herself to give him an enticing smile.

She returned to their table, hoping the hook had worked. Sure enough, just moments after their glasses were empty and

Barbie had refreshed Bina's lip gloss, Billy appeared at their table, a pitcher of beer in each hand. "Welcome to the Barber Bar," he said, and put down the pitchers. He smiled at Kate. "So, you weren't lying about your posse at the wedding."

All eyes at the table focused on Kate. She hadn't mentioned their little pas de deux on the terrace to anyone. Now, she regretted that. Across the table, Kate saw Bev dig an elbow into Bina's side.

"Hey, Billy," Bunny said, "business looks real good."

"You gotta pretty full crowd," Bev said approvingly. "And dancing."

"Yeah," Billy said, and then looked back at Kate. "We do a little hokey-pokey."

"Don't you get a night off?" Bev asked.

"Usually Saturdays. But one of the guys called in sick. Lucky I was here and got to see all you beauties," Billy said.

Above the general noise, Pete, the older bartender, bellowed, "Yo, Billy! This ain't a one-man band. Where's Joey?"

Billy didn't turn around. Bunny, clearly desperate, grabbed his hand. "This is my friend Bina," she said. "You two ought to get together."

Billy looked at Bina blankly for a moment. "Yeah. Nice to meet you." He turned back to Kate, who felt desperate herself.

"How about bowling with Bina and me next Wednesday?" she asked.

He blinked, then smiled. "I wouldn't have guessed you for the bowling type," he said.

Barbie, always prepared, pushed Bina's phone number scribbled on a piece of paper into Billy's hand. "Here," she said, "give Bina a call to set it up. She's in charge of all the bowling events with Kate." There was another yell from the bar, and this time Billy turned.

"Coming," he said, and gave the group a dazzling smile before he disappeared into the crowd.

"My God," Brice said. "He's gorgeous. Can I come, too?"

Elliot gave Brice a look, then turned back to Kate and gave

her a more searching one. Before he could say anything, Bev began to high-five everyone at the table. Next, Kate thought, they'd do the Wave. "Nice work," said Barbie, slapping Kate's palm.

"Good save," Bunny agreed.

"I think he believes he's going out with you, Kate," Brice said.

"Well," she told the table, "he'll find out differently when he meets Michael. Anyway, he has Bina's number."

"Thanks, Katie," Bina said, and looked totally exhausted. Kate smiled at her but wondered how she would talk Michael into a Wednesday night of bowling.

Chapter Twenty-two

Kate felt guilty as she pressed the buzzer, then she remembered she had Michael's keys. Silently she cursed herself. She checked her watch and was even more concerned when she realized it was a quarter to one. She was sure he was sleeping and equally sure she had more beer on her breath than she would like him to smell. Somehow it was all right to go out with friends because of obligation but not to have a good time.

When Michael came to the door, still dressed but obviously rubbing the sleep out of his eyes, she greeted him with a quick hug and passed him in the narrow foyer.

"You shouldn't have waited up," she said. What she meant was, she should have gone home to her own apartment or, better yet, not gone to Brooklyn at all.

But Michael just yawned and stretched. "Time to go to bed," he said. Kate agreed with a nod but headed to the bathroom.

"I have to pee," she said.

Once she had the door closed, she washed her face, brushed her teeth, gargled, and then brushed her teeth again. She caught a glimpse of herself in the mirror as she reached for the face towel. She looked so . . . furtive. For a moment, Kate saw—in her jaw, the set of her eyes, and her hairline—a frightening similarity to her father. It sent a shiver through her. Then she realized that more than the physical resemblance, it was the guilty, skulking body language and expression that had conjured up his image. She stood immobile under the light of the bare bulb in Michael's bachelor bathroom and looked herself in the eye. You have nothing to feel guilty about, she told herself. If Michael is rigid with his schedule, there is no reason for you to feel guilty. Having drinks with your girlfriends is nothing to feel guilty about.

But Kate knew it wasn't just that. Her thoughts about Billy Nolan were unsettling. She didn't want those thoughts; she didn't want the feeling she had had as she'd flirted with him. And even if she had done it for Bina, and even if she was only tricking Billy, the fact was she had acted as if she were making a date with another man and the other man had believed it. Wasn't that kind of cheating on Michael? Raised as a Catholic while her mother was alive, Kate had never quite gotten over the concept of sins of commission and omission. Was she guilty of the latter?

Now she was returning to sleep with her lover, and she felt uncomfortably like a slut. It wasn't the beer on her breath or the smell of cigarette smoke on her clothes that embarrassed her. It was her own feelings.

Kate washed quickly and emerged from the bathroom in her panties and bra. As she walked into Michael's bedroom, she was dismayed to see that he was completely undressed under the sheet and had lit the candle on his nightstand. Michael usually slept in pajama bottoms and a T-shirt. The lack of them and the lighted candle sent a clear signal.

"May I borrow a shirt?" Kate asked meekly.

Michael nodded and gestured to the bureau. She took out a plain white Fruit of the Loom and slipped into it, then slid into bed beside him.

"Was it fun?" Michael asked, putting his arm around her.

"Not really," Kate said. "And I'm so exhausted." She paused. Michael was good with this kind of sexual nuance. She waited a minute. "Can we just spoon?" she asked, and turned her back to him, feeling his chest against her shoulder blades.

"Sure," Michael said, and Kate was relieved not to hear disappointment in his voice. He shifted for a moment, blew out the candle, and pressed his body up to hers. Kate sighed, and out

of either shame, exhaustion, or too much beer, she closed her
eyes and was asleep in moments.

Sunday morning, she and Michael fell into their comforting ritual. He had bought *The New York Times* and bagels, and they
spent two hours reading bits of the paper to each other and
nibbling on cream cheese and pumpernickel. Kate opened the
"Styles" section to read a continuation of a story about beauty
parlors in Afghanistan and accidentally ran into the Weddings/
Celebration page. It was something she tried to avoid, something unsettling, like stepping around a dead pigeon on the
sidewalk.

She then went on to read the rest of the section, as she
always had to when she forgot to avoid it. It was a bad mistake. Column after column describing happy unions, listing
the groom's parents, the bride's family, with quotes from their
siblings and descriptions of the celebrations that always left
her feeling depressed and different from everybody else. If
she married Michael, what would the *Times* possibly run
about her wedding? "The bride, close to her 32nd birthday
and an orphan, elected to have a small wedding. 'I couldn't
really afford a big party, and I don't have enough family and
friends to attend one,' Katherine Jameson-Atwood said. 'In
fact, I'm not sure I'm doing the right thing, but then, who is?'"
Covertly, she peered over the top of the paper at Michael and
wondered how he would look in one of the grainy gray photos, his head leaned toward hers. She closed the paper and
put it aside.

Restless, she got up and went to the window. Michael's
building, a large white brick postwar complex, consisted of
several hundred boring apartments, but the views from the
upper floors were spectacular. She looked out the window
down at Turtle Bay. She could even see a glimmer of the East
River. "It looks like it's clouding over," she said.

Michael came up behind her and wrapped one arm around
her chest and shoulder, like a high collar on a coat. "Well," he

said, "we could either go out and skateboard competitively or we could lie down in the bedroom. The choice is yours."

Kate laughed and let him take her hand, leading her to the bed, though she wasn't certain she was in the mood. But when they were lying down and he had undressed her, she relaxed into his kisses. When he bit her, gently, on the back of her neck, it sent a pleasant shiver down her spine. She began to forget herself in the trance of sexual pleasure that began to rise slowly like a tide at full moon. She felt his hands slide over her, deft and knowing, if a little predictable. When he rolled from his side on top of her, she wanted him. Swept away by the rhythm of his movements and her hungry response, Kate felt good for the first time that weekend. She closed her eyes and felt the rise of an orgasm about to take place. At the edge she whispered, "Yes." She squeezed her eyes shut, and then Billy Nolan's face flashed before her, as clear as it had been the night before. She caught her breath and groaned, but it was not with pleasure.

When Michael came, Kate realized to her dismay that she was relieved.

As they lay there together, she thought about the bowling plan. She couldn't imagine Michael running down the lane, but she had to go with him or Billy would continue to believe that she was his date. She couldn't take Elliot, because any man could tell there were no vibes between them—at least not the sexual kind. And her guilt compelled her to end the charade as quickly as possible. "Michael," she whispered, "are you asleep?"

"Not quite," he murmured.

"I want to ask you something."

He turned to her with that deer-in-the-headlights look men got when they thought you were going to talk about "the relationship."

"How do you feel about bowling?" Kate asked.

Chapter Twenty-three

Pee-yeuw!" Bina said as she, Kate, and Michael struggled to get their rented bowling shoes on.

"Strike!"

"You lucky son of a bitch!" Behind them, a bunch of blue-collar bowlers were in some sort of fierce competition, either bowling or drinking—or perhaps both.

They were at Bowl-a-Rama. The noise was thunderous as pins fell and madmen screamed. "The thrill of victory, the agony of defeat!" Kate chirped.

"The agony of de feet is only starting," Michael quipped, looking down at the smelly shoes. It seemed that Bina had qualms, too, but they were more fashion-related.

"Do you think this red goes with my outfit?" she asked Kate nervously.

"Sure," Kate told her, though the shoes were hideous, as was Bina's new outfit. Kate could see that Barbie had "helped" dress Bina for the big occasion.

Thinking of that, Kate scanned the crowd, looking for Billy Nolan. All was chaos. In the lanes next to them, a league was just finishing up, and the clash of orange-and-brown shirts was almost nauseating to look at. Kate herself was wearing a simple white shirt and jeans, while Michael was wearing a sports coat, perhaps the only sports coat in a ten-block radius.

Bina stood up. Kate reassessed her outfit and realized that the short black miniskirt would reveal all when she bent over to release the ball. Her clingy green top was set off by a fuchsia scarf, Barbie's trademark color. Unfortunately for Bina, the scarf gave her face a mauve cast that clashed with the blouse. Oh well, Kate thought, nothing would make this double date from hell work anyway.

They were assigned an alley, and as they slipped into the molded plastic seats, Michael, ever the gentleman, asked if they would like something to drink. Bina asked for a cola, and before she thought about it, Kate ordered a beer. She imagined that Michael raised his brows before he went off to the bar.

The moment he was gone, Bina turned to her. "Where is he, Katie?" she asked, eyeing the entrance. "He said he'd be here on time. Maybe he's going to stand me up. Oh, I'm so nervous."

"Calm down, honey," Kate said. "He'll be here." In truth, she was nervous herself. She knew she had deceived Billy, though Bina hadn't a clue. And if she couldn't make the transition gracefully and make it look as if any confusion were a natural mistake on Billy's part, she was afraid of the fallout. Billy Nolan wasn't going to be thrilled when he realized that he'd been tricked into an evening with Bina.

"God, I'm sweating through my blouse," Bina said. "I'm going to run to the ladies' room and check my makeup one more time." She stood up and wound her way through the bobbing heads and fat bellies in the crowd.

Michael returned with the beverages, and Kate saw he had also bought some snacks.

"Bina's looking . . . um, different since the last time I saw her," he stammered.

"Well, I think you only saw her when she was having a case of the hysterical fantods," Kate reminded him.

"No, that's not what I mean," Michael said. "She looks . . . jazzier."

"Please! She looks like she belongs in the cast of *Forty-second Street*," Kate told him. She realized she sounded as tense as she felt. She put her arm out and took Michael's hand. "It was sweet of you to come," she said. "Launching Bina in her new life is really important after what she's been through."

"Well, it didn't seem to take her long to recover," Michael said. He sat down and picked up a paper cup of soda. For a moment Kate felt irritated. Because of her background, she had always looked for a man who avoided drinking to excess, but perhaps never drinking at all was a bad thing. It occurred to her for the first time that Michael might be terribly afraid of losing control.

He squeezed her hand. "It was sweet to see you at work last week," he told her. "I suppose that you could do that any-where. Or even have a private practice."

"I like working in the school setting," she said, her mind else-where. "You get more feedback about behavior and change."

He didn't respond, and she craned her neck, looking first to the ladies' room and then to the door, hoping that this mad scheme with Billy would work out. At that moment, Billy walked into the bowling alley. He spotted Kate before she could even raise her hand and walked over to their lane. Damn Bina, Kate thought. It was going to be difficult enough to subtly show him who his date was; now it would be virtually impossible. What the hell was she doing in the ladies' room for so long, taking a shower?

Kate introduced Billy to Michael. They shook hands. Kate couldn't help but notice how incredibly attractive Billy looked. He was wearing very old black jeans and a slightly clingy T-shirt of the same color that revealed the body of a natural athlete. She could see his arms and figured the guy didn't have 2 percent body fat. Typical narcissist, she thought. He must be a gym rat to have that kind of bicep definition. And she was amused to see that he had his own equipment. She hadn't known anybody who owned their own bowling ball in fifteen years.

Billy dropped his bowling bag on the seat next to Kate. "Let's rock and bowl!" he said, looking down at her a little too intensely.

Kate stood up quickly, scanning the bowling alley. "Bina will be back in a moment," she told him.

"Fine," Billy said, clearly not at all interested in Bina's whereabouts. To her alarm, he put his arm around Kate's shoulder. "Hey, you look great," he said, his voice way too personal.

Kate quickly stepped out of his embrace and moved closer to Michael, who was still seated. She put her hand on Michael's shoulder. Billy paused for a moment, then sat down and began to put on his own shoes. Kate, feeling both guilty and awkward, sat beside Michael. Michael, as if in response to Billy's overly warm greeting, put his arm across the back of the seats and rested it on her shoulder.

Billy looked up from his laces and eyed the two of them. "You two just meet?" he asked. "Or are you related?"

"No. We've been going out for a while now," Michael replied innocently. Kate thought she saw Billy's face color up, but he looked down again at his shoes.

Just then, to Kate's enormous relief, Bina returned to the lane. She looked as if the entire research staff of Max Factor had worked her face over. A great look for bowling. But when she smiled, her natural warmth showed. "Well, hey," she said to Billy as she sat beside him.

Billy looked from Kate to Bina. And then he looked back across at Kate, leaning against Michael's proprietary arm. "I was afraid you weren't going to make it," Bina told him. Kate tried to avert her eyes, but not soon enough. From the look on Billy's face, she knew that he now understood what was going on and was clearly unhappy with the territory as it was currently staked. She decided to hope for the best.

"Okay," Kate said, sliding into the double seat behind the scorekeeping board. She quickly entered their information into the keypad, and their names lit up on the overhead screens—hers with Michael's and Bina's with Billy's. "Now we can get started."

"Yeah," Billy said, looking at the screen, "but what are we starting?"

Kate thought she heard some anger or maybe bitterness in his voice but felt it was best to just ignore it.

"We can't start," Bina whined. "I haven't found a ball." She looked at Billy and did everything except bat her eyes. "Would you help me?" she asked. Then she licked her lips. Kate wondered if she had confused Elliot's ridiculous instructions and was trying to annoy instead of arouse.

Billy shot Kate a look, and it said everything. Then he grabbed Bina's hand and, without taking his eyes off Kate, stood up. "Sure," he said. "I'm no expert with balls, except my own, but I'll try. Though it often seems to me that other people have a lot of balls."

Kate blushed. She knew this type of behavior; she had seen it with her child patients. He was going to act out and make sure she paid for her little deception by being as horrible as possible. Billy and Bina left the pit, and Michael waited until they were out of earshot.

"Charming," he said. "Will he discuss other parts of his anatomy as the night progresses?" He sat beside Kate in the scoring seat. "How long have you known him?" he asked, echoing Billy, consciously or not.

Kate was surprised to feel a slight surge of pleasure at his possessiveness. "Oh, he picked up Bina at that wedding I went to," she replied.

"A friendly guy. And well equipped," was all Michael deigned to say.

Then Bina and Billy returned from the rack. Bina was carrying a hideous-looking bowling ball, blue with patches of fuchsia. "We finally found a ball that matches my scarf!" Bina said with excessive enthusiasm. "Billy helped me." Kate restrained herself from shaking her head. Bina was acting as if the selection of a piece of sporting equipment were akin to slaying a dragon. She held up the hideous ball, then nearly dropped it. Kate remembered, all at once, just how klutzy Bina was. "Klutzy, smutzy," Mrs. Horowitz used to say. "As long as you get good grades." Bina then attempted to stick her plump fingers into the tiny holes.

Billy, meanwhile, unzipped his bag and took out a much larger black ball. "And look," he exclaimed, laying on the sarcasm, "I found a ball that matches my outfit, too!"

Kate, concerned about hurting Bina's feelings, decided to comment. "Well, *you're* wearing all black and you coordinated by bringing your own ball."

Billy served Kate an insincere smile. "That did make it less of a challenge." He looked over at Michael. "Hey, Mike, how big is your ball?"

"Ten pounds," Michael answered. "And I prefer to be called Michael," he added flatly.

Kate saw him narrow his eyes. It was clear that he wasn't enjoying himself. But it seemed as if he also sensed or observed that something was going on between her and Billy.

Bina reached over for her cola. "I haven't been bowling since Annie Jackson's sixth-grade birthday party. Remember, Katie?"

"How could I forget?" Kate said, smiling at the memory. "I threw up Pop Rocks all over myself."

"Oh, yeah!" Bina squealed. "Gross." She looked over at Billy, licking her lips again.

Billy joined the two of them at the scoreboard. "Oh, I don't know," he said, and put his foot down right beside Kate's and on her shoelace. Kate moved her foot away, pulling out the bow. "I think some women look cute in their own vomit." Kate, totally nonplussed, pulled her foot up to the seat and quickly retied her shoe.

"Well, I'm sure you've had plenty of opportunity to see it," she said, and turned to Michael. "Billy works in a bar."

"Lots of chances with drunken women," Billy said. "Right, Mike?"

"Michael," Michael corrected. "Not in my experience."

"Well, owning my own bar, I'm sure I have more experience," Billy said coolly.

Kate was surprised to hear that Billy owned the Barber Bar, if that was, in fact, the truth.

Billy stared her down for a moment and then wrapped his arm around Bina. "I'm sure I have a lot more experience in quite a few things," he said.

Chapter Twenty-four

Ouch!" Bina yelled. "Ow. Ow." She shook her hand as if it were a limp fish at the end of a pole, then put her index finger into her mouth. Kate hadn't been looking, but as Bina had tried to retrieve her ball from the ball return, her finger had been crunched by another ball spewed from the maw of the machine.

Billy bent over her hand, taking it in his. "Are you okay?" he asked.

Kate turned away from the two of them and looked at Michael, who was sitting beside her. When she had put together this ridiculous scheme, she had thought of Billy and how he might be angry and difficult. She had thought of Bina and how she might be disappointed. But she hadn't thought of Michael and the effect that a night of Brooklyn bowling might have on him. She put her arm around him. He was a lot quieter than usual and obviously disturbed by his poor performance. While he was not a jock, Michael was fit and played squash regularly, where, she knew, he was a tough competitor. He didn't like to lose.

Kate looked down at the board, then put her head on Michael's shoulder. "The score doesn't matter," she cooed, realizing at once that her tone was the one she used when she was talking to her young patients. "Are you having fun?"

Michael ignored the question, as he so obviously was not. "I can't believe I'm coming in third," he said, and shook his head. Kate wondered if she should try to do poorly, just so Michael would have a shot at second place, but she knew that her score and Bina's didn't matter. Michael was pissed because Billy was beating him, and doing it by so wide a margin.

Just then Billy approached them. He picked up his drink from the holder, then shook his head as he took a look at the scoreboard. "Well, we're all having a pretty dismal night," he commented, but Kate thought she saw him smirk as he went up to help Bina prepare for what would almost certainly be yet another gutter ball.

Kate ignored them and turned back to Michael. She felt responsible for this and didn't like to see him upset. If she was completely truthful with herself, she'd have to admit she also didn't like to see him bested by Billy. It was foolish, she told herself, to feel that way or to allow Michael to have that view. It was some vestige of the *Homo sapiens* fight for alpha male position. "People often confuse athletic scores with personal identity," she said.

"Sure. When the Cubs lose my world falls apart," Michael said, almost sneering.

Michael was from Chicago, and the fact was that he did root for the pathetic Cubs. But this wasn't the Cubs pitted against another, superior baseball team. This was Michael pitted against Billy Nolan. And Michael, in a word from her youth, was getting *shmeisted*.

"This isn't that hard. I can't believe I haven't rolled a strike."

"Oh, it's just for fun," she tried to remind him. "Bowling was never your game. Anyway," she said, waving toward Bina, who was still at the line, dithering, "no one does worse than Bina."

Billy, sipping his soft drink, overheard her, grinned, and laughed. "Eye on the head pin, Bina," he encouraged. Then he put back his cup. "Hey, wait!" he called. He left the pit and stepped behind her, put his arms around her, and changed her stance.

Kate, watching them, felt a twinge of what she wouldn't admit was jealousy. Then Bina, guided by Billy, released the ball down the lane—this time with her eyes closed. The group watched as the ball rolled directly down the middle of the lane and almost miraculously knocked over all the pins. Kate's mouth dropped, but not as much as Michael's pride.

"Omigod! Omigod! I hit them! I hit them all!" Bina shouted. She did a victory dance that involved reaching both arms up to the ceiling and incidentally exposing a significant part of the fuchsia underpants beneath her tiny skirt. Kate watched as bowlers from other lanes smiled, pointed, and gave her a thumbs-up sign.

"Touchdown!" Bina yelled. She gave Billy a big hug, then ran over to Kate. "Katie, I can't believe it," she said, her arms under Kate's while she jumped back and forth. "I knocked them over!" Then, flinging her arms wide, she accidentally knocked the beer out of Kate's hand and all over the front of Michael's shirt.

"Bina, you seem to be on a roll at knocking things over," Kate said as Michael jumped up.

"I'm so sorry," Bina said to Michael, flushing bright red. She grabbed for the already damp Bowl-a-Rama cocktail napkin that was lying on the scoreboard top. Michael was holding his shirt away from his body, his elbows extended like a man impersonating a rooster. Kate could see the beer had soaked not only his shirt, but also his pants. When Bina began to dab ineffectually at his chest and crotch, Michael took a step backward.

"No. Let me help," she begged. "I can get it right out. Club soda on the shirt. Club soda and salt on your pants."

Kate almost smiled, despite Michael's discomfort. The Horowitz family were experts at removing every stain from every possible material: wine on linen, ballpoint on silk, tar on leather. The list was endless and often discussed. Kate took Michael's arm. He looked at her helplessly.

"Hurry up," Bina insisted, taking his other arm. "We have to do it before the stain sets. Trust me, I know."

"She does," Kate said, nodding at him.

"Maybe it's all right," Michael volunteered, but then he looked down at himself.

"Go with her," Kate said.

"Yeah. Let's get you cleaned up," Bina told him as she led him away from the lane.

Kate watched him go and felt deeply sorry for having invited him. He disappeared into the crowd like a damaged ship being pulled by a determined little tugboat. Kate sighed.

"Not Mike's day."

Kate turned around to face Billy, who was leaning on the side of their banquette, his legs crossed and his eyebrows raised. "Not much of a player."

"Just because he's in third place . . . ," Kate began.

"Last," Billy corrected her.

"Excuse me?" Kate asked. Billy pointed at the electronic scoreboard. He took a step closer to her. She felt his arm against her shoulder. She also felt heat rise up from her chest to her neck and hoped he wouldn't notice the blush on her face.

"Last," he said again, and leaned forward to tap the score. "Since Bina's strike, he's in last place." Kate felt a little light-headed. Billy Nolan was so close to her, she could smell his soap and the heat of his body. For an insane moment she had an impulse to close her eyes and fall into his arms. Instead she took a step away and picked up a bowling ball.

"You're just jealous," she said without thinking, not quite sure what she meant.

He turned to face her instead of the score. "You're right, I am," he said in a steady voice.

"You are?" Kate asked, but she couldn't match his steadiness. She was surprised at this admission.

"Yeah," Billy said. And then he continued, a lot less casually. He lowered his voice, but it rose in intensity. "I thought I was going on this date with you. And you knew that. I can't believe I fell for the old bait and switch, or that you played me that way."

Kate dropped the ball back into the ball return. Despite the truth of what he said, she felt indignant. She'd done it for the best of reasons, and who was he to claim a higher moral ground? "You're on a date with my best friend," she said defensively.

"Really?" Billy asked, his voice heavy with sarcasm. "Is that what you thought?"

"Yes," Kate lied. "And then you insult my boyfriend and come on to me. What is wrong with you?"

"Well, for one thing, I like to pick my own women," Billy said. And he looked her over from head to toe. He paused, took a couple of steps away from her, and sat on the banquette, crossing an ankle over his knee. "For another, I certainly wouldn't pick Bina," he said bluntly.

Kate felt a surge of anger on behalf of her friend. She had feared something like this would happen, and now her main concern was that Billy would humiliate Bina. She silently cursed Elliot, Barbie, and the whole bunch of them. Playing with people's lives was always dangerous, and right now she was the one about to face retribution for their stupidity. "That is just plain rude," she told him.

"Rude to be angry when I'm tricked? I'm just calling it as I see it," Billy said.

"I guess that's why everyone calls you like they see you," Kate snapped.

"What's that supposed to mean?" Billy said, sitting upright and putting both feet on the ground.

Kate controlled herself, but with difficulty. She didn't want to see Bina hurt, and she had to try to get out of this somehow. She turned away from him. "It means every woman in Brooklyn, perhaps with the exception of Brooklyn Heights, knows your reputation," she said, and went to pick up her purse.

"What reputation?" Billy asked. He stood up and followed her. When she didn't answer him or turn around, he put a hand on her shoulder and turned her to him. "What reputation?" he asked again.

"Oh, come on. Don't you know everyone calls you 'Dumping Billy'?" Kate answered, exasperated.

" 'Dumping Billy'? Why?"

Kate looked up at him. He was tall, at least seven or eight inches taller than she was, but she could see his eyes cloud. He seemed to have been completely unaware of his nickname.

"Why the hell would they call me that?" he asked.

"Because you dump every woman you date." Kate looked toward the bar and the rest rooms beyond. When would Michael and Bina return? She was tired of this conversation and wanted only to salvage the rest of the evening.

"I don't dump women," Billy said. For the first time, he seemed defensive. "I mean, I've broken up relationships, but I don't dump people."

"Oh, come on," Kate said. "My friends know a dozen women you've dumped. I didn't make up the nickname. Anyway, your behavior is pathological."

"What?" Billy demanded. He'd clearly gone from defensive to angry.

Kate knew she'd gone too far and spoiled what was left of the evening, but she couldn't resist taking a deep, annoyed breath. "Path-o-log-i-cal," she said slowly, as if for a child. "It means—"

"Any abnormal variation from a sound condition," Billy finished for her.

Kate blinked, taken aback. Billy pushed past her, grabbed his bag, and turned back.

"It also means I'm out of here. The bad news is, I did just dump Bina, but I wish I could've dumped you. The good news is that now your friend Michael has a chance of coming in third."

He was gone in a minute, and Kate stood beside their almost deserted lane, wondering what she could possibly say when Bina and Michael returned.

Chapter Twenty-five

The next morning, Kate sat in her office face-to-face with a young girl. Tina, a high-spirited third grader, was sitting in one of the tiny chairs with a big bandage on her arm. Tina had injured herself over and over, but Kate didn't think clumsiness or a need for self-mutilation were behind the injuries. She thought Tina probably had a repetition compulsion: For some reason she had to keep acting out the trauma of being challenged and frightened and forced to respond. While many professionals in her field dismissed the idea, Kate had always found the concept valid.

She had been talking with the child for over an hour and she felt some progress had been made. "So you won't do that again?" she asked Tina.

Tina looked up at her and smiled. "No," she said, then added, "Not unless Jason dares me."

"If he dares you to jump off the roof . . ." Kate stopped herself. Where had that come from? It was the kind of line her father might have used. Instead, she smiled, almost closed her eyes, and leaned forward toward Tina, the girl who couldn't refuse a dare. "I dare you not to," she said. "I bet that you have to do anything Jason dares you to."

"Do not," Tina said.

"Dare you not to," Kate said.

She wasn't sure the counterdare would work. Tina really might jump off the roof. Just then the bell rang and interrupted her thoughts. "We'll talk about your friendship with Jason next time, okay, Tina?" Kate said.

Tina nodded again, slid off the chair, and bounded from the room.

"I told you, it just won't work." Kate said each word slowly and distinctly so Elliot might possibly get it through his mathematical head. "Zero, null set, no way. *Impossible*. Finished. Kaput."

"But are you sure?" Elliot asked.

She gave him a look. They were going to their gym, Crunch—a place that ran cool ads on television and that had as its motto "No judgements." But Kate was ready to make a few judgments now. Even for him, Elliot looked awful. They were walking up Eighth Avenue, and he was wearing baggy shorts, a torn T-shirt, and a madras fishing hat that must have come from some thrift shop, while his feet displayed two mismatched socks. "You know," Kate said, trying to change the subject, "you look like a recently released mental patient."

"Thank you," Elliot said. "It was the look I was going for. Brice helped me."

Against her will, Kate smiled. How a guy as fashion impaired as Elliot could couple up with stylish Brice was inconceivable to her. But they were a solid and happy couple with enough things in common to make their lives congenial and enough respect for their differences to make life interesting. It was hard to imagine Brice letting Elliot out of the house dressed like this, but she knew that he'd probably just shrugged, laughed, and hugged Elliot. Then the image of Michael and his sports jacket the night before came unbidden to her mind. Just because Michael dressed inappropriately was no reason for her to judge him, but somehow she did.

"I want to find out exactly what happened, sentence by sentence, word by word, act by act." They turned west on 18th Street, and Kate looked at Elliot with hostile amazement.

"If you think I'm going to go through last night one more

time, you can think again." They reached the door to the gym. "And you can warm up by yourself."

They had both gotten memberships at Crunch so that they could work out together and force each other to go. It usually worked pretty well, but Kate was in no mood to dissect the previous evening. The fact was she was a little bit ashamed, both of her ruse and of her behavior. But that didn't mean she had to tell Elliot that. At the door to the women's locker room, she turned to him and said, "Spot yourself. I'm going to find a straight guy to work out with."

After she had changed into her workout pants and loose top, twisted her hair into a scrunchie and stuck it on top of her head with hairpins, then stowed her stuff in the locker, she came out to find Elliot standing there, just where she'd left him.

"Oh, come on," he pleaded as if she hadn't just been gone for ten minutes. "You never tell me anything anymore."

"Oh, for heaven's sake." Kate laughed, exasperated. But she couldn't refuse him. So she went into detail about the whole awful night—how Barbie had dressed Bina up like a Las Vegas showgirl, how Billy had showed up thinking he was her date and not at all happy to find out he was Bina's, and how they'd finally gotten into an argument at the end of the evening.

By then they had reached the mats, and Kate grabbed a big blue plastic ball to begin their warmup. She leaned backward over it to stretch the front of her body. The stretch felt good, and she took a deep, soothing breath. Stretching was the only part of working out that she actually enjoyed, and she needed it after last night and today. While Brian Conroy had improved and was able to cry over the loss of his mother, a new child, Lisa Allen, had been sent to her because she seemed "withdrawn." And Tina Foster had been sent to her for the second time because she had taken a ridiculous dare and jumped off the top of the playground wall. Kate sighed.

She and Elliot now clasped hands and bent away from each other in order to stretch out their backs. They had been coming to the gym together for seven months now and had their routine down pat. They continued to pull each other—first arms, then legs—around the big blue ball. "Well, you know," Elliot said, "I got a partial report from Bev last night, who got it from Bina."

"Bev called you?"

"Oh, yeah. She and I are bonding. I want to be godfather to the baby."

"God forbid," Kate said. She really felt irritated that Elliot was so . . . integrated with her Brooklyn friends and pissed that Bev would stick her two cents in. "Look, I didn't think Billy Nolan would like Bina. It turns out that he resented the way I manipulated him and—shock, shock—he doesn't want to go out with Bina despite Barbie's outfits, Brice's haircut, and your plan. Not only that, *I* don't like him. He isn't a nice person."

"*You* don't have to like him," Elliot began. "*I* don't have to like him. Even *Bina* doesn't have to like him. She only has to date him for an average of two point four months. That's roughly ten weeks, or seventy days—give or take."

"But he has to like Bina," Kate pointed out. "And he doesn't. Case closed."

"Technically we don't know that," Elliot gurgled with his head tilted backward. He was arching himself in a back bend.

"What do you mean?" Kate asked, standing upright again.

"I mean, from your retelling it sounds like he had the argument with you," Elliot said.

"Yes. So?"

"So his problem is with you, *not* Bina." Elliot looked at her sternly.

"Elliot, trust me. There was no chemistry between them."

"Kate, from what you told me and what Bev said Bina said, I think last night was an opener. The fact is, you did trick the guy and he was angry at you and he doesn't like you, but he might, given the chance, like Bina—at least long enough to date her for seventy-three days."

"Oh, Elliot, don't be ridiculous," Kate snapped. She let go of his hands, and he went sprawling, his butt hitting the mat with a splat. "Are you trying to tell me the fiasco was my fault?"

Elliot rose slowly from the mat, his hands rubbing his backside. "That's exactly what I'm telling you. That and the fact that you owe him an apology."

Kate stared at him in amazement. "That is the most outrageous thing I ever heard," she told him. "I would never apologize to that insufferable, arrogant . . ." She turned and began to walk away.

"You like him, don't you?" Elliot asked.

Kate stopped where she was, swung around, and stared at him. "I do not!" she said.

Elliot shrugged. "Just asking," he told her. "It's just that I've never seen you this excited about Michael." He threw his towel over his neck and sauntered toward the treadmills.

"Leave Michael out of this," Kate snapped. She took a deep breath. Elliot, who probably knew her better than anyone, was pressing all her buttons. But she wouldn't let him. As she watched him set the program on his treadmill, his back turned to her, she made herself slowly and carefully go over the facts and feelings from the previous night. Maybe she *had* been both a catalyst and a stumbling block. Maybe if she hadn't been in the way, Billy would be interested in Bina. He seemed to have dated every other woman east of Court Street. However, even if she had gone about it badly, she knew her intentions had been good. She got onto the treadmill beside Elliot and punched in her own stats and program.

As she started walking, she said, "If you believe in this and Bina believes in this, I'll do what I can to make it work. But I can't make him date her." And not for two point four months, she thought. I don't believe he can rise to the challenge. The image stopped her in her tracks, and she almost flew off the back of the treadmill.

"Have you just thought of something, or are you just being klutzy?" Elliot asked as she regained her position and matched her stride to his.

"Maybe I have," Kate admitted. "But I hate the idea of apologizing to him. Do I have to?"

"Kate," Elliot said, ignoring her tone, "I don't see that you have much of a choice. It doesn't matter that you don't believe in the 'silly' plan. Bina does, you are her best friend, and you alienated Billy. You have to apologize."

God, Kate thought. I hate how Elliot is always right.

Chapter Twenty-six

On Tuesday morning, Kate stood in her bedroom before a full-length mirror, holding a hip but dignified blouse up to herself. Deciding against it, she threw it onto the pile of rejected clothes that had already formed on her bed. "What am I going to wear?" she asked her reflection. She turned away and paused for a moment. Why did she even care? Billy meant nothing to her, despite his obvious attractions. She went to her tiny closet and began to look for the green crew-neck top that looked so good on her. As she pulled it off the hanger, she stopped dead. Billy Nolan was taking up more space in her mind than he ought to. And he had seen her before. It wasn't as if she were going to make a different impression on him this time.

She took a deep breath and looked back steadily at herself. "Hello," she said as if talking to someone else. "Billy, I wanted to apologize for my behavior the other night. . . ."

She gritted her teeth. This was more difficult than she had imagined. She thought of all the children she had asked to engage in role-play: children who were supposed to talk to the fathers who had left the family, children who were tired of being scolded, children who had to practice asking for what they wanted. Now it was her turn, and the experience was humbling. It was leaving her with a deeper sense of compassion for her little clients.

The phone rang and she was relieved for the distraction, until she saw the phone number. Somehow, she didn't feel like speaking to Michael right now, and it was odd for him to be calling her on a school morning. Reluctantly, she picked up the phone.

"Hi," he said cheerfully. "Did I wake you up?" Kate assured him that he hadn't. "Look, I just thought that we might get together tonight."

For a moment, Kate was confused. They never got together on Tuesdays. It was always Wednesdays. "Is something wrong?" she asked.

"Yeah. I miss you," Michael said.

"I miss you too," she replied automatically. Then she paused, surprised to realize it wasn't true. But why not? she wondered. Would she perhaps be missing Michael right now if she weren't so focused on Billy? She felt a stab of irritation. No, of course not! It was ridiculous. "I'm sorry, but I . . . I have errands I have to run tonight."

"Oh. Okay. No problem. See you tomorrow, I guess."

"Yes," Kate said. "I'll see you tomorrow." She hung up the phone, sighed, and went back to the task at hand.

Later that day, after school, Kate arrived at the Barber Bar, her hair perfectly coiffed, looking as if she were about to take over a Fortune 500 company. She'd taken the subway from school to the closest stop. All was quiet in the area, and the bar itself looked closed, but she knocked on the door anyway. A woman's voice called out.

"We ain't open until—" The door jerked open and a tall, skinny woman in her late thirties in old jeans and a cut-off top stood before her. She was polishing a glass with the apron she had on and looked at Kate suspiciously. "Hey, listen. If you're lost, I'm dyslexic, so I don't give directions. And unless you're a customer you don't get to use this toilet." She was about to slam the door when Kate put up her hand and held it open. Then the woman paused. "The redhead," she said as if she already knew everything about her.

"Excuse me?" Kate asked. Had her reputation preceded her? "Actually, I'm looking for someone who works here . . . Billy Nolan." She blushed, thinking of all the women who must have turned up on this doorstep and said the very same thing.

"Of course you are," the woman said tiredly. "But he ain't on tonight until six."

Kate looked at her watch. She had almost two hours to wait. She sighed, more aggravated than ever. "Well, thank you anyway," she said, and turned to leave. She'd find somewhere in this ruin of a neighborhood to have a cup of coffee.

But before she'd taken more than three steps, the barmaid called after her. "Hey! You the one who told him his nickname?"

Kate turned around and nodded. "Dumping Billy," she said. "Isn't that what everyone calls him?"

"Yeah. He just didn't know it." She laughed. "Put him in quite a spin." She looked Kate over again.

"Well, I'll come back later," Kate said. At least she'd had some impact on the arrogant bastard. That might help her on this errand.

"Look, if you gotta see him now, he lives above the bar." She pointed to a buzzer on the other side of the doorway.

"That's okay. I'll come back another—"

Before Kate could get the words out, the woman rang the buzzer and shouted into the intercom. "Hey, Billy! You got company and—surprise, surprise—it's a woman."

"Thanks, Mary," Billy's voice said through the speaker. "I'll buzz."

Kate gave Mary a small half smile. "Thanks," she said, although she wasn't sure she meant it.

"Don't mention it, Red," the barmaid replied.

"I'm Kate," Kate told her.

A smile spread across Mary's face. "Oh. Kate . . . ," she said knowingly, and she went back into the bar.

The door buzzed open. Kate smoothed her hair once and put her hand on the doorknob. She ascended the steps to the landing of the first floor, where a door stood open. She peered in at the room before her. It was not at all what she would have predicted. Instead of being a "bachelor pad" filled with empty pizza boxes and furniture that looked as if it had fallen off a truck, the room had a polished wooden floor, a shabby but attractive Persian rug, a big worn brown leather Chesterfield sofa, and two walls of bookshelves filled to the ceiling with hundreds of books. A window seat was built into one bookshelf wall, and the window was open. Through it there was the view of a tree and a bit of the sky, though the blowing white curtains kept obscuring the small vista. Altogether it was charming and far more homey and sophisticated than Kate would ever have given Billy Nolan credit for.

Billy sat at a mahogany desk with his back to her, transfixed by the laptop screen in front of him. Kate entered the room and looked around. Her surprise continued to grow. Almost half the books on the shelves were in French, and she now could see two nicely framed Daumier prints. A woman must have furnished this place, she thought. "Hello," she said.

Billy did not take his eyes off the monitor. "Hold on. Hold on. I'm just catching up on my e-mail," was all he offered as a greeting.

"This won't take long," Kate began. Billy pulled his hands off the keyboard and spun around. There was an awkward silence.

"I d-d-didn't realize it was you," he stammered. "I thought I had to interview a n-n-new barmaid."

"I don't think I'm qualified for the job," Kate said, and was then ready to bite her tongue. She sounded snotty, and she really hadn't meant to.

Billy stood up. "So did you just come over here to turn down a job offer, or is there more to this unexpected visit?" he asked.

The two of them stood across the room from each other, the sofa and plenty of tension between them. Kate tried to decide whether it would be best to just blurt out her apology and throw out her dare or first try to bridge the gap between them. Everything she had practiced seemed inappropriate. "I wanted to . . . ," she began.

"Yes?" Billy raised his eyebrows. It was annoying to see how attractive he was, even with his hair in disarray and his shirt untucked and open to the third button. She tore her eyes away from him.

"I wanted to apologize for . . ." It was coming out wrong. "I wanted to apologize for not telling you the truth the other night."

Billy laughed. "That doesn't sound like much of an apology to me."

"I realize after what happened I may not be your favorite person, but that's not what counts," she explained. She put her purse on the desk.

"It isn't?" Billy asked.

"No. What counts is that Bina really likes you," Kate said. This was going badly. She was being either too direct or too indirect and was annoyed at her inability to really express herself to this guy. "And I think you might like her."

"Oh, really?" Billy smirked. "And what would give you insight into my feelings?"

"Look, it's none of my business, but—"

"Well, you finally got something right," he said, and sat on the Chesterfield. "What is your business, anyway?"

"I'm a psychologist," she said.

He shook his head. "I should have known," he muttered. "Nothing worse than a psychologist except a psychiatrist."

"How would you know?" she asked. "Have you dated both?"

"No. I consulted both. A long time ago. And they were ineffectual intellectuals."

She wondered what a mook like him had gone into therapy for but knew better than to ask. She just walked over to the little window seat and tried again.

"I don't like this 'Dumping Billy' stuff," he said.

"I'm sorry. I shouldn't have said anything, but I'm not responsible for the name. Apparently, everybody uses it."

"Apparently," he said dryly. "As if my personal life is anyone else's business."

Here was her chance to put in one more plug for Bina. She pushed forward. "Well, that's why I dropped by. Of course, it's none of my business, but I think you two would be very . . . you know . . . good for each other . . . which would be quite . . . something . . . so what I'm saying is basically what I have already said . . . you know?" What the hell had she just said? she thought. She'd never been less articulate in her whole life.

"Actually, no," Billy said, smiling gently at her obvious unease.

"Oh, I just knew you would make this difficult!" Kate stood up and walked to the door in frustration. It was never so hard to speak with children. Or to Elliot. Or Bina, the girls, or even Michael. Why was she having such a hard time talking to Billy Nolan?

"Why should I go out with Bina? I pick my own women. And she looks like a husband hunter," Billy said. "Not my type."

Kate could take his slight mocking of her, but how dare he insult her friend! "That is totally out of line. You're the loser!" she almost shouted at him.

"Me?!" Billy asked. He got up from the couch and faced her. "Hey, I own this place. I built it up from nothing. I've got bigger plans, too! I'll be opening a restaurant next year."

"Yes. But can you manage one decent relationship?" she asked.

"And I can date anyone I want!"

"Not anyone. You can't date me!" Kate flared. "You are still just a Mick who never even got out of Brooklyn. The trick with you is you are slightly better looking on the outside than you are on the inside, and the inner and outer you are in constant conflict. That's why you don't know you're a loser." Kate was out of breath, and her face was hot. This was not going well. She looked at Billy, who was surprisingly cool.

"Are you speaking as a doctor or as a bitch?" he asked with a coldness that cut right through her.

Kate opened her mouth, then checked herself, remembering her mission. She crossed to the desk, picked up her purse and muttered loudly enough for Billy to hear: "You couldn't do it anyway."

"Do what?" he demanded.

Kate turned around to face him, eyes blazing. They stared each other down as they had in the bowling alley the other night. "Nothing," she spat. "Absolutely nothing."

"Tell me," he said through clenched teeth, leaning across the back of the sofa toward her.

Kate almost smiled, because she knew that she'd be victorious. He was no more difficult than Tina Foster. "It's just that when I came here I knew you couldn't date Bina for more than a week or two," she said, self-assured. "You obviously have a repetition compulsion."

"A what?" Billy asked, indignant.

"A repetition compulsion," Kate replied impatiently.

"What's that? Some jargon from the *DSM-Four?*"

Kate was surprised he knew about the *Diagnostic and Statistical Manual of Mental Disorders.* The *DSM* was the bible of mental dysfunctions that was compiled regularly for mental health professionals. Still, she didn't let him see her reaction. "It's not a *DSM-Four* construct. It's an older Freudian theoretical position."

"I thought Freud was unpopular these days. Oedipus complex, penis envy. Isn't that all pretty much out-of-date? After all, he was a guy who didn't know what women wanted."

Once again, Kate was surprised by his casual familiarity with things she figured he had never heard of. "I think it's still valid," she said. "Especially in your case. It's roughly defined as compulsive neurotic behavior in which a person repeats an altered version of traumatic events from his past. Once it starts, the compulsion requires the person to keep doing the maladaptive behavior."

"Oh, really?" Billy asked. As she hoped, he was becoming belligerent. "And what maladaptive behavior would I be repeating?"

"An attempt at intimacy that has to be followed by abandonment. And each time you pick an inappropriate partner to ensure the eventual split."

"And how do you know all of this about me?" he asked.

"Well, I am a doctor," she said, "and I do know several of the inappropriate women you've played the pattern out with. I just thought Bina might be a real person, someone you could actually bond with. She isn't one of your typical Brooklyn big-haired bimbos. And she's quite sad at the moment. Anyway, it didn't work, and it doesn't matter to me or to Bina. I'm just sorry I gave you an easy excuse not to conquer it."

"You didn't give me anything but a headache," he shot back.

"Well, we're not really talking about me, are we? We're talking about you. And you find it impossible to date a nice girl with whom any kind of commitment might be possible."

"That isn't true," he told her.

"I guess that isn't why you have the nickname, then," she said.

"I'd have no problem dating Bina. She's a nice enough girl, and she knows how to have a good time. Unlike some uptight, word-dropping psychologists I've met. And I don't have a . . . petition . . . whatever."

"Sure you don't," she said.

"I don't," he insisted.

"Great. Then prove it," she said. "Date her for a couple of months without dumping her, and I will be proven totally and utterly wrong. Well, if you can manage a real relationship, you might also lose the nickname. But I don't think you can do it."

"Done," he declared. "And only because I want to. And because she's a nice girl. Not my type, but nice. And I'll see her as long as I want to. I don't need a shrink to manage it, or to psychoanalyze me later."

"I wouldn't dream of it." Kate smiled and headed to the door. She put her hand on the knob, but before she turned it, she looked back at Billy.

"I can give you Bina's number," she said.

"Thanks, but I already have it. And it's memorized: Bina Horowitz, on Ocean Parkway." He looked at her with a glint of triumph in his eye. And Kate, for some reason she didn't quite understand, was annoyed.

Well, her feelings didn't matter in this ridiculous escapade. She'd accomplished what she'd set out to do. So she simply opened the door, exited, and slammed it behind her.

Chapter Twenty-seven

Kate was almost a quarter of an hour early at LaMarca on Wednesday evening because she didn't want to be late. The restaurant, an unpretentious bistro in Chelsea, was not the kind of snotty place where you had to "wait at the bar until your party has joined you." Kate was seated at a window table and had a chance to freshen her lipstick and twist her hair up into a knot. Then she waited, trying hard not to think. Nestled next to her lipstick in the makeup bag she carried in her purse was a pretty blue box that contained a pair of new keys on a silver Tiffany key ring. The ring was actually more like a U than a circle, with sterling silver balls at each end that unscrewed so that keys could be added and subtracted easily. It also had a small silver dogtag on it. The number engraved on the sterling was registered at Tiffany's, and if the keys were ever lost and dropped in a mailbox, Tiffany's would return them. Kate felt that perhaps she had gone overboard, that she might be compensating with the gift for a diminution in her passion for Michael.

She'd tried over and over to analyze why she seemed to have cooled toward Michael. Certainly their sex was fulfilling and their relationship sound and based on shared interests, though she had never felt truly passionate about Michael as she once had for Steven. That, however, she had considered a good thing. After Steven, Kate had promised herself she would never allow an obsession with a man to take over her life. And until now she had been more than happy with Michael. Despite Elliot's prejudice against him, Michael was a grown-up—perhaps the first male grown-up in her life—and he respected and liked her. Unlike a lot of guys, Michael wasn't intimidated by her work, her looks, or her independence. And he was not the kind of man to run from intimacy. So why, she wondered, did she find herself resisting? Was she afraid of the next step in their relationship? She didn't think so. But as Anna Freud had pointed out, resistance was an unconscious thing.

"Would you like something to drink while you're waiting?" the waiter asked, startling her.

"A glass of Chardonnay, please," she said, and then felt a bit guilty, which in turn made her feel annoyed.

As she was taking her first sip of the wine, Michael strode in, an unusually wide smile on his face. He was, she reminded herself, very nice looking. Not dramatically gorgeous like that idiot in Brooklyn, but handsome in an understated way. His hair was thick, and a little silver was mixed prematurely with the brown. The steel-rimmed glasses he wore went well with his hair, and Kate had sometimes wondered if he knew that. If his shoulders were a little narrow, he made up for that with his height. Now, he bent over her, took her chin in his hand, and turned her head so he could kiss her on the mouth. She smiled at him, and he slipped into the banquette opposite her.

"Very nice choice," he said, looking around. They alternated in choosing restaurants, Michael most often referring to *Zagat* on-line, while Kate depended on Elliot, her own personal restaurant rating service.

"You seem in a good mood," she said.

"Better than good!" Michael told her. "I've gotten the offer from Austin." He beamed. "It's almost too good to be true."

"It's official?" Kate asked. She felt her stomach tighten.

"Well, as good as. I got a call from Charles Hopkins at the Sagerman Foundation, and he told me, in complete confidence, of course, that they had selected me and that I'd hear from Austin soon."

"Wow. So you'll chair a department?" Kate was impressed and delighted for Michael, but her feelings were mixed and she felt a kind of tension in her chest, as if her bra had suddenly become two sizes too small. Austin, Texas, was supposed to be a lovely place, with a great university and very pretty country-side. And for someone as young as Michael to get the chair-manship of a department was almost unheard of. But Kate didn't want to think of the ramifications: If Michael chose to go, would he ask her to go as well? And if he did, what would she say? She loved her job and her friends and . . .

The waiter approached again. "Something to drink, sir?" he asked.

Michael nodded. "A bottle of champagne, please."

Kate was startled, but she merely smiled. Michael was obvi-ously very excited.

When the champagne came, Kate toasted him. "To the smartest, most deserving man I know," she said, and she thought she saw Michael blush. The moment seemed appropriate, so she reached into her purse and took out the little blue Tiffany box. "I'm not sure these will be useful in Austin," she said, and placed the box between them on the table. "I would have picked something else, if I had known."

Then Michael did flush, either with pleasure or embarrass-ment—some men were awkward with gifts—and Kate felt that he would surely be disappointed. But he opened the box, held up the key chain, and grinned. "How nice," he said. "How very nice."

They ordered dinner, and Michael actually took a sip or two of champagne. He spent most of the time chatting about the Sagerman Foundation and the University of Texas. She was sur-prised to discover how unprepared she was for this eventuality, something that a part of her had been expecting for months. Why was that?

She had been waiting for a moment when he would ask her her opinion about what he should do or, at least, tell her his plans and ask if she might consider joining him. But it didn't seem to happen. He continued talking and it was hard for her to tell whether he had no intention of asking her to come or if he was simply taking her for granted.

After dinner they walked to her apartment. It was a balmy night, and Michael, swinging his briefcase with one hand, held her hand with the other. When they got to her door he reached into his pocket and took out the keys. "Allow me," he said, and opened the door for her. As they walked up the steps, Kate reached into her bag. For some reason she wanted to open her own apartment door, and she managed to beat him to it.

When they entered the living room, Michael threw his briefcase onto the sofa and immediately pulled off his tie. Kate thought he might be a little bit high from the bit of champagne that he had drunk. She, on the other hand, was as sober as a judge. In fact, she felt like a judge, busy weighing the pros and cons of the situation before her. When Michael took her hand and led her to her bedroom, she simply followed.

He began unbuttoning his shirt, sitting on the side of her bed. He took off his shoes, unsheathed his feet from their socks, and tucked the socks carefully into his shoes. When he stood up and undid his belt buckle, his chest bare, he looked over at her and smiled. "Do I have to undress you?" he asked.

Kate smiled back and hoped the smile didn't reveal her uneasiness. She wasn't uneasy because Michael would leave her. His great good humor was certainly inappropriate, and Michael was not an insensitive man.

Yet, like most men, he didn't feel her mood as he began to make love to her. She felt his hands on her waist, then lower, and he slipped her panties off. Then he moved his hands upward to cover her breasts. He kissed her, long and deeply, but Kate felt unmoved. When he began to touch her, she realized there was no way she could possibly have an orgasm. Ashamed to reveal herself, she simply eased herself into position over him and worked to make sure he achieved pleasure. But later, when they were finished, Michael sighed and dropped his head deep into the pillow. "You'll like Austin," he said.

Kate wasn't sure she'd heard the words. "What?" she asked.

"You'll like Austin," he said. "It's really great." Then he turned on his side and after a few deep breaths she knew he was sleeping.

She lay there silently but a storm of feelings swept through her. Had she just been proposed to? Clearly, Michael assumed not only that she was coming with him but that he didn't need to ask her to do it. He had talked plenty about the Sagerman chair and what it meant to him but never about what it might mean to her. She supposed that was because he knew it meant nothing. To him she meant nothing. She was someone who would go where he wanted. She couldn't believe his presumption or how little he knew her. Suddenly she felt deep shame, though she wasn't sure if it was for him or for her. How could she be sleeping with a man—how could he be intimate with her—when they didn't know each other at all?

Kate looked over his head at the dresser and the statue of the Virgin on it and wondered what was wrong with her.

Chapter Twenty-eight

It had been a few days since Kate had heard from Bina. When Bina did call, she just chattered on, not leaving a moment's opening for Kate's news. Apparently, she had been kept pretty busy by Billy. Kate supposed that was a good thing, since she needed time to figure out her own emotional landscape.

Still, after a few moments, Kate found herself feeling oddly resentful of Bina's harmless blather. She went on and on about Billy: how funny he was, what a good time they'd had over dinner, how sophisticated he seemed to be, and, last, what a gentleman he was. This, Kate knew, was Bina talk for him not jumping her bones when he said good night. "I can see why he gets all the girls," Bina said. "He just seems to really listen when you talk. You know how guys are so busy talking or else they kind of glaze over when you start talking?" Kate, thinking of Michael, reluctantly had to admit she knew. "Well, he doesn't do that."

"How refreshing," Kate said dryly. "So all is going well." Not that she was coming to believe in Elliot's ridiculous plan, but Billy's attentions must at the very least be a welcome break from the recent drama of Bina's life.

"Oh, we had the best time," Bina was saying. "He's just so much fun. When we went to this club that he knew, he . . ."

Kate found it hard to listen. Besides, she had her own tribulations. She hated to admit it, but she was beginning to believe that Elliot's assessment of Michael had been right. Although sweet and caring in some ways, Michael was self-involved, and lately she had found him . . . dull. In the past week, he had called her daily, giving her updates in what Kate was beginning to think of as the "Sagerman Situation." Since their dinner, he had spent most of their time together talking about nothing else.

". . . So then he goes, 'I would if I was crazy,' and I go, 'You are crazy. . . .'"

Kate had spent only a half day at Andrew Country Day today as the school year was winding down, and she had another half day tomorrow. She'd asked Michael over, but he had to attend a business lecture. Suddenly it came to her that tonight would be the perfect evening to take a break from her own relationship and catch up with Bina's. And as a psychologist, she was interested in seeing how well Billy was handling himself with Bina. So far all seemed well, but she would find out this evening, if Bina had the time and inclination to see her.

"Hey," she said, breaking into Bina's monologue, "you wanna walk the bridge?"

Since they were teenagers, Kate and Bina had found pleasure in walking from one side of the Brooklyn Bridge to the other. Now, since Kate had moved across it, they occasionally met in the middle and then walked to one side or the other.

"You kidding?" Bina said. "God, we haven't done that in ages."

"Why not?" Kate asked. "I'll buy you dinner in Brooklyn Heights. At Isobel's." They both loved the restaurant, and Kate knew it would be great bait.

"Same old Kate," Bina said. "Let's go Dutch."

"Same old Bina." Kate laughed, and they agreed to meet in the middle of the bridge.

The walk was good for Kate. It felt as if it blew some of the cotton out of her clogged head. She thought about some of the children and how they might get through the summer; she thought about Michael and his "proposal"; but mostly she thought about herself. She had to be prepared to talk to Michael. She felt as if she should be happy. After all, wasn't this possibility what she had been hoping for? Even if it was, though, something nagged her about the way Michael was going about it. It wasn't that he was cold, exactly. It was more self-centered—but then weren't all men? If she was brutally honest with herself, she also had to admit that she didn't like the idea that he might be assuming she would just drop everything and go with him. Still, she had no one to blame but herself for that. And why shouldn't he assume (if he was assuming) that she would be willing to go to Texas with him? Unfortunately, there were plenty of dysfunctional families and a need for child psychologists everywhere. She could set up her own practice. She would be the first member of her family not only to become a doctor, but also to marry one. The Horowitzes would be so proud! And if there was something, well, something missing in her relationship with Michael, wasn't everything imperfect in some way or other? Relationships were built over time, with both people willing to listen and try to understand each other. Michael would certainly listen.

Kate, her thoughts tumbling about in her head, walked faster than she expected. When she hit the midpoint of the bridge, she was alone and couldn't even see Bina in the distance. She stopped for a moment, turned north, and looked up the East River. The water looked almost blue, and the Williamsburg and Triboro Bridges sandwiching Manhattan created a magical illusion. When she looked to the right, Brooklyn seemed flat and dull in comparison. Kate felt a little tug on her heart. She looked back at Manhattan. There, small as it was, she had a place of her own, a place she had created and lived in. Could she leave it? Why should she? She was so deep in thought that she didn't hear Bina until her friend was beside her and put her hand on Kate's shoulder.

"A nickel for your thoughts," Bina said.

"A nickel? I thought it was a penny."

"Inflation. Plus your thoughts are better than other people's."

Bina took her hand and led her away from Manhattan, just the way they used to do.

"So how's it going?" Kate asked. "Have you been proposed to?"

Bina laughed. With the wind catching her hair and the sunlight glancing off the blond streaks, she looked almost as good as a shampoo ad.

"That guy is crazy," she said. "We went to this club where they know him. Well, they know him everywhere. So everyone was saying hello. We didn't even have to wait to get in." She began to ramble on with details that Kate found tedious. ". . . and then they start playing 'Flavor of the Week' . . . you know the song?" she asked Kate.

"Yeah. I know it," Kate said.

"Well, it must be like his theme song. And everyone in the bar starts shouting: 'Billy! Billy!' And at first he's like brushing it off, you know what I mean?" Bina asked.

"Yeah. I know," Kate replied. She was feeling odd, as if Bina's simple story were upsetting her on some high school level.

"Anyway, they won't stop. So he gets on the bar and starts singing at the top of his lungs. It was such a riot." Bina laughed at the memory.

"Sounds like one," Kate said dryly.

"He's so not like Jack!" Bina said. "Can you imagine Jack . . ." A look came over her face, as if she had just heard her own words.

Kate knew her friend well enough to recognize conflict. Could Bina be falling for Billy? "Thank God he's not," she said, looking at Bina. "Right?" Bina nodded, but she looked slightly dejected.

Max had dropped by several times to inform Kate of Jack's latest bulletins. It was hard to tell if he did it because he was trying to be helpful, was horrified, or was just gossiping. Certainly he seemed outraged as he told her about Jack's barhopping and his delight in the beauty and apparent availability of Hong Kong women, both Asian and Caucasian. She wondered whether Bina had heard anything, but she guessed that Bina still hadn't heard from Jack, who had been gone for so many weeks now.

They had come to the end of the bridge. "Do you want to walk on the promenade before we eat?" Kate asked.

"Sure," Bina said, and they made a right, crossed Cadman Plaza, passed Isobel's, and walked up Cranberry Street. This was the charming part of Brooklyn, which looked virtually unchanged since the late 1800s. Brownstones lined the blocks, complete with little gardens in the front, and the trees arched overhead. "So how are things with the fruits and nuts?" Bina asked.

Kate raised her eyebrows, taking Bina's remark as a comment on Elliot as well as her little clients. Then she realized that Bina probably didn't know the connotation that "fruit" had. "They're not nuts," she said. "Although their parents sometimes are."

"Sorry," Bina said. "Didn't mean to hurt your feelers."

Kate had to smile. She and Bina had replaced the word *feelings* with *feelers* when they were ten years old, and Bina still used the joke. Kate decided to change the subject. "What have you bought Bev for the shower?" she asked.

"Omigod! Omigod!" Bina exclaimed, a new level of animation lighting up her face. "I went with my mother to the Macy's on Flatbush. We got the most adorable outfit you've ever seen. Tiny little booties, a matching sweater, and a bonnet. You should see the stitches, they're tiny. You know, everyone's knitting now. You think Bev would believe me if I told her I knit it myself?" Kate shook her head. "I showed them to Billy and you should've seen the look on his face. I don't think he believed a real person could be that small."

"Why in the world would you show baby clothes to Billy?" Kate asked, and was surprised by the irritation in her voice.

They reached the promenade, and Kate looked around appreciatively. Bina didn't pay much attention. She chatted on about the shower and then suggested they walk back to Isobel's to eat.

Brooklyn Heights was not really part of Brooklyn, Kate had always thought. It was Manhattan once removed, and the view of the island from the promenade was breathtaking. They were quiet for a little while, and then Bina broke the silence. "All I've been doing is talking about myself. So," she said with contrived casualness, "where did you and Michael go last night?"

"We went to a movie," Kate informed her friend, and realized she had said it with about as much enthusiasm as if they had gone to a funeral.

"The new George Clooney?" Bina asked, her eyes lighting up. To Bina, George Clooney was a walking god.

"Not exactly," Kate began. How could she explain their visit to the Film Forum? "We went to see a documentary."

"Oh," Bina said. "About what?"

"Afghan women and their struggle for literacy," Kate said flatly.

Bina looked confused by the very thought. Kate figured that the last documentary Bina had seen was something they'd had to watch in grade school.

"That sounds . . . serious," Bina stammered, apparently unsure how to respond. She paused and looked across the bay at the Empire State Building, whose red, white, and blue lights had just been lit. "So, are you two getting serious?"

Kate could hear Mrs. Horowitz's voice channeled through Bina's lips. "I'm not sure," she said.

"There's not a serious bone in Billy's body . . . and what a body," Bina added.

"Bina!" Kate exclaimed. She looked over at her friend, whose change since Jack's departure seemed to be a lot more than physical. "You didn't . . . I mean, you wouldn't . . ." The thought of Bina with Billy disturbed her deeply. She tried to decide whether it was fear for Bina or envy.

"Of course not. I still love Jack," Bina said. Kate breathed a sigh of relief. "But I've got eyes. And he's got hands." Bina raised her brows playfully.

Kate was not sure this talk was as lighthearted as Bina was

making it out to be. She herself had felt Billy's devastating, if shallow, charm, and Bina was nothing if not inexperienced. "Bina, remember you are not supposed to be getting attached to this guy. He's only a means to an end—at least according to you and Elliot."

"I know. Believe me, I know. This whole plan is going to work. I just have a feeling." Bina paused. "And there's something else. Billy makes me feel . . . well, it's like I feel prettier when I'm with him." She looked away for a minute, and her face reddened. "I mean, I know people are probably looking at him, not me. But it makes me feel special, too." She smiled as if remembering something. "He always tells me how nice I look, and he notices things, like if I wear a barrette." She paused again. Then she lowered her voice, as if what she had to say were fragile and could be broken easily. "You know how much I love Jack." Kate nodded. "Well, I saw Max—you know, he's so nice. I don't understand why he isn't hooked up with someone. Anyway, he told me that Jack was sending him e-mails."

Kate managed not to gasp or show any emotion. A single one of those pictures would break Bina's heart.

"Anyway, I'm certain he misses me. And when he comes back, I'm sure he'll ask me to marry him."

The two of them walked down Henry Street. Kate was afraid to say a word to her friend. She didn't want to encourage her about Jack, and though she did want to discourage her about any attachment to Billy Nolan, she was not sure of her motives. They came to Henry's End restaurant, which was already bustling even though it was early for dinner. Well, Kate reminded herself, people ate earlier on this side of the river. "Are you hungry?" she asked. "Shall we eat here instead of Isobel's?"

"Sure," Bina told her. "Just don't make me eat a Bambi—and don't you eat Thumper." Henry's End was famous for wild game, though Kate would settle for steak.

"You can trust me on that," she told Bina.

Her friend took her arm. "I'll always trust you, Katie." They paused for a moment. "Hey, maybe you and Michael will get married and we could have a double wedding. My parents would love that."

Kate had a flash of an overdone ceremony, with the two of them walking down the aisle on Dr. Horowitz's arm. After that it would be a life full of documentaries, talks of anthropological discoveries, and Texas cocktail parties.

"Please, Bina," Kate said. "Not when we are near a very high bridge with a lot of cold water underneath it."

Chapter Twenty-nine

There's a possibility you're actually going to get engaged?" Elliot asked Kate, his face pruning up with disapproval. They were sitting in the Starbucks located exactly halfway between his apartment and hers.

"You better stop disliking him," Kate told Elliot. "If I *do* marry him, and you stay snotty, I won't be able to see you anymore."

"Wedding bells are breaking up that old gang of mine," Elliot warbled. Kate shook her head. "Like I'm really threatened that you'd give up our friendship," he continued. "Who else do you have to talk about every detail of your emotional seismograph and Barbara Pym, too?"

Kate smiled. It was true she described every tremor to Elliot, and like a geophysicist, he had predicted when the earthquakes were coming to rock her world. And Barbara Pym, a British author she and Elliot both reread frequently, was one of her secret addictions. Kate found her novels soothing because almost nothing happened in them; no one's feelings were hurt, and very little changed. A big event was a visit from the vicar, and most chapters ended with someone having a hot, milky drink. Which reminded Kate about Elliot's beverage.

"Did you know that there are more calories in that coconut frappuccino than three Big Macs?" Kate asked.

"Speaking of Max," Elliot said, ignoring her concern, "is he still sniffing around? And is he sniffing around you or Bina?"

Kate made a dismissive gesture. Like a good mom, Elliot always thought every man was in love with Kate, and if they weren't, he was offended. "He seems to be busy carrying news about Jack to anyone who'll listen. I think he still feels guilty because he introduced Bina to him. Anyway, he's harmless." Kate grimaced as Elliot used his straw to suck up every last molecule of liquid at the very bottom of his cup. "That is truly disgusting," she said.

"Well, I promise not to do it in front of your friends at the shower."

"Bev's shower?" Kate asked, her voice rising. "You're invited to Bev's shower?"

"You sound surprised," Elliot said. Then, in a mocking tone, he added, "You know, Bev and Brice and I are *very* close." Kate merely rolled her eyes.

"Hey, I saw Brian Conroy at lunch today, and he was actually laughing with two other little bandits," he continued. "I think they were slinging tunafish salad at the girls' table, but I didn't catch them at it. You might actually be doing some good work," he said.

They looked at each other for a long moment, Elliot smiling at her, his brown eyes warm and affectionate, and Kate basked in his approval. Then, as was their custom, they simultaneously shook their heads and bleated, "Nah!!"

"So what is it with you and Michael?" Kate asked, returning to the subject. "He's the kind of stable, nice guy you've wanted for me. And he likes me." As she looked down at the bracelet hanging from her wrist, her cell phone rang. She was expecting a call from Rita about drinks after Rita got out of work, which wasn't usually until six or seven o'clock. She pulled out her cell phone and, without even glancing at the caller ID, hit the green button.

"Hi," she said cheerfully, fully expecting Rita's nasal voice.

"Hi back atchya," said Steven's voice.

Kate felt her stomach contract and drop. Suddenly there wasn't enough air in her lungs. "Oh. Steven. Hello." She opened her eyes wide, but not as wide as Elliot's.

"Steven? *The* Steven?" he mouthed.

Kate, already rattled, looked away. She could feel her throat tighten.

"Am I getting you at a bad time?" Steven asked.

She wanted to say, "No. The bad time was the six months after you stopped calling," but needless to say, she didn't. Any time was a bad time to talk to Steven, as far as she was concerned. "No," she said. "I'm just having coffee with Elliot." She could have bitten her tongue. Why couldn't she have said she was with a date?

"Good old Elliot," Steven said, which made Kate even more annoyed with herself. "I miss him." His voice dropped a half register. "I miss *you,* too," he said.

Kate felt a flush spreading to her neck and chest. Meanwhile, Elliot was crouching in front of her, pulling his index finger across his throat to get her to cut off the conversation. She turned her head to the right.

Kate didn't need to be reminded of how dangerous Steven was. She had really loved him, and he had encouraged her attachment. Long ago, Kate had made a rule never to care for any man more than he cared for her. But Steven had cared for her—at least as long as the early lust stage had lasted. Then, after eighteen months his ardor and his commitment had dropped off. Kate hadn't felt it at first, and by the time she had realized that he was not still focused on her, she had run into him walking with the woman to whom his focus had shifted. When Kate, humiliated, had confronted him, he had been reluctant to admit the truth and had reassured her that nothing had happened between him and Sabrina, but after Kate broke up with him, a miserable six weeks later, he and Sabrina had hooked up. Now, the question Kate longed to ask was, "What's happened to Sabrina?" But she wouldn't let her curiosity overwhelm her common sense and pride.

"Look, I thought we might meet for a coffee or something," Steven said.

"I don't think so," Kate said. "I'm having coffee right now."

"You're not making this easy," Steven said, and the depth of feeling in his voice gave Kate a little thrill. All at once she realized what she had felt was missing in Michael—access to deeper feelings or the ability to express them.

But Steven's feelings, deep or not, had not been dependable. He was either an excellent actor (Elliot's opinion) or a man afraid of his own emotions, longing for connection and then backing away from it (Kate's theory). Kate still believed that Steven had loved her but had been afraid.

"Was it my job to make it easy?" Kate asked. Elliot rolled his eyes and put a hand over his own mouth to indicate that she should shut up—as if she didn't know that already. She swatted at him.

"Kate, you have every right to be pissed at me. But I swear that a day hasn't gone by that I haven't thought of you, or missed you, or even tried to get up the courage to phone you."

"It must have been a tough year," Kate said.

"Don't tell me you haven't thought of me," Steven said, and all of it—the miserable nights, the lonely weekends, the mornings she woke up alone and missing him—came rushing back.

"I've been pretty busy," she said. "And I'm about to get engaged. . . ."

Elliot bolted upright, gave her a thumbs-up with both hands, and then sank back into his chair as if exhausted.

There was silence at the other end of the phone, and Kate was torn between two emotions: She wanted Steven to give up and feel just a little bit of pain on her account. She also wanted him to try harder, and she was ashamed and embarrassed by that.

"Would that stop you from just having a drink with me?" Steven asked. "I really feel as if I need to tell you what happened. I mean, I'm in therapy now and . . . I just understand a few things that I didn't know before."

Kate wasn't sure she wanted to know what Steven had learned about himself. And she knew it wasn't a good idea to see him. But she felt an irresistible pull toward him. "How about next Monday," she said. "About four o'clock."

"That would be great," Steven said. "Onieal's?" It was a restaurant on Grand Street, a cool but lush bar and dining room. It had been a place they often went to, not far from his loft.

"No," she said. She didn't want to be seduced into drinks

followed by dinner followed by anything else. It was out of the question. She thought as quickly as she could about a more neutral site. "How about Starbucks?" And after he agreed she hung up and threw her phone into her purse.

"You are not going!" Elliot said. "You know why you're not going? Because I cannot hear one more word about that stupid fucking ass-fuck. Do you know how much Steven I had to live with last year? How many times can a man—even a gay man— sing 'I Will Survive' with you?"

Kate didn't know if she wanted to laugh or cry. They did actually sing Gloria Gaynor's song a few times, but only at Elliot's demand and because it always made her laugh.

"We wore out three CDs, and speaking of wearing out, you might be self-destructive, but I have a life and I can't go through another Steven bout. Maybe you don't remember what it did to you, but I do. And I just can't take it. Neither can you."

"I'm not going to go through another Steven 'bout,'" Kate snapped. "But he's in therapy and he probably needs some closure."

"What he probably needs is some pussy," Elliot said. "And that's fine with me as long as it isn't yours."

"Elliot!"

"I can't believe he calls you for the first time in a year in the middle of the afternoon on your cell phone and you make a date with him. Have you no pride?" Elliot asked, then continued without waiting for an answer: "You're a disgrace to your sex. It's because of you that women need to read *The Rules* and those other stupid self-help books." He moved his arms in a spasm of disgust and completely upset Kate's drink. "Oh, shit," he said, and Kate wasn't sure if he was referring to the spill or her mistake.

Because it was a mistake. Wasn't it?

Chapter Thirty

It was crowded in Bunny and Arnie's new apartment; everyone sat or stood in perfect silence in the dark. Which was quite a trick when Kate considered the compulsive talkers she was there with. Bunny, Barbie, Mrs. Horowitz, Bina, two of Bev's cousins, Bev's mom and two aunts, assorted friends from work, and Bev's astrologist, not to mention Elliot and Brice, were all there and quiet. But only for a moment.

"Surprise!" the entire crowd shouted as the door opened. The lights went on and pink and blue balloons—big, but not as big as Bev's third-trimester belly—cascaded from the ceiling. Flash-bulbs went off all around the room, capturing forever Bev's rictus of fear as she screamed and jumped. Guests screamed and jumped as well. After the explosions were over, Kate watched as a palpitating Bev leaned on her mother's arm.

She took a seat, from where she surveyed the scene of laughing friends and relatives. She clutched her face and screamed, "Aah, you guys," as soon as she could speak. "I swear my water almost broke! You shouldn't have." She'd been told to "drop over at Bunny's new apartment for a look-see."

Kate agreed with that. There was something sadistic about surprise parties, but, "Yes, we should have and we did," Barbie told Bev, joining her on the sofa, a hideous blue three seater.

In fact, virtually all of Bunny's new apartment was in blue, and most of it was hideous. Kate had forgotten that nobody in Brooklyn south of Prospect Park believed in antiques—things were either new or junk. Kate considered the royal blue rayon-damask upholstered furniture in the living room new *and* junk, but everyone else had oohed and aahed over Bunny's new marital home on the obligatory tour before Bev's arrival. Even Elliot, not only color-blind but largely tasteless, had raised his eyebrows at the smoked mirror framed with golden cherubs and the Museum Shop lamps with fake busts of antiquity mounted under the shades. Brice, however, was in ecstasy. "Just like Picasso," he had murmured to Kate and Elliot. "She's having her blue period."

The wall-to-wall carpet was a peacock blue in the living room, a Madonna blue in the master bedroom, and a royal blue in the second bedroom. The bathrooms, one full and one half, were also, needless to say, blue. One was papered in periwinkle with green vines and matching green towels, "the essential accent" (as Bunny had explained). The other was done in navy foil. "I wanted something masculine for Arnie," she'd told them, though why shiny dark walls were manly was something Kate couldn't fathom.

"I didn't know they still made foil," Brice had said, marveling.

"I know. I had to go on-line to find it," Bunny had confided.

But Kate wasn't looking around only at the apartment, she was also looking at her friends. Each one was committed to a life that would almost inevitably include children, PTA meetings, family holidays, trips to Disney World, and all the trimmings that came not only on the Christmas tree (or Hanukkah bush), but also with the comfy order of family life. She wondered if she would ever leave the little nest she had carved out for herself in Manhattan and, if she did, what she would trade it for. Somehow the prospect of doing it in Austin without either her Manhattan or her Brooklyn friends to support or encourage her seemed grim. At least when she had been with Steven she knew that her future—if there was one—would be in New York.

Once Bev got over her surprise, all of the guests felt free to tear into the platters of food. Set out on the dining table and credenza (both covered with sky blue cloths, with napkins to match) was a truly impressive spread. Everything from bagels with four varieties of cream cheese to pasta salads, Thai sate, canapés, and cannolis was arrayed in overwhelming profusion. Elliot picked up a plate and heaved a big sigh of happiness. "I love it here," he said.

"Oops. He's up another waist size," Brice said, and patted Elliot lovingly.

Everyone seemed to be enjoying themselves enormously, except Bina. Kate didn't want another recitation of Billy Nolan's charms, so she had avoided Bina just a little. But it didn't seem necessary: Kate realized that Bina was avoiding her. She was sitting, her plate heaped high, next to one of Bev's cousins, but she wasn't talking or eating. Only Bev's nephew, a four-year-old who sat on the floor dutifully chewing whatever his grandma or mother put in his mouth, seemed capable of bringing a smile to her lips.

"Okay. Let's get down to business," Barbie told everyone once the food frenzy had subsided. "Open the presents! Open the presents!"

Everyone cheered and agreed except Bina. Kate kept an eye on her as box after box was unwrapped.

All the gifts had been opened, and Bev's mother was wrestling in the wrapping paper as if it were a pile of leaves that had been raked up in the fall. Bev was holding up a tiny sweater and examining the knitted bonnet that went with it.

Kate touched the tiny piece of hand-knit material, and all at once, she was almost overcome by a wave of feeling so unexpected and so strong that she had to sit down. Up till now, for some inexplicable reason, Bev's pregnancy had been just that—a swelling stomach, a few inappropriate outfits, and some complaints. Holding the tiny sweater, Kate realized that very soon, Bev—and Johnny, of course—would have a new person as tiny as the little bit of wool, to hold and love and care about for the rest of their lives. Kate felt so very far from that reality that tears of envy and despair filmed her eyes. She had to turn her head away so no one would notice her sudden rush of emotion.

I want a baby of my own, she thought, and realized at the same time that she was further away from that possibility than she had been for a long time. Because she suddenly knew, absolutely knew, as she held the little sweater, that she wouldn't want to be putting it on Michael's child. The very idea was . . . well, it just wasn't possible.

"Have some rugelach, Katie," Mrs. Horowitz offered, and Kate looked up. She must have appeared as dazed as she felt, because Mrs. Horowitz exclaimed, "You're so pale. Are you all right, darling?"

The answer, of course, was no, but how could she explain that to kind, concerned, simple Myra Horowitz?

Now that all the gifts had been opened, the women went back to the food. Soon, overfilled paper plates were being balanced precariously next to plastic cups of juice, margaritas, or New York State champagne. The Bitches, Brice, and Elliot gathered in a small group in the corner near the easy chair that Bev had settled into.

"So, is it a girl or a boy?" Barbie asked, taking a bite of her bagel.

Bev looked at her mother, than shrugged. "Johnny and I want a surprise," she said, but Kate saw the look that passed between them and knew better.

"I think you should name him William," Elliot said.

"After the prince?" Bev asked.

"No. After Billy Nolan. The man who made all this possible," Elliot told her.

"See, Elliot's theory works. Just think. You're next," Brice told Bina with frightening assurance.

"That's right, Bina," Bunny agreed.

"Jack'll come around," Bev's mother told Bina in a comforting tone. "Remember how hard it was to get her Johnny to propose? I'm glad you stayed local, Bina, and didn't go into Manhattan like Katie."

"Yeah," Barbie echoed. "It's even harder to get them to commit."

"That's not true," Kate began to protest, "I don't think that location has—"

"Kate's doing okay," Elliot cut in defensively.

"Yeah," Brice echoed. "She's getting a proposal from this doctor guy."

Kate felt the blood leave her face.

"Get outta town!" Barbie cried.

"You sneak! You didn't say a word," Bunny squawked.

"What's his sign?" Bev demanded.

Kate was kissed and pummeled for a few minutes, until she could get a word in. "I'm not 'getting a proposal,'" she told them all, then gave Brice a dirty look. He shrugged an apology. Kate tried to find words to describe her situation with Michael and put out the blazing fire of curiosity around her. "We're talking about options."

"Options, schmopshins," said Mrs. Horowitz. "So what kind of doctor? Not a surgeon," she warned. "Surgeons are cold, Katie."

"He's not a medical doctor," Kate said, then heard all the sighs of disappointment that moved through the room like a summer breeze.

"It doesn't matter if he's not a *real* doctor," she said to Kate, her voice low. "As long as you love him." Kate managed a smile and took a pastry.

Then she shot Elliot and Brice a murderous look. "They don't know what they're saying. Anyway, we were talking about Bina."

"Maybe we shouldn't," Bina said quietly.

"Oh, everything is going to work out fine," Bunny said, and she put her arm around Elliot. It seemed to Kate that the group had adopted Elliot and Brice as girlfriends in drag.

"She's got Dumping Billy on her side," Barbie said.

"He hasn't dumped you yet, though, has he?" Bev asked Bina.

"No. Not yet. But I'm really looking forward to it," Bina said, obviously uncomfortable.

"Well, it's been a long time," Barbie pointed out.

"According to Elliot's theory, that makes sense," Barbie said.

"No. Actually, it doesn't. This whole thing doesn't make sense, and it's making me crazy," Kate told the women irritably. Somehow everything seemed wrong: her with Michael, Bina with Billy, Jack with a bevy of foreign beauties, Steven calling her from out of the blue. It was like a French farce. Looking at Bina and suddenly feeling sorry for herself, Kate blinked back tears and took a piece of the shower cake to comfort herself.

"Oh, well, it has to be at least two months or else it doesn't work. And I'm a little uncomfortable," Bina admitted.

Bev put her hand on the back of the chair to help herself up. "Honey, you don't have any idea what uncomfortable is. You *cannot* give up now," she said matter-of-factly.

"Stay the course," Barbie advised Bina. "Billy can't last much longer. You're not his type."

"Oh, no? He's asked me to the Hamptons this weekend," Bina said without enthusiasm.

The Bitches squealed with delight, wisecracked, elbowed, and laughed to one another.

"What's so funny?" Bina asked them.

"What you don't know about men could fill a library," Bev said.

"A big one. A Manhattan one," Bunny added.

"What don't I know?" Bina demanded.

"Bina, honey, this will be the end. Men like Billy freak out after a weekend alone with a woman," Barbie said. "He's sure to drop you after that."

"But then why would he ask me?" Bina did look really upset. Kate wondered again if her friend was falling for that self-centered idiot. "It wasn't my idea."

"That's the point," Bunny told her.

"They like the idea of intimacy . . . ," Bev began.

"But the reality is they freak out because of all the one-on-one time," Barbie continued.

"Really, Bina. Go to the Hamptons and you are as good as dumped," Bunny assured Bina.

"I don't know. It seems like false pretense," Bina told them.

"Maybe it is, but you can't turn back now," Bev said as she walked to the refreshments table.

Bina had been juggling her plate of food on her lap and suddenly lost control of it. The entire thing fell down her dress and onto the floor. The Bitches fell silent and stared at her.

Kate had felt something was wrong with Bina's behavior since they'd arrived, and now, as if to confirm that, instead of cleaning up the mess, Bina took Kate's hand and began to pull her down the hall. "I have to talk to you," she whispered.

"Wait a minute," Kate said, and put down her glass of red wine as they passed a side table, afraid that a spill would turn the carpet an irrevocable purple. Bina pulled her into the guest bedroom and sat her down on the sofa bed.

"I can't believe it, Katie," she said, and her voice caught on a sob. "I'm so ashamed. I never thought . . . I could never believe that I . . . Omigod, Jack."

Kate had no idea what Bina was going on about, but she was upset to hear her so upset. And in a different way from her usual innocent hysteria. "What *is* it, Bina?" she asked gently.

"If my mother knew . . . Oh, Katie! I cheated on Jack."

"Bina, a few dates doesn't mean—"

"No. I mean I really did. I had sex. I mean the whole thing. And it was . . . wonderful."

As Bina burst into tears, Kate felt the room and the noise of the party receding. And this new information, this sexual misadventure of Bina's, was exactly what she had been afraid of. She felt herself becoming angry but wasn't sure whom she was angry at or with. Elliot should never have proposed this, she should never have allowed it, Bina shouldn't have fallen for Billy's empty charm, and she was most angry that Billy, in true Lothario fashion, had taken advantage of Bina's inexperience.

What had she done? She and Elliot and the Bitches had interfered in Bina's life, and the results were this: a girl awash in guilt and tears and confusion. Hadn't they all succeeded in ruining Bina's loyalty and single-minded devotion? Perhaps it was a bad thing, to count on one man to come through for you and to believe there was nobody else. Still, Bina should have been left to make her own choices. Setting her up with a man like Billy Nolan was sure to be her undoing. And now, what if she decided she loved him? What if after the heartbreak of Jack's desertion she was dumped again, as was inevitable? It would destroy her self-confidence. Kate didn't even want to imagine what Bina might do.

She took her friend by the shoulders and stared into her eyes. "Listen to me, Bina. Whatever you did is all right. Jack has been off sleeping around, and if you had a slip, so—"

"But I don't feel like it was a slip," Bina said, and began crying anew. "I feel as if he appreciates me. He says that since he saw me he's felt that not grabbing me up was a mistake."

Kate recalled how she'd had to challenge Billy even to consider Bina as date material. She was furious at everyone—at Jack, at Elliot, at the Bitches . . . even at herself. But beneath all of that, there was another feeling. "Bina, you can't believe everything men say," she began cautiously.

"Katie, I never doubted my love for Jack. I mean, I do love Jack. It's just that now that I've had some more experience . . . well, I just can't explain it. He's so understanding. And it's like we never run out of things to talk about." She paused.

"Look, Bina, you have not been disloyal. Just don't confuse this, this little adventure with real love."

Bina looked at Kate solemnly. "You're right," she said, and nodded. "I won't let it happen again. Because I really, really do love Jack."

"Good girl," Kate told her. "Now, just don't think about it anymore. You don't have to do what you don't want to do."

Bina nodded, then wiped her eyes. "But he was so very, very good in bed." She blushed, and Kate felt her own face color because she realized what the other feeling was.

She was envious.

Kate left the shower before Brice and Elliot. She was too despondent to take the subway, so as an indulgence, she looked for a taxi. It wasn't easy in Brooklyn—another reason to stay in Manhattan, she reflected sourly. But at last she flagged down an off-duty taxi who was merely avoiding a fare that would take him deeper into Brooklyn.

Kate sat in the backseat, grateful for the time alone. Though she loved both Brice and Elliot, she simply wasn't up for their chatter. She had a lot of thinking to do, and though she had put off dealing with her reality until now, she would have to come to terms with it. What was it that she really wanted? Of course, that was easy to answer: a perfect life with a rewarding job, a loving, dependable, and passionate husband, healthy children, and good friends. Good fucking luck, she told herself. She couldn't see any indications in her future that would promise it all. If you got one part, you wouldn't get the other. Yet Kate had promised herself for all these years that she wouldn't compromise.

As they crossed the Brooklyn Bridge, she stared at the city. The skyline, as always, moved her deeply. But now she had to admit that she was even more deeply moved by Bina's revelation. How could she go on with Michael when she felt drawn to someone as useless as Billy Nolan? His behavior with Bina had only further convinced her of his heartlessness, and the fact that a part of her—not the good part—still desired him was shameful. One thing she was certain of: She wouldn't become confused and reassess Steven's actions in light of Billy's. What did it matter which of them was worse?

Kate looked out the taxi window and wished that she could stay forever suspended on the bridge between the two boroughs in her life.

Chapter Thirty-one

Kate sat at a window table in the Chelsea Kitchen and played with her fork, laying it down, picking it up, tapping the bottom, and then touching the tines to her water glass, her plate, and even the folded napkin. She was uncomfortable in the restaurant, but she had decided that she would do this in a public place. That's what men do, she thought, and remembered Steven. Probably it was because they were afraid of scenes. Kate knew that wasn't a realistic threat with Michael, but she couldn't imagine having this talk and then moving through his apartment on her way to the door or, worse, asking him to leave her place. Since yesterday at the shower, Kate had known with blinding clarity that Michael was not for her. And today she'd asked Michael to meet her here, to avoid having to engage in senseless chatter as they walked along.

Beside her on the floor was a Big Brown Bag from Bloomingdale's. When she forced herself to put down the fork, she used the same hand to check again that the bag was there—as if anyone would want to steal folded shorts and athletic socks, a razor, half-used-up toiletries, and an old tie Michael had left at her house. She wiped her palms on the napkin, surprised to find how sweaty they were. The truth was that she had little experience in being the initiator of a breakup.

When the waiter came over, she asked for vodka on the rocks. She didn't usually drink hard liquor, and when she did it was generally a cosmopolitan, a drink that had come in and gone out of fashion but that she still liked. Today, however, she needed a jolt of something. She remembered a phrase her father used to use—"Dutch courage"—and for the first time she really appreciated its meaning. She needed courage, Dutch or otherwise.

When the waiter returned with her order, she downed it in two long gulps with barely a breath between them. Only then did she realize that she didn't want Michael to see her drinking, and she also didn't want him to smell alcohol on her breath. Why? That had always been a strained part of their relationship. Though he had never tried to intimidate her or force her to change, Kate realized she had often walked on eggshells with Michael. She wondered now if she had ever really been herself with him. She wasn't sure if it was his personality that had imposed restraints on her. Perhaps that wasn't fair. Perhaps his academic credentials and his comfortable suburban back-ground had created a sense of inferiority in her. Maybe they both had a classic fear of intimacy. But whatever it was, Kate knew something was not right, something not fixable, about their relationship.

She waved to the waiter and handed him the evidence. "Can I get you another?" he asked, no doubt taking her for a heavy drinker, but she shook her head. Then she picked up a piece of the garlic bread from the basket on the table. Better to smell of garlic than vodka. People mistakenly thought you couldn't detect it on a person's breath, but Kate always could—maybe because of her father.

She munched on the bread and looked out the window. In the late afternoon, there weren't many people on West 18th Street. She wondered where the man with the red tips at the ends of his black hair was going and whether the woman who looked like a real estate broker in her fake Chanel suit actually was one. Kate sighed. She'd probably never be able to afford to buy an apart-ment or own her own home. Here in Manhattan, it was difficult enough as a couple. As a single person, it was impossible.

She had no home of her own, no summer plans, and soon she'd have no man in her life.

Kate took a sip of her water and looked out at the traffic. It was a wet day, and though the drizzle had stopped for the moment, it had put a sheen on the macadam, the trucks and taxis, and even the sidewalks and buildings across the way. She loved Manhattan, and this simple silvery scene outside the restaurant window calmed her. Could she leave this for Austin, or anywhere?

On the other hand, she could be completely crazy. Aside from the Arnies, Johnnys, Eddies, and the rest of the Brooklyn world, it seemed there were no marriageable men. Rita and every other one of her Manhattan girlfriends complained about how the men here were players or neurotics or commitment phobes. She thought back to Steven and the pain she had gone through after he left her. She wasn't having this talk with Michael just because of her upcoming meeting with Steven. Steven was out of her life, although she couldn't help feeling a bit of excitement, the old buzz, when she thought of seeing him. It would be nice to look at him, talk with him, and feel nothing. She hoped she could manage it. She looked down and saw that the fork in her hand was actually trembling. Could she hurt Michael like this? Could she bear to be alone, start dating again, and risk being hurt again?

The waiter returned with a pitcher of water. Her glass was half-empty, or half-full. She supposed, as he poured out the water, that it was all in the eye of the beholder. If she discussed what she was about to do with Barbie, Bev, or even Mrs. Horowitz, they would tell her she was crazy. Her glass was half-full. Still, while she knew that Steven was dangerous and not for her, simply hearing from him had reminded her of how much she had felt for him when they were together. The disparity between that feeling and the pale echo of it that she felt for Michael frightened her. She just didn't think that she could bear to go through life without stronger feelings for her companion.

Kate couldn't suppress the surge of feeling she was experiencing not only from Steven's call, but also from the overwhelming envy she'd felt when Bina told her about her actual affair with Billy. Kate knew she couldn't stay with Michael. Michael was a safe, dependable partner, and yes, he'd make a responsible father. But for someone else's children, not hers.

Even if she was ruining her last chance of settling down, Kate couldn't settle for him. She placed the fork she'd been holding back in its proper place. A young woman, obviously an au pair, walked by with a little girl who looked about four. Both were wearing yellow raincoats. Kate smiled and thought of the children she was working with at Andrew Country Day. Everything about her job, from her little office, to Elliot down the hall, to the easy commute from home, to the children she worked with, seemed precious to her. Now, at the thought of losing it, she could feel just how precious it was. Even Dr. McKay seemed lovable in his ridiculous way. And Michael believed it was nothing to her? Did he know her at all?

When Michael walked in, Kate was still staring out the window. She jumped when he put his hand on her shoulder. "I got caught in the rain," he said as he shook his umbrella and took the seat across from her.

Kate looked at him. His jaw was still strong, his nose still regular, his eyes a warm brown. But as if a spell had been broken, Kate no longer found him the slightest bit attractive. As he set his briefcase on the empty chair, she wondered whether this kind of reversal had happened to Steven: whether one day he had just looked at her and felt nothing but . . . a mild distaste. The idea made her skin crawl. The combination of the drink and what she was about to do made her stomach feel queasy.

"Would you like something to drink?" Michael asked her.

She managed a weak smile. "No, thank you," she told him as soberly as she could manage.

The solicitous waiter appeared unbidden, and Kate hoped he wouldn't blow her cover by asking if she wanted *another* vodka on the rocks.

"A cup of tea," Michael requested. "Earl Grey, if you have it."

"Nothing for me," Kate said.

After the waiter moved off, Michael looked out the window, as Kate had been doing. "Well, we won't have to put up with this kind of weather in Austin."

"Why?" Kate asked. "Doesn't it rain there?" But she didn't pursue it. Why be unpleasant? She didn't know how to begin, so she just launched into her prepared speech. "Michael, I can't go to Austin. First because I don't want to; I like it here. Secondly, because you didn't ask me. You *assumed* I could come with you. We had no discussion. It was as if you were granting me some kind of favor. You just thought I would jump at the chance."

Michael blinked and put down the cup that was halfway to his lips. Kate saw some of the tea splash over the lip and onto the tablecloth, but Michael didn't seem to notice. "Kate. Kate, I just felt—"

"I'm not sure what you felt," Kate said. "But it isn't what *I* felt. And you didn't know it."

Michael sat absolutely still, and the table—no more than twenty-six inches wide—seemed to Kate to be expanding to tundra proportions. She could almost see Michael receding into the distance, his face bluish in the reflected light from the white cloth that stretched between them. "Kate, I never meant to be presumptuous. I just thought, well, I thought you wanted what I wanted."

"That may be true, but since we never actually spoke about what we wanted, how was I to know?"

Michael sat still and looked at her as if he were seeing her for the first time. Had she been guilty of trying too hard to please? Had she kept her feelings and fears from him? Somehow it didn't seem to matter anymore. Even if Michael now told her he was willing to give up the Austin job and make a home with her here, Kate was no longer interested. Am I fickle? she thought. She couldn't answer the question, but she knew that a single life, alone and with no children, would be better than a half-life with Michael. He simply wasn't the man for her.

"Kate, I can't tell you how floored I am by this. I mean, it's coming out of nowhere. I've been busy making plans, assuming—"

"Never assume, Michael," Kate said. "Never presume. My life is just as important to me as yours is to you. I'm not sure you ever recognized that."

"Of course I did," Michael said. "But you could make new friends and set up a practice in Austin. You could visit back here whenever you wanted. And it's not as if you have family here."

"Oh yes, I do," Kate said. She thought of Elliot and Brice and Bina and the Horowitzes. Even the Bitches meant a lot to her. "They might not be DNA related, but I have family all the same." She paused. "I don't know whose fault it is, Michael; let's not talk about fault, and let's not blame each other. It isn't as if I've felt this way for months and withheld the knowledge from you. It's just that once you told me about Austin and made your decision unilaterally, I guess I made mine. I'm very sorry." She reached across the tablecloth to touch his hand, but he pulled away, spilling the tea in the process. It spread, like a brown blot, across the pure white space between them. For a moment Kate was reminded of the bowling alley and her spilled beer. "I'm sorry," she repeated, "because there's nothing else to say." She stood up, holding the shopping bag. "Here are your things," she said. "If I've forgotten some of them, let me know."

Oddly, she didn't feel sad, and she didn't feel free. She felt nothing. Michael was still looking at her, his face torn between disbelief and anger.

"Good luck in Austin," she said, and walked out of the restaurant.

Kate walked in the drizzle, which had started up again and now perfectly reflected her frame of mind. She felt she'd be miserable for the rest of her life, but she couldn't imagine Michael feeling too bad for too long. It wasn't his style. That was the reason she'd left him: He didn't feel things.

After about half an hour, she found herself in front of the gym. She walked in in time to see Elliot just finishing up his cardio on the StairMaster. Once he caught sight of her, he became instantly concerned.

"What have you done? You're supposed to take your clothes off before you shower." He led her over to one of the leather banquettes and helped her out of her sodden raincoat. "You're wet right through," he said, and fussed for a few minutes with towels. When Kate's wet hair had been wrapped in a turban and the towel hugged her neck, Elliot was ready for conversation.

"I broke up with Michael," Kate said.

"Good." Elliot nodded, then put his arm around her. "It was only a matter of time. And this saves you a ticket to Austin, which you can spend on a share in our house this summer."

Kate, who had expected more surprise and a lot more sympathy, shook her head. "I don't think being the only woman in a house full of gay men in Cherry Grove would be the thing for me right now."

"Oh, come on. You'd have more fun than you would with any of your straight boyfriends. When did Michael ever make you laugh the way Brice does? When did Steven *ever* make you laugh?" Elliot stopped and stared at her so intently that she knew she was in trouble. He leaned forward, his elbows on his knees, his nose an inch away from hers. "You're not still going to meet up with Steven, are you?"

And, of course, Kate was.

Chapter Thirty-two

Kate expected nothing from the meeting with Steven the next afternoon, but her pride made her primp. She was vain enough to want to look her best, and she put on extra mascara and French-braided her hair. Steven had always liked it like that.

As she was leaving her apartment and pulling the door shut behind her, she stopped, gazing out into space, remembering too vividly the last time she'd seen Steven and the way they had parted at this door.

"Forget something?" Max asked from behind her.

Startled, she spun around. "Oh, no, just thinking is all. What's up with you lately?"

"Not much. How about you?" He lounged against the wall.

Now was not the time to explain what she was doing or going to do, and Max certainly wasn't the person she should confide in. "I'm actually going to be late for a meeting," she said, and tried to step by him. Max wasn't exactly a nuisance: He was a nice guy, but she didn't have time for him.

But he wouldn't let her go. He reached out and touched her arm. Again, she was startled. "I've heard from Jack again," he said, and shifted from foot to foot. "Or should I say, I've gotten e-mails. He sent me more pictures."

Kate sighed. It was bad news that didn't have to be shared.

As if he could read her mind, Max looked away and said, "I still don't think I should show them to Bina."

"Absolutely not," Kate told him. "You know she's pretty tight with Billy now, and I don't want her to get upset about Jack again."

"Billy? Who's Billy?" Max asked, his forehead wrinkled.

"Oh, that's a long story you don't have the time to—"

"I'll listen. Try me. I've got the time." He sounded more anxious than casual.

God, he was such a gossip! "Unfortunately, I don't," Kate told him. "I'm going to be late." She made her way to the stairs at the end of the hall, then looked back to see Max sliding down the wall to sit on the floor. Since when was Max so compassionate about her friends? Sure, Jack was his cousin and he might feel some responsibility for Bina, but not to this extent.

"You know, I worry about Bina," Max said. "I need to talk to Jack."

"No, you don't," Kate called to him as she ran down the stairs. "Leave well enough alone."

Steven looked terrific. Well, Kate reflected, Steven had always looked terrific to her. As he stood up, his length unfolded, reminding Kate of one of those hinged yardsticks. He smiled, and his smile broke the parentheses, the lines on each side of his mouth that looked so attractive on men.

"Hi," he said. "What can I get you?"

Kate was glad she hadn't committed to dinner. Though he lived in the East Village, Kate had selected the Starbucks near her apartment. It was safe: Steven wouldn't expect her to have a meal with him, and Elliot never frequented that place. Steven had what looked like a very large caffè latte in front of him, half of it gone. He must have arrived early. "An iced tea," she said in answer to his question, and took the seat across from him at his tiny table in the corner. He nodded and was at the counter in a moment. It gave Kate a chance to smooth her hair and look at him from behind.

He was still long and lean—at six feet three it was easy to be long, but perhaps he wasn't quite as thin as he had been. His hair, however, was still as beautiful: a thick black waterfall that gleamed like a crow's wing. Kate remembered too vividly how she had loved to stroke his hair. He turned and came back to her, the iced tea and a paper plate of biscotti in his hands. They were the anise ones that she liked. She was touched and surprised that he remembered, but when he picked one up himself, she thought that perhaps he'd gotten them for himself.

It was the time of day when few people dropped in for coffee: after the rush that followed lunch, but before the rush that followed dinner. No clients lingered except for the inevitable madman writing in something that looked like a journal and an older gentleman—obviously—who sat in a plush chair near the window, reading a rumpled copy of *The New York Times* in the waning afternoon light.

She took a sip of her tea and they sat for a moment in silence. Kate had promised herself that she wasn't going to do much talking. She felt him looking at her and returned his gaze passively.

"You look terrific," he said.

Kate smiled and hoped the smile was what art historians and novelists called "enigmatic." "I'm glad you could meet me," he added. He paused, but Kate maintained her silence. "Well, enough about you," Steven said, "how do I look?"

"I think you've grown," Kate said, tongue-in-cheek. "Do men have growth spurts?"

"Sure, but only emotional ones. And it's pretty rare." He stopped smiling, and his face took on the lean and hungry look that Kate remembered from their lovemaking and his talk about his ambitions. He wore it, she knew, when he wanted things. But she remained silent, waiting to hear what it was that he wanted now.

"Kate, do you ever think about how it was . . . I mean, how it was between us?"

She was grateful that Elliot wasn't there to smack his forehead and whine about the months she had relived every detail of her time with Steven. "I've been busy," she said.

Steven nodded. "I deserved that," he said. "But I've been thinking about you. Actually, I can't stop thinking about you. I do it all the time."

"That isn't good," Kate said in exactly the same tone of voice Elliot would have used.

Steven didn't seem to notice. "I'm here to tell you I was an asshole. I would say cad, but it's too archaic. Asshole covers a lot of territory, but you know what I mean."

Kate nodded and took another sip of her tea. "I think lying asshole would be more accurate," she said. She turned her head toward the window so that she wouldn't display any visible emotion to him. To her horror, out of the corner of her eye she thought she saw Max walking by. Was he with a woman? She couldn't see them as they turned the corner, but she prayed they wouldn't step into the shop. Max had met Steven more than once and would definitely agree with Steven's current self-assessment.

"I don't know what to say, exactly," Steven told her. "Except that I've been reading Piaget and I think I'm a case of arrested development. I was emotionally somewhere between seven and nine years old when we were going out." Kate raised her eyebrows. She'd expected an apology, but not such a complete and accurate one.

"Kate, I don't regret anything in my life as much as I regret letting you go."

Kate tried not to let his words sink in. There had been so many weeks, months, that she had hoped to hear them. Now she told herself to stay cool and calm.

Steven looked around. "God, this place is murder," he told her. "Please, Kate, let me take you out for a drink and dinner. Just give me a chance to explain everything."

Kate meant to say no. She meant to shake her head. She had gotten the satisfaction and closure that she craved, and now she only had to be cold and polite and negative. Just one shake of the head. "My job is very demanding right now," she told him.

"When will it let up?"

"With term-end reports, maybe a month."

"So if I call you, could we see each other?"

When she found herself nodding, she was as surprised as Steven appeared to be.

Chapter Thirty-three

Kate barely had time to shower and get into bed, totally exhausted from her meeting with Steven, when the phone rang. She looked at the caller ID, wondering, and when she saw that it was Bina's number she heaved a sigh of relief and answered.

"I can't believe it!" Bina almost yelled. "It's working! It's working almost too good! And he hasn't even broken up with me yet."

Kate was totally confused. "What are you talking about?" she asked.

"He called! He's going to ask me to marry him!"

Kate felt a jolt of jealousy mixed with complete surprise. "Billy is proposing?" she asked, incredulous.

"Not Billy! Jack! Jack called from Hong Kong." Bina was almost shouting. "He said he's flying home the day after tomorrow and he's doing it to see me. Kate, don't you get it? Elliot's plan worked. Jack is coming back to me."

Tired as she was, Kate had trouble digesting this news. Her head was a jumble of Max's e-mails, Elliot's numbers and graphs, Bina's gossip about her dates, the recent shocking news from the baby shower. All of it seemed to converge, making her dizzy. "Jack called and proposed?" she asked.

"Well, yes and no," Bina said, sounding slightly less joyous now to admit the truth.

"Okay. Tell me exactly what happened," Kate said, and wished that she hadn't given up smoking years ago. This was going to be the kind of long, involved description that only a cigarette could help get you through. "And tell me it in order from beginning to end."

She heard Bina take a deep breath. "Well, first the phone rang."

Kate realized it was just as well she'd given up cigarettes: She'd probably need a whole carton for this. "Yeah. Then what?"

"Then I picked it up. No, actually my mother picked it up. Then she handed it to me and said, 'It's for you.'"

"Did she know it was Jack?"

"Not then. Not until I screamed. Well, maybe she did, do you want me to ask her?"

"No." Kate pushed an extra throw pillow behind her head and wished she had a glass of beer. "Just tell me what he said and what you said, Bina."

"Okay, so he said, 'Bina, is that you?' So I said, 'Who wants to know?' But I knew it was him because I knew his voice right away. You know, it sounded like he was calling from Coney Island or something, not from the other side of the world."

Kate sighed. "Then what did he say?"

"He says, 'Bina, I got to talk to you,' and I say, 'I'm listening,' and he goes, 'I've made a big mistake, Bina.' And I go, 'Well, how is that my business?' So he says, 'This is Jack.' And I say— you're gonna like this, Katie. I say, 'Jack who?' Wasn't that good?"

"Great," Kate said.

"So he says, 'Jack Weintraub.' And I go, 'Oh, I was confused. I thought it was Jack Marco Polo.' And he's like, 'What?' And I'm like, 'You know, the single guy that discovered a whole new world in the Orient.'"

Kate thought for a moment of hurrying Bina along, but now was no time for lessons in geography and political correctness.

"So he says, 'Bina, don't mock me. Have you been going out with someone else?' And I say, 'What's it to you?' And he says, 'Now I know you are.' And I say, 'Think what you want, but I know the truth.' And then he's like, 'Bina, I really have to talk to you.' And I say, 'Whatever.' And he says, 'I know you're probably angry at me and everything—' And I interrupt him and I say, 'Think again, because I hardly remember you.' Hey, Katie, do you think he heard gossip all the way in Japan?"

"He's in Hong Kong, Bina."

"Isn't that a part of Japan?"

Kate just shook her head. "So what happened then?" she asked.

"Now it gets really good. He goes, 'I have to talk to you.' And I say, 'Isn't that what you're doing now?' And he says, 'I've got to talk to you face-to-face.' So I go, 'That will probably be difficult since you're so two-faced.' And he says, 'Meet me at the airport on Thursday, Bina. I'm flying into JFK just to see you. Please don't say no.'"

Kate waited. There was silence at the other end of the phone. "So what did you say?" she asked, hesitating.

"I said yes!" Bina almost yodeled into the phone. "And he says, 'I have something I want to ask you and something I want to give you.' Isn't that great? So do you think it's too late to call Elliot and Brice and tell them, or should I wait until tomorrow morning? I mean, if it wasn't for Elliot's statistics, I never . . ." She paused. "Omigod, Katie! Omigod! I have to get Billy to dump me for this to work, right?"

"Come on, Bina, that's all nonsense. Jack called you because he loves you and misses you."

"Forget that. This is because of Elliot. If I didn't go out with Billy . . ."

Kate flung off the blankets and stood up. "Don't be ridiculous," she said. "You don't have to do anything now but show up at the airport."

"I'm calling Elliot," Bina said. "I have to find out how long I have to date Billy, and then you and Elliot have to figure out how we break up."

"Oh, come on," Kate said. "You can just tell him it's over."

"Nahuh," Bina said while Kate stomped into the hall and

across to her tiny kitchen, phone in hand. She prayed there was just one beer left somewhere in the back of the refrigerator. "He has to break up with me, remember?" Kate opened the refrigerator door. It shone that lonely light that illuminates single women at one A.M. after they've had some horrible disappointment.

"I have to figure out a way for him to dump me, Katie," Bina continued. "And I have to do it by Thursday. Otherwise . . ."

Behind the mayonnaise jar, Kate glimpsed the brown neck of a Samuel Adams. She uttered a silent prayer to the god of alcohol and grabbed it. "Look, Bina, you don't have to believe me," she told her friend as she poured the beer into a glass. She never drank from a bottle; it reminded her too much of her father. "Jack has just about proposed. I don't know if you should accept him, but if that's what you want, that's what you're going to do when you see him."

"I'm calling Elliot," Bina said. "I'm calling him and then I'm calling Barbie and then—"

"Fine," said Kate. "Call them all, but leave me out of it." After the baby shower, she didn't think she could do one more function with the Bitches. She hung up the phone and chugged all the beer. Then she put down the glass and left it on the counter while she went, alone, to her bed.

Chapter Thirty-four

The morning dawned beautifully. Kate knew because she was awake—as she had been, on and off, for most of the night. The window in her bedroom faced east, and she saw the murky brown that passed as darkness turn first beige, then pink, and then, last, salmon as the sun rose. The light would last till past eight that evening, but there was no light in Kate's heart. Though this was Kate's favorite time of year, she woke with a heaviness in her chest and a gray despair that no dawn could affect. For the past few days she had been working and eating—though without an appetite—and walking to and from school, but she felt barely conscious of any of it. Although she didn't regret breaking up with Michael and she didn't expect anything from Steven, she felt lonely and hopeless. Like so many women in Manhattan, she would go without a partner because either she wasn't good enough or they weren't. Her Brooklyn friends had exhausted her, and like a sore spot on her gums that she couldn't keep her tongue away from, there was something annoying and painful about Billy Nolan and Bina's affair with him that she preferred not to think about but kept going back to over and over. Perhaps worst of all, she couldn't talk to Rita or her other Manhattan friends about it because they would never understand, and she couldn't talk to Elliot about it because he was the instigator, and the truth was she didn't want him, like a dentist with a fine instrument, picking at this sensitive spot.

She drifted into a light sleep. It was a quarter after six when the phone rang. She couldn't imagine who it would be. She picked up the phone to hear Bina's imploring voice at the other end. "Please, Kate, help me! I couldn't do it right, and now I have to go to the airport. I went out with Billy last night and I acted as snotty as I could, but he just laughed. I flirted with another guy, but he didn't seem to mind—"

"Whoa. Bina, slow down."

"Kate, I tried everything everyone suggested. You have to help me. Billy hasn't dumped me, and Jack lands in an hour and a half, and . . ."

Bina began to cry. And while Kate had heard Bina cry through almost every phase of their lives, there was an element to this that was new. Kate made shushing noises while she tried to wake up enough to figure out what was different. And then it came to her. For the first time, Bina was crying like an adult. Gone was the hysteria that allowed Bina to be so infuriating and yet sweet. Instead, Kate heard overlays of guilt, and shame, and anxiety.

"I made a mistake, Kate. But I don't want to have to tell Jack, and if Billy doesn't dump me, Jack won't propose and I've ruined my life."

"It's all going to be all right," Kate assured her. "I'll get a limo and pick you up this afternoon. I'll drop you at the airport. Just look good. I'll take care of everything. I promise you, it's all going to be all right."

"Cross your heart and hope to die?" Bina asked. Kate smiled. Same old Bina, she thought, and reassured her friend.

Dressed, made-up, coiffed, and scented, Bina sat beside Kate in the limo. Kate had done some deep thinking, called the car service, picked up Bina in Brooklyn, and swept her into the backseat. Although she was impressed with the car, Bina was still nervous.

"But what are you going to do?" she asked.

"That's for me to know, and for you to never find out," Kate said, and leaned forward. "Take the BQE," she told the driver, who seemed to be taking the scenic route—as if there were one—to JFK.

"Do you know which terminal he's coming into?" the driver asked.

"International arrivals," Kate said. "Follow the signs." She leaned back into the leather of the seats and turned to her friend, looking into her eyes. "Listen to me," she said.

"I am," Bina told her.

"Okay, really listen to me. You have nothing to tell Jack. You have nothing to confess." Kate paused. The idea of Bina and Billy together, the idea of him, of her . . . She repressed both the thought and her jealousy. "It only happened that once."

"Well, no. Last week I saw him and we got caught in the rain, and he took me to his apartment to towel me off, and . . ."

Kate imagined the scene too vividly. The image of Billy gently drying her hair and other body parts was disturbing and arousing. She could see why Bina would fall from grace again. "It doesn't matter. You and Jack broke up. He's been a free agent, and so have you. Remember the army had that policy: 'Don't ask. Don't tell'?" Bina nodded. "Well, follow it. And if you're asked anything by Jack, remind him that you love him. Ask him if he loves you."

"But I slept with—"

"There are no buts."

"But even if I don't tell him about the sex . . . Okay, I won't tell Jack anything."

"You promise?"

"I promise. But to make this work, I have to get Billy to dump me."

"I'm going to take care of that," Kate said. "Now, fix your makeup." Obediently, Bina rooted around in her huge purse and pulled out a cosmetics case. Kate helped her with her primping and then turned the mirror on herself. She looked a little pale, and there was bruised-looking skin under her eyes because of her lack of sleep, but she would take care of all that later.

"Okay," she said as they pulled up to the sidewalk at the airport. "You look great, you should feel great, and Jack is coming here just for you. Because he loves you."

Bina hesitated. "But I'm not sure—"

"I'm sure," Kate said. "Now go to the arrivals waiting area, where passengers get out of customs. He'll probably be out of there in less than thirty minutes or so."

"Aren't you going to wait with me?" Bina asked, her eyes opening wide.

"No. I have something else to do," Kate said, and gave Bina a hug. "Keep your cell phone on and your powder dry. Call me the moment anything happens."

Bina got out of the car and walked through the sliding glass door entrance, then she turned and waved and gave Kate the thumbs-up sign. As soon as she disappeared, merging with the crowd inside the terminal, Kate leaned forward to speak to the driver. "Take me back to Brooklyn," she told him.

Chapter Thirty-five

Kate rang Billy Nolan's bell. It took several minutes before he responded. Kate put her hands over the intercom and murmured something, pitching her voice higher than normal. Surely this wasn't the first time that he'd had an unexpected visit from a woman at an inopportune time. The more realistic worry was that some other woman was there. But, as she'd hoped, the door buzzed and Kate pushed into the hallway. I'm only doing this for Bina, she told herself, but she knew it was a lie.

Since Bina's confession at the shower, Kate had felt herself possessed by her desire for Billy Nolan. No matter how hard she had tried to deny it, she had been jealous and intrigued by Bina's flirtation with Billy. To be brutally honest, from the first moment she had met him on the terrace, she had felt an almost irresistible pull toward him. She had tried to resist it, knowing that he, like Steven, was not "relationship material." However, she reasoned, if she did this for Bina, maybe she would also be able to get Billy Nolan—his smile, his charm, and his easy physical grace—out of her system once and for all. She wasn't going to waste time in a meaningless relationship, but if this would precipitate a breakup with Bina and give her confidence, then . . .

Kate stopped to look in the mirror at the stair landing. She wasn't wild about what she saw. Her face was pale, and there were still dark circles under her eyes. Well, it would have to do. She pulled out a brush from her purse and puffed up her hair.

Her lipstick was still holding up, but she did a full-face smile to see if there was any on her teeth. Walking up the stairs, Kate caught herself licking her lips. Then she remembered Elliot's absolutely ridiculous acronym and regretted it. Well, she told herself, I'll regret more than that after this day is over. She got to Billy's door, took a deep breath, and knocked.

Billy, his hair tousled and a loose cotton robe drawn around him, obviously just out of the shower, opened the door. "What . . . ?"

His physical presence was almost a blow to her. She could smell shampoo on him. It was better than any cologne.

Kate pushed in past him. She walked across the room, put down her purse, sat at the edge of his bed, and crossed her legs.

"Sit down. Make yourself at home," Billy said with as much sarcasm as he could muster. He closed the door behind him. "To what do I owe . . ." He gave up trying to be urbane. "You want a cup of coffee?" he asked, and, scratching his head, began to move toward the kitchen.

"No, thank you," Kate said, trying not to lick her lips. "I didn't come here for coffee."

Billy stopped at the sink, his hand midway between the coffeemaker and the faucet. She had not gotten an opportunity to look at his hands since the dreadful bowling evening. Kate had always been interested in men's hands. She considered herself a sort of connoisseur, disliking short, stubby, or hairy-backed hands, yet equally turned off by overly slender, almost feminine hands. Now she was transfixed by Billy's. They were perfect, strong yet sensitive, the hands of competence and sensual knowledge. She blushed. He walked toward her slowly, pulled a chair opposite her, and sat down. "What did you come here for, doctor?" he asked. "Is this another consultation?"

Okay. She deserved that. And probably more. If he was going to make her eat humble pie, she would. But couldn't he feel her almost ridiculous longing? She was grateful that it wasn't palpable to him, since it suffused her being. "Look, I was wrong," she admitted, then paused. She'd rehearsed this coming from the airport, but all that she had prepared seemed to have evaporated. "The thing with Bina isn't working, is it," she blurted.

Billy looked at her. "Have I missed something? Are we still in high school?" he asked.

Shit! Jack should be walking with Bina at this very moment. "Just tell me the truth," she said. "Bina means nothing to you, does she."

"Bina is a very nice girl," Billy told her.

"I know that, but that isn't the question I asked you." She looked down at her exposed toes, and the Pre-Raphaelite painting titled *King Cophetua and the Beggar Maid* appeared before her eyes. She'd always found it erotically charged. "Look," she said, "I came over here to admit that I made a terrible mistake. Bina is beginning to be really attached to you, and it isn't fair. She's going to get hurt, and it's going to be my fault as much as it is yours."

For the first time since she had arrived, Billy actually looked alert. He looked down at the floor for a long moment, then back at her. "Look, I never meant to hurt her. I go out with women who know how to take care of themselves."

"Well, Bina isn't a woman like that."

"I know. That's why I never slept with her. Not that it's any of your business."

Kate looked away from his beautiful face. So he was a liar as well as a flirt and a serial dater.

"Don't waste my time with lies," she told him.

"Hey!" He stood up. "I don't lie. I've never dated more than one woman at a time, and I break up with one before I start in with anyone else. I never promise what I don't deliver. I own a bar, for God's sake. They know I'm . . . well, not serious right now. And if that's a repetition compulsion, well, that's my problem. Meanwhile, I make them feel good about themselves."

"It's time to break up with Bina," Kate said firmly. The fact was she felt anything but firm. She was more frightened than she could ever remember being. What if he was disinterested or, worse, if he laughed at her and threw her out? At that moment she felt it would be unbearable. Yet she couldn't show her fear. She looked at him, his hair still messy from the shower but as adorable as ever, his brow wrinkled in incredulity. "It's time," she repeated.

"What are you? Her social secretary or her mother? And how do you know how I feel?"

Kate stood up, leaned forward, and looked into his eyes. She felt the heat from his chest, and she could have melted. There was a place beyond words where honesty and intention are felt. Kate did more than apologize. She bared herself and let him in through her eyes. Silently, she kept her eyes on his and let him feel her intentions. All of the sexual heat, all of the longing that she had repressed, was there, visible to him if he would look. Billy actually pulled back for a moment, then leaned forward.

"Doctor, are you . . . ?" His expression changed from confusion to incredulity to . . . well, it looked like delight.

Kate stood up, took the sweater off her shoulders, and tossed it onto the chair behind her. Then she sat back down on the bed and unbuttoned the top button of her blouse. "I think you should call Bina," she said. "She won't be home now, but you can leave a message."

"That seems pretty cold," Billy ventured.

"Her old boyfriend is in town. She won't mind if you break up with her right now."

"B-b-but over the phone?" he stammered.

Kate looked him full in the face. She felt surprised at his sense of honor and guilt at her own manipulativeness. But she put both emotions out of her mind. "I promise this way is best. I wouldn't hurt her for the world."

And, as if hypnotized, Billy did just that. He picked up the phone, and Kate had the delicacy to leave the room while he left the message that Bina felt was so crucial. In the bathroom, she called in sick—only the third time she'd missed a day of work. Then she had a moment to look at herself in the mirror. What are you doing? she silently asked her reflection. She couldn't convince herself that she was giving her body to this man simply to ensure the ending to a crack-brain scheme that she certainly had never believed in. She wanted to sleep with Billy, but she was already afraid that she wanted more. And she knew his record with women. Could she afford to spend more of her time in a relationship that would lead to nothing in the end?

She looked away from her own pale blue eyes. She knew she didn't really have a choice. She wanted Billy Nolan more than she had ever wanted anyone. But this has to mean nothing, she told herself. There is no future, only the present. I won't make the mistakes I made with Steven and Michael. This isn't a relationship, she told herself firmly. This is what other people call "fun."

Fun was not exactly the word Kate would use for coupling with Billy.

"I've wanted you since the first time I saw you on the terrace," he said.

Kate felt something within her tighten. They were the words she wanted to hear but didn't dare believe. They were true for her, though she had not admitted it to herself and she certainly wouldn't admit it to Billy. That way lay madness. She just smiled enigmatically and tried to put all thought out of her mind. That was easy to do, because no one had ever made love to her the way Billy did. She wasn't surprised by his strength or his skill, but his tenderness took her aback. He cradled her head with both hands and held her face to his as he kissed her. He stroked her hair. "It's so beautiful," he murmured. "I love your hair." He buried his face in it, just beside her ear. "I love how it smells and how it feels. I wanted to touch it, but I didn't think I'd get the chance."

Kate turned to him, and he put his mouth on hers. She couldn't decide what she liked better, when he used his mouth to kiss her or when he used it to speak to her. His hands spoke to her as well. They moved miraculously from her breasts to her thighs and up again to her mouth, each time going further, becoming more probing, more intimate, and even more responsive to her.

Kate had always found the first few times she made love with someone to be a little awkward and unsatisfying. But with Billy it was different. He heard and registered every intake of her breath, the slightest movement of her hips or shifting of her body. She felt she could ask him for anything without speaking a word. But she didn't have to ask. He was slow and practiced and skillful, but she also felt such a flood of feeling, such an exchange of emotion, that she lost herself. As they made love, Billy kept his mouth on hers, and it seemed as if he had a hundred variations of kissing, all of which were in sync with his movements and her own. He took his mouth off hers only when he paused to look at her or when he moved his mouth to her nipples and then lower.

He brought her to the brink with his hand and with his mouth and then moving against her and then again with his hand, until Kate was trembling all over. She almost couldn't catch her breath, but the feeling was wonderful, not frightening. And when she put her hand on him, his gasp was so deep that she felt an almost greater pleasure in touching him than she felt when he moved on her body. She had no idea what time it was when he finally slipped inside her for the last time, and when both of them fell asleep, exhausted and satisfied, he kept his arms wrapped around her waist, holding her to him even as they slept.

Chapter Thirty-six

Kate opened her eyes. She had one of those moments of waking dislocation. Where was she? It wasn't her ceiling or Michael's. Then she turned her head and saw Billy, still sleeping. The events of the previous day flooded back. Kate smiled and felt her cheeks flushing, but, uncharacteristically, she didn't mind.

While they had slept her hair had fanned out, and now a red tendril was curled around Billy's upper arm. Simply looking at his arm lying on the sheet, bathed in the sunshine that spread from the window across the upper part of the bed, made her feel . . . extremely happy. It was a feeling she wasn't used to.

Kate stretched and luxuriated in the feeling. Happiness this deep was something you could not hold on to, and she was wise enough not to try. She only drank in the sunlight, the clean white sheets rumpled around them, and cherished the moment. She wasn't thinking about the sex, though it had been exquisite. It was simply looking at Billy and experiencing the feeling of warmth, comfort, and protectiveness that staring at the hairs so perfectly aligned on his forearm seemed to give her. It was a moment of pure joy.

Slowly, so as not to wake him, she lifted her head to look at his sleeping face. Even without animation, his features had a beauty and liveliness that made her wonder. From their conversation the previous night, she felt Billy Nolan was not just another pretty face. After all, in his own way, Steven had been very handsome. But Billy seemed to have a depth of feeling, a sense of compassion and understanding, that had been blocked in Steven by his narcissism.

As if feeling himself observed, Billy opened his eyes. "Hello," he said, his voice dipping somehow in the middle of the word, making it sound like a self-assured and very happy greeting. Kate felt herself blush again, and this time it did embarrass her. She fell back on her pillow. Billy raised himself on one elbow, bent over her, and kissed her. His kisses were so sensitive, so searching and gentle. That reminded her of the way they had made love, his lips almost never leaving her own—except when he was kissing some other part of her. He lifted his head.

"Good morning," Kate said, and tucked the sheet in on either side of her.

"Now you're my prisoner. Stuck in my bed for life."

Kate thought that that sounded like a delicious idea, but she only smiled.

"What time is it?" Billy asked, then fell back and yawned.

Kate hadn't a clue. At the moment, she couldn't even remember what day it was, and that also felt delicious. Lying in his bed, she felt suspended in time. If she could have asked for one place and feeling to have for all eternity, this moment would be a good choice. Then she forced herself to turn and look at the clock on the bedside table. "Oh, God," she gasped. "It's Friday! And almost nine. I have to call the school," she told him, and fell back onto the bedclothes in horror. She couldn't go running out of his apartment, scuttling like a bug to gather up her belongings, because she was way too late to get to school. She *never* missed work two days in a row; even when she'd had the stomach virus that had torn through the school, she'd still managed to come in after one day off. The children had to be able to count on her. But it was the end of the term, a half-day, and she had her reports to write up and the summaries that would go to the administration and the children's parents. She ought to be at school, going through her notes, but for once she was tempted to think of herself first. Dr. McKay, on the other hand, would have to be told, and he wouldn't like it. She knew her contract was being considered for renewal right now, and it was not a time to screw up. Still, she couldn't leave. Billy was looking at her, his eyebrows raised in question.

"My job," she said. "I have to make a call."

He picked up his phone and handed it to her. "Feel free," he said. "As long as you don't call another man, my minutes are yours."

"He isn't exactly a man, he's a principal," Kate told him.

"Well, I'm glad you've got at least one principle," he said, and kissed her again as she was punching in the Andrew number. "When you arrived I wasn't sure." She made a face and pushed him away. He lay down, holding a curl of her hair between his fingers and playing with it.

When Vera, Dr. McKay's secretary, answered the phone, Kate was relieved. She asked for Dr. McKay but hoped he might not be available so that she could just leave a message.

Unfortunately, Vera put her right through. Kate heard the principal's nasal voice at the other end of the phone. "McKay," he said. "Yes?"

"This is Kate Jameson. I'm very sorry, but I won't be able to come in again today." There was a pause at the other end. It was amazing how powerful silence could be. She wanted to fill it, to blurt out excuses, but didn't let herself.

"Are you still ill?" Dr. McKay finally asked.

"No," she said, "but I have a personal emergency." She looked over at Billy, under the sheet and clearly aroused. "Something's just come up." Billy gave her a look. Kate would have smiled, but she felt McKay's silent curiosity move like a snake through the telephone lines. Stalwart, she kept silent on her end. She watched Billy, who picked up the ends of her hair and held them to his mouth in a kiss.

"I'm sorry to hear that," Dr. McKay intoned, and Kate thought he sounded sorry about it, although she wasn't sure why.

"Because it's half a day, I'll be able to catch up easily. Most of my reports on the children are done."

They discussed scheduling for a few moments, and then Kate

was able to hang up. She gave a sigh of relief, and Billy grinned at her. "Playing hookey?" he asked. She nodded. "I'd like to play something else as well," he said. "And if you don't agree, I'm afraid I'll have to call the truant officer and report you."

Kate giggled. "I'm not in school anymore," she said.

"Oh, we'll see about that," Billy told her.

She supposed if she thought about it, she'd get crazy. After all, here was a man who had slept with half the women in Brooklyn, including her best friend. The idea did make her a bit queasy, so, like some of her young patients, she compartmentalized. She simply put that thought in a mental box, which she closed tightly and put aside. It wasn't possible that Billy Nolan could fake all of these feelings, or could he? His vast experience showed in the skill he displayed when they made love. Every touch, every movement, felt wonderful, perfect almost. If it got any better, it would be frightening. As it was, it was spooky. He seemed to know almost before she did where to put his hands, how hard to press, where to put his mouth, when to be playful, and when to be intense. If she compared his lovemaking to Michael's, which she was trying with little success not to do, she felt as if Michael were only a sandwich while Billy was a Thanksgiving feast.

The two of them spent the morning making love. Then Billy made breakfast. He was a good cook, and Kate was hungry. She looked around the sunny living room. "This is a really nice place," she said as she finished the last of her bacon.

Billy laughed. "You sound surprised," he said.

Kate blushed. "Have you lived here long?" she asked.

"My dad moved in when he got sick. Emphysema. He didn't like being alone in our old house after my mom died. He couldn't work as a fireman anymore, so he began working full-time in the bar, and I helped him turn this into an apartment."

"So you can cook and do carpentry?" Kate asked as she brought the dirty dishes to the sink.

"Yeah," he said. He paused and looked away from her. "It

was fun to work with my dad, but we barely got the place finished before he died."

"Was it from the emphysema?" Kate asked.

Billy nodded and grimaced. "Well, complications thereof. It's a terrible way to die. Terrible to watch."

"I'm sorry," Kate said.

Billy shrugged and began to scrape a plate. "You shouldn't be a fireman and smoke," he said.

"My father was a policeman who drank, and you shouldn't do that, either," Kate said.

Billy nodded, filled the sink with hot water, and put the dishes in to soak. He looked around. "Anyway, I liked this apartment, and when I took over the bar, it seemed handy to live here. This place still reminds me of him." He turned back to the sink and added some dish detergent. Then he wiped his hands on a paper towel and turned back to her. "Funny thing," he said. "We just had breakfast, but I'm hungry again." He raised his brows suggestively, put his arms around her waist, and nuzzled her neck. Kate felt herself responding to the pressure behind her, and with his arms still around her waist, they went back to bed.

It was after their encore, when Billy had gone off to shower, that Kate's cell phone began to ring. She saw that it was Bina and picked it up.

"Katie? Katie?"

"Yes, of course it's me," Kate said.

"Omigod, Katie! He proposed. Just like Elliot said. I couldn't believe it, but Jack proposed."

Kate was flooded with a kind of horror as she remembered—for the first time since she had gotten to Billy's place—that she had originally come to facilitate Bina's long delayed engagement. Was she a selfish or selfless friend?

"That's great! That's really, really great!"

"And you won't believe this," Bina continued. "This is how I know Elliot was right. You won't believe it."

"Try me," Kate said dryly, knowing what was coming. Just

then her phone starting beeping for a call waiting. She glanced at the caller ID and didn't recognize the number, so she let it go to voice mail.

"Well, I had a message from Billy breaking up with me—just in time! Jack asked me to marry him right after I checked my voice mail and got Billy's message!"

"Congratulations. Or best wishes. Or *mazel tov*," Kate said. "Your mother must be thrilled, and your father. And me. I'm thrilled for you."

"I'm thrilled, too. And the best part is that he apologized for what happened, you know, about him not, well, you know. He said he just panicked. He got frightened and couldn't get the words out." She paused. "Do you think that's true?"

"I'm sure that was part of it," Kate said, remembering his request for exploration. It seemed Bina hadn't forgotten it, either.

"And he said he wanted just a little more time to, well, you know . . . we've been going out so long, and he's never cheated on me, and he just wanted to be sure. I don't blame him for that. Would you?"

"No."

"Yeah, but . . ." Bina paused, then lowered her voice. "But I can't forget what happened. You know, about . . . well, you can't imagine how fantastic it was with—"

"I think I can," Kate said as she glanced toward the bathroom. "Look, I gotta go. I'll talk to you tonight."

Kate had just stepped out of the shower herself when her cell phone rang again. She looked at the caller ID and knew she was in trouble. She thought for a moment that she would just ignore it, but she knew Elliot would never give up.

"Where are you?" he asked without any preamble. "You're not here at work and you're not at home. You're out, so you're not sick. Unless you're at the doctor's. Are you at the doctor's?"

"No," Kate said. "And I can't talk right now." She was self-conscious. She felt Billy listening, even though she wasn't sure that he was.

"Okay, so where are you?"

"I'll tell you later," Kate said, lowering her voice.

"What?"

"I'll tell you later."

"Oh, God. You're in bed with Steven."

"Not exactly," Kate said.

"What is that supposed to mean?" Elliot asked. "Oh, I knew it. This is really terrible. So you are with Steven."

"No."

Elliot paused, doing the math. "But you're in bed with someone."

"Yes, Einstein."

"I can't tell you how relieved I am," Elliot said. "At first I was going to call all the hospitals, then, when I thought of Steven, I was going to call all the mental hospitals. But instead of getting neurotic, you just got lucky."

"This may not qualify as luck," Kate said.

"Well, girlfriend, I want to hear all of the details the minute you get home."

Chapter Thirty-seven

W e're coming to a rise. You ready?" Kate nodded.

It was hot, and the heat was already radiating up from the macadam they were skimming over. Kate had been in-line skating once or twice before but had never felt really secure. Now, on this beautifully warm afternoon, everything seemed easy as the two of them skated in Prospect Park, their hands intertwined behind their backs. Billy was a surprisingly good and patient teacher, coaching her until she felt secure enough to lean into her strokes. But the fun was doing it with Billy. He held her with the gentlest pressure, but his support gave her confidence. He warned her of every hill and curve before it came up and tightened his grip when they swooped down an incline. It was exhilarating. Kate believed their skating was almost as sensual as their sex.

"You skate so well," she murmured as they glided into the tree-shaded part of the road.

"Six years on the hockey team and only one chipped tooth to show for it," Billy told her.

Kate looked up and smiled at him. She had wondered about the tooth. It was the imperfection that made the rest of his perfection bearable. She was reminded of the Brad Pitt film in which he had played a boxer. Special makeup had transformed his nose and given it a broken jauntiness. Kate had read somewhere that more women found him attractive in that movie than in any other.

"I like that chipped tooth," was all she said and then felt his arm push her slightly. She thought for a moment it was a reaction to her compliment, but, "Eyes forward," Billy said as he avoided a stumbling skater, and then moved Kate smoothly through a crowd of children crossing the road ahead of them. Out of the shaded alley, the sun beat down fiercely, but their gathering speed created a pleasant breeze. Once they were on the flat open stretch, they really began to move.

"I can see you've had a lot of practice," she noted while she kept her face forward as instructed.

"Hey," Billy said, "you're no virgin yourself."

"I wasn't any good," she told him truthfully. "It's because of you."

Everything was different because of him. It had been over a week since Jack's return and Kate's visit to Billy, and in that time she had spent every free moment with him. The first weekend had been spent being deliciously idle. Then, after work on Monday, he had made her dinner. She'd stayed at his place, but the following evening—traditionally a slow night at the bar—he had come to her house and they'd eaten takeout pizza and one of her great salads. And they'd been together ever since. She had seen Elliot at school but had ducked him, her friend Rita, and the entire Brooklyn cadre. Now they were spending their second weekend together.

Kate was amazed by how much she and Billy had in common. It wasn't only the French. He had also lost his mother early, although he never spoke about her death. He had spent his teenage years being raised by his father. They were both only children and both orphans.

Kate had to admit that she had been prejudiced about him; he wasn't a dunce, and he didn't get by just on his good looks. In fact, if she could put aside his appalling record of conquests, he was the most compatible male companion she had ever spent time with. Kate's work for the semester was ending, and with more time for shopping and cooking, she found that she enjoyed having Billy to her place for dinner.

Over the past week, when it was Billy's turn to close the bar, she'd gone to his apartment early and worked or read until he was through. He'd come up intermittently for quick kisses, usually bringing a treat or a drink. On nights he got off early, he'd made the trip to Manhattan, driving into what he referred to as "the city." Kate remembered when she used to call Manhattan that, and it made her smile every time he said it.

"Another hill," Billy told her now. "Let's put our backs into it."

Kate did. It wasn't just his skating that was impressive. There was almost nothing about Billy Nolan that did not impress her. He wasn't at all what she had thought; he didn't seem glib, or shallow, or arrogant. Not once you knew him. And his affection for her seemed so warm and real. Could he be acting? Kate hated to doubt him. He seemed so sensitive, not only to his own vulnerabilities, as Steven had been, but also to the feelings of others.

The only cloud over her happiness was the nagging thought of the host of women he had previously conquered. In the time she spent away from him, Kate sometimes wondered if all the women he had known had felt like this and, more important, if he had felt just the same about them as he seemed to feel about her. It was hardly the kind of question she could ask, and even if she did, it was not the kind of question that would elicit an honest answer.

They crested the hill, and the long slide down actually made Kate scream, partly with pleasure and partly with fear. Not so different from the way she felt about this relationship. At the bottom of the hill, Billy released one of her hands and coasted over to a bench beside an ice-cream vendor. Just behind them was a field for roller hockey and beyond it a park exit. Kate was grateful for the sit-down. "I'm exhausted," she admitted.

"So am I," Billy told her, though she doubted that was true. There didn't seem to be an ounce of body fat on him, and Kate knew that under his clothes he was lean and powerful without any extra bulk. Thinking of his body gave her a momentary frisson of desire.

"Thirsty?" Billy asked, and she nodded. "Let's go." They took off their Rollerblades, put on their shoes, and bundled their gear into his backpack.

They were just leaving the park when her cell phone rang. She pulled it out and saw that it was Elliot. For the last week she had been ducking his calls when she could and had been equally evasive when she saw him at school. She had talked about Bina's engagement, the shower they were going to throw for her, Elliot and Brice's plans for the summer—everything but the identity of her new boyfriend. She hadn't wanted to lie to him, but she knew how strongly he would disapprove of the truth.

"Are you going to pick it up? Or is it another boyfriend?" Billy asked. Just then the phone stopped ringing.

"It's a he, and he's a friend, but he's gay," Kate told Billy. "Does that count?"

Kate and Billy made their way to Jo's Sweet Shop for some ice cream. Jo's was an institution, the old-time confectionary where parents brought their kids for hot chocolate after winter skating and for sundaes when the weather turned warm. Kate had always envied the kids who got taken to Jo's. A game broke, and behind them an after-the-skating/roller hockey crowd complete with blades, skates, and Prospect Park parents swarmed in to get drinks and ice cream to cool off. With the usual pattern of bullying, the bigger kids elbowed the smaller, some parents pushed ahead of other parents, and chaos reigned. Billy and Kate watched as a seven- or eight-year-old boy was virtually trampled. He began to cry.

"Oh, God!" Kate cried. She worked her way over to him, knelt, and put her arm around him. "Oh, sweetie. Are you hurt?"

"He stepped on me!" the boy sobbed, pointing upward. Kate looked up at a big hulk of a teen hockey guy still in his gear. From low vantage point, the guy looked like a giant. But Billy grabbed him by the back of his hockey shirt and tugged him.

"See? He's gone now." Kate comforted the child.

People began screaming their orders. "Two cookies 'n cream sugar cones with sprinkles!"

"A vanilla Coke!"

"Three large chocolate cones and an iced tea!"

The shouted orders were almost drowned out by the kids' excited yelling and by loud complaints about people pushing ahead and whose turn it was. The adolescent working behind the counter was clearly overwhelmed by the crowd. Kate reunited the little boy with his dad, while the poor soda jerk tried and failed to gain control. With more parkgoers pushing in from the back, those in the front got even rowdier. "Please form a line!" the teen shouted desperately. No one was listening.

Billy returned to Kate's side. He positioned her at the entrance to the work space behind the counter. "This is madness," he said. Then he leapt over the counter and moved to the center, facing out to the crowd.

"All right," he began in a voice loud enough to be heard all the way into the park. "All right now! Kids with hockey sticks on the left. Kids with skates on the right."

There was silence for a moment, and then pushing and shoving began as the crowd tried to part.

"Keep it down! I mean it!"

As if he were Moses and the crowd were the Red Sea, his will was done. Kate smiled as the two lines formed. Billy leaned toward the poor, overwhelmed kid in the apron. "You take the so-called adults and I'll do the Mighty Ducks."

The teen nodded and began taking orders from the line on the right. Billy looked at the children and gestured to the eight-year-old who had been crying. "Service first to the player who was body-checked."

His dad brought the little boy up to the counter. Kate couldn't help but glow. Billy leaned toward the little boy. "What position do you play?" he asked him.

"Goalie," he replied, and looked at his father as if he weren't completely sure.

"Your lucky day!" Billy exclaimed. "Goalies get free cones! Wanna double scoop?"

The teenager behind the counter gave him a look of "No

way." Billy ignored him, took out his wallet, and placed it beside the ice-cream tubs. "What's it gonna be?" The little boy asked for a vanilla cone with sprinkles and hooted with joy when he saw the double dipping he received. Billy moved to the next in the line.

"What's it gonna be?" he asked.

"A cup of chocolate with nuts and whipped cream," the next kid said.

"You got it. And it's on me." Billy sprayed some of the aerosol cream on his shirt. "Get it? It's on me."

The portion of the crowd that was up front laughed. Kate watched Billy with a combination of astonishment, awe, and delight. When he took his next order, he smiled at the kid. "Position?" Billy asked him.

"Guard," the boy said proudly.

"Whoa!" Billy pretended to be taken aback. "Guards get free toppings."

"Wow!" the boy cried. "Hey, Mom! I get a free topping."

Billy leaned over to Kate and gave her a quick kiss right below the ear.

"What do I get?" she asked him coyly.

Billy was already busy making up a cone, but he looked up at her.

"Depends on what position you play," he said, and smiled.

The thing about him, Kate thought, was that he knew the way things worked. He wasn't a macho guy, but he was strong enough and confident enough to be willing to take chances. When the manager of the shop came from out back, leaving the booths and table behind, he took over for Billy. Thanking him, he insisted on giving Billy and Kate free cones.

As they finally made their way out of the sweet shop, Kate looked at Billy. "That was quite a scene, Mr. Nolan," she said. "You're a take-charge kinda guy."

"Hey, what would you expect from a bartender who has dealt with bachelor parties?" Billy said.

"Well, you really managed that crowd."

Billy looked down at his cone, melting over his hand in the heat. "Yeah. If only I could manage my own ice cream."

"Okay. This I know how to do," Kate said, and moved him over to a trash bin. She knocked two scoops off his cone and into the bin, did the same with her own, pulled a Wet-Nap out of her pocket, wiped his hand, and then, with her finger, cleaned up the last trace of whipped cream from his neck.

"Hey, no fair," said Billy. "That was mine."

Kate just smiled and put her ice-cream-covered finger in her mouth. Billy took her hand and licked the remaining ice cream off her finger. Then he gently pinned her against the wall of the sweet shop and, keeping her left hand in his, lifted his arm and pushed his weight against her. Kate thought of Victorian heroines and how they "swooned." She was feeling pretty swoony.

"What do you call this position?" he asked her, his voice low.

At that moment the door of Jo's opened and a bunch of kids streamed out. When a couple of them saw Billy, they began hooting.

"Exhibitionist," Kate told him, and smiled.

On the subway, the unruly park crowd pushed as the train doors opened. Kate was about to be crushed against a pole until Billy corraled her, placing her in the corner of the car against the front window. He protected her with his body, but the crowd had the two of them pushed against each other. She was shocked when his hands disappeared under the back of the waistband of her jeans. He leaned forward to whisper in her ear, "What do you call this position?"

"Tight. Very tight," she said.

Back at Kate's apartment, Billy undressed her slowly. She was surprised and touched by his tenderness: He took off her sandals as if she were a very young child. But by the time he had worked his way up from her feet and unbuttoned her blouse, she knew he considered her grown-up. Then he was on top of her, kissing her neck and making his way to her breasts. She could barely manage to hold back a moan of pure pleasure. Then he stopped, took each of her hands in his, and held them beside her face on the pillow. He looked at her. "And what do you call this position?" he asked.

"Perfect," Kate whispered.

Chapter Thirty-eight

Despite his nose for news and Kate's constant exposure to Elliot at school, she had managed not to raise his suspicions or start him questioning her on why she seemed so happy. If he wrote it off to relief at her breakup with Michael, it was just as well. Although she and Elliot often fought and sometimes didn't speak for a day or two, they had never lied to each other, and Kate did not want to set a precedent now. A sin of omission, however, was less than a fib. But Elliot would be a veritable bloodhound if he got wind of a juicy tidbit like this, and Kate was afraid it was only a matter of time before he sniffed her out. Sooner or later, he would discover the reason for her sunny disposition, and when he did, thunderclouds would gather.

Kate stood in a patch of sunshine and watched the kids all around her. Andrew Country Day was one of the few city schools that had been able to maintain an almost campuslike setting. Old trees, including a giant willow, and a perfect border of manicured lawn gave the enclave the beauty and dignity of a New England college quad.

She felt her first year had been successful but wasn't quite certain that Dr. McKay and the board shared her view. When Michael had assumed she would leave Andrew Country Day, she had suddenly realized how much the job meant to her, the deep pleasure it gave her. The scene around her was so lovely and her work with the children so meaningful that she felt she couldn't part with them. A small but dark voice within her whispered that she would never be allowed so much personal happiness without suffering a professional loss of some sort. Of course, she recognized the fear as superstitious nonsense, something from her childhood that would probably always haunt her when things went well.

Kate brushed a wisp of hair from her face and drew it back into her barrette. A group of fifth-grade girls sat in the grass in the sun, as languid and colorful as the women in a Monet painting. "Hi, Dr. Jameson!" Brian Conroy yelled as he streaked across the lawn, and Kate winced. Dr. McKay was somewhat obsessive about "his" lawn, and running on it was strictly against the rules. But Kate didn't have the heart to scold him. He looked happy, at least for the moment.

The breeze died down and the sun grew warmer. Kate took off her sweater, tied it around her shoulders, and surveyed the schoolyard.

She thought of Billy and smiled. Of course, if she allowed herself to think too much, doubts and questions crept in. Was she deluding herself about Billy being the right sort of man for her? Brooklyn, alcohol, Irish men, dysfunctional families—how could she go back to everything she had run from?

To retain her happiness, Kate put Billy and the future out of her mind, simply watching over the children running and playing in front of her. She smiled. It was almost like watching seawater eddy in tidepools—the children's allegiances, posses, and games changed at different rates, making swirls of motion that were faster in one corner, slower in the middle, and stagnant at one side.

Again her hair escaped from its mooring and blew across her face. As she grabbed it, her fingers brushed her jawline in exactly the way Billy's had stroked it just hours ago. A little shiver ran down her spine, and she felt a flutter in her stomach. Sleeping with him had been so extraordinary, so passionate but tender, that thinking about it seemed dangerous—Kate was afraid she might discover that it was all a dream and have to awaken to a much colder reality.

She walked over to the willow but didn't take a seat on the bench beside it. It was well-known that Dr. McKay frowned on staff sitting when on playground duty. Instead she leaned one hand against the bench, picked up a tendril of the willow in the other, and again lifted her face to the sun. It amazed her how life could change in such sudden, profound ways. She felt, for once, like one of the lucky ones, one of the people in the world for whom things worked out, someone who could simply exist and breathe warm air without struggling. She felt as if everything she wanted would come to her.

Although she wasn't sure she wanted Dr. McKay, when Kate turned her head she saw him scuttling toward her on the flagstone path across the lawn. She straightened, and the bit of the willow wand still in her hand broke off. She hadn't talked to him since she'd called in her absence. The thought made her blush.

"Dr. Jameson," Dr. McKay began, "I've been wanting to talk to you."

Kate felt another flutter, but this one was not nearly so pleasant. Was he going to criticize her for daydreaming or for neglecting to scold the girls who were sitting on the lawn despite the interdict against it? Worse yet, was he about to reject her contract renewal? Was the small, dark voice the voice of truth?

But Dr. McKay looked at her with something approaching a smile, and to her relief he ignored his precious sod for once. "I'm glad I caught you here," he said, and for a moment his voice sounded almost cordial. "Your contract is up for renewal, and the board and I would like to extend it." He paused. "We feel that you are becoming an important part of the Andrew Country Day School tradition."

"Thank you," Kate said. "I'm very happy here, and I hope I'm making a contribution."

Dr. McKay nodded, his face once again poker straight, as if he had lost all his cordiality chips. "Good. Vera will have your renewal contract."

As he walked away, Kate watched his narrow back and managed to feel some affection for him, even when he waved the fifth-grade girls off the lawn.

The bell rang, the children began to line up, and Kate was free to go back to her office. But on the way down the hall, Elliot appeared at his classroom door.

"Are you trying to avoid me?" he asked.

She averted her eyes. "No, of course not."

"Look, I figured it out. I know who your mystery man is and why you're embarrassed to tell me."

"Shh," Kate said anxiously, and took hold of his sleeve. "Come into my office." She was filled with dread. Elliot knew, and he would tell everyone, and Brooklyn would be abuzz with the news.

Once in the office, Elliot closed the door and she turned to face him. "I figured it out," he repeated complacently. "It's Max. You're sleeping with Max and you're embarrassed. But there's nothing wrong with him. I've always thought he was kinda hot myself. It might be a little awkward after you end it, since he lives just upstairs, but any port in a storm."

For a moment Kate was tempted to let him think he'd found her out. But she simply couldn't lie to such a close friend.

"Okay. What is it, then?" Elliot demanded as she shook her head.

"Dr. McKay wants to renew my contract," Kate told him.

"That's not what I'm talking about." Elliot stopped and looked her over. "You're seeing *him,* aren't you?" he said accusingly.

Once again Kate felt her complexion betray her. As a blush suffused her cheeks, she turned her eyes away. "Yes," she said.

For a minute, Elliot was stunned into silence. Then he shook his head. "You little sneak. I should have known you were up to something," he said. "I thought, well, I suspected you might be thinking of that idiot Steven. But no, you have to sniff out worse trouble. And I didn't think there could be worse trouble than Steven Kaplan."

Kate, who thought she was prepared for Elliot's anger, was taken aback. "You don't even know Billy," she said. "To you he's some kind of magic charm, some statistical improbability."

"And what is he to you? A good bonk? Because that would be all he's good for."

Kate felt herself go livid, and the blood that drained from her face actually made her almost dizzy. "I appreciate your concern," she said, her voice cold. "But I don't think you know what you're talking about."

"Right! I haven't been around for the last ten years to witness and dissect every bump and curve in your so-called love life. You forget whom you're talking to, Kate." He pointed to the drawings on her walls, many of them new, farewell gifts from children who would not see her until the autumn. "You want to mess up your life?" Elliot asked, his voice lowered. "I've watched you grow in the last year. Michael might not be right for you, but he was stable and a professional and probably a good father-to-be." He moved closer to her, but Kate pulled away. If he touched her, she was afraid she might slap his hand away.

"You're being unfair and horrible," she said, and realized she sounded like a child. She took a deep breath. She owed a lot to Elliot: his loyalty, his friendship, his help in graduate school, and his assistance in getting her this job that she loved. But it didn't give him the right to judge her let alone Billy in this way. "You don't understand," she said.

"Oh, yes, I do. I know masochism when I see it. And I'm staring at it right now."

"Shut up," Kate told him, her voice lowered to a hiss.

Elliot shrugged and turned away. In the midst of walking out, however, he turned back to her. "Out of the frying pan and into the furnace. This is going on your permanent record, missy."

Chapter Thirty-nine

Kate looked at the pan bubbling on Billy's burner. It certainly didn't look appetizing, but it smelled pretty good, though she couldn't honestly say she was hungry. Her argument with Elliot that afternoon had not only upset her (and her stomach), it had also made her nervous. What was she doing here? Elliot had told her this was only a get-over-Michael fling, but it didn't feel like one. It felt . . . well, she needed to hear that this feeling she had for Billy, who was poking at the contents of the pan with a fork, was mutual.

He was cooking dinner for the two of them. Kate was keeping out of his way while he worked over the shallow pan, in which he seemed to be simmering a lot of tomato sauce, meat, and capers. "What is it?" she had asked him, looking at it doubtfully.

"An old Nolan family recipe. Hey, don't judge it until you've tried it." He grinned at her expression, then reached around her for the bottle of red wine he was using in the sauce. "Listen, before I forget, would you like to go out for lunch on Saturday? I'll have to work Saturday night."

Kate shook her head. "I have a previous engagement," she said. "Bina's bridal shower. How about Friday?"

"That sounds good," he said. Then he shrugged. "We've got the bar booked for Bina's fiancé's bachelor party. Let me tell you, I'm not looking forward to that."

Kate looked down at the pan again and thought about Bina and how upset she seemed. Between the end of school and her time with Billy, Kate hadn't had much time for her friend and couldn't bear to hear all the ongoing wedding preparation details. Bina was obviously bewildered about her seeming indifference.

Seeing the look on her face, Billy patted her shoulder. "Don't you worry, everybody likes it. It's a guaranteed way to tenderize the toughest meat. My mom used to make it." He had never spoken of his mother before, except to say she was dead. For a moment Kate considered asking about her but decided against it.

She took the glass of red wine Billy had poured her in between doctoring the sauce and wandered over to the window. After her fight with Elliot, he had called to make up. He'd asked her to meet him for a drink, but she'd been forced to admit that she was spending the night with Billy. Elliot had made his disapproval obvious and vocal. Kate had tried to ignore all of the calmer, more logical things he had said to dissuade her: how Billy was a playboy and she was barking up the wrong tree, how Elliot loved her but didn't want to have to "pick up the pieces." Then he had stopped, as if at a sudden thought. "You're not doing this just to get a proposal, are you?" he'd asked. "After all, you turned Michael down and you don't know what the cat might drag in after Billy dumps you."

The words had chilled her. "I never believed that ridiculous theory," she had snapped.

"How can you say that?" he'd asked. "It got Bina engaged. Proof positive."

With a lot of effort and sidestepping, Kate had managed to convince him that she was not taking this affair seriously. Now, as she stared out the window at the rain, she admitted to herself that she had lied. She was taking Billy seriously, and she was beginning to hope that his feelings for her were totally sincere. Elliot's assured assumption that Billy would, of course, dump her had shaken her more than she liked to admit. Was it possible that she was nothing to him but another notch on his belt? She looked over at him, busily throwing far too much pepper into the pan. He wasn't even wearing a belt, for God's sake, and his Levi's rode his hips in the most provocative way. Kate turned away. She'd never looked at Michael with this kind of carnal longing.

She gazed around the room. Steven's West Side apartment had always looked like a student's place with its sprung sofa and the books he still had in cartons, while Michael's place, though it was neater and furnished with new Ikea pieces, looked in comparison temporary. But Billy's three big rooms indicated that he had put down deep roots. Beneath her feet, the Persian rug in blue and maroon looked faded and worn, as if his grandmother might have walked on it. The Chesterfield sofa didn't look as if it had been bought from a catalog—the oxblood leather didn't appear to have been professionally "distressed" at the factory before it was shipped. But there were new things, too: On one wall there was a big art piece—Kate couldn't call it a painting or a collage because it was something in between, a crazy-quilt consisting of torn bits of white paper glued to a white canvas. On the wall between the windows there was a small abstract of a woman lying under what looked like a very fluffy duvet. And over the sofa, hanging in a row, was a series of lithographs. Kate studied them.

"What do you think?" Billy asked her. He had come out of the kitchen. "Are they art, or did the artist who owed me a big tab rip me off?"

She smiled at him. "I like them," she said.

He took an appraising look. "I think I do," he said, and indicated the art on the walls with a flourish of the meat fork still in his hand. "Valuable art or bad debts. You be the judge." He smiled. "Dinner's almost ready."

Kate nodded, and Billy disappeared back into the kitchen. Watching him, she had to admit that Billy Nolan was the first man she had felt this kind of desire for. It was too comfortable to be infatuation, but too passionate to be completely comfortable. Most likely, it would end in tears. And the rain against the window seemed appropriate.

"Hey! How about a little help here?" Billy asked, coming out of the kitchen again, this time with plates and flatware. "You set the table." He went to the mantelpiece and took down two candle-sticks, the candles in them stubby and of two different heights. "Spare no expense," he said. "Candlelight. Paper napkins. The works."

Kate smiled and set the table. She fetched a wineglass for him and put out the salt and pepper. A matchbook from the bar lay on the coffee table, and she used a match to light the two black wicks. As she did, it occurred to her that the last time Billy had used these candles it might have been to dine—and sleep—with Bina. She stood absolutely still until the match burned down, almost to her fingernail. Then she dropped it, just the way she dropped the idea of Billy with Bina or anyone else, and moved away from the table.

To distract herself, Kate looked around at all of the French volumes lined up neatly on Billy's bookshelves. She reminded herself not to be too inquisitive, not to bring up the past or the future, but she couldn't help being curious, and it seemed harmless enough to ask. "What's with the French?" she called to him in the kitchen.

Billy emerged with his mystery dish and began to fill her plate. "Oh. I like it. It's not as rich a language as English, but it has subtleties that we lack."

Kate sat at the table and placed her napkin on her lap. "Did you learn it in school?" she asked, accepting her plate and eyeing its contents with uncertainty.

"A little," said Billy. He filled his own plate, then took a seat.

Gingerly, Kate tasted the stew. It was delicious, the meat so tender it fell off the bone. She looked across at him and smiled.

"Good?"

"Very. Really." She leaned back in her chair and smiled at him. "You must have been a terror growing up. A real class clown," she said.

He shook his head, his mouth full. He had to swallow before he could answer. "No. I didn't even talk in class. I had a stutter so bad that I was really self-conscious. I didn't want to talk to anyone."

Kate put down her fork and stared at him. She had almost forgotten his slight stammer. But stuttering, she knew, was almost impossible to cure completely, and many of the treatments had only a temporary effect. "How did you . . . when did you lose the . . ."

"Oh, I went all through high school with it. But when I was a junior, I had a good French teacher, and I noticed that in French I didn't stutter. It was strange, to be able to say whatever I wanted to without worrying about certain words and letters I always got stuck on."

"It must have been amazing."

"Yeah. I felt like I was being let out of a prison. Man, I learned every word I possibly could in French. I wanted to know how to say 'dude' in French."

"What is 'dude' in French?"

"There's not really an equivalent. Believe me, I looked. Senior year I really didn't study anything else. And I didn't care about the grade. I just wanted to be able to speak whenever I felt like it."

Kate was fascinated. "What happened then?" she asked, like a child being told a bedtime story.

"My teacher introduced me to some of her French friends, and she helped me get into L'Ecole des Beaux-Arts in Paris. I was supposed to be studying French history, but what I was really doing was reinventing myself. I felt like I was reborn. I wasn't the kid who stuttered. I was the American who spoke French as well as any Parisian. Sometimes people I met wouldn't believe I was American."

"And what happened to your stutter? In English, I mean?" Kate asked.

Billy shrugged. "When I had to come back because of my father, it just seemed to be gone. Sometimes when I'm tired or under a lot of stress, I stammer a little bit."

Kate remembered his speech at the wedding. He had stammered a little then. "How do you control it?"

"I just relax and it goes away."

"You never had speech therapy? No one ever tried to help when you were younger?"

"Oh, there was some attempt in grammar school. You know, a speech therapist. She used to come and take me out of class. I was mortified."

"Didn't your parents try to help? I mean, was there any other—"

"Well, both of them were very concerned. Every time there was an article about stuttering with some new cure, they got excited. But it was expensive and nothing really worked for long, and by the time I got to junior high I just told them to forget it."

"And you found a way to cure it yourself," Kate said. His resourcefulness amazed her.

"Well, I kind of fell into it, didn't I? I shouldn't get full credit. I just wasn't so stupid that I ignored the possibility of change."

"And what did you study in Paris?"

"Girls. I mean, for the first time I could talk to them. I also studied cheap train tickets. I got to Berlin and Bruges and Bologna for about a dime."

"Only places that began with Bs?" Kate asked with a smile.

Billy stared at her. "B was the letter I had the most trouble with," he said. "I wonder if that was just a coincidence."

Kate shrugged. "Jung would say no," she told him, "but I'm not sure."

"What did Jung say about repetition compulsions?" Billy teased, and Kate didn't know if she should laugh or cry. But she didn't have to do either, because he rose and cupped one hand around her neck, then combed his fingers through her hair. "I have ice cream," he told her, "but I can think of a much more delicious dessert." Kate smiled up at him.

Chapter Forty

The afternoon was lovely, warm in the sun but cool in the shade of the buildings, with a breeze that kept the slightly humid city air from being uncomfortable. "Let's take a walk," Billy suggested. "I'll show you some parts of Brooklyn you might not know."

Luckily, Kate had worn her Nikes and felt energetic. "I'm sorry that we can't spend the night together this Saturday," Billy told her as they left his apartment. "I'm always on watch during bachelor parties."

Kate nodded. Billy seemed completely accepting of Bina's nuptials. Had their relationship meant absolutely nothing to him? She shivered, though the weather was perfect. Surely what she felt for him was not unrequited.

Always sensitive to her movements, Billy put his arm around her. "Yeah," he said, "those bachelor parties make me shiver, too, but I just close my eyes and think of England."

Kate hadn't even considered the kind of raunchy goings-on that were typical. She didn't want to ask if Jack would have lap dancers or strippers or even worse. The sun and the cloudless sky were so lovely that she decided to put the whole idea out of her mind and do her best to live in the present. The present was perfect.

Billy took her hand, and although it was sentimental and wrong of her, Kate felt protected and loved just because he cradled her hand so safely in his own.

"This is Windsor Park," he said as they turned a corner and walked along a block of small houses, each with a garden in front of it. "Mostly Italian. Cops. Plumbers. A nice family neighborhood, but the yuppies are moving in from the north."

Kate enjoyed the gardens, some of which were planted with so many colorful flowers that they were almost in bad taste. In some front yards, as if the flowers weren't enough, stood garden statues of everything from Bambi to the Blessed Virgin. They walked past a big Catholic high school and crossed a walkway over the BQE.

"This is the edge of Park Slope," Billy told her. "You can't touch a house here for less than eight hundred thousand dollars anymore."

Kate looked from side to side at the brownstones and brick facades. Billy pointed to one where, unlike the others, the paint was peeling off the front door and the windows were old metal casements instead of the elegant flat expanses on the other houses. "You can always tell a holdout from the old days," he said. "The old lady who owns that place probably hasn't painted her kitchen in a decade."

They came to a corner where a tavern had set a few tables outside. "Not quite a café yet," Billy said with a smile. "Wanna drink?"

Kate nodded. They shared a beer and sat on a bench, watching women with strollers and kids with bikes and dads move past them. "So you drink?" Kate asked, though it was now obvious that he sometimes did. She had feared he might be a sober alcoholic and not drink at all. Or a control freak like Michael.

"My father told me there were two kinds of people not to trust: the ones who drank too much and the ones who didn't drink at all." He stood up. "You ready to continue?" he asked. Kate stood and took his hand.

They walked for another half hour until they reached a building that was neither as perfect as the gentrified ones nor as run-down as the one he had pointed out to her. He stopped and searched in his pocket for a moment. "Come over here," he said as he ran down the three steps and stood in the doorway. For a moment Kate thought he was only looking for a slightly private place to kiss her, but before she reached him he had inserted a key into the door. He took her hand and led her down the hallway of the brownstone, which had been divided into apartments. At the back he used another key to open another door. Inside there was an empty white room.

"Come through this way," he said, and led her across the gleaming wood floor to a back door.

Once through it, Kate felt as if she had entered another world. It was a backyard garden, but what a garden. A small lawn was perfectly tended. It made Dr. McKay's patch of grass look bald. Here and there, the lawn had bluestone placed in it, like islands in a green sea. They led in a lazy, curving path to a bower of trees that were in bloom. Behind them was a tiny pond surrounded by iris and fern. Kate could see goldfish darting under the lily pads and duckweed. Two chairs, their wood weathered to a silvery gray, sat beside the pool. Behind them, ivy crawled up the brick wall that divided the yard from whatever lay on the other side.

But Kate didn't care what was on the other side or anywhere else. It was the most serene, most beautifully groomed city garden she had ever seen. She didn't want to be anywhere but here. She looked at Billy, who had stopped in the sunshine on the lawn and was watching her. She walked back to him. "How did you know about this place?" she asked.

"It's mine," he said.

"What do you mean?"

"Well, when I was a kid we lived here. It was my grandmother's house. She lived on the ground floor and we had the top. But my mother took care of the garden. She taught me, and then I started to like it." He took her hand and led her to one of the chairs. "Do you like it?" he asked.

"It's breathtaking," Kate told him. She thought of *The Secret Garden,* her favorite book when she was growing up. "You've kept it up? Do the people who own the house now—"

"I own the house now," Billy told her.

"But you live—"

"Yeah, I live over the bar because it's convenient and it's the right amount of space and it reminds me of my dad. I've been renting out this place, but I keep the bottom floor empty so that I get the garden. I renovated the house—I mean, not by myself, but with a carpenter friend and a plumber who used to work with my father. Anyway, it's apartments now, but easy to turn back into a family house, maybe someday."

Kate sat, trying not to show her amazement.

"Ça te plaît?" he asked.

Did she like it? *"Je l'adore,"* she told him. *"C'est un vrai paradis."* She didn't want Billy to see just how impressed she was because it would embarrass her and possibly embarrass him. She was a psychologist and supposed to be aware of people's psychological depths, but she had misjudged Billy at every step. The idea of him tending the grass, planting flowers, and raking leaves had never occurred to her. Why should it? She wasn't yet sure about all that this garden revealed about Billy, but she could see how much it said to him. More important, she already knew what it meant to her. A man who could create and tend a garden like this was obviously very special. Why hadn't she been able to see? Was it because he acted so casual, so carefree? But a garden like this took care and . . . diligence. It also took vision. She looked around again at the perfectly tended beauty. Kate caught her breath. A man with such tenderness as this could surely be a good father, husband, best friend.

She dared to look at him. He shrugged. *"Il faut cultiver notre jardin,"* he said, quoting Voltaire. "I used to work here with my mother."

Billy had told her about his father's death, but she hadn't yet asked him questions about his mother's. Now she did. "Pancreatic cancer," Billy told her, and Kate winced. She knew it was a particularly ugly and painful death.

"I'm so sorry," she said. "When?"

"Quite some time ago. The day before Thanksgiving. It still makes the holidays tough."

Kate nodded. Although she didn't miss her father, and she was always included at the Horowitz table, she felt like the orphan she was from Thanksgiving to New Year's. They sat for a while, both silent, but it wasn't an uncomfortable silence. Kate felt that by bringing her here, Billy had shown her more than his landscaping skills. She took his hand, and the two of them watched the fish move in golden darts under the surface of the water.

Chapter Forty-one

My God! These girls and showers! They are the cleanest people in the city of New York. Not to mention the ones with the most gifts."

Despite his sharp tongue, Brice was smiling. He sat between Elliot and Kate in the cab, a big, beautifully wrapped gift sitting on his lap. Kate wasn't sure she could face everyone in Brooklyn, but Bina's bridal shower couldn't be missed.

Elliot was silent. She knew he was angry at her, but there was nothing she could do. She thought of the Pascal line *Le coeur a ses raisons que la raison ne connaît point*. The heart has its reasons that reason knows nothing of.

The story of Billy's French lingered in Kate's mind. She tried to imagine what a silent, humiliated young Billy Nolan had been like. She couldn't. It was either a failure of imagination or too sad to visualize. Somehow, his history changed her view of him in the present. Instead of cocky and too self-assured, she saw his outgoing personality as a celebration of his freedom. It made her feel far more tender toward him, as if he needed protection. This was ridiculous, of course, since the days when he was a vulnerable child and adolescent were long over. Billy Nolan could certainly take care of himself, but despite her intentions to keep a lid on her feelings, she found herself feeling more and more for him.

They were crowded in the back of the taxi, and Kate was relieved when the cab pulled up in front of the Horowitz house.

Before they even reached the front door, it was flung open by Mrs. Horowitz. "Come on," she called. "Hurry up or you'll spoil the surprise." Kate would never tell her that she had already "spoiled" the surprise by telling Bina in advance about the party. The two of them had made a pact long ago that they would never allow either one of them to show up badly dressed and be scared out of their wits by a "wonderful surprise."

Kate and the guys walked in and joined the others. There were kisses and hugs and introductions. Kate added her gift to the big, colorful pile already stacked on a card table. Then Mrs. Horowitz called out, "Sha! Sha! They're coming!" Kate sighed while everyone else in the room seemed to suck in their breath so they could shout more loudly. Dr. Horowitz flung open the door and made way for Bina. Kate thought Bina did a miserable imitation of a surprised person, but no one seemed to notice. When Bina gave her a special look, Kate smiled at her.

The party went through each of its traditional phases: the weren't-you-surprised-yes-I-was part; the no-you-shouldn't-have-this-wasn't-necessary section; and the oh-let's-eat-isn't-this-delicious portion (and they were big portions). The party culminated in the traditional oohing and aahing over gifts. Kate knew she was watching an important female rite of passage, but she just wasn't in the mood. She regretted giving up the day with Billy, she was annoyed by all of the Horowitz extended family and their questions about when it was her turn, and she was bored by the chatter and old jokes, not to mention resentful of the way Brice and Elliot seemed to relish it all.

Kate wondered why Bina kept throwing looks at her and hoped that Elliot hadn't told her about what he was now referring to as the "Billy thing." Several times Bina seemed to try to get next to Kate and talk to her, but Kate managed to slip away. Elliot wouldn't—couldn't—break the confidentiality of her private situation without her permission.

When the cake was cut and being passed around, Kate could take no more and went into the bathroom to revive herself. She looked about as lousy as she felt. She put on some lipstick and a little blush, but it didn't seem to do much. She decided it didn't matter. She had been so happy for the past few weeks that her discomfort seemed especially painful. Why was seeing her friends such an onerous task? She thought about it for a little while. Kate believed she wasn't like her friends. She had a career and loved her work. She hadn't been out looking for a husband from the time she was twenty. She didn't feel as if she needed a man to protect her or to support her. But somehow, because of breaking up with Michael or seeing Steven or because of this . . . thing with Billy Nolan, she felt as insecure and lonely as she used to feel back in high school.

Since her talk with Elliot, she had felt more and more doubt. Somehow, being here with Bina and all her married Brooklyn friends made it seem more unlikely that she would ever get to share their experience of this kind of group celebration. Billy wasn't "a safe bet." He was not the kind of man women got to marry or men threw bachelor parties for. Kate imagined his whole life had been a kind of bachelor party, and Elliot was right: There was no reason for her to think that would change. She began to feel extremely sorry for herself and realized it was best to leave the bathroom now before the tears set in.

As she walked into the hallway, Bina sidelined her. "I have to talk to you," she hissed. "Quick, before anyone notices." She took Kate's hand and drew her down the narrow hallway to her bedroom.

Nothing had changed. The same flowered pink curtains hung at the window, the same matching wallpaper covered the walls, and the print repeated itself on Bina's bedspread. The dressing table with the pink skirt that Kate had envied so when they were in seventh grade still sat between the two windows. Kate herself sat on the bench in front of it. "What is it?" she asked.

"Oh, Katie, I just can't keep this lie going," Bina said.

Kate took a deep breath. She loved her friend's simplicity, but sometimes it was just too much. "Oh, Bina. Nobody cares. If you just act normal now and carry on, everyone will be thrilled."

Bina's face registered horror. "I can't believe that you would tell me to do that," she cried.

"Bina, it's just a party. It's not a lifetime."

Bina's mouth dropped open. "I'm sorry," she said. "I beg to differ with you. I think a marriage is supposed to last a lifetime."

Kate stopped examining the pictures and mementos on the dressing table. "What are you talking about?" she said. "Just because you pretended to be surprised doesn't mean you're starting your marriage with a lie. For God's sake, have a sense of proportion."

Bina took a step backward, as if Kate had physically attacked her. Then her lips began to tremble. "Is it really you saying this?" she said. "Max thought you would understand, but even if you don't, I can't go through with it. I can't marry Jack. It's not like he really loves me. I know what he was up to in Hong Kong. Max showed me."

Kate sighed angrily. After all that Bina had gone through to finally get Jack, it seemed a little late in the day to find a misplaced sense of pride. "Well, that was very wrong of Max. Remember, you were dating, too."

"Yeah, but I didn't want to."

"Oh, come on, you had a lot of fun with Billy."

"But that was just fun."

Kate raised her brows. "And why are you feeling guilty about that little sexual escapade?"

"Because it wasn't an escapade," Bina said. "I keep comparing it to being with Jack, and . . ."

Kate certainly doubted that Jack could be anywhere near as erotic and imaginative and warm in bed. But she certainly couldn't tell Bina why she suspected that. And it was hopeless for Bina to think about Billy as an alternative to Jack. Kate truly believed Bina loved Jack, and with a little time she would get over this guilt and unhealthy comparison and settle down.

"Bina," she said, rising and taking her friend by her shoulders, "you have to get over this guilt. You have to move on. This is what you have wanted your whole life."

"But I was wrong," Bina wailed.

"No, you weren't," Kate told her. "You're wrong now. So just calm down. Enjoy all this."

Just then the door opened. "Oh, here they are," Mrs. Horowitz sang out. "The best friends are at it in here," she called, and lifted her camera to take what would develop into a hideously unflattering picture of both of them.

Chapter Forty-two

Kate fumbled with the lock to her door and pushed in. The lights were on, and she gasped and almost jumped when she realized that her living room was filled with people. For a moment she was terrified that Elliot, Barbie, Bina, and the rest would scream, "Surprise!" But no one yelled—in fact, no one said anything. She couldn't believe that Elliot—whom she had trusted with a key—would invade her nest, bringing a flock of raptors with him. She would get her keys back, and she would get him back some other way. Before she had a chance to ask what the hell was going on, Elliot, who was perched on a windowsill, spoke.

"Some of you might ask why we are gathered here today," he said in a pretty good imitation of Dr. McKay's pompous tone.

"What's going on?" Kate asked. Her stomach sank, as if she were in a plunging elevator. But at the same time, she felt her rage ready to choke her. She didn't even have a place to sit or put her bag down.

"We're worried about you," Bina said. She was the only one there who looked apologetic.

"Katie, look, you're allowed to go out with him, and you're even allowed to sleep with him, but you're not allowed to fall in love with him," Barbie added.

"What are you talking about?" Kate asked. But of course, she knew. Elliot must have told everyone, and now they were trying to do some kind of . . . intervention, or something, as if she were a drunk who needed to be confronted with her self-destructive behavior.

"Time to go now. Party's over," Kate told them, using the phrase Billy did when he was ready to close the bar. She turned into her little hallway to get to the bedroom and away from all of these so-called friends. Unfortunately, Brice was standing there, leaning against the wall.

"Sorry, girlfriend, you have to hear this," he said, and gently turned her around, marching her into the middle of her living room. Bina got out of the wicker chair, and Brice maneuvered Kate over to it. Bev leaned forward as far as she could given the state of her belly and took Kate's hand.

"I know how it is, Katie," she said. "You want a home of your own. You want a wedding and a husband and a baby."

Kate snatched her hand away. "I have a home," she said. "It's right here, and I would like you all to do me a favor and get out of it. Please," she added so that she didn't sound quite so rude. After all, they probably meant well.

Elliot came up from behind her and put his hands on her shoulders. His face was beside her own. "I wouldn't have done this if I didn't think it was really serious," he said.

"I want my keys back," Kate told him, and extended her hand. "I mean now." It was better to lock him out permanently, she thought, than ever to walk into a scene like this again.

"Look, you moved out of the old neighborhood. You might not remember what players in Brooklyn are like, but you've wasted enough of your time on jerks. You're not getting younger this week," Bunny said. "Or any other week."

"Yeah. A fling is okay, but once you're thirty your flings are flung," Barbie added. "Whaddya think? A blow job's a commitment?"

"Shut up, Barbie," Kate told her. "None of this is your business." She turned and looked around at the room. She couldn't defend herself with logic. And a part of her knew they were probably right. But that was a part she didn't want to listen to.

Elliot sighed. "I told you this wouldn't be easy," he said to the assembled bunch of gossips, yentas, and morons that up till now Kate had considered her friends. He leaned toward her again. "Kate, I'm not saying you did the wrong thing in turning Michael down."

"I am," Bev interrupted. "He was a doctor and a Pisces. Perfect."

Brice silenced her with a look. "I think what Elliot is trying to say is that you can waste a lot of time with men like Steven and Billy, but you get propositions, not proposals, from them."

Kate could feel her face getting warm with anger and embarrassment. "We only want what's best for you," Elliot said.

"We're worried about you," Barbie added. Then she looked down at Kate's feet. "Where did you get those shoes?" she asked. "Are they Ferragamo?"

"Not now, Barbie," Brice admonished. "This isn't *Full Frontal Fashion.*"

"No. It's *Full Frontal Confrontation,* and it's over." Kate took a deep breath. She looked at Bina, who had been the quietest. "How was the bachelor party?" she asked.

"Didn't you hear?" Bev asked.

"There was a fistfight."

"You're kidding?" Brice said. "Why haven't I heard about this?"

"My Arnie said it was incredible. Max and Jack really went at each other."

"Yeah, my Johnny said Jack's black eye probably won't heal before the wedding. And if Billy hadn't of broken it up . . ."

Once again Kate felt her stomach lurch, this time over the scene in a Brooklyn bar during a bachelor party. She knew Billy kept a baseball bat beside the cash register, but she wondered if he had been hurt. This, however, was not the time to ask.

"So what happened?" Elliot wanted to know.

"Oh, Max called Jack names and he got mad and took a

swing at Max, but then Max got wild and jumped him. Whaddaya expect? They were all drunk."

Kate stood up. She wanted to call Billy and find out if he was okay. She also needed all of these so-called friends of hers to leave her in peace. But Elliot had other plans. "Kate, you have to promise us all that you'll break off this thing with Billy," he said. "I mean, what's the point? After he dumps you, you don't want to get proposed to by a stranger."

"Will you stop that!" Kate told him. "What makes you so sure he'll dump me? And if you believe that garbage about proposals . . ."

The room filled with half a dozen hushed oohs. "Jesus," Barbie said. "Do you actually think he's serious about you?"

"Kate, this is a guy who has made fear of commitment a permanent lifestyle," Bev said. She stood up with difficulty. She opened her mouth, but before she could continue her rant, a strange look came over her face. "I feel a little twinge." She put a hand on her belly, and as she did her water broke.

Chapter Forty-three

It was the last day of school, and Kate was straightening out her files, packing her two plants, and saying good-bye for the summer to the children who dropped in. Once she was finished, she knew she should go to Bev's to see her baby. Though she was curious to see it, her resentment of the Bitches still lingered, and to be brutally honest, she was also afraid she'd feel some envy.

Not that she was unhappy. She had the children at the school. Overall, she was very pleased with her work at Andrew. Though she hadn't made any progress with the Reilly twins, she had convinced their parents to dress them in different clothes. It hadn't stopped them from continuing to pull the switcheroo, but at least now they had to go into the bathroom or gym and swap their outfits to do it. If there was a darker side to their masquerading, she would have to find it in September. But most of her other work had gone well. Tina Foster was no longer taking dares or launching herself out into space. Though she was still a tomboy and preferred to chase boys than sit with the girls, she didn't seem at all self-destructive.

As Kate put some papers into her backpack, Jennifer Whalen appeared in the doorway. Jennifer had stopped her exaggerated lying, and Kate smiled at the little girl. "Coming to say good-bye?" she asked. Jennifer nodded. "You know, I'll see you in September." Jennifer nodded again and then rushed into the room and hugged Kate.

"Thank you for helping me with my shelf-esteem," Jennifer said.

Kate looked down at her, suppressing a smile. "You're very welcome," she said.

Jennifer nodded wisely and gestured to all the empty shelves in the office. "Do you have shelf-esteem, too?" she asked.

Now Kate allowed herself to smile. "Plenty," she told the little girl, and Jennifer smiled, too, turned, and skipped out of the room.

"See ya next year," she called.

Kate had just knelt down to straighten the dollhouse when she felt someone else's presence behind her. Still on her knees, she turned and was totally surprised to find Billy standing in the doorway. He took a step into the room and closed the door behind him. His face was bruised, with a swollen patch on one cheek and a scratch over his eye. She jumped to her feet. "Are you all right? I kept leaving messages on your machine. Where have you been?" she asked, and moved toward him. He must have been hurt in the imbroglio at Jack's party, as she had feared. She wanted to hold him and touch his face, but he put up a hand to stop her.

"So who do you expect a proposal from?" he asked. His face was pale, and the bruise seemed even darker against his livid skin.

"What do you mean?" she asked.

"What kind of game were you playing with me?" he demanded. "Don't try to deny it, because I heard all about it at the bachelor party. Those assholes called me Dumping Billy for most of the evening. And when one of them finally told me the score, I couldn't believe it." Kate realized she was holding her breath but couldn't seem to do anything about it. "Bina got that jerk-off Jack. Who are you expecting to get?"

For a moment Kate considered saying, "You. I want you," but she knew this certainly wasn't the time for an admission like that. She moved toward him and tried to take his hand, but again he extended his arm, silently telling her to back off. She could see the anger on his face, but beyond that she could see real pain in his eyes. He must truly care for me, she thought.

"It's not what you think," Kate began, and then tried to figure out how she could possibly explain all the machinations and manipulations that had gone on since the fateful day of Bunny's wedding. Before she could launch into an explanation, Billy spoke.

"Did you all do research? You know, to find out about the women I'd dated in the past and what happened to them after we broke up?"

"I didn't," Kate said.

"Don't become a lawyer," Billy snapped. "If it wasn't you, it was someone in your posse."

Kate looked away. She should have seen this coming, but somehow she had just thought things would continue as they were going or that Billy would tire of her the way he had with so many other women. She wanted to wiggle out of this, but she couldn't lie. The problem was, she also didn't want to tell the truth.

"My friend Elliot . . . ," she began.

"Is he the one you expect to propose to you after we break up?"

"Billy, he's gay, hooked up, and my best friend. He's a mathematician, and, well, he noticed . . . he discovered that after you left girls they immediately got married. He thought there was a cause and effect. And he convinced Bina that—"

"And you convinced me to go out with her. Repetition compulsion, my ass. The whole thing was a setup. And I have no goddamn idea why it worked, but Bina is marrying Jack and I figure you've got someone on the hook. . . ."

"Billy, you really have this wrong."

"Oh? I had three hours of bullshit from every guy at the party, all of them blaming me for their marriages."

Kate felt herself begin to lose her own temper. "I think you made a reputation for yourself long before I came on the scene," she snapped. "I just didn't know when you were planning to dump me."

"How about right now?" he asked. "And best wishes on your upcoming nuptials. I hope whoever your victim is richly deserves you." He spun around, opened the door, and virtually smashed into Dr. McKay.

"Am I interrupting something?" Dr. McKay asked, his eyebrows raised and his eyes darting back and forth between Kate and Billy.

"No," Billy told him. "We're finished." Kate could only watch his back as he strode down the hallway.

Chapter Forty-four

Kate cried for an hour in her office. Then, when Elliot found her and bundled her in his arms to take her home, she cried in the taxi all the way back to his apartment. She cried when Brice got in, and she cried over the dinner he made. At last Elliot took her to the sofa, sat her down, and put his arm around her. "Kate," he said, his voice warm and compassionate, "I know how you hurt. And I hurt for you. But are you sure this isn't just a Bina Horowitz impersonation you're doing?"

Despite her pain, Kate almost laughed, and that made her choke, snorting tears up her nose.

"You also have to consider my rug," Brice added, sitting beside them. "It's a faux antique Tabriz."

Kate took a shuddering breath. She couldn't go on crying forever, though she felt as if she wanted to. But what was the point? She'd ruined her life. She'd hurt the man she loved, and now he despised her. Still, she might as well stop crying. She managed a wet grin. "There's my good girl," Elliot told her.

"Why don't you try to pull yourself together?" Brice suggested. "Go on into the bathroom and clean up your face?"

Kate nodded and stood up.

"Do you want me to help?" Elliot asked, but Kate shook her head.

"I'll brew up some teabags for your eyes," Brice told her, and patted her arm in a comforting way. "It will take down the swelling. Believe me, I know."

Looking at herself in the bathroom mirror, Kate couldn't help it: She began to cry again. Her face was a ruin, her eyes red and minuscule in the puff pastry around them. Her nose, especially around the nostrils, almost perfectly matched the color of her hair. God, she was ugly! She filled the sink with cold water, took a deep breath, and lowered her face into it. The shock felt good, and she stood, bent at the waist, her face in the sink, for what seemed like a long time. Maybe, she thought, she could drown this way.

She thought of Billy in bed, his arms around her. She thought of him from the back, moving shirtless as he cooked breakfast. She remembered every book and picture in his apartment, their walks around Brooklyn, and his garden. Without ever admitting it to herself, she had hoped that garden, that house, would be one they would share and fill with their children someday.

Kate's body shuddered for air, and she lifted her face out of the sink. She looked back in the mirror as she gasped for breath. She knew this breakdown was more than just about Billy. She had been crying because she'd hurt him and because she herself was hurt. But she felt she had also been crying for her past as well as her future. All the tears she had held back in grammar school, on lonely holidays, in high school, through the struggle of college and graduate school, all of the unshed tears seemed to be leaking out of her now. She filled the sink again and immersed herself. She opened her eyes under the water.

She could see now that Billy had been a chance to regain the good part of her background, to heal a lot of her wounds. She had changed her style, perhaps, but despite the education and the move to Manhattan, her roots were showing. She blinked. Underwater, with her eyes painful from crying, she could see that Billy had been a unique opportunity to love and be loved by an equal, by a partner who would truly know her.

Kate burst up out of the water like a submarine exploding onto the surface of the sea. She was about to begin crying again when she heard her cell phone ring. She ran out of the bathroom.

Brice framed her with two hands. *"Ophelia, Drowned for Love and Answering a Phone,"* he said. "Pre-Raphaelite school."

"Want to stop running the marathon and help clean up dinner?" Elliot asked.

She paid no attention. She got to her purse and began scrambling through it. Her phone was still ringing. Billy had changed his mind. Somehow he had realized that it had all been a mistake, that she loved him and wanted him, and that everything else that had happened was nonsense.

She was on her knees, her makeup bag and change purse and wallet spread all around her on Brice's carpet. But when she finally managed to find the phone, the caller had hung up. She quickly punched in the request for received calls, but she didn't recognize the number. It was a 212 area code, not the 718 of Brooklyn. It didn't matter. It had to be Billy. He had come looking for her. She pressed the call button and waited, literally holding her breath. It would all be all right, she told herself. It *had* to be all right. In a moment someone answered the phone.

"Hello, Kate?"

It was a man's voice, but her stomach lurched when she realized it wasn't Billy.

"Yes?" Kate said, though she wanted to hang up and throw the phone into the sink of cold water. If Billy didn't call, what did she need a phone for?

"Kate, it's me. Steven."

"Steven!"

At the sound of his name, both Elliot and Brice nearly dropped the plates and silverware they were clearing from the table.

"*That* Steven?" Brice whispered.

"Drop the phone into this soup right now," Elliot said, holding out a full bowl. "I mean it, missy."

Kate motioned for them both to shut up.

"Did I get you at a bad time?" Steven asked.

Kate almost laughed aloud. She couldn't remember ever crying for this long in her whole life. "A bad time" was a massive understatement. "No," she said. "I can talk."

Elliot shook his head wildly, but Kate paid no attention. She remembered how she had lived for his calls. And now the deadness she felt talking to him was new and curious. Maybe in two years I could feel this way talking to Billy, she thought. Maybe I can learn eventually not to care about anyone. But where was the benefit of that?

"Look, if you're not busy, would you consider meeting me for a drink?"

"Now?" Kate asked. She looked down at her watch. It felt like midnight, but it was only eight-fifteen. Typical Steven move: calling with no warning and expecting her to jump. But she felt no resentment. "I don't think so," she said.

"It's really important," Steven told her. "I'm sure you have other things to do, but I have something I have to tell you."

Kate couldn't think of a single thing that Steven could tell her that would be of any interest, unless he had taken a job distributing Publishers Clearing House lottery checks and she was a winner. And even then, what would she do with the money? Buy a big apartment to be alone in? Thinking of her empty apartment made her say yes. "Where?" she asked while Elliot shook both his head and his finger at her.

"Can you come downtown?" Steven asked.

Typical. He wanted a favor, but she had to go out of her way. She looked like shit and she felt like shit and she told him yes. What did she care? He gave her an address and she hung up.

"Kate, don't tell me that you're going," Elliot said.

"I am," Kate told him. She fumbled through her makeup bag, took out a mirror, and smeared concealer under her eyes.

"Rebound therapy is not a legitimate approach to this," Elliot told her.

Kate stood up, threw her scattered things back into her bag, and looked at Brice and Elliot. "I'm not going to rebound. I'm not a damn basketball." She walked to the door, then turned back to them, a happy couple in a world of couples. "I've already ruined my life," she said. "You don't have to worry anymore."

Chapter Forty-five

Kate sat beside Steven, her purse on her lap, her legs crossed. One foot was perched on the bar rail. She was actually grateful he had asked to meet at Temple Bar because it was probably the darkest boîte in Manhattan. It was so cool that the entrance didn't even have a name. It was the kind of place that Steven would know about and frequent. It was all dark velvet, elegant uplighting, murmured conversation, and $7 cosmopolitans. Nothing at all like the Barber Bar. It was pure Manhattan.

Steven hadn't seemed to notice her disarray, or if he did, he had the good grace not to mention it. But as she sat there and looked at him, she realized that he was more about being noticed than about noticing other people. There was something in the way he flipped the dark wing of his hair away from his face, the way he held his head, even the way he gestured, that made Kate think he was always performing for an audience, real or imagined. How had she missed that? She simply sat there, tired and sad, and tried to listen to him. It was a long harangue and had gone on for some time now.

". . . and I deserved it. I really did," he was saying. "I know I hurt you, and I know now that I was a fool. I guess I just wanted to prolong my childhood." He looked away from her, but she could see his expression across from the two of them in the mirror behind the bar. She wondered, in a kind of disinterested way, why he was bothering to go through this again. Elliot didn't have to worry. The good news was there was no way she was going to sleep with this player, no way she was going to let herself be hurt again. The bad news was she was so numb that nothing could ever hurt her again.

"I've done a lot of soul-searching," Steven continued. "I didn't really like what I found." Join the club, Kate thought, but she only nodded. "I've been irresponsible," he said. "The fact is, I've behaved like a boy, not a man."

You and five hundred thousand other single men in Manhattan, Kate thought. But again she just nodded. How could she have put up with him? The idea of beginning to date again, of having to meet new men and sit in bars like this and listen to their ruminations and take them seriously, seemed not just more trouble than it was worth, but a kind of torture that no one should be subjected to. Where was Amnesty International when you needed them? Kate supposed she could get used to going out again or she could simply give up, wait until the rest of her friends had babies, and make a career of being a dedicated aunt.

Surprisingly, Steven reached out then and took her hand. Kate jumped a little but managed to keep her purse on her lap and her perch on the bar stool. "I know you're not listening, and I don't blame you," he said. That brought Kate's attention back to him. Perhaps Steven was more aware of others than she'd given him credit for. "Kate, what I'm trying to say is that when we were dating we had different goals. At least I thought we did. But I've had a long time to think about it, and I spent most of that time regretting losing you."

Kate looked at him, face-to-face, for the first time. What was he doing?

Steven sighed. "I can't believe how stupid I was when we met for coffee," he said. "It was arrogant of me to think that an apology would be enough to put us back where we left off." He looked away for a moment. "Sometimes I lack . . . well, there's probably a lot that I lack. But because I lack you, I'd like to try, slowly, to prove I've changed."

Despite her pain, Kate tried to remember if he'd been more stupid than usual. She supposed asking her out at all had been arrogant, but nothing she would not have expected from him. The problem with Steven, she realized, was that everything came too easily to him. He had never had to suffer or work to get anything he wanted, so it was only to be expected that he believed he could get whatever he wanted simply by asking for it. Kate took her hand back from his. He looked down at the bar for a moment, recognizing her rebuke.

"Kate, you shouldn't waste your time on any man who doesn't value you. Who isn't willing to commit to you."

Tell me about it, Kate thought, and idly wondered whether Steven had decided to become a counselor for single women. Maybe he wanted her as a client. But, once again, he took her hand in his. Kate felt nothing. But because of her purse and her unsteady seat, she couldn't easily pull back.

"Kate, I'm asking for your hand."

"You have it," she said.

"No. I mean . . . I mean I'm asking for your hand in marriage."

Kate couldn't—didn't—believe what she'd just heard. Was she having an aural hallucination, projecting this onto Steven, or was he making some bad-taste joke? But, to her utter amazement, he reached into his pocket and took out a ring. Before she had a chance to do anything, he slipped it onto her finger. Kate stared at the diamond flanked by two smaller emeralds, her favorite stone. "Do you like it?" Steven asked.

She stared up at him. What in the world was he thinking of? His audacity, his presumption, were enough to infuriate her, but then she stared down at her hand. The diamond seemed to wink at her in the reflected light of the bottles behind the bar. And then she began to laugh. Once she started, she couldn't stop. Her foot slipped and her purse fell to the floor, but she couldn't silence herself. She wasn't trying to be cruel—she had lost control.

At first, as she began to laugh, Steven looked at her with a smile. Then, as her laughter continued, he stopped smiling. Patrons' heads began to turn and look in their direction. She didn't want to humiliate him, but he had already done it for himself. Why is life like this? Kate thought. When you really wanted something, you didn't get it. Then when you did get it, you didn't want it anymore.

With a tremendous effort she got herself under control. She stopped laughing and thought about all the things she could say, all the things she could tell Steven. In the end, she decided his education and therapy were none of her business. She simply took her hand from his, pulled off the ring, and handed it back to him. "I'm afraid not, Steven," she said. "It wouldn't be good for either one of us."

His face immediately took on the stricken look she knew all too well. For a moment she felt sorry for him. Pain was as hard to inflict as it was to bear. But she knew Steven. In a few days he'd find some other woman who would comfort him, trying to get that look to change. Good luck to her, Kate thought. Then she stood up and patted Steven on the shoulder. "I have to go," she told him. Her empty apartment suddenly seemed like a haven.

"Be well," she told him. Then she turned and walked down the long bar to the door. It wasn't the best exit line, but it would have to do.

Chapter Forty-six

Kate lay on her bed. The oppressive heat had closed down on New York. The temperature and stagnant air made it feel more like mid-August. Kate was unprepared for this kind of heat. She felt unprepared for everything in her life right now; she had an air conditioner stored in the basement but hadn't asked Max to help her bring it up to her window; she hadn't folded and put away her school clothes and refilled her tiny closet with her light summer things; she hadn't made plans for the July Fourth weekend. In fact, summer had come and Kate felt as unprepared for her whole life as she did for her vacation. Somehow, without planning any of it, she had wasted too much time with Michael, revisited a ridiculous relationship with Steven, inappropriately fallen for and been blown off by Billy. Meanwhile, everyone she knew was moving forward with their lives. Brice had gotten a promotion, Elliot was teaching a course at the New School, the two of them had rented a share on Fire Island, Bina was endlessly preparing for her wedding, Bev's baby was keeping her busy, and—the latest news flash was that Barbie had announced that she was pregnant. It seemed as if everyone had a direction and only she was rudderless.

Kate thought about the reasons she should get up. She had laundry piling up, she should go to the gym, she ought to try to get the air conditioner in somehow. There was a pile of books she had been saving to read over the summer. The plants in the living room needed watering. Still, she couldn't force herself to move. She tried to think of something she had to look forward to and failed miserably.

What came to her mind instead were thoughts that didn't bear thinking about: Both her parents were dead, she had no sisters, no brothers. Elliot would be gone for the whole summer. Her friends were married. She'd cut off Michael and was glad of it, but the proposal from Steven had thrown her. She didn't want Steven—but she had once. And she didn't want Michael, but she'd once thought she might have. She obviously didn't know what—or whom—she wanted. Maybe she never would. She was becoming more and more convinced that she would always be alone. Something must be wrong with her, something deep, no doubt caused by the traumas of her childhood. Her mother had died; her father had been emotionally unavailable, and then he'd died. She had chosen abandonment or abandoning as a way of life.

She threw the sheet off of her and was exhausted by the effort. Why had she moved to Manhattan? Why had she struggled through school? Even her work with the children, over now for the summer, seemed hopeless, useless, and second-rate.

But it was the scene with Billy that made her inconsolable. Thinking about it was almost unbearable, but she played the scene over and over in her mind. Now she thought of the day they had gone skating in the park and his easy leadership when the crowd became unruly at the ice-cream store. She wondered if his garden was still so cool despite the day's heat. Thinking of the grass, the fish glimmering in the water, the canopy of leaves, she felt again how special Billy was and what a perfect idiot she had been. She had sent him two notes: One was a simple apology and the other a longer explanation. She hadn't gotten a reply. It wasn't possible to know if he had really loved her, if he'd read her letters, or if—regardless of the nastiness— he would have dumped her anyway; but falling in with Bina's crazy superstition and Elliot's plan had been madness. She thought again of his face when he had confronted her at school. She had seen real pain there and couldn't bear knowing that she had caused it. And she had hurt Michael. And she had hurt Steven, though he had deserved it. Still, she had never meant to hurt any of them and certainly didn't want this pain she was in.

Her loneliness was too big for her little bedroom. She felt it expand out the door and into the living room, until the place felt like a vacuum of love. Kate turned on her side and thought again of Billy. It was always Billy. She began to cry, and the tears were absorbed by her already damp pillow.

When the bell rang, Kate awoke with a start. She felt sticky and disoriented but managed to rise from the crumpled bedclothes and move toward the door. Who would be visiting her, unannounced, at one o'clock on a weekday?

She opened the door, and Max stood there with Bina beside him. Both should have been at work. It was Monday, wasn't it? Her terrible weekend had seemed endless, but it couldn't possibly still be Sunday?

"Katie, we have to see you," Bina said.

"Can we come in, or did we get you at a bad time?" Max asked.

Kate was too sad, dispirited, and confused to tell him that any time was a bad time for her. She just stood aside and let them walk past her into the living room.

"God, it's hot." Bina sighed and took a seat on the sofa.

"Oh. I should have remembered to bring up your air conditioner," Max said. "Why didn't you ask me?"

"I've been busy," Kate told him, but the sarcasm was lost on both of them. She must look awful, but neither of them seemed to notice. Instead of looking at her, they seemed to be either exchanging looks or avoiding her glance. She thought of the Reilly twins and their bad behavior, but what did Max and Bina have to be guilty about, and what naughtiness could these two possibly be up to together? Kate sank into her wicker chair. "What's up?" she asked.

"It's just that . . . well, I can't . . ."

Bina's mouth began to tremble. Kate wasn't sure that she could sit through one more of her friend's cloudbursts. After all, she was getting everything she wanted and needed. She'd have the Vera Wang knockoff dress, the bridesmaids, a wedding with all her family there, the down payment on a house, a husband who might now appreciate her, and, no doubt, babies on the way. And, as always, after the flood of tears Bina would be cheerful and sunny again. It was Kate who would be drained.

Before she could manage to say anything or get up from her chair, Max put his arm around Bina. "It will all be okay," he said. "I promise. It will all be okay." He looked up at Kate. "Tell her it will be okay."

"What will be okay?" Kate demanded. "Bina, stop crying and tell me what's wrong."

"Everything. Everything is wrong," Bina sobbed. "I don't want to marry Jack. I can't marry him. But I have to."

"No, you don't," Max told her.

"Omigod!" Bina said. "What will people think?"

Kate tried to keep her mouth from dropping open. Why in the world would Bina . . . Then a hideous thought occurred to her. Could she be pregnant? Pregnant by Billy? "Bina, you have been using birth control, haven't you?"

Bina looked up for a moment and wiped her eyes. "Yeah. Sure. Why? Do I look like I'm bloated?" Max handed her his handkerchief, and she wiped her eyes. "My mother sent out three hundred invitations," she said. "A calligrapher wrote the addresses."

Kate leaned forward and took one of Bina's hands in her own. "You shouldn't feel guilty. Just because you slept with somebody else doesn't mean you can't marry Jack. It's not like you had a real relationship. Or that you loved him."

"It is a relationship," Max said. "A serious one."

"And I do love him," Bina said, and began sobbing again. "I love him with all my heart." Now Max took Bina's other hand, which left her none to wipe her nose with.

Kate turned away, feeling sick to her stomach. She and Bina both hopelessly in love with Billy Nolan. It was ridiculous. "Look, it's just an infatuation. It's a physical thing. It isn't real love," she said, trying to convince herself as well as her friend.

"It is real love," Bina said, and looked at Max. "It's real, isn't it, Max?"

"Of course it is," Max said.

Kate was wondering where the hell Max got off encouraging Bina's delusional behavior when, to her utter amazement, he leaned forward and gave Bina a deep, soul-searing tongue kiss that left Kate reeling. Then he turned and looked at Kate.

"It isn't just an infatuation, Kate. We're sure of it. I love Bina and she loves me. We didn't mean to do anything behind Jack's back. I mean, after all, he's my cousin. But he was, well, playing around and telling me all about it, and—"

"Wait!" Kate wasn't sure she was hearing this correctly. "You slept with Billy Nolan and now you're sleeping with Max?" she asked Bina.

"Billy Nolan? Why would I sleep with Billy Nolan?" Bina asked. "I just needed him to dump me. Then he did and Jack proposed, and I said yes, and you said it was all right even though I slept with Max, but . . ."

Kate tried to think back. When Bina had told her about her "indiscretion," she hadn't been talking about Billy. Kate had misunderstood. And she had spent all of this time tormenting herself about Billy's promiscuity while he and Bina had never . . . "Oh, my God!" Kate said.

"See. I told you. Omigod!" Bina echoed. Max smoothed Bina's hair and kissed her on the top of her head.

"Look," he said, "I don't mind telling Jack, and I don't mind telling Bina's parents, but she's afraid that it will cause a big to-do and that they'll hate me."

Kate felt so hot and so confused that she was actually dizzy. The room was airless, but her mind kept working while she struggled for a breath. If she could possibly feel more regret about the end of her affair with Billy, she felt it now.

Billy had never slept with Bina. Her doubts about his charac-
ter, all her suspicions, had no basis in reality. Billy had gone out
with innocent Bina and had seen and respected her innocence.
She could barely take it in. "But the towels. The night in the
rain when he dried you off."

"Bina told you about that?" Max asked, and looked at Bina.
"Did you tell her what we did afterwards?"

"That was you and Max?"

"That's the point," Bina said. "I want it to be me and Max, not
me and Jack. But I have Jack's ring and the rabbi is scheduled
and we picked out the flowers and hired the band . . ." She
began to cry again.

"Do you two want to get married to each other?" Kate asked.

"Of course," Max and Bina said simultaneously.

Kate took a deep breath. She looked at the two of them and
remembered the way Max had looked at Bina after her makeover, and the time she had once met them sitting together on
her stoop, and the night she had met Steven and seen Max with
a woman, and even the noises she had heard upstairs. "How
long has this been going on?" she asked them.

"Shortly after Jack left," Max told her.

Kate thought back. She realized that virtually the entire time
that Bina was dating Billy she had been interested in Max, and
Kate had been jealous and . . . Oh, the whole thing was too
ridiculous. She looked across at her friend. "Not the same old
Bina."

Bina shook her head.

"Okay," Kate continued as the reality sank in. The truth was,
she had never liked Jack. She had never thought he was good
enough for Bina. And Max was perfect. All of this was a good
thing—just because she had totally fucked up her life didn't
mean that Bina had to follow in her footsteps. "Max, you take
care of Jack and your family. I'll take care of Bina's side. And
it's best to do it right away." She looked at Bina. "But you'll
have to give him back the ring."

Bina nodded.

"I'll get you a bigger ring," Max told Bina.

"I don't want a ring. I just want you," Bina told him, and they kissed again.

Kate reached for her phone. She dialed the number she knew so well. "Mrs. Horowitz, it's Kate." She was greeted with the usual effusive hellos, invitations to come over for a meal, and questions about her health, her job, and her dating life, all without a pause or the opportunity to answer. "I'm just fine," she finally managed to say. "But I have some news for you."

Chapter Forty-seven

God, it's hot," Elliot said, as if they didn't already know that. He and Brice were in formal dress again, and once again they were in Brooklyn. But this time both of them were tanned, and the contrast of their sun-burnished skin with the blazing white of their shirtfronts made them even more attractive than usual. Kate, wearing a lilac silk strapless gown, was roasting.

Outside the Brooklyn Synagogue, dozens of friends and relatives milled around, greeting guests in voices as shrill as the call of mynah birds.

"Howahya?"

"Waddahya doin'? We haven't seen ya in three Passovers."

"So she's finally getting married. I tell ya, her mother was *plotzing*."

"Are the Weintraubs here? You know the story, don't you?"

The crowd bean to move up the steps and into the building. Kate hung back while Brice moved with the press of people. "I'll get us good seats," he told them.

Kate stood alone with Elliot. She took a deep breath. "Another wedding," she said, and tried to keep her voice cheery. "At least this is the last. I'll never have to buy an ugly bridesmaid's gown again."

"Hey, you're not a bridesmaid," Elliot told her. "You're an old maid of honor."

"Thanks for reminding me."

Kate sighed. She knew that both Elliot and Brice were trying to keep her cheerful, but this was really hard. She was still unable to pull herself together about Billy. Although she knew that there was no such thing as just one person for any other person, she felt that for the rest of her life, she would be comparing Billy to every man she met. And the others would suffer by comparison. She had been stupid and she was being punished, and there was nothing she could do about it except pretend she didn't hurt as much as she did and wait for time to take the sting out. Having to participate in this wedding, however, wasn't helping her to have a sense of proportion.

As if he knew just what she was thinking—and he usually did—Elliot took her arm. "Okay, Katie," he said, making her grimace at the name. "It's show time." They began to move up the stairs together. "Look on the bright side," he told her. "It's not a three-hour Catholic mass." He lowered his voice as they entered the sanctuary. "It actually looks more like a Jewish mess. Check out the outfit on the old lady with the walker."

Kate glanced in the direction Elliot indicated and saw the old woman with a fur piece draped around her neck. "Is it living or dead?" Elliot continued. "And I mean the lady, not the fur."

"Shut up," Kate hissed. "That's Grandma Groppie. She's Mrs. Horowitz's mother and bakes the best *mondelbrot* in Brooklyn. She used to send me care packages when I was away at school."

"And for that you're grateful?" Elliot asked.

Brice called out to Elliot before Kate had a chance to smack him. People were talking, waving to one another, and having mild disagreements over where they should sit. Behind her, two old yentas were busy gossiping. ". . . so, *takka,* he changes his mind, but he doesn't know she's going to change hers." The woman, her hair fifty years older than Heather Locklear's but the exact same shade, nodded. Her companion, short and dumpy but wearing a regal beaded dress, shook her head and tsked.

"After all those years, you would think Jack Weintraub knew what he wanted."

"Oh, the Weintraubs. For them it's a crisis to pick towel colors."

"These kids today. What a *shanda*." Heavily, she took her seat. But the elderly blonde wasn't finished.

"Don't judge like that, Doris. I lost Melvin after forty-one years of marriage, and if I had to do it over again, better I should have eloped with Bernie Silverman like he asked."

"Bernie asked you, too?" Doris asked in a shocked voice.

Kate was fascinated, but she, of course, was part of the wedding party and had to join them. "Can I leave you here?" she asked Brice and Elliot. "Or will you misbehave?"

"You can trust us," Elliot said.

Brice nodded. "I've never seen a Jewish wedding, except in *Crossing Delancey*. Will they really hold Bina in a chair in the air and dance around her?"

"This isn't *Fiddler on the Roof*," Kate snapped, and left them. By the time she found Bina and her mother, the hysteria had already begun. Somehow Bina had forgotten one shoe. "I must have left it on the dressing table," she was telling her mother.

"Omigod! What are we going to do?" Mrs. Horowitz whimpered.

"Myra, it's not a tragedy," said Dr. Horowitz. "If it was a foot she lost, it might be a tragedy."

"Arthur, what is she going to do? Hobble down the aisle like a cripple? And do you know how much we paid for these shoes? You have to go back to the apartment and get the other one."

Kate looked at Bina and figured she was about to begin crying. But today she saw a different Bina. It was a cliché to say that the bride was glowing, but between Bina's obvious joy and the heat, her face looked beautiful and incandescent, almost as if a candle burned within her. "Forget about it," Bina said. "I'll just go barefoot."

"Are you *meshuge*?" Mrs. Horowitz asked. She turned to Kate. "My daughter, the bride, has gone crazy. Talk to her, Katie."

"I think it's a great idea," Kate said. "After all, Julia Roberts did it."

"Another *meshugene*," Mrs. Horowitz said. She looked at

Kate. "You look beautiful, darling," she said, and kissed Kate on the cheek. Just then a sweating man in a shirt opened at the neck came in.

"We're ready to go," he said. "The cameras are set up, and we've put the lights on. You better start before the congregation melts."

"Where are the girls?" Mrs. Horowitz asked.

"They're in the ladies' room. Where else?" Dr. Horowitz asked.

"Go get them and I'll get the flowers. Katie, you keep an eye on Bina so she doesn't decide to marry a third guy."

Kate and Bina were left alone. "You look beautiful," Kate told her friend. "Are you as happy as you look?"

"Omigod! I'm so happy. And it never would have happened without you. Thank you, Katie." Bina's eyes filled with tears. "I love Max so much. I didn't know it could be like this."

Kate knew exactly what she meant but said nothing. Just then the girls arrived, looking like a bunch of tangerines that had rolled out of a broken bag. "Katie!" they called.

"Shh," Mrs. Horowitz said. "They'll hear you. With decorum."

"And the bouquets," Dr. Horowitz called. "Refrigerator fresh." All the bridesmaids received the same nosegay of orange orchids with glossy lemon leaves. Kate got a larger bouquet of lilacs, lianthus, and white roses.

"That's not the only thing that's fresh," Mrs. Horowitz whispered into Kate's ear. "I made kugel just for you. Just don't tell the caterers." She pushed back Kate's hair and then looked up at Bina. "Time to go," she said.

"Exactly," Dr. Horowitz told her. "Now go sit down where you're supposed to, Myra. I walk her down the aisle."

"See you at the *bima*, Bina," Mrs. Horowitz said, and cackled. "I waited thirty years to use that line," she told them as she went to take her place.

Kate stood under the traditional canopy in front of the whole congregation with the Bitches arrayed behind her. There wasn't a lot of room, and the brims of their picture hats were bumping into one another as well as into the back of Kate's neck. She had her hair up and was actually grateful for the tickling because it kept her distracted. Max and Bina stood on either side of the rabbi. Kate couldn't take her eyes off Bina. She looked so happy and stared adoringly at Max. He was a little pale, but he returned the passion of Bina's looks. In fact, it seemed to Kate that they were unaware of the rabbi, the wedding party, or the couple of hundred guests before them. Kate looked out at the crowd. She wondered how many of the couples sitting in the rows loved one another. She also wondered if Jack was feeling desolate on this day. Along with his family, he had decided to boycott the wedding, and Kate couldn't help thinking that he had no one but himself to blame if he had lost the most precious thing in his life.

Most of the ceremony was in Hebrew, and Kate was clueless as to what it meant. But she did know that it meant that Bina had gotten the man she loved and that Max was a kind, loving, and dependable man. Kate supposed that she would never find a man she could look at the way Bina was now looking at Max. When the wedding vows were repeated in English, Kate couldn't keep the sadness at bay any longer. Bina would now join the sisterhood of young wives and mothers. . . . How ironic that just when Kate had merged her old friends with her newer ones, she would lose Bina to housekeeping, motherhood, and preschool.

"Do you, Max, take Bina to be your lawfully wedded wife . . ."

Kate heard the words, and this time it was not Bina's but Kate's own lips that trembled. She thought of Billy, now lost to her, and the way he'd looked at her when her face had rested beside his on the pillow. Had his eyes shone with as much warmth as she now saw in Max's eyes?

"I do," Max said.

"So do I," said Bina, jumping the gun. People throughout the temple laughed, and Kate, who had been on the edge of tears, had to laugh as well. Same old Bina.

The heat and the noise at the reception were almost overwhelming. It didn't help Kate's mood that the reception was being held at the same banquet hall where Bunny had been married and where all of the Billy Nolan nonsense had begun.

Elliot and Brice were doing their best to keep her diverted, but it wasn't an easy assignment.

"When do we Elders of Zion do the blood ritual with a little Christian baby?" Brice asked.

"That's *after* the appetizer," Kate told him.

Unfortunately, the two of them couldn't keep up the bodyguard act because Kate had to sit on the dais with the wedding party. That left her open to the women who kept accosting her, wanting to know, "When is it going to be your turn?" Kate wanted to tell them she was a lesbian and had already had a civil union with a lady gym teacher performed in Vermont, but she wasn't sure there was oxygen and an EMS team nearby. As soon as the bandleader announced that the dancing was about to begin, she stood up because she couldn't bear to sit there like a target any longer.

"And now, ladies and gentlemen, for the first time on the dance floor, let us put our hands together for Mr. and Mrs. Max Cepek."

The room was filled with the sound of applause, shouts of *"Mazel tov!"* and the dinging of forks against glasses. Max stood up, put his arm around Bina's waist, and swept her onto the dance floor, where the two of them began to waltz. Kate applauded along with the rest, despite the tears in her eyes. Over Max's shoulder, Bina threw Kate a kiss and mouthed, "Thank you." Kate nodded.

To the end of her life Kate couldn't remember how she got through the next couple of hours. Part of the time she hid in the ladies' room, part of it she spent woodenly smiling, feeling like a target at a carnival shooting range. Occasionally she danced with Elliot or Brice but could barely acknowledge their jokes. She did remember how tired her face got from holding grimly to the smile she kept plastered on it. Finally, the cake was served and she saw that there might eventually be some escape. At last Bina came over to her. "We're going to go soon," she said. "Get ready to catch the bouquet because I want you to be the next one married. Meet us downstairs." Kate nodded.

Then, because she could bear no more, she stepped off the dais and, as unobtrusively as possible, opened a door to the terrace.

Chapter Forty-eight

Kate slipped out onto the terrace unnoticed and leaned against the closing door. She was dizzy and having trouble catching her breath. She knew that most likely she was having what psychologists would term "an acute panic attack," but at the moment she was more woman, less psychologist. She took a moment or two to calm herself. Behind her in the hall, she heard the band begin to play "If I Loved You." Kate walked through the heat to the end of the terrace, but there was no escape. It was a corny song, and she didn't like ballads from musicals. That was more in Brice's department. But there was something undeniably poignant about the unexpressed fear and longing in the song. She felt her own loneliness welling up inside her.

She'd never get married, and even if she did, she had no parents to throw her a wedding. Not that she wanted a wedding thrown for her any more than she wanted the damn bridal bouquet that Bina was conniving to have her catch. She sighed, a catch in her throat.

Then, just a few feet away, there was a shaking of the ivy along the balustrade. Kate stepped away, expecting to see a squirrel or a chipmunk. Instead, the trembling became wilder, and the vines beneath the ivy actually jumped back and forth. Kate watched, fascinated, until a hand grabbed the railing. It was followed by a second hand, and then Billy Nolan's head and shoulders appeared. He hoisted himself up by his arms, then threw his long legs over the balustrade.

Kate couldn't tear her eyes away from him as he stood there, breathing heavily, recovering. He was wearing jeans, a white shirt, and loafers—obviously not wedding attire. Finally, after what seemed like an eternity of staring at him in silence, Kate found her voice.

"What are you doing here?" she asked, working hard to sound perfectly at ease, as though something like this happened to her all the time.

"I might ask you the same question," Billy said.

She blushed. "I'm here to see Bina celebrate."

"Out here on the terrace?" Billy asked.

It was too much. She didn't need to be teased by the man she'd loved and lost.

"I just . . . I have to go back now," she told him. "Nice seeing you."

She got as far as the door, her hand actually on the knob, when his arms came around her and his hand rested over hers. "Don't touch the dial," he said.

Kate watched, her face reflected in the glass of the terrace door. Her lips were trembling. It wasn't a pretty picture. Inside, everyone was on the dance floor, celebrating with Max and Bina. Why was Billy torturing her like this?

In the reflection of the glass, she saw him lean forward. She felt his face beside hers. "Kate," he whispered in her ear, "want to dance with me?" Without turning around, Kate shook her head. "Oh, come on," he said, the familiar coaxing tease in his voice. "You know you want to."

Kate turned to look at him. They were face-to-face, an inch or two of space between them. She could feel the stream of air from his nose on her forehead. She might not be able to have him, but for now she could inhale the same air he breathed. Then he took her in his arms and they began to move to the music.

Kate was stiff at first but soon couldn't help but relax into his body. God, she missed his smell, his skin, his clean heat. This was breaking whatever was left of her heart, but she couldn't help it: She moved her arms up so that they draped over his shoulders.

"Kate," Billy said, pulling back slightly, "tell me you missed me."

"Missed you?" Kate echoed. Could she—or should she—describe the ache and emptiness and regret she'd felt since . . .

"Look, I don't know how the whole thing started, or whose idea it was, or whether it started as a joke," Billy began, "but I heard about your proposal."

She looked up at him. How did he know about Steven? She'd told only Elliot. But then, she reflected, he'd probably told Bina, and she'd told . . . well, everybody. "It was ridiculous," she said. "It had nothing to do with you."

His shoulders, under her arms, shrugged. "Maybe yes, maybe no," he told her. "You know what happens after you date Dumping Billy."

"Stop," Kate told him. "I never dated you because of that. It's a stupid nickname."

Billy shrugged again. "Everyone called me that. And everyone knew its truth but me."

"You don't think you've got some kind of . . . power, do you? I mean, to get people married?"

Billy laughed. "Don't worry. I'm not delusional. At least not in that way. I watched as one by one, all the guys I knew got married. And I wondered, What was I waiting for? What was wrong with me?" He looked down at her. "I had a prolonged adolescence. And I knew how much my dad loved my mom. I . . . I had fun, but I didn't want to settle. You know what I mean?"

Kate nodded up at him.

"You were different. You had the courage to leave, to raise yourself above what you came from. You, well, you're accomplished." He paused. "And I probably shouldn't say this, but I think we have a lot in common. I'm not saying I have your education or anything. But we both overcame a lot of early loss. You know what I mean?"

Kate nodded again, speechless, listening. His body against hers, moving to the music through the heat, felt like some kind of delicious dream. She didn't want to think about waking up.

"I think people who haven't suffered, well, good for them, but they're different from those of us who have," he said. "I don't know all the psychology, the way you do, but I know that people like us, we're always going to be scared that we're going to screw up, that we're going to make the wrong decision and wind up where we started. You know?"

Kate nodded. She knew too well. She felt her heart begin to beat faster. Was it possible that he wasn't just forgiving her, but . . . She couldn't think. The heat and her excitement seemed to close in on her.

"I don't know why I had higher ambitions than the guys I know. Or why I went to France. I don't know why when I came back I wouldn't settle for a job working for someone else. Why I took over the bar and changed the clientele. I just wanted to be . . ." He paused. "It seemed like I wanted something more than Arnie and Johnny did, not that . . ." He took a deep breath. "I mean, how do you pick a partner not just for a few months, but for life?"

Kate nodded. Steven had done for months, and so had Michael . . . but for life? How did one know?

Billy continued. "It's not like I'm a snob, or I look down on the guys I know or the women I dated. We had fun. When we broke up I didn't hurt them. I liked them."

"I know you didn't hurt them," Kate said. "They all like you."

"Good. And it seemed to help them resolve things." He smiled. "I mean, they did all get married. My magic touch?"

Kate felt her face get hot again. "You know I never believed that nonsense. . . ."

"Until it happened to you."

"It didn't happen to me. I had known Steven for years. And I wasn't interested in him."

"Really," Billy said. And at that moment the band inside began to play the hokey-pokey.

Kate pulled herself away from him to stare into the room. "How did you do that?" she asked.

Billy just looked at her and smiled. "Coincidence."

Kate wouldn't accept that. Had he timed this? Did he know the band? He seemed to know everyone. She continued to stare at him. "How did you get them to play that just now?"

Billy shrugged. "Magic?" He leaned forward and nuzzled her ear. "You put your left foot in, you put your left foot out. You put your left foot in and you shake it all about," he murmured. "You do the hokey-pokey and you turn yourself around."

He swung Kate out away from him but held her hand tightly. Then he pulled her back into him, this time closer than ever. He stopped dancing and put his arms around her. He kissed her, and she let him. She kissed him back passionately, even if this was the last kiss he gave her. Even if he'd shown up only to punish her for her deceptions. "This is what it's all about, Kate," he said. Tears came to her eyes. Billy kissed her again.

"You're not angry at me?" she asked.

"Well, of course I was angry with you. I was furious." He paused. "You know how it is. The truth hurts. But I figured the entire thing out, and the parts I didn't know, Barbie and Bev were happy to fill in."

"They were?"

"Sure. And you know what the French say: *Tout comprendre c'est tout pardonner.*"

To understand all is to forgive all. Kate, for the first time, began to feel flooded with hope. "But we, well, we tried to use you for Bina, and I, well, I . . . I didn't mean to hurt you, it was just . . ." She didn't get to finish. Billy put his hand over her mouth and then kissed her again.

Kate looked through the terrace door to see a large crowd of women gathering around a barely visible Bina and Max. She knew the couple planned an early escape to get the last minute flight they'd booked for their honeymoon.

"Kate," Billy said, and she turned back to him. "I know I just own a bar in Brooklyn, that I'm not as educated as you are, but

I can't stop thinking about you. From the first time I saw you, I—" He was interrupted by a hubbub below them.

The wedding crowd was streaming out the front doors. Billy and Kate watched from above as Max covered Bina's face. The two of them were pelted with confetti and flower petals. (Mrs. Horowitz had not allowed rice. She said it was too dangerous and could put somebody's eye out.) The driver of the wedding limo was holding the door open, but the guests and family were shouting and blocking the couple's way. Billy looked down and grinned. "Ah. The usual gauntlet."

Kate watched her friend. Bina was laughing and struggling to get into the car. "Throw the bouquet! Don't forget the bouquet!" yelled Barbie.

Bina looked around wildly. "Where's Katie? Where's Katie?" she yelled back. "*She* has to catch it."

Same old Bina, Kate thought. She knew she should be there seeing Bina off, but she'd never make it downstairs and outside in time—and most of all, she couldn't bear to leave Billy.

"Let's go, Bina," Kate heard Max urge. "We'll miss the plane."

Meanwhile the crowd was getting rowdy. Arnie and Johnny were "decorating" the limo with shaving cream and streamers. Mrs. Horowitz was giving a bag—probably full of kugel—to the driver, while Dr. Horowitz tried to confiscate the aerosol cans.

"Throw the bouquet! The bouquet!" Bev screamed.

"Katie!" Bina shrieked.

At that Max took the flowers from her hand. With all his strength, he wound up to pitch and tossed the bouquet in a wide arc high into the blue, blue sky. All eyes followed it.

With a somewhat violent *whoosh,* Bina's bridal bouquet hurtled through the air toward the terrace. Kate stepped back in time to avoid being seen by the crowd below. To her amazement, the bouquet fell with a splat at her feet. Startled, she and Billy stared at it silently. She felt paralyzed with embarrassment and . . . fear. Her longing was almost too much to bear. Then Billy broke the moment by stooping gracefully, picking it up, and offering it to her. Kate accepted it as if in a dream. She stared down at the bouquet in her hands, then at Billy, then back to the bouquet. She said a silent prayer that this moment wasn't just a coincidence. That it meant something real and lasting. She knew she was blushing, but she forced herself to look at Billy Nolan, even if it gave her away.

"How did you manage that?" Billy asked. "Was it magic?"

Kate, no matter what the cost, nodded, because it was.

"Kate, will you marry me?" Billy asked.

And, of course, she did.